Praise for *On a Coastal Breeze*

"Christy Award–winner Fisher delivers a delightful second installment to her Three Sisters Island trilogy. . . . This winsome tale will hit the spot for fans of contemporary inspirationals."

Publishers Weekly

"A lively, witty, and charmingly entertaining read from cover to cover."

Midwest Book Review

"This book was such a delightful read, and so is the author who wrote it. I love anything she writes!"

Interviews & Reviews

"Everything I wanted in a book. . . . I cried, I laughed, and I fell head over heels in love."

Urban Lit Magazine

Praise for *On a Summer Tide*

"Fans of Suzanne Woods Fisher will love this story of three sisters coming together on a rugged Maine island to refurbish a camp. *On a Summer Tide* is an enduring tale of love and restoration."

Denise Hunter, bestselling author of *On Magnolia Lane*

"*On a Summer Tide* is filled with memorable characters, gorgeous Maine scenery, and plenty of family drama. I can't wait to visit Three Sisters Island again!"

Irene Hannon, bestselling author of the beloved Hope Harbor series

"Fisher creates a vibrant cast of charming, plucky characters set on redefining themselves."

Publishers Weekly

"Suzanne Woods Fisher offers a contemporary novel of a family rebuilding their connection, adding a touch of suspense and just enough spirituality to make this a heartwarming read."

New York Journal of Books

At Lighthouse Point

Novels by Suzanne Woods Fisher

LANCASTER COUNTY SECRETS

The Choice

The Waiting

The Search

SEASONS OF STONEY RIDGE

The Keeper

The Haven

The Lesson

THE INN AT EAGLE HILL

The Letters

The Calling

The Revealing

AMISH BEGINNINGS

Anna's Crossing

The Newcomer

The Return

THE BISHOP'S FAMILY

The Imposter

The Quieting

The Devoted

NANTUCKET LEGACY

Phoebe's Light

Minding the Light

The Light Before Day

THE DEACON'S FAMILY

Mending Fences

Stitches in Time

Two Steps Forward

THREE SISTERS ISLAND

On a Summer Tide

On a Coastal Breeze

At Lighthouse Point

The Moonlight School

At Lighthouse Point

SUZANNE
WOODS
FISHER

Revell
a division of Baker Publishing Group
Grand Rapids, Michigan

© 2021 by Suzanne Woods Fisher

Published by Revell
a division of Baker Publishing Group
PO Box 6287, Grand Rapids, MI 49516-6287
www.revellbooks.com

Printed in the United States of America

Library of Congress Cataloging-in-Publication Data
Names: Fisher, Suzanne Woods, author.
Title: At Lighthouse Point / Suzanne Woods Fisher.
Description: Grand Rapids, Michigan : Revell, a division of Baker Publishing
    Group, [2021] | Series: Three Sisters Island
Identifiers: LCCN 2020047619 | ISBN 9780800735005 (paperback) | ISBN
    9780800739973 (casebound) | ISBN 9781493430376 (ebook)
Subjects: GSAFD: Love stories.
Classification: LCC PS3606.I78 A93 2021 | DDC 813/.6—dc23
LC record available at https://lccn.loc.gov/2020047619

Some Scripture used in this book, whether quoted or paraphrased by the characters, is taken from the Amplified® Bible (AMP), copyright © 2015 by The Lockman Foundation. Used by permission. www.Lockman.org

Some Scripture used in this book, whether quoted or paraphrased by the characters, is taken from the Holy Bible, New International Version®. NIV®. Copyright © 1973, 1978, 1984, 2011 by Biblica, Inc.™ Used by permission of Zondervan. All rights reserved worldwide. www.zondervan.com. The "NIV" and "New International Version" are trademarks registered in the United States Patent and Trademark Office by Biblica, Inc.™

Some Scripture used in this book, whether quoted or paraphrased by the characters, is taken from the New King James Version®. Copyright © 1982 by Thomas Nelson. Used by permission. All rights reserved.

Some Scripture used in this book, whether quoted or paraphrased by the characters, is taken from the *Holy Bible*, New Living Translation, copyright © 1996, 2004, 2007, 2013, 2015 by Tyndale House Foundation. Used by permission of Tyndale House Publishers, Inc., Carol Stream, Illinois 60188. All rights reserved.

Published in association with Joyce Hart of the Hartline Literary Agency, LLC.

21 22 23 24 25 26 27   7 6 5 4 3 2 1

Cast of Characters

Paul Grayson (age 62)—retired sports announcer; father of Cam, Maddie, Blaine; grandfather of Cooper

Camden Grayson Walker (age 32)—eldest daughter of Paul, adoptive mother of Cooper, wife of schoolteacher Seth Walker

Madison Grayson O'Shea (age 28)—middle daughter of Paul, marriage and family therapist, married to Pastor Rick O'Shea

Blaine Grayson (age 22)—youngest daughter of Paul, graduate of Le Cordon Bleu culinary school in Paris

Cooper Grayson Walker (age 10)—son of Camden and Seth Walker

Seth Walker (age 32)—schoolteacher at Three Sisters Island

Rick O'Shea (age 29)—husband to Maddie, pastor to the small church on Three Sisters Island

Artie Lotosky (age 24)—college friend of Blaine, now a doctor to the outlying islands

Bob Lotosky (age 50-ish)—Artie's dad, a potato farmer from Aroostook County, Maine

Peg Legg (won't reveal her age)—runs the Lunch Counter, mayor of Three Sisters Island (though it's too small for a mayor)

Walter Grayson (age 80-ish)—estranged father of Paul Grayson

Captain Ed (ageless)—runs the Never Late Ferry between Mount Desert and Three Sisters Island

Tillie (somewhere in her 50s)—the übervolunteer church secretary

Maeve O'Shea (mid-60s)—Rick O'Shea's mother

One

It was a long way home. Blaine Grayson stood on the bow of the Never Late Ferry to fully appreciate this moment of coming home, breathing deeply of the salty ocean air, listening to the screech of the seagulls, the hum of the lobster boat engines as they chugged toward the dock with the day's catch. What was it about this crazy little island? Why did it always seem so remote from the rest of the world, so far away? Probably because it was.

With her long blonde hair whipping about her face, Blaine tipped her face back to look at the blue sky. The midmorning sun had lifted well above the trees—glinting off the water's surface. There was no place more special on earth than Maine . . . especially with summer coming.

Two years ago, Blaine had left Three Sisters Island to travel through Europe for a little while and find herself. Her dad thought she'd only last a few weeks, and during that entire first month in Paris, she worried he was right. The cost of living was exorbitant, even on the cheap. Broke, she'd maxed out her credit cards, had worn out her welcome at the apartment where she was couch surfing, and had no idea what to do or where to go. She hit a low point. Lower than low. But then a single moment changed everything, gave her life meaning and direction. She glanced at her friend, sitting inside the ferry, eyes closed because of his mal de mer. She pressed her hand over her heart, so thankful for him.

And here she was, two years later with a diploma from Le Cordon Bleu in hand, returning to her family and the little island in Maine she had missed so terribly.

Standing behind the wheel, Captain Ed caught her eye and motioned her over. As she drew near, he took his pipe out of the corner of his mouth. "Bah's gone."

"The sandbar? It's gone?"

"Big storm took it out." He stuck his pipe back in his mouth.

That bar, during low tide, was a lifeline. You could walk across it to Mount Desert Island, or even drive your car back and forth. If the tide was high, there was Captain Ed's ferry for passengers. If you were in a hurry, wanted your car with you, and didn't mind a steep fee, he also had a car ferry. The sandbar was gone?

As the ferry slowed to reverse its engine and ease into the slip, Blaine gazed at the little harbor, trying to assess other changes. Boon Dock still looked about the same: a floating dock with fishing boats and rowboats lining the finger piers. Then she spotted something off in the distance, a sleek yacht anchored in the harbor. A *yacht*. On Three Sisters Island? Her mouth dropped open. She turned to catch Captain Ed's eye—the one that wasn't in a permanent squint.

He took his pipe out of his mouth. "Did I not tell you so, girlie?"

Her eyes moved toward Main Street, rising above Boon Dock, and she felt the first hitch in her gut. This was not the island she remembered. Gone was the look of an abandoned ghost town. The street—which Blaine remembered as cracked pavement with grass growing in the middle of it—had been recently tarred. Black and shiny, with a crisp white line running down the middle. The business buildings that lined Main Street were no longer shuttered or boarded up or covered with flaking paint and rusting gutters.

Her dad had kept her in the loop about Camp Kicking Moose. Her sister Cam told her, ad nauseam, about the wind turbine that was creating power for the little island. Maddie told her about the growth of the church and lots about her husband Rick, who was pastoring a second island church. Blaine had heard plenty of news from her family, but they didn't prepare her for *this* kind of change to Three Sisters Island. Not for prosperity.

Shouts and waves caught her attention. There on Boon Dock was Dad (so much more gray in his hair!) and her nephew Cooper (so tall!) and Peg from the Lunch Counter (no change there—Blaine felt a sweep of relief as she spotted Peg's bright purple headband) and her brothers-in-law Seth and Pastor Rick and . . . *Oh my gosh*. Her two sisters! Cam and Maddie waved and waved with one hand, the other pointing to their basketball bellies. Both! They hadn't told her *that* news either. *Oh wow*. She should have realized change would come; after all, she was returning as a different person.

As the ferry came to a stop, Blaine got choked up, bombarded by mixed feelings: joy at being home, sorrow at what she'd missed, a familiar and vague unsettledness about where she belonged in this expanding family.

But as she jumped onto the floating dock, she knew one thing for sure: She was not ever going to leave this island again. No matter what.

She stopped and turned to offer a smile. "Jean-Paul." She reached out to grasp his hand. "Take a deep breath. It's time to meet my family."

It wasn't often that Paul Grayson felt blindsided, but his youngest daughter Blaine had a knack for it. He kept waking up last night to check the clock, so excited for this day. His little girl was coming home! If he'd known she would've been gone such a long time, he probably would never have let her go in the first place. When he had said goodbye to her, he was convinced she'd be back in a month. And here it was, nearly two years later.

The family had kept in regular contact with Blaine. Paul had heard so much about Le Cordon Bleu that he felt as if he'd been there himself. Blaine gave blow-by-blow accounts of the demanding instructors, how they liked to weed out inferior aspiring chefs, how often she cried after a disappointing dish or a tongue lashing by an instructor.

Paul had heard so much about Paris, its monuments and museums, that he thought he could navigate the city without a map. He knew about Blaine's quirky roommates and her weekend trips to other European cities. But he'd never heard a word about a French boyfriend, a skinny fellow who looked like he needed to get outdoors more often. And she brought him all the way from France to Three Sisters Island to meet the family. Good grief. What did that mean? What was he to her?

Paul watched Blaine for a moment as she swirled Cooper around in a hug, exclaiming over how much he had changed. She was the tallest of his three girls, and Cooper had been a small boy when she left. No longer. He was ten now, starting to spike, long limbs and a skinny middle. Blaine looked the same to Paul. Beautiful.

The French boyfriend stood at a distance, watching Blaine twirl Cooper, an enigmatic look on his face.

"Paul Grayson?"

Paul spun around when he heard someone call his name. He tented his eyes to see an older man walk up the hill from Boon Dock and suddenly recognized the gait of the man. "Oh no," he murmured. "It can't be him." *Not him. Please don't be who I think it is.*

The man stopped a few yards away from the big cluster of Graysons still absorbed in celebrating Blaine's arrival. They hadn't noticed him.

Paul separated himself from his family and walked toward him. "What brings you here?"

The man cocked his ear. "Pardon?"

Paul cleared his throat and tried again. "Why are you here?"

The man swept a hand toward the big group of Graysons. "Family. What else?"

He took his hat off and Paul could see how much he had aged. A shock of white hair. Wrinkled, leathered skin. Tired eyes. When had he seen him last? Ten years? Fifteen? Maybe longer.

"Well, son, aren't you going to introduce me to my granddaughters?"

Blaine breathed in the sharp, familiar tang of salt air and sighed. It felt great to be back on Three Sisters Island. Back home. Her whole soul felt settled, as if a part of herself had been restored.

"Glad you're home, Blaine." Seth, Cam's husband, gave her a welcoming hug. "Gotta go for now, but we'll catch up later."

Rick, Maddie's husband, gave Seth a gentle push out of the way to embrace Blaine. "I'm leaving with him on the ferry, but we both wanted to be sure to welcome you home."

And with that, they were both running down Boon Dock to catch the ferry.

"What about dinner?" she called to them.

Seth turned around, walking backward. "Won't be home till late! But save us leftovers!"

Oh. Blaine had big plans to cook a gourmet meal for the family for tonight. She had left Three Sisters Island to find her culinary voice, and she wanted her family to know she'd found it.

Boy, had she ever found it.

For tonight's family dinner, she'd planned a menu that she had once served to her favorite instructor Chef Henri, a man who was terribly hard to impress, and yet even he was impressed by it. Lamb loin in Socca; a demi-glace over fingerling potatoes, sprinkled with Maine Sea Salt; baby vegetables with a grand aioli; and a bittersweet chocolate mousse for dessert. Perfection on a plate.

Disappointed, Blaine turned around. Dad was trying to shepherd everyone up to Main Street to have lunch at the diner before heading back to the camp. Cam peeled off to walk down the beach, cell phone glued to her ear. Blaine picked up her pace, reached the street, and suddenly saw her grandfather—a man she barely remembered and wasn't even sure what to call him until Maddie shouted out, "Granddad Grayson!"—go pasty white and faint on the sidewalk. He plunged face forward right into Jean-Paul, and both went sprawling to the ground, arms and legs splayed.

Cushioning Granddad Grayson's fall, Jean-Paul's knee had bent in an odd twist and his eyes were closed in a grimace as he writhed in pain.

"Jean-Paul!" Blaine ran and crouched down beside him.

Two girls riding bicycles down Main Street stopped and stared, and a couple sprang out of a shop to see what had happened. Everyone started talking at once.

"What hurts?" Blaine said, as she and her dad helped shift Granddad Grayson, who had quickly regained consciousness and was surprised to find himself smothering Jean-Paul.

"*Mon genou*! Oh no, no, no! *J'mal au genou*!"

"It's his knee. He has a weak knee from an old injury." Blaine looked up at Peg Legg, the likeliest to know what to do. Peg ran the Lunch Counter, the island's only diner—a ten-table establishment that served locals.

Short-haired and stocky, her sleeves perpetually rolled up, Peg took charge. "Cooper, honey," she said, "go call Artie on the kitchen phone. His number is tacked on an index card right next to the phone. I saw the *Lightship* down at the dock. He's gotta be somewhere around here."

"Artie?" Blaine said. *My Artie?*

Dad was sitting on the sidewalk, checking his father's pulse. "Artie's the doctor for outlying islands."

Artie . . . was *what*? He'd never told her, but then again, they didn't talk. Not anymore. Two years ago, Blaine and Artie had parted on a sour note. His sour note, not hers. Artie Lotosky had been her longtime friend, her very best buddy, and she had invited him to join her in Europe. Since he was a struggling medical student, she'd even offered to buy his plane ticket, which she thought was a very generous offer, especially because she would've added it to her considerable credit card debt. Artie turned her down flat. He wasn't at all grateful for her invitation. He should've been, she thought, but he just wasn't. He even implied she was irresponsible. A few months later, she had called him on his birthday and he never bothered to return her call. *That* stung.

Peg pointed up the road. "Cooper, there he is now."

Blaine spun around to see her nephew dash up the street to greet a man coming out of a store—hold on! That man was *Artie*.

She'd had no warning. Her mind was completely focused on the crisis at hand, and the next moment, here came Artie Lotosky, striding confidently down Main Street, one hand grasping a medical black bag.

Blaine stared. He'd lost weight. A lot of it. He used to be kind of chubby. No longer. And he sported a beard. Even his clothes were an upgrade. Gone was the faded sweatshirt with the stretched-out neck, replaced by a smart button-down. Gone were the worn sneakers, replaced by trendy L.L.Bean boots. Gone was his scruffy, unkempt appearance. He looked like a completely different person. Rakish. Stylish.

Goose bumps broke out on her arms. Man, he looked *good*.

Artie didn't notice Blaine at all. His attention was focused on the clump of people down on the ground. "Who's hurt here? Paul, what's happened?"

Dad patted his father's shoulder. "This elderly man fainted."

"I did nothing of the kind." Granddad Grayson batted his hands away. "I tripped on the sidewalk." He shared a few choice words about the uneven concrete.

"I saw it all," Peg said. "He dropped like a stone and fell right on top of this poor little skinny fella. Twisted his leg something fierce."

Jean-Paul moaned, trying to raise himself to a sitting position, then gave up. "No worry. Eez fine."

15

Artie crouched down to run his hands over the swelling knee. "I don't think anything is broken. If the knee distended, you might have sprained the ligaments."

Gradually Jean-Paul sat up. "See? All better now." But his face grimaced in pain.

"Sprains can be worse than breaks. You'll have to stay off your feet for a while."

"No, no," Jean-Paul said. "Eez okay." He tried to rise and quickly gave up again, clutching his knee with a groan.

Artie turned his attention to Granddad Grayson. "So, what's going on with you?"

"I'm just fine."

Artie took his wrist and felt his pulse. "Do you faint often?"

Granddad Grayson yanked his hand away and tried to get up.

Artie helped him to his feet. "When was the last time you ate?" When he didn't answer, Artie glanced at Peg. "Can you bring him something to eat?"

"Also for me. *Merci*," Jean-Paul piped up, between moans. "I starve."

"You just polished off my entire sandwich on the ferry," Blaine said, and she felt the tiniest bit of pleasure spiral through her when she saw Artie's hands, rifling through his medical bag, still at the sound of her voice. Then he resumed his search in the bag and pulled out a bottle of aspirin.

"Take two of these, every four to six hours." Artie handed Jean-Paul the bottle. "Practice RICE."

Jean-Paul lifted his head, confused. "*Pardon?*" He pronounced it with a lift on the second syllable.

"Rest. Ice. Compression. Elevation." Artie turned to Paul. "He'll need a bag of ice. And maybe a glass of water for the aspirin."

"Done and done," Dad said and hurried into the diner.

Blaine should have been the one to get those things for Jean-Paul, but she remained where she was, transfixed by Artie, the

16

doctor. Artie, so confident, so authoritative. No one questioned him, they just took his directives.

Artie closed his medical bag and rose, chin tucked, before he looked Blaine in the eye. "So, you're back."

"I'm back."

"I suppose you brought him back with you." He glanced down at Jean-Paul, who remained on the sidewalk cupping his knee with his hands, moaning softly.

Artie made it sound like she'd brought home a stray puppy. "Yeessss," she said cautiously, drawing out the word.

"Then, I'll give you the instructions. Keep him from putting any weight on that leg for forty-eight to seventy-two hours. He should be fine, but call me if it doesn't seem to improve." He glanced at his watch. "Gotta go. Remember to RICE." And he jogged down toward Boon Dock without a look back. Without a second thought for Blaine, his dearest friend, whom he hadn't seen in over two years. He did have the wherewithal to take a moment to wave to Cam, who was still glued to her cell phone down near Boon Dock. But nothing more for Blaine.

Blaine's dad came out of the Lunch Counter with a bag of ice and a glass of water, and Peg followed with a hastily made sandwich on a paper plate.

"Oh, merci," Jean-Paul said, grabbing half the sandwich. He took a bite, swallowed, paused. "Eez possible to add a dash of Dijon mustard?"

"I only have hot dog mustard," Peg said. "The bright yellow kind."

Jean-Paul looked aghast. "Maybe, then, a spoonful of aioli?"

"A-what?" Peg asked.

"It's a fancy type of mayonnaise," Blaine said.

"*Très important*," he said.

"No Dijon. No aioli." Blaine gave him a pat on the shoulder. "Sorry, Jean-Paul." She saw Peg and Maddie exchange a look. "What? What was that look for?"

"Nothing," Maddie said. "Jean-Paul seems . . ."

"Hungry," Peg finished. "Poor little fella."

Jean-Paul had swallowed the sandwich in two bites and was eyeing the other half in Granddad Grayson's hand. "His metabolism," Blaine explained. "It's very high. Like a hummingbird."

Peg patted her rather well-cushioned hips. "Ah, must be nice."

"I've always thought gals look better with a little meat on their bones," Granddad Grayson said.

Peg beamed. "Then, honey, you and I are gonna get along just fine."

Blaine watched her dad roll his eyes. She wondered what that was all about. Did her dad have romantic feelings for Peg? What had she missed? Two years ago, Artie's dad, a potato farmer from Aroostook County, had started courting Peg. Dad didn't seem to mind, though Blaine did. Bob Lotosky was a very nice man, but he lived and breathed potatoes. She knew he'd never, ever leave Aroostook County, which meant Peg might leave Three Sisters Island. That was unfathomable.

As Peg showed Granddad Grayson into the Lunch Counter, Blaine and her dad helped Jean-Paul get to his feet, or rather one foot, to hop into the diner where it would be easier to ice his knee. She crossed the threshold and stopped abruptly, startled. Her first thought was that her eyes were playing tricks on her from the bright sunlight. Her second thought was, *What in the world has happened here?*

Two

WALKING ALONG THE BEACH by Boon Dock because it was the best place to get reception, Cam finished the call, stuffed her phone in her purse, and watched Artie Lotosky stop and turn abruptly as he reached the dock, then gaze up at the Lunch Counter. At Blaine. If ever a heart was in a look, it was in his.

Cam sighed. Why didn't Blaine tell the family she had a French boyfriend? Or that she was bringing him home? During weekly Sunday-afternoon-with-the-family phone calls, Blaine had shared everything about her Parisian experience with them—mimicking the arrogant chef instructors to a tee (which made them all laugh) and providing lengthy descriptions of the new dishes she'd tried, then mastered.

But she had never mentioned the French guy in skinny jeans. She didn't tell anyone she'd be bringing him home! What did that mean, anyway? Were they serious? Was it even possible for her little sister to be serious about a man?

Cam's baby gave her a kick and she rubbed her tummy. "I'm with you, little guy. I'm still holding out hope for Artie." She didn't actually know her baby's gender, but from the constant tap dancing on her pelvic floor, she thought *boy*. The ferry tooted its horn and pulled away from the dock, as her baby kicked again, she thought *soccer player*. Then Cooper called to her from outside the Lunch Counter, and Cam turned away from fretting over Blaine, hurrying up the hill as quickly as she could, which was rather slow and cumbersome. These days, she shuffled. Cooper met her halfway up the hill to tell her all that had transpired in the last fifteen minutes.

Cam stopped to catch her breath. "I missed all that?"

"Yes, Mom," he said in that annoying preteenagey tone. "You're always missing stuff cuz you're always on the phone about that cell tower."

She sputtered a defense—no one in her family seemed to understand the pressure she was under to bring this cell tower to the island—but gave up. Cooper wasn't listening. He was already in front of the diner, holding the door open for her. Inside, the family was huddled around Blaine's French boyfriend, who lay prostrate in a booth.

Maddie saw Cam and hurried to join her. "Did you talk to Artie?" she whispered.

"No. Did he see Blaine?"

"Yes. Hardly any reaction, from either one of them." Maddie crossed her arms. "She's probably mad at us for not telling her Artie is working as a resident on the island."

"Then we're even. I'm mad at her for not telling us about the French boyfriend." Cam didn't get it. He just didn't seem like Blaine's type. Her sister was tall and lean and drop-dead gorgeous. She towered over Jean-Paul—a short and skinny guy who wore super-tight jeans with a cliché-kerchief around his neck.

Blaine saw her sisters by the door and crossed the room. "Why has Peg let this place get so run-down? When I left, the vibe was hip and cool."

"Peg doesn't know the first thing about hip and cool," Maddie said. "You're the one who gave the diner that vibe."

So true. The diner had returned to its former dumpy, drab pre-Blaine look. The food too. Cam knew Peg did the best she could, providing simple fare, but it was just that. Simple. Bland. Peg didn't have Blaine's magic in the kitchen. No one did. Not even Mom. Blaine's talent, even at a young age, surpassed Mom's.

"Seems odd to have Granddad show up out of the blue." Blaine glanced over at him, seated at a table, reading a newspaper he'd found. "You really had no idea he was coming?"

Cam shrugged. "None. But we had no idea you were bringing home a boyfriend either."

"He's not my boyfriend and his name is Jean-Paul."

"Hold it," Cam said. "If he's not your boyfriend, then . . . why is he here?"

"To meet my family. And for my family to get to know him."

"But why now? There's so much to do to get ready for the summer season. This is no time to be playing hostess."

"Don't worry," Blaine said, patting her shoulder. "Jean-Paul won't slow anything down. I'll explain more at dinner tonight, okay?" She held up the ice bag. "Excuse me. Jean-Paul needs fresh ice."

Cam watched Blaine plop the fresh ice pack on Jean-Paul's knee. "Think he's really not her boyfriend?"

Maddie gave her a gentle jab with her elbow. "That's what she said."

Cam sighed. "So suddenly we have two houseguests, just as we're trying to expand the camp *and* get ready for the coming summer season."

"Maybe our houseguests will help," Maddie said, ever the optimist.

"Maybe." But Maddie gave people a lot of margin, a lot of grace. Not Cam. With that, her baby gave her another swift kick.

When Maddie had woken this morning, she knew this day would be full of surprises with Blaine's homecoming. Good surprises. The family had intentionally kept some news from Blaine, like the coming babies and Artie Lotosky's position as outlying island doctor. And the kitchen remodel at Moose Manor. They weren't trying to keep Blaine out of the loop but to help her stay focused on finishing her culinary degree in Paris. It was the first thing Blaine had started on her own . . . and finished! It was cause for celebration. Her baby sister was growing up.

Now as the car turned onto the gravel driveway that led to Camp Kicking Moose, Maddie watched Blaine's reaction. In Maddie's eyes, the transformation over the last four years was astonishing. She had to give props to her dad for the vision of resurrecting the dumpy old camp. And credit Cam for bringing structure and style to Dad's vision. But Maddie had to give herself a little pat on the back . . . she was the one who helped to bring the vision to life. She was the one who paid attention to the endless little details of managing the camp. Nothing fancy or flashy, just steadily advancing the plot. Keeping the family together, united in purpose.

Having Blaine home again meant they could expand dining service at the camp. So far, they'd only been able to offer a continental breakfast. No longer! They'd been waiting for Blaine to return to move forward.

Maddie could hardly wait for the big reveal. She, Cam, Dad, and Cooper had a one-minute planning session about the sequence of events before they left the diner, while Blaine focused on Jean-Paul. Cam would get Granddad Grayson settled somewhere, Maddie would help Jean-Paul onto the couch with a fresh bag of ice on his puffy knee, and Dad and Cooper would keep Blaine distracted and not let her get near the kitchen. Not until the time was right.

Maddie wondered what her little sister would say when she saw the new state-of-the-art kitchen in Moose Manor—a major gut and remodel job, with all kinds of stresses and setbacks that the family endured during a bitterly cold Maine winter. She shuddered at the very recent memories: a freezing cold house because of a kitchen under construction, snow and mud and dirt traipsed in by workmen, endless family disagreements, costly change orders.

A major kitchen remodel was not for the squeamish. And Blaine, lucky girl, had missed it all.

Blaine stood in the new kitchen of Moose Manor, fighting back sudden tears. Why had no one told her? This kitchen remodel was supposed to be *her* project, suited to her specifications. *This* was why she had returned to Three Sisters Island. She was finally qualified, both in skills and in confidence, to turn Moose Manor into a destination fine dining spot. She'd been schooled in how to create a commercial kitchen. Trained in how to run it, how to staff it. And no one in her family had even asked her for input? For suggestions?

She walked around the room, trying to hide her mortification from her dad and sisters. They were so excited, sure she'd be thrilled.

"Isn't it beautiful?" Maddie said.

"Beautiful," Blaine echoed. And it was. But beauty was not the goal. Professional kitchens were designed for function, not aesthetics. For food safety. For ease of production. She gazed at the porcelain farmhouse sink. It was stunning, and completely impractical. Soon it would be covered in scratches. It should've been made of stainless steel. There should've been more than one sink. What kind of kitchen designer did they hire?

"Cam chose everything," Dad said. "All the textures and colors and appliances."

In other words, no kitchen designer was involved.

"Cam thinks the trend for open shelving is attractive," Maddie said, "so she opted to skip upper cupboards."

"So I see," Blaine said. Attractive, yes. Functional, no. Open-shelved baker's racks, now *that* would have been helpful. Those little decorative pieces of wood couldn't hold more than a small houseplant.

"Look at the wood floors," Dad said in his husky voice—though not as husky as it used to be. "All pine. You can see the grain."

"Very nice wood grain." Pine! A soft wood. Blaine could imagine how quickly the floor would show wear and tear, how water would destroy it. Never mind that there were no floor drains, no slip mats.

Smiling broadly, Maddie stood next to the four-burner stove top and waved her arm like Vanna White. A professional kitchen should have at least six to eight burners. At least. Blaine felt tears sting her eyes again.

"Check out this refrigerator," Cam said, opening one door wide.

Cooper burst into the kitchen and had to stop short.

Blaine felt like screaming, though she'd never been much of a screamer. The refrigerator was placed right next to the door that led to the dining room. Each time the fridge door opened, it blocked the passageway.

Cooper waited until Cam closed the door, then grabbed a bag of potato chips off the top of the refrigerator. (Seriously? Where was the pantry? Then she realized . . . there was no pantry!) He threw open the freezer door of the refrigerator and pulled out ice cream. (No commercial ice maker! Even the Lunch Counter had a commercial ice maker.) "Walter sent me to get some food."

"Walter?" Dad said.

"That's what he said to call him. I asked." Cooper cocked his head. "He said he didn't know about me. Said he's not old enough to be a great-grandfather, so just call him Walter."

"He's plenty old enough," Dad said, irritated, his voice now raspy. "Call him Granddad Grayson."

Cooper nodded, vanished through the door, popped back in, and grabbed three spoons. "For me, Jean-Paul, and Walter . . . I mean, Granddad Grayson."

It suddenly occurred to Blaine that the door leading from the kitchen to the dining room was not a swinging door, as one would expect in a restaurant. It was just a hinge door with a handle, opening *into* the kitchen (what were they thinking?!), right next

24

to a refrigerator. It was the worst possible way for servers to bring food in and out of the dining room. She squeezed her eyes shut. The dream of creating high-end dining service in Moose Manor fizzled like a Fourth of July firecracker tossed in a bucket of water.

"Well," Maddie said, tugging on Blaine's arm. "What do you have to say?"

Blaine just shook her head, eyes wide. This was a lot to absorb. This kitchen was designed for a home cook, a hobbyist, a dabbler. She could just imagine what her favorite chef instructor, Henri, would have to say, his hands chopping the air in agitation: "Do over! Eez all wrong!"

But she couldn't say that to her family. She couldn't admit what she was really thinking. Clearly, this was a costly project, a time-consuming effort, during what sounded like one of the longest, coldest winters in Maine's recent history.

Blaine turned away from everyone, cringing. Why couldn't they just have asked her before they started? They never asked. Never said a word about this kitchen. Her kitchen. She thought there was an unspoken agreement that she would return to create both the kitchen and the high-end dinner service at Moose Manor. She'd even created a recipe book.

But in this kitchen? This kitchen belonged to Cam. To be honest with herself, that's what irked Blaine the most. Cam, who couldn't even heat up canned soup properly, had *designed* the kitchen at Moose Manor. It was like having a non-driver design a freeway overpass.

Stalling, she peered out the kitchen window and noticed something that wasn't there before. Concrete. "What happened to the garden?"

"We turned it into a pickleball court last summer," Cam said. "They're all the rage. The campers love it."

Blaine had tagged that area as the best place on the property for a big garden. Lots of sun, flat land, close to the kitchen. Her garden. The garden she had planned in her mind, right down to the type of trellis to support the pole beans. A tear rolled down her cheek and she quickly brushed it away before anyone would notice. She'd had such high hopes for her homecoming. She'd needed to be away from her family these last two years to find her footing, to become an independent adult. And she'd done just that. But nothing had really changed in their family dynamics. Cam was in charge of everything. Dad and Maddie went along with Cam's plans, like they always did. Blaine was left out, rendered as a permanent child whose opinions didn't count.

"Well?" Dad said, a little impatiently.

So what should she say? What could she say?

"Hey," Maddie whispered, slipping up beside her. "You okay?"

Blaine leaned her head against Maddie's shoulder for the briefest of moments. She had learned much from her time in France, and perhaps the best lesson of all was the awareness that there was a time and place for all things, including conflict. And this wasn't the time for it.

She reached deep, pulled out a smile, and turned to face her dad and sisters. "This kitchen is . . . truly . . . absolutely . . . magazine-worthy."

They beamed.

BLAINE, AGE 12

It seemed to Blaine as if Cam and Mom were going off together on errands all summer long and offered up vague excuses each time she asked where they'd been. Blaine didn't mind so much until the week Maddie went off to summer camp. Then she was alone all the time, and she didn't like to be alone.

On a hot, muggy August morning, Blaine woke up late to an empty house. No note was left under a refrigerator magnet, where Mom usually put one if she had to go out. Blaine took the dog for a long walk, but when she came back and Mom still wasn't home, she started to feel scared. They'd planned to make a key lime pie this morning, Dad's favorite, because he was due in this weekend. They even had all the ingredients gathered on a tray. She decided not to wait for Mom.

Boy oh boy, that was a mistake.

She burnt the shortbread crust, nearly caught a rag on fire by leaving it too close to the flame, and curdled the custard with the limes. Don't even ask about the meringue—it was a disaster. Wet and white and gooey, like Elmer's glue.

She looked at the lumpy, gloppy effort. One tear started, then another, and soon she was weeping, overcome with self-pity. She was always left out. Maddie was having fun at camp, Mom and Cam were buddy-buddies, and she was home with a slobbery dog for company. Winslow licked the sticky floor around her. And where was Mom, anyway? It was her fault that this pie was so hard to make.

By the time Mom did walk through the door, it was after three o'clock, and Blaine was nearly hysterical, frightened and worried and furious.

Mom sat down at the kitchen table with a sigh. "I'm sorry, Blaine. I should have left a note."

That wasn't good enough for Blaine. She went on a rant of tears and accusations. "Why don't you just admit it? You love Cam more than me!"

Her mother sat back in her chair with a surprised look on her face, and it was then that Blaine noticed how exhausted she looked.

"Where have you been? Tell me the truth."

Mom rubbed her face. "Honey, you're too young for this."

"I am not! I know there's something going on, and I know it has something to do with Cam."

Mom dropped her hands, watched her for a while, then pulled out the chair next to her and patted it. "Not Cam. It has to do with Libby. She had a baby today. A beautiful little boy. She named him Grayson, after our family. Grayson Cooper."

Blaine's anger melted away. It just now occurred to her that she hadn't seen Libby in months. "But she's only Cam's age."

"That's right. Cam and I, we've been taking her to appointments all summer. Doctor visits and birthing classes. Cam and I acted as her labor coaches. Cam even cut the umbilical cord."

"Libby's not married."

"No, there's no dad around for this baby."

"Mom, she's going to need our help."

Mom reached out and pulled Blaine into a hug. "I owe you an apology, Blaine. I'm sorry you felt left out and alone. But please don't ever think you are less loved than your sisters. It's not true. You have no reason to be jealous of your sisters. You're loved because you're you." She kissed the top of her head. "Jealousy is a slippery slope that leads nowhere good." She sighed. "Never forget that you don't really know what's going on in people's lives. Only God knows."

"I tried to make our pie. It didn't turn out."

Mom looked over at the kitchen counter. "Let me have a piece. I'm starving."

That was a kindness. Even her dog Winslow wouldn't try it. Mom got up and cut off a slice, put it in her mouth, and puckered. "Did you remember to add sugar to the lime custard?"

Blaine hit her forehead with the palm of her hand. "Oh man. Sugar! Shoot."

Mom smiled. "Let me change clothes and we'll start again."

The next night, Dad said it was the best key lime pie he'd ever eaten. And they took half the pie over to Libby, to meet her new little baby boy.

Three

It was Paul's idea to be in charge of dinner tonight. He shooed everyone out of the kitchen and dug a pizza out of the freezer. While he turned on the oven, another brainstorm hit him—eating picnic style in the living room, complete with paper plates. That way, Jean-Paul—stuck on the couch—would feel included. His father, too, because that was pretty much Paul's fare through childhood.

It surprised him that Blaine didn't insist on cooking a big meal, that she didn't seem as eager as he thought she'd be to try out the new kitchen. Jet lag, probably. There would be plenty of nights to come for her to practice her culinary school education on them. Tonight, he thought, make it easy.

In the refrigerator, he found a salad-in-a-bag and tossed it in a bowl, squeezing out the orangy-looking salad dressing over it. The oven timer went off. He cut the pizza in slices, stacked them on a tray, and took it out to the living room, pretty darned pleased with himself.

Sitting cross-legged on the living room floor, Blaine tried not to burst into laughter as Dad handed Jean-Paul a paper plate with a slice of pizza on it.

29

"This eez *what*?" Jean-Paul asked, peering at it curiously.

"Pizza," Cooper said. "From the freezer."

"From my favorite box," Granddad said, helping himself to another slice.

"Blaine," Cam said, "tell us how you and Jean-Paul met."

Blaine shot a look at Jean-Paul, wondering how much she wanted to say and if he was going to volunteer anything, but his attention was fixed on the pizza, as if he was still trying to determine if it was edible. She glanced down at her plastic-looking pizza, aware of three pairs of eyes on her—Dad's, Cam's, Maddie's. They wanted to know who this guy was and what he meant to her and why she had brought him here. Why now, during the busy preseason time?

She'd thought this all through, and even had a little speech prepared, but the entire homecoming had gone sideways. Not now. Not with Granddad here. She just couldn't say more. She was afraid she might start crying, weary from jet lag, disappointed about the kitchen.

Cooper jumped up and ran to the kitchen, bringing back a big bottle of Pepsi.

"Blaine. . . ," Cam prompted. "You met Jean-Paul . . . where?"

Blaine looked up to see Cam check the time on her watch. That settled it. *Not now.* The whole story could wait. "We met on a bridge overlooking the Seine River. Jean-Paul's father has a bistro, and when he knew that I needed a job, he introduced me to his father. I cooked something for him—"

"A strawberry cake. *Magnifique*."

Blaine smiled at Jean-Paul. So he was listening. "—and he gave me a job. Which . . . led to Le Cordon Bleu. He's been a wonderful, amazing friend to me."

"That's it?" Dad said.

"*Oui*," Jean-Paul said, watching Blaine. She sent him a silent thank you. "And Blaine eez returning the favor to me. She invites me to your quiet little island as I ponder my future."

"Ponder your future?" Maddie said. "Like, you're at a fork in the road?"

"Oui—"

Before Jean-Paul could expand on the topic, Cooper opened the Pepsi bottle, oblivious that he had shaken it while he ran in from the kitchen. It exploded, spraying all of them with brown soda. It brought the moment of sharing to an abrupt and sticky end.

Yesterday had been such a wonderful day. Today was already starting out horribly. Maddie had been woken by a nightmare of that horrible fire that killed her mom and Libby. She hadn't had one of those in such a long time.

She glanced over Rick's shoulder at the clock on the night-stand. Three a.m. She'd hardly slept. Nor had Rick. He tossed and turned, jostling the bed. Jostling her.

In the quiet, Maddie rubbed her tummy, wondering what life would be like if Mom were still alive. This little baby would be her mom's first biological grandchild. It kind of pleased Maddie to be the first at something so significant, even if it was only by a few months. Cam was always first at everything in their family. Not this time. In fact, Maddie had a hunch that it took the announcement of her own pregnancy to spur Cam along to try to get pregnant. She'd been hemming and hawing, and Maddie knew that Seth was super anxious to have children. He didn't want Cooper growing up as a lonely only.

Rick flopped over, startling her out of her reflections.

She lifted her head. "What's wrong?"

"Just . . . a little . . . heartburn," he said.

"Do you want to go sleep on the couch?" It often helped if he could be in a more upright position.

"I would, but Blaine's friend might get the wrong idea."

Smiling, Maddie gave Rick a gentle kick, and he responded by putting her arm around her, pulling her close. She heard his heart beating, steady and regular, a sound that brought her enormous comfort. She closed her eyes and tried to sleep, but her mind kept spinning. Sleepless nights were happening too often for Rick lately.

Maddie knew she was a natural-born worrier. She had worked diligently on mastering that tendency. She hadn't had a panic attack in over three years; she handled unexpected crises with calm and aplomb, she straddled that thin line of too much/not enough empathy for her clients, she tried not to jump to the worst-case scenario in future matters. And then she became pregnant and slid right back into those same habits she thought she'd conquered. Like a default setting on a computer.

She worried about the baby's health, about being a good mother, about juggling work with motherhood, about whether or not they should remain at Moose Manor after the baby was born—but they really couldn't afford to live anywhere else. She worried about the life her baby boy would have, she wondered what this little boy would look like, who he would *be* like. From her basement office, she often heard the children playing in the schoolyard across the street. The boys were always shrieking, chasing each other around the yard, never still.

How would she be able to survive raising a boy?

She even worried about Cam's pregnancy, because her sister didn't seem to worry about it herself. Why *was* Cam so big? She was barely into her second trimester. Could her due date be mistaken?

Mostly, Maddie worried about Rick.

When Maddie had married Rick, she was fully aware of what risks lay in store, even with the ICD that monitored his heart. Despite a serious heart condition, he lived life at full throttle. A zest for life was his very essence and she loved him for it. She had made a promise to God that she would not try to change her husband and she meant to keep it. In their first year of marriage, demands on his time began to pile up and she said nothing. His reputation grew. A second church on another unbridged island was added to his preaching responsibilities, plus numerous out-of-town speaking engagements. Maddie battled her increasing fear for him. Still, she kept those worries to herself.

But after she became pregnant, her firm "hands-off" resolve went out the window. She tried reasoning with him, tried to get him to reduce his commitments. He always listened calmly to her and promised to try. But nothing ever really changed as a result of their talks.

Finally, Maddie drifted off when she heard a noise. Her eyes opened to light peering through the window shade. Rick was changing into clothes. "Where are you going?"

Bent over to tie his shoes, he said, "Early meeting." When he sat back up, he let out a sharp gasp.

"What?"

Slowly, he let out a breath. "Just got up too fast."

Maddie sat up in bed. "I'll call Dr. Turner and see if she can fit you in today."

"No, no. I have a checkup in a month or so. It can wait."

"Your heart is nothing to mess with, Rick. Even your mom . . ."

He turned to face her, eyebrows lifted. "My mom?"

"I called her yesterday. I invited her to come up for a visit before the season starts, but she's worried she'll be in the way. By that . . . she means you and your busy schedule."

"Nonsense. Tell her to come. I'll clear the decks."

Sure you will. Maddie bit her tongue.

"You two could shop for baby things. She could help you set up the nursery."

"I love your mom. I really do. I couldn't ask for a better mother-in-law. But she's not coming to see me. She wants to see her son."

He shook his head. "Not true. She's crazy about you, Mads. You know what she always says." He lifted his voice an octave to mimic his mother's voice. "Rick is my son, but Maddie is the daughter God gave me."

"Don't make fun of your mom."

"I'm not! I owe her everything. She took my sister and me to church every Sunday and injected the fear of God into the marrow of our bones."

She looked intently into Rick's brown eyes. Eyes that had the same irresistible twinkle that stole Maddie's heart when they first met—all the way back in kindergarten. It was a mighty powerful twinkle. "Richard O'Shea. Stop deflecting."

"I know perfectly well that you're trying to protect me, Madison O'Shea."

"Why not take the day off? I only have two afternoon appointments today. We could spend the morning together."

"I'll be back before you can miss me."

She plopped back on the pillow. "Right. I've heard that line before."

He bent over to kiss her, but she rolled over, angry with him. He kissed her on the top of her head. "I love you."

"If you loved me, you'd listen to me and go see Dr. Turner today."

"Ah, there you have it. Flawed thinking. Love isn't conditional."

She groaned. That was a line she'd heard him spill plenty of times too. He had all kinds of sayings to assuage her, but it really boiled down to Rick refusing to slow down. Nothing seemed to matter to him but doing the work of God as hard and fast as he could.

Maddie wasn't quite so convinced that it was God who was asking so much of him.

Blaine woke up in an introspective, sulky kind of mood. Somehow she had managed to get through her homecoming with calm dignity. Those two words were her focal points, grasped on to when she walked into the new kitchen. *Stay calm. Keep my dignity.*

But that kitchen! That impractical, inefficient kitchen. And the gorgeous sunny spot behind the house that was just aching to become a vegetable garden . . . had been paved over for pickle-ball. Blaine knew her reaction to these changes was childish, but she couldn't seem to be able to move past it. She felt as if she were seven years old again: Cam in charge, Dad oblivious, Maddie on the fence, trying to see each situation from every angle. Blaine thought she was ready to come home again. But maybe she wasn't.

She had waited to return to her family until she was confident that the girl who was permanently insecure and easily offended, terrified of failure, sniveling herself to sleep at night because she felt so insignificant, was no longer. She was coming home with hard-earned maturity, something that had started during that terrible, terrible time at the beginning of her stay in Paris and blossomed over the next two years. Blaine Grayson was a different person now. After all, had she not just graduated from the most famous culinary school in the world? Not only graduated, but received honors. And magnanimous job offers! All of which she turned down, determined to keep her promise to her dad to help him start the restaurant at Moose Manor.

She pulled the covers over her head. Here she was, a grown woman thinking like a peeved teenager. A complete regression to her childhood role. Unfortunately, self-pity was the first place Blaine went whenever she felt diminished by others, real or imagined.

Blaine pulled the covers off her head. The important thing was that she was only *thinking* that way. Not acting that way. She could let her feelings about the kitchen and garden stew in the back of her mind, but they needed to stay there, because, really, that was all she could do about them.

She threw the covers off and jumped out of bed. What she needed was a distraction. To get out of the house and away from this mood. She needed to go see Peg. She wanted to find out what had happened with Peg's romance with Bob Lotosky. She wanted to find out what had happened to Artie.

Minutes later, Blaine rummaged the kitchen cupboards to find something acceptable for Jean-Paul's breakfast. He was on the couch with his tender swollen knee and deserved a decent meal for cushioning her grandfather's fall.

She thought she'd make Jean-Paul a sumptuous omelet with minced *fines herbes*, filled, perhaps, with grilled asparagus and Swiss cheese, yet the ridiculously small refrigerator was shockingly bare of necessities. No eggs, no cheese. Cooper had used the two remaining pieces of bread—the heels—for his school lunch. Didn't anyone shop for food in this household? Did they all just eat at the Lunch Counter? Probably.

Blaine was actually impressed that Cooper was willing to eat the heels from a loaf of bread. Two years ago, he would have first drilled Blaine with questions about how old the bread was and examined it carefully for signs of mold. But her delight in seeing him make a significant stride over anxiety dissipated when she saw him take a can of Lysol and spray down his backpack—including the zipper—before tucking his lunch bag inside and running out the kitchen door to join Seth for a bike ride to school. So, his tendency toward anxiety wasn't *completely* gone. Well, to quote Chef Henri, "Little steps, little steps."

Blaine grabbed the milk container, a bowl and spoon, and Cooper's cereal box of Fruit Loops. "Good morning," she said, putting everything within Jean-Paul's reaching distance on the coffee table. "How's your knee today?"

Jean-Paul squinted at the box. "What eez zis?"

Seeing the look of horror on his face, she quickly reassured him. "Cereal. Children's cereal. I'm heading into town this morning. I promise to bring back food you'll approve of." She gazed at him, lying there. He looked so pathetic, so pale and uncomfortable. His knee had puffed up to the size of a grapefruit and looked red and angry and sore. "How are you feeling today?"

"Much better."

"Liar." She went back to the kitchen and returned with a bag of ice, draping it gently over his knee. "Did you sleep well?"

"At times, it eez so quiet here. Other times, eez loud."

"Different sounds than city living. You'll get used to them." Blaine loved mornings in Maine, waking to songbirds.

"Blaine, what does zis word 'ay-up' mean?"

"Ah! You're noticing the secret code. It's the Maine way of saying, 'Why yes, indeed, I agree wholeheartedly.'"

"It means all zat?"

"Ayup." She reached for the remote and turned on the TV. "This might help pass the time until I get back from town." She handed him the remote. "You can change channels to find something you'd like to watch."

At first, he seemed completely mystified by the numerous controls on the remote. Then he wrinkled his nose. "TV eez junk food for zee soul." He lifted his cell phone off his lap. "Does not work."

"Didn't I warn you? There's no cell phone service on the island."

He gasped in horror. "Non! *Tu es sérieuse?*"

"Jean-Paul!" Blaine laughed. "You're the one who always says"— she lowered her voice and added a bad French accent—"zee cell phone eez no substitute for zee face-to-face."

Blaine heard Maddie pick up her car keys, so she waved goodbye to Jean-Paul and followed Maddie out the door to catch a ride to the Lunch Counter. A twinge of guilt pricked her; she should stay home to keep Jean-Paul company, but she did need to stock up on real food for this family of hers. And she needed some time alone.

Besides, Peg needed her more. The condition of the Lunch Counter was alarming and Blaine felt responsible for its decline. When she left, just two years ago, she had set things up for Peg to continue its success. But no. It had reverted back to a tired old diner, serving pale, weak coffee. Watery scrambled eggs with limp bacon. Biscuits that could chip a tooth. Blaine shuddered. Yes, Peg needed her more than Jean-Paul did right now.

Normally, Maddie would have filled the car ride to town with probing questions, trying to coax Blaine to share her innermost feelings and reflections. All counselor-y. Happily, today her sister was completely focused on her pregnancy, although not in a good way. Heartburn, hemorrhoids, weight gain, fatigue . . . on and on and on.

Nearing town, Blaine was starting to rethink whether she'd ever want to have children. But on a cheerier note, Maddie's attention was not on Blaine. As soon as her sister pulled the car to a stop and finished her lament over her swollen ankles, Blaine jumped out and turned to her with a smile. "Thanks for the ride. Remember to elevate those fat ankles in between customers!"

"Not fat!" Maddie said. "I never said fat! I said swollen. And they're *not* customers. They're clients."

Blaine lifted her hand in a friendly wave. As much as Maddie complained, she shouldn't worry. She looked great. But Cam looked *huge*. And no wonder, Blaine thought, if last night was any indication. Cam ate enough for an army. It surprised Blaine that Cam, who was so self-disciplined, would let herself balloon like this.

Blaine peered into the Lunch Counter to see Peg at the stove and she paused, the sight calming her for a moment. She yanked open the door to the diner as Peg bent over, poking at something in a big pot.

Peg had taken an interest in Blaine, had noticed her talent in the kitchen and given her a job, when no one else seemed to give her a second thought. Often, after closing time, while they were cleaning up, she'd put down the broom and say to Blaine, "Pull up a chair, honey. Let's have a chat."

As they talked, Blaine would study Peg, trying to decide what made her so wonderful. Peg Legg was somewhere in her fifties, comfortably, bouncily plump, happy by nature and endlessly kind. She wore her dyed red hair pulled back in two pigtails, held with a variety of hair clasps, finished off with a brightly colored headband. But it wasn't just Peg's cheerful appearance that fascinated Blaine. It was how she listened, focusing all her attention on her, often remaining silent for a minute or two while she contemplated Blaine's words.

"Uh-huh," Peg would hum. "Let me think on that a bit." And she would.

She had a kind of patience with not having all the answers, with not being in control, and Blaine worked to achieve that in herself. Peg had two solutions to most of the problems in life: God loved her, and it was all going to be okay.

Peg turned at the door's jingle and, seeing Blaine, her face lit. When Peg smiled, something shone from her face, something generous and welcoming and gentle. "Hey there, honey! Aren't you a sight for sore eyes."

Blaine's heart melted. Then she sniffed. Her nose, always hypersensitive, was on high alert. "What's that smell?"

"I'm making grits for Captain Ed."

Blaine sniffed the air again and realized, with horror, that the aroma wafting from the bubbling pot on the stove was not something anyone would associate with humble grits: the corn smell of stone-ground grits, nor the hearty smell of homemade chicken stock, nor the sweet scent of cooking cream.

No. This . . . this smell . . . it was a mixture of Play-Doh and stale beer. "What cheese did you add in?"

Peg scanned the ceiling as if counting something up there.

"Peg . . . ," Blaine said in a warning voice.

"Well, honey, I ran out of cheddar cheese, so I swapped it out with something else." Blaine saw the empty jar of Cheez Whiz and shuddered. "Peg, we've gone over this. Stick to the recipe. Then, after you've made it successfully dozens of times, *then* and only then are you allowed to make substitutions." That very concept had been drilled into her at Le Cordon Bleu: Master the basics. *Then* you will learn to intuit how to apply basic principles in new circumstances.

Peg's usually cheerful face reddened. "Everybody swaps ingredients. I call it a switcheroo."

Blaine grabbed a potholder and dumped the disgusting glob of grits into the sink. Take two. She grabbed another pan to start over. This time, she made a show of turning the burner on low with a small whoosh of air. "Once your grits reach the boiling point, you want to turn the heat way down, to keep them from burning. Stir, stir, stir."

"So why do you think your cute little grandpa is here?"

Blaine glanced over at Peg. *Cute* and *little* weren't words she would attach to Granddad Grayson. "Actually, I don't really know."

"I think it's nice."

Nice, Blaine supposed, but also kind of weird. Granddad Grayson had never seemed to be terribly interested in any of them.

She handed the spoon to Peg and went to the fridge. The large, two-sided, commercial refrigerator. But searching for cheese, any cheese, made her cringe. What had happened to the labels she'd carefully stuck on every flat surface? What had happened to the organizational system she had set up? She gasped. On the bottom shelf of the fridge was a platter of green Jell-O with canned peaches suspended inside. She sighed. Everything she'd done had been undone.

"Keep stirring?"

"Keep stirring." Blaine found one package of moldy Swiss cheese and tossed it in the trash. These grits might have to be cheese-less. Wait, hold on. She found a container of grated Parmesan cheese . . . and it hadn't expired. Triumphant, she took the spoon back from Peg. "We're stepping things up a notch."

Peg sighed. "Story of this island. Thanks to the summer people."

Blaine stirred the grits slowly. "I noticed lots of change going on around here." After she had said goodbye to Maddie this morning, she walked down Main Street, astounded at the little boutiques that filled the empty buildings. Even the humble grocery store looked like someone had given it a makeover. Green-and-white-striped awning, wooden stands of colorful fruit. "Nancy's grocery store sure looks pretty spiffy." She glanced at Peg, wondering why she had let the Lunch Counter slip back to its 1950s look. Not in a chic vintagey way, just in a drab, colorless way.

"Spiffy?" Peg gave a humorless little laugh. "That's because Nancy sold it and moved to the mainland to live near her daughter." She pointed to empty baker's racks lining the walls. "You probably noticed those."

"I did." When Blaine had left the island, those racks were strategically placed around the diner, filled with tempting, high-end picnic food products. Peg's sales had skyrocketed.

"That new grocery store owner stocked everything I carried, and marked it down to crazy-low prices."

Blaine sighed. "Loss leaders." A well-known grocery store marketing tool to coax a shopper into the store. Poor Peg.

"I couldn't sell a blessed thing. Those fancy schmancy cracker boxes you ordered grew dusty." Peg stood next to the ancient cash register, inputting numbers into a credit card processor. Mumbling to herself, something that sounded like a cuss word.

Blaine paused, midstir, eyes wide. Credit cards! "Peg! You *are* entering the twenty-first century."

Peg waved Blaine off with a flick of her wrist. "Mind your grits."

Oh! The grits. Blaine reached for the container of Parmesan and whisked it into the grits, stirring rapidly. Peg came over to peer into the pot.

"If it looks too thick," Blaine said, "you can add more broth to make sure you've got the right consistency."

"Broth?"

"What were you using?"

Peg's eyes darted toward an open can. "Condensed milk?"

Blaine cringed. "Ohhh, I have so much work to do."

Peg pushed the back of her hand against the bow of her purple headband. "Honey, it's so good to have you home." She took a fresh spoon and dipped it into the grits. Her blue eyes went wide as she swallowed. "I could eat my weight in that." She tried another spoonful. "How do you do it? You didn't even glance at the recipe."

"Experience."

"I've been cooking for thirty years and I don't have what you have."

Blaine turned off the burner and put a lid on top of the grits. "At Le Cordon Bleu, we had something called '*travaux pratiques*.' In English, it means practicals. The instructor would prepare a dish a day or two ahead, and we were graded on how well we followed his techniques and how well the recipe turned out."

"Bet you crushed it."

Blaine gave a modest shrug of her shoulders. Yes, she had crushed travaux pratiques. Chef Instructor Henri said she was the most gifted student he'd ever had, and he was stingy with compliments.

Peg handed her the coffee beans to grind. "Are you glad you're back?"

"Yes," Blaine said, but without that confident sound. She pressed the button to grind and waited for the right sound of crushed beans. Just enough and not too much. "It's just that . . ."

Peg sighed. "It's that kitchen."

Blaine spun around. "Yes!"

"Honey, I told them." Peg put her hands on her hips. "I told them to wait until you came back. But once Cam and Paul Grayson get their mind set on something, there's no way to change it. It's like trying to flag down a bullet train. You just get out of the way."

Scooping coffee into the filter, Blaine pondered Peg's insights. She'd never thought that she and Maddie shared any similar traits, but they did both hop out of the way of the coming train. Dad had bought Camp Kicking Moose without telling anyone, even though it profoundly affected the entire family. Cam had adopted Cooper without any discussion, even though it meant they would all be raising him. Dad and Cam together? They were a formidable force. Peg knew them all so well.

Blaine poured water into the container and waited for the black stream of coffee to flow into the pitcher. "Have you seen the kitchen?"

"Sure have. Real pretty."

"Pretty. Not at all practical." Peg set two mugs on the counter and Blaine filled them. "Thank you for trying, Peg." For understanding.

"Hon, that kitchen would scare me to cook in it. Everything looks breakable."

Pretty much. "I'm stuck between a rock and a hard place. I feel like a heel by complaining. I sound so ungrateful. Dad must have spent a chunk of change on the remodel. I know that it was done for the right reasons. Everyone's heart was in the right place. But there's no way that kitchen can support a restaurant—even a small one. I don't see how Moose Manor can be what we planned it to be."

Peg didn't respond, which was unlike her. Blaine glanced at her, wondering just what she was thinking. Brows furrowed, she had a look on her face as if she were trying to figure out how to phrase something.

"Go ahead, Peg. Say what's on your mind."

"Honey, life doesn't always turn out the way we plan."

"Huh?" Was Peg talking about herself or about Blaine? Before she could ask, the bell over the door jingled as two customers walked in and Peg swept into action.

Feeling melancholy, Blaine walked around the kitchen, letting her fingertips trail across the cheap laminate countertop with curled seams. She gazed at the painted plywood cupboards with pegboard facing, at the cooktop that, as far as Blaine was concerned, was ready for a trip to the dump.

Fretting over Moose Manor's nonexistent restaurant could wait. This might be a crummy little kitchen compared to the new one in Moose Manor, but it was Peg's crummy little kitchen. And for that alone, she loved it. She loved being here. She loved Peg, had missed her so much.

Out of her oversized purse she pulled her prized possession: her chef's whites. A jacket with her name embroidered on it. She slipped it on with reverence, carefully buttoning each button down the double-breasted front. She knew what she had to do. She was going to get the Lunch Counter back on track before the summer people started sailing in.

Four

WHEN COOPER TOLD CAM that other kids at school called his mother the Queen of the Summer People, she was shocked. On this island, there was no greater insult. Summer people were a different kind of tourist than the typical day-trippers from Acadia or the campers. Tolerated, but not particularly liked. Welcomed, but not wanted.

Cam couldn't deny that many summer people—not all, but many—gave off an attitude. Summer people wanted a good time; they didn't really care about the island or the locals, or the wildlife and fauna, or the three other seasons of the year. They were on vacation in a place where the islanders made their home.

Cam knew she wasn't truly accepted yet, still viewed as an outsider. She knew the locals viewed her with suspicion. Skepticism. And she was aware that she might come across as a tiny bit condescending or overbearing. Still, she was shocked to be considered the flavor of snooty that gave certain summer people their reputation. To be called the Queen of the Summer People? Wow, *that* smarted.

Cooper stood in front of her, waiting for a response. "So what should I tell the kids?" He pushed his glasses up on the bridge of his nose. "You know, when they call you that."

"Tell them, um . . ." Frankly, she didn't know how to respond.

45

Seth appeared at her side with glasses of ice water. "You need to drink more water. Eight glasses a day, the doctor said."

"Why, thanks," Cam said, happy for the interruption. Helping herself, she took a sip, then another, stalling. She'd never been particularly good at this kind of thing. But Seth . . . he was great at it. "Honey, we need your input here. Apparently, some of the kids at school are teasing Cooper about the cell phone tower."

"Not the cell phone tower," Cooper said, shaking his head like a dog out of a lake. "And not me. It's about Mom. The kids all call her the Queen of the Summer People."

"Yeah, so I've heard," Seth said, avoiding Cam's eyes. "Coops, your mom is doing her best to help the island. There are always a few people who resist any kind of change, so that's why you heard someone make that comment."

"It wasn't just one kid, Dad. It was a lot of them. They even have a song they made up."

"A song?" Cam said, her voice cracking a bit.

"It goes like this." Cooper cleared his throat. "Cam the Ham—"

Seth held up his hand like a stop sign. "That's enough, Cooper."

"But I didn't finish the song."

"I get the general idea," Cam said.

"Look," Seth said, "there were a lot of insults tossed at your mom before the wind turbine and solar panels and hydro dam went in—"

"There were?" Cam said. How had she missed those?

Cooper nodded. "A lot."

"This is the same kind of thing," Seth said. "Change is hard for people, but later, they're grateful for it. People love having reliable energy to power the electricity to their homes and businesses now."

"Not everyone," Cooper said. "Not Mr. Phinney. He says Mom is out to ruin the island."

"You just can't please everyone," Seth said.

"Especially Baxtor Phinney," Cam added.

Seth ignored her. "But your mom is trying to do a good thing *for* everyone, even if some will always complain about it. Those kinds of comments don't bother your mom at all, so don't let them bother you either."

"Mom's tough."

"Ayup. Mom's tough." Seth clapped his hands. "You know, I think I saw some blueberry tarts that Blaine brought home from the diner. Cooper, let's go check it out." The two of them left Cam at her desk, staring at her PowerPoint presentation on her computer.

Seth, as usual, said just the right thing to help Cooper. He had a knack for seeing the big picture. But one thing he was wrong about. Cam wasn't quite as tough as everyone thought.

Small raindrops were starting to hit against the windowpanes. Paul was grateful there'd been a few days of bright blue skies for Blaine's homecoming before the more typical spring weather returned. He hoped it wouldn't be a rainy summer, like last year. After a couple of days with lots of sunshine, the campers at Camp Kicking Moose didn't mind a rainy day as a change of pace. But if there were too many rainy days in a row, they would glare at Paul, as if he had caused the gloomy weather.

"Dad, are you listening to me?"

Paul turned from gazing out the window at the rain and looked at Maddie. He was half listening, mainly because he didn't like what she was telling him. He had never thought of himself as passive-aggressive, or as an avoider, but those were the labels his therapist daughter Maddie had just slapped on him.

"Talk to Granddad Grayson," she said as she handed him a cup of coffee. "He's your father. Find out why he's here."

Standing by the farmhouse sink in the magazine-worthy kitchen—now *there* was a label Paul liked—he knew Maddie was right. Two days had passed and he had made himself as scarce as a man could be, which wasn't at all difficult, or even suspicious. It was March; opening season for Camp Kicking Moose was just two months away. This last winter had been particularly cold, snowy, windy—which Paul felt he'd somehow conjured up by choosing to have the kitchen remodeled. It made no sense, but he felt as if he'd annoyed Mother Nature in some way and was getting a payback.

Winter always took a toll on the camp. Loose shingles, leaky windows, frozen pipes, and then came spring rains, like today's, which often brought flooding as an abundance of water tried to find a place to go. Never Enough Thyme, his favorite cabin, seemed to have a pond settle beneath it each spring.

So why did his father pick this time of year to show up? Why did he come at all? The last time Paul had seen his father, he'd told him he never wanted to see him again. Swirling his coffee, he practically cringed at the memory.

"Dad!"

Paul snapped his head up. "I'll talk to him, Maddie."

"You're acting really weird."

Paul wasn't acting weird. He was acting normal. It was the sudden appearance of his father that was weird. It was Blaine's friend stuck on the living room couch with his knee elevated—*that* was weird. But to explain all that to Maddie would be asking too much of his easily strained vocal cords.

Maddie poured a second cup of coffee and handed it to him, along with today's newspaper. "Take this to Granddad. He's out on the porch. Go talk."

His father seemed to like the front porch, even in the rain. He had spent the last two days there since he'd arrived, reading the newspaper and doing crossword puzzles.

Paul crossed through the living room, past the boyfriend on the couch, and out to the porch. He handed his father the coffee cup and sat down in a rocking chair beside him.

"So," he said. A good start to an honest conversation, he thought.

"So?"

"So what brings you here?" he asked his father, a man he hardly knew anymore.

His father eyed him. "So . . . your voice is still a mess. And you're living on an island. What brought *you* here?"

Stalling, Paul took a sip of coffee. True, his voice wasn't what it used to be, but it was a whole lot better than it had been the last few years. He'd had a successful career as a radio sports announcer, a job he'd loved, until that one Christmas when a severe case of laryngitis arrived and never left. What did leave was his career. He became a radio announcer without a voice. So he did what any logical man nearing the age of sixty might do. He retired early.

Then Paul did something totally illogical. He used his 401(k) and savings to buy a bankrupt camp on a remote island off the coast of Maine.

To explain all that to his father would use up his words for the day—something his speech therapist had drilled into him. *Choose carefully what you want to say,* she often reminded him, *because you should only say so much. Don't waste your words. Save them for what's truly important.*

Not such a bad theory for everyone to abide by, he had realized.

Too bad such heightened awareness had come so late in life. He could have used that filter as a husband, and as a father to three daughters.

It occurred to Paul that his father seemed to know a lot about him. They hadn't spoken since that last time, long before Corinna had died. How did his father know to find him at Camp Kicking Moose anyway?

He tried again. "What brings you to the island?"

His father peered at him over the corner of the newspaper. "Can't a father visit his son without a reason?"

Not if they haven't spoken in over fifteen years. But his father knew that. There was some reason he'd come to the island, something that was behind this. But that might have to wait. Something more important was pressing on Paul's mind. "Dad, are you still drinking? Because if you are, you can't stay here."

His father put down the newspaper and glared at him. "Been sober five years now."

Paul sucked in a deep breath. That news was not just a relief, but a miracle. He'd love to know how his father came to sobriety after a lifetime of alcoholism. For now, Paul felt satisfied with this first stab at a conversation. He tipped the rocking chair forward and rose. "Breakfast should be served soon."

"Who's cooking?"

Paul crossed his arms. "Blaine. My youngest daughter."

"She's the one who made those splendid sticky cinnamon rolls yesterday?"

"Yes, that's her."

His father folded down a corner of the newspaper.

"She's the only one who looks like your mother."

"How so?"

"Tall. Willowy. Blonde."

Interesting. Paul's memories of his mother were vague. In them, she certainly was not willowy, tall, and blonde. Beaten down, shoulders slumped, *that* he remembered.

One more question. "How long do you plan to stay?"

His father dropped the newspaper in his lap. "You kicking me out?"

Paul shook his head. Not yet. "Season starts on Memorial Day. There's a lot of work to do to get the camp ready. And even more work after it opens." He cleared his throat, something his speech therapist had warned him not to do because it caused injury to fragile vocal folds. "If you plan on staying, you'll be expected to earn your keep." He didn't even look at his father for an answer. His voice sounded like gravel, he needed to rest it, and he wanted his father to think long and hard before he responded.

But that didn't stop his father. "About that little boy with the glasses . . ."

"Cooper. Your great-grandson."

"So he's the eldest girl's son?"

"Her name is Camden. She's your first granddaughter. And yes, Cooper is her son."

"He doesn't resemble her in the slightest."

"That's because she adopted him. Cooper is her best friend Libby's son. Libby died in the fire with Corinna." *Oh boy*. Paul's voice had ground down to a scratch, and it wasn't even eight o'clock in the morning. He'd been doing so much better lately. Just as his father opened his mouth to ask another question, Paul flagged him off. "Ask Cam," his voice near a whisper, "if you want more info."

Thank goodness Paul didn't have an appointment today with his speech therapist. She would read him the riot act. He could imagine how she would lecture him, holding three fingers in the air. "Steam, water, vocal naps." He knew, he knew. "First thing in the morning," she would say, wagging a finger in his face, "first thing! Your voice needs warming up. Slow starts. Hot water with honey."

Had he started slow today? Did he have a cup of hot water with honey?

No. He'd had coffee, a forbidden love. "Anything," his bossy speech therapist would scold, "*anything* that dehydrates is going to increase the closed phase, creating wear and tear on the edge of the vocal folds."

Yup, yup. Paul understood. But he did love that first cup of coffee.

"That little kid with the glasses needs a dog. He's at the perfect age for it. Every boy should have a dog."

Paul shot out of the chair. Seth's dog Dory had passed away last summer and it broke Paul's heart. The last thing he needed to worry about was a dog. Good grief, he had a camp to run. And now that Blaine was back, the time had come to expand Moose Manor's dining services. He gave his father a brief wave and hurried into the house. That was enough for now.

Later in the day, Cam was working at the kitchen table when Jean-Paul hopped in on one leg. "Hi, Jean-Paul. Can I help you with something?"

"No, no. I am just getting a glass of water. Where eez Blaine?"

"She's in town, visiting Peg. The diner's owner." Cam's focus returned to her computer as he hopped from one part of the kitchen to another to fill up a glass of water.

"Eez good zis kitchen eez so"—he squeezed his thumb and index fingers on his good hand together—"minuscule." In his thick French accent it sounded more like *mini-school*.

Minuscule? This kitchen wasn't small! It was plenty big. "I like to think of it as compact and efficient." She leaned back in her chair and stretched. "Would you like to sit down?" She really, really needed to work, but she knew she should be hospitable. Seth had given her a warning, just last night, that she was starting to go into a default mode of snippiness—her stress handle.

"No, no. Merci." He refilled his water glass and Cam went back to work. A moment later, she realized Jean-Paul had leaned against the beautiful farmstead sink, watching her type. When she looked up, he said, "You work very hard."

"Well, yes. Especially now. I'm preparing a presentation to the island residents to allow for a cell phone tower, so we can finally, finally, get cell coverage and Wi-Fi. Right now, you have to go down to a certain place near Boon Dock and wave your phone in the air, hoping for a signal."

He nodded his head from side to side, very French-like. "Zat would be nice."

She looked back at her screen to see where she had left off.

"And zee island residents, zey want zis?"

"Sort of," she said, not even looking up, hoping he would take the hint that she needed to work.

"What does zat mean . . . 'sort of'?"

Inwardly, Cam sighed. She really needed to get this presentation done so she could ask Peg to call for a village meeting and get this cell phone tower approved. As soon as she checked that off her list, she and Blaine could drill down on Moose Manor's fine dining plans.

She felt a kick from the baby. And then there was that too. She had so much to do before the baby arrived.

"Sort of? It means . . . that the locals will need a little persuasion. They tend to say no to new ideas, but later on they're grateful for them." She thought so, anyway.

Jean-Paul listened to her with a pensive look on his face. "So zese locals . . . zey do not know what zey want?"

"Exactly. They're a little like children."

"And you are zee parent."

She paused. Put that way, it did seem like an odd analogy. One that would offend Peg and deeply insult Baxtor Phinney. "Let's just say . . . I've seen this situation play out before." She glanced at her computer hoping Jean-Paul would hop away. She really wanted to get back to work.

"Your little boy, Cooper. Each time I see him, he likes to scrub down surfaces. Scrub, scrub, scrub."

"Yes. Cooper has, um, a tendency toward repetition and some irrational fears. It's much better than it used to be." Though this germ phobia was a new twist. It started when the kitchen remodel began last winter. "He thinks germs are everywhere—"

"He eez not wrong."

"—and that all germs are bad and going to make him sick."

"So he eez on high alert."

"What?"

"His mind. It eez on high alert, all the time."

"Yes, I suppose that's one way of looking at it."

"You talk to him about it, oui?"

"Do I talk to him about germs? Oh yes, of course. I tell him that there are good germs and bad germs and that there's nothing to worry about and to only wash his hands before meals or after he goes to the bathroom."

"Oui, oui. I hear you talk to him. Talk, talk, talk. It causes me to wonder if, maybe, zee talking so much makes it worse. Makes him stay on high alert. All zee time, he stays on high alert."

Oh. *Oh*. She hadn't thought of it like that. She assumed it would be wise to get his germ awareness out in the open. Hmm. She'd have to run this by Cooper's therapist. She turned back to her computer. "I'm sorry to cut you off, but I'd better get back to work."

"*Pardon, pardon.* My apologies for interrupting."

Cam watched Jean-Paul hop away. As soon as she heard the TV turn on in the living room, she tiptoed to the landline and called Cooper's therapist.

Three Sisters Island was a small island, a small town. Sooner or later, Blaine would run into Artie. But days were passing and she'd seen no sign of him. Heard not a word from him. *Man.* Two years ago, they told each other everything. Pretty much everything. What had gone so terribly wrong between them? She had no idea.

Early in the morning on the third day after her homecoming, she popped in the kitchen to grab her purse and keys. Dad was at the table, drinking coffee. "Since when are you allowed to drink coffee?"

He frowned. "Since when did you agree to work full-time for Peg?"

"Dad, the diner is a wreck. Obviously, she needs me full-time."

"As soon as Cam gets the green light from the town for the cell phone tower, she'll turn her focus to setting up dining service this summer. We'll need to get rolling."

"Well, first things first. After she's done with the cell phone thingamajigee, then we'll talk."

"What about him?" He pointed to the door that led to the living room, where Jean-Paul was asleep on the couch.

"His knee looks a little better, don't you think?"

"Not really. More importantly, I wonder how he feels about being here when you're gone all day."

Jean-Paul had never complained that he felt she had ditched him. Then again, he wasn't a complainer. But there was no way she was going to sit at home while his knee mended. Peg needed her, and she needed to be needed. "Don't worry about Jean-Paul, Dad. Artie told him to rest two or three days. Maybe tomorrow he can come with me into town." She hoisted her big purse over her shoulder. "I'd better go. I'm covering Peg all morning. She and Baxtor have some big important meeting."

"Baxtor Phinney?" Dad's eyebrows shot up. "What kind of meeting?"

"Not sure." Blaine shrugged.

Dad's chin was tucked, and he was drumming his fingers on the tabletop. A sign that his mind was elsewhere. She took advantage of his distractibility to vanish.

After parking her car near Boon Dock, she paused. It was her favorite place in town to park. At just that moment, the sun found an opening in the gray clouds. Sunrays poured down on the little village, illuminating the dark water in the harbor, casting shadows, glinting off windows along Main Street. The power of light gave Blaine goose bumps. It seemed holy.

Off in the harbor, she heard a lobsterman call out and another answered, breaking her reverie. She was eager to arrive at the diner before the first wave of customers started coming in—the fishermen returning from the morning's catch. She had woken in the night with an idea for a new scone recipe she wanted to try out: cheddar cheese, jalapeño, scallions.

Rummaging through her purse for Peg's key, Blaine stood in front of the diner under the awning, trying to imagine how nice it would look if the window boxes were filled with lavender plants, so that passersby could brush up against them, leaving a soft, dusty scent in the air. Instead, walking by the boxes stirred up swirls of dust from the plastic ivy. She wondered if Peg would be open to change—because she seemed to be resistant to anything new. In the last few days, Peg had made quite a few disparaging remarks about change—all aimed at the summer people.

Such an attitude puzzled Blaine. The island had always welcomed vacationers. Camp Kicking Moose relied on campers. When Blaine said as much to Peg, she received a curt reply. "It's different here, now that the bar is gone. You'll see. These summer people aren't the type who give to Three Sisters Island. They only want to take something from it."

That was hard for Blaine to get her head around, because she thought dropping buckets of tourist dollars was a fine way to give to the island. A win-win for everyone.

As soon as Blaine's fingers found Peg's key, she inserted it into the lock of the door. When she felt it click, she paused, squeezing her eyes shut. She imagined every chef in the world enjoyed the same satisfying tingle as the door to their kitchen opened in the morning. A momentary rush of pride and satisfaction. Of anticipation.

It was silent inside. Morning light streamed through the windows. Blaine inhaled a deep breath. Yesterday afternoon, she had mindfully filled the coffeemaker with water, a simple trick that allowed chlorination in the water to evaporate, providing a better taste. She poured coffee beans into the grinder and smiled at the familiar whirring sound, waiting until it was just so. As she took off the lid of the grinder, she inhaled deeply, with great pleasure. Ah, the aroma of fresh-ground coffee. No better smell in all the world.

She grabbed her chef's white jacket off the wall peg, slipped each arm into it, and buttoned each button. A grin tugged at the corners of her mouth. The chef was in the house.

BLAINE AT LE CORDON BLEU, AGE 20

Day one of culinary school. Blaine sat in the far back corner of the classroom, taking copious notes. Chef Instructor Henri stood at the bottom of the lecture hall, sweeping the room with his piercing gaze, a cleaver tucked under the tie of his apron.

"Put away your notes. Forget everyzing you have ever learned. Everyzing. From now on, what will guide you eez your heart." He thumped his chest with his fist. "Your palate will be your educator. Your instincts will be your teacher." He snapped his fingers and suddenly the room was in full swing. Waitstaff poured into the room, delivering a small plate with a slice of cheese, and two small cups. One was filled with red wine, one with green tea. "If you please," Chef Henri said, waving his hand at the students, "a bite, zen . . . a sip. Bite, zen a different sip."

The students, Blaine included, did as he asked. Patiently waiting for everyone to finish, the chef walked slowly back and forth, watching the faces of the students.

"Now," Chef Henri said, "if you please . . . explain."

No one spoke. Chef Henri glared at the students, then lifted his cleaver from his apron. "You," he said, pointing the cleaver right at Blaine.

Facing the sharp edge of that cleaver, Blaine could not for the life of her remember anything at all. Shakily, stalling, she rose to her feet. And then she remembered being in a kitchen store with her mom one rainy summer day, when a demonstration was going on about food pairing. No one had come to the demonstration. "That poor lady," Mom had whispered. "Let's sit down so at least there's two people in the audience."

At the time, Blaine hadn't wanted to, but afterward, she was so glad they'd stayed. Mom even let her take a sip from her wine sampling as the woman described . . .

"Astringents!"

Chef Henri's eyebrows lifted at Blaine's enthusiastic response.

"The cheese," Blaine said, "is full of fat, which lubricates the tongue. The wine and green tea act as astringents."

"Why does zee cheese taste better with wine zan with zee tea?"

"Some fatty foods just pair better with certain astringents."

Chef Henri's eyes narrowed. "Name another."

"Sushi and pickled ginger." Blaine remembered the lady at the kitchen store had served them tiny samples of sushi and pickled ginger. It was the first time she'd ever tried sushi.

Chef Henri stared at her, then gave a slight nod of approval. Slight, but huge.

"Zis," he said to the class, "eez the mystery of gastronomy. And zis eez why you must learn to rely on your heart as you cook. Because no matter what skills you learn at Le Cordon Bleu, no matter what a recipe instructs, zere will always be an inexplicable part of creating the dish. Inexplicable to here." He pointed to his head. "But not here." He patted his heart. "True chefs cook only with zee heart." He shrugged his shoulders. "If not with zee heart, one should not cook at all."

And there it was. Blaine found herself transported, as if a lever had been pulled. In a strange way, she sensed her mother's pleasure, beaming down at her from Heaven. She felt a closeness to her mother that she thought was lost to her forever. She smiled.

Blaine was no longer a cook. She was becoming a chef.

Five

THE AIR IN THE BEDROOM was hot and sticky, or maybe Cam was just hot and sticky. She couldn't breathe, let alone sleep. She kicked the sheets off her clammy skin and stood in front of the little fan, letting it billow the folds of her cotton nightgown. She glanced past Seth, sleeping soundly, to the clock on the nightstand. It was only midnight. Cam walked to the window and saw something move on the lawn. A doe, nibbling on the grass. She held her breath when two small fawns pranced out of the pine trees to join their mother, the moonlight shining down on their dappled backs. Startled by something, the doe lifted her head, then bounded into the pine trees, into the shelter of darkness, the fawns following right behind her.

Cam sighed. Even in nature, female animals had a maternal instinct. What if she had none? She had a strong sense of duty and obligation, but motherhood required more. It required instinctive love.

Her hands rolled over her round tummy. What if she didn't love her baby? It had taken a long time to love Cooper. She loved him through sheer willpower; she loved him because he belonged to Libby, whom she loved as a sister. Better than a sister.

"But I didn't *feel* love for him, not for a very long time," she whispered into the night air.

Cam wondered if there might be something seriously missing in her. Whenever Maddie showed her what crib she had chosen, or what stroller was the best one, she told her to order two. She had absolutely no interest in becoming well versed in baby paraphernalia. After all, most everything would be needed for a few years, then gone. Instead, her head was filled with thoughts of getting that cell phone tower approved by the town.

Sometimes Cam felt as if she were dragging the island into the twenty-first century kicking and screaming. When she thought back to how frustrating daily life used to be on the island when they relied on the ancient rusty electricity cable under the harbor, it made her shudder. Brownouts were a regular occurrence; everyone had to wait until evening to run their washing machines or dishwashers. How had they tolerated it for so long? How had Peg, trying to run a diner, put up with such dodgy power?

Cam had figured out a way to create consistent, renewable energy on the island, and had even financed it herself by cashing in her stock options. Even then, it was no small task to turn it into a reality. The locals objected to every single location. They didn't want to see it, and they didn't want it to be visible from the harbor.

Cam was teetering on throwing out the whole idea when Seth came back from a long hike around Camp Kicking Moose. In a seldom explored, difficult-to-get-to section of the eastern side of the island, he'd found a flat meadow on a cliff, with a small reservoir below. The *perfect* setting needed to create renewable, sustainable energy for the entire island. It was the best day of Cam's life (next to adopting Cooper and marrying Seth, of course). As if that location had just been waiting to be discovered. There was no way anyone with a reasonable bone in his body could object to it. (Baxtor Phinney did, of course, but that was to be expected.)

So on a rocky cliff overlooking the Atlantic Ocean, on land that belonged to Camp Kicking Moose, were solar panels, a wind turbine, and, just below the cliff, a hydroelectric dam with a small powerhouse that contained the hydroelectric turbine generator. The panels soaked up every bit of sun that shone on Three Sisters Island and converted sunshine into usable electricity. The wind, which increased in strength in the early afternoon and late evening, filled in when fog or inclement weather blocked the sun. The hydro dam captured rainwater in a "run-of-the-river" style of a hydro plant. Some water was diverted and piped to the powerhouse which contained the hydroelectric turbine generator. After spinning the turbine, the water returned to the ocean. Separately, each component couldn't provide enough power for the entire island. All together, they did the job nicely.

Now, the island itself was humming along nicely, helped dramatically after the dissolution of the sandbar in the harbor. What a boon to the commercial industry of the island! Who could have seen *that* coming? Mother Nature provided a very nice boost. And Cam was ready to implement Phase 2 of her plan—bringing reliable cell phone service and Wi-Fi connectivity to the island with a cell tower. It had taken all fall and winter, but she'd finally convinced a telecom company that a cellular tower should be built on the island, that there *were* enough customers to support it, which meant that it would make financial sense for the company.

If only the cell phone tower could be put somewhere on Camp Kicking Moose's property. Unfortunately, the carrier had specific expectations for the location of the tower. It would need to be accessible to construction crews, as well as maintenance and repairs, and in the highest spot on the island. The place they chose was the top of Main Street, next to the old Unitarian church, which was currently the home for the island's public school. The carrier promised it would hardly be noticeable after a while.

Cam was readying her report to present to the village selectmen, and since Peg Legg ran the council, she was sure they would give her the green light to go ahead. No doubt.

She was pretty sure, anyway.

Seth rolled onto his back and she snuggled up next to him, re-assured by his solid, steadfast presence. After a while, she settled into a fitful sleep.

⁓

Now that April was here and the weather was warmer—as in, no longer snowing—Seth and Cooper rode bikes to school, so Paul lost his daily excuse to drive to town, have morning coffee at the Lunch Counter, and head to the beach to make a phone call to a certain friend. Today, Cooper left his lunch on the kitchen counter—the brand-new granite counter, he revised his thought with a smug smile—so Paul grabbed the paper-bag lunch in one hand, the keys for his pickup in another, and took off. He parked near the church office because it was getting hard to find a park-ing spot on Main Street, even at this hour of the morning. What would it be like when the summer season opened?

Cooper was playing tetherball on the school playground across the street, so Paul stopped a moment to watch. Ten years old now, and growing big and strong in every way. Mostly in his confidence, his sense of security, his joy. That pleased Paul to no end.

Paul well remembered being ten years old and feeling as if he didn't matter to anyone. It was the year his mother left, and his father's alcoholism took a nosedive from weekend benders to nightly ones. It wasn't until Paul's voice changed, deepened to that low baritone, that he started to get noticed. His voice change surprised everyone, especially him. It had been a gift, lifting him out of a dead-end life like his father had lived, giving him purpose. Opening the door to a wonderful career in radio. He rubbed his throat, missing that voice of his.

But that was then, and this was now.

The beeping of a car horn brought him back to earth. He lifted his head to see Blaine wave to him as she passed by.

Blaine!

She was really back, home to stay. Tears pricked his eyes. The joy of having her home more than made up for the sudden and unwanted appearance of his father, plus the hard-to-understand French boy parked on his sofa. Both.

Cooper's turn at tetherball ended. When he stepped out of the game, Paul called out to him and tossed his lunch over the fence before heading down Main Street to the Lunch Counter.

It was a wonderful day. The air smelled sweet, slightly scented with salt and sea. It was a pleasure to stroll down Main Street. It had gone from a neglected-looking place filled with shuttered storefronts to a thriving and charming business district. Some of the stores had American flags flying above the doors. Most had window boxes spilling over with bright red geraniums or fresh-faced pansies. He passed what used to be the food store run by Peg's friend Nancy. She'd left the island and sold it to a young couple; they'd turned it into an upscale grocery store, filled with pricey, high-end products like Stonewall jams and air-chilled chicken. He preferred waiting for a reason to go to the mainland and making a stop in Costco.

In front of the grocery store sat a large gray cat, as still as a work of art, whose gray eyes watched Paul carefully as he passed. "I don't like cats," Paul said, just to be clear. The cat narrowed its eyes into a haughty stare.

Washing dishes by the diner's sink, Peg waved as he came through the door, and he felt his spirits lift.

Paul often wished he was more like Peg, with her attitude always turned toward the sun. Her smile seemed to warm the entire room, and he felt immeasurably cheered, glad he'd come to town. Peg's smile had that effect on him. "Good morning, Peg Legg."

"Call me that one more time and I'll start a rumor that you're on the FBI's Ten Most Wanted List."

Paul grinned. It was the emptiest of empty threats. "One cup of coffee, please." He sat on a stool, pleased with how the day was taking shape, grateful that the Lunch Counter had only a few customers, savoring the aroma of freshly brewed coffee.

Peg finished washing a bowl and set it out to dry. She folded the dishrag and draped it over the faucet's neck. It occurred to him that Peg always seemed unhurried, and how nice it was to have a friend who wasn't in a rush.

She turned to Paul. "I was just thinking . . . you've got a pretty full house out there at Moose Manor."

Paul nodded. "Full to the brim." As he hoped a cup of coffee would be, just as soon as Peg got around to filling it. Again, she was in no hurry.

As for the house, it was jam-packed. When he had bought Camp Kicking Moose, he had a hope that his daughters would come to Three Sisters Island, but he hadn't really thought that through. He hadn't considered where everyone would live. They lived with him, with no plans to leave, not even after the babies arrived.

"How's it going with that cute little French fella?"

"He's still on the couch with an elevated leg." Where he would remain, Paul hoped. He'd never had to worry about visiting boyfriends with Cam—she scared most men away—or Maddie—she stuck to very high principles. But Blaine? He was never really sure where she stood on this issue.

"So, Paul, I've got a gal for you to meet. She's in her midfifties, divorced, a bunch of grown kids but no grandchildren yet. Oh, and she likes to hike."

Paul said nothing, hoping she would take the hint. Peg had been trying to set him up with women all winter. He never took the bait.

Peg handed him a mug of hot water and a jar of honey and grinned at his look of disappointment. "That's all you're going to get here. No coffee. Strict orders from Maddie."

He frowned, pouring the honey into the mug. Maddie meant well, but he didn't need her meddling any more than he needed Peg's matchmaking. He loved his middle daughter, but he bristled at the way she fussed over him, like he was an old man in need of minders. He was hoping that, come September, she could shift all her caretaking tendencies to fuss over the baby.

"So how's it going with your father? Seemed like the two of you weren't exactly chummy." She gave a brief laugh. "I figured that out when I realized he didn't even know Cooper, the world's best boy."

Paul didn't like to talk much, or think much, about his father. "We parted ways a long time ago. He preferred the bottle to having a son."

Peg tilted her head. "And now?"

"Says he's been sober five years."

"Think he's here to make amends?"

Paul shrugged. If so, it would take more than an unannounced visit to make amends. His father had missed his entire life.

Peg's eyes were fastened on him, which kind of threw him off. He'd never known anyone with such blue eyes. Like blueberries. "Paul, let me give you a piece of advice. Never be too hard on the man who gives up the drink."

He stilled. Peg was usually right about such things. Maybe he needed to stop thinking about his father from a disappointed son's point of view. He swirled the water in his mug, staring down into it. Good grief. He was over sixty, and he still felt affected by his father's bad choices. When did it end?

Time to switch the subject. "Is Bob Lotosky coming out?" For the last few years, in May and again in September, Paul counted on Bob Lotosky's help to open and close the camp. He was Artie's dad, and one of those guys who could fix anything and was generous with his time. He hadn't heard Peg mention Bob's name lately. Come to think of it, he couldn't remember when she last spoke of him.

"No."

"Not this May?"

"No."

He glanced up. "Or not ever?"

"Not ever."

Paul sat back, surprised. He had relied heavily on Bob. Quite

65

frankly, he felt a little hurt. He'd like to know what had happened, why Bob had deserted them, but unlike his daughters, he was a firm believer in not asking people about their private business. Especially female people.

Hands on her hips, Peg said, "Aren't you even going to ask?"

Blast. He would never understand women. "None of my business."

"What's that supposed to mean?"

Just what he said. But it worried him to say anything more and end up in trouble, so he pointed to his throat. His cop-out method, Maddie called it.

Peg sighed. "Bob loves Aroostook County. I love Three Sisters Island. It's as simple as that."

"Not as simple as that. Bob always loved his potatoes best of all." Oh no. Why did Paul say *that*? Where was his filter?

She stared at him, eyes wide, shocked. Then her face crumpled and she burst into tears and he felt a familiar panic spiral through him—despite being married to Corinna for twenty-two years, despite being a father of three highly passionate daughters, he never knew what to do when they cried. Peg turned and hurried away into the back room. Paul waited, then when he realized she wasn't coming back anytime soon, he left an overly generous tip for his mug of hot water and left the diner.

Blaine heard her dad's truck drive up the gravel driveway to Moose Manor and opened the front door to see Peg's green mini-van pull in behind it. Artie climbed out and headed toward the house. She rubbed her arms to get rid of the goose bumps that had appeared. "Well, well. Look who's here."

Dad closed the truck door and joined Artie at the bottom of the steps. "Bumped into him in town."

Artie looked past Blaine up at the house. "I'm here to check on the patients."

"Who?"

Artie looked at his clipboard. "The sprained-knee guy and the fainting guy."

Since when did Artie need an excuse to come out to the camp? He'd always loved visits to Moose Manor. That first summer, he'd even helped paint the house gray, covering up the horrid Pepto-Bismol pink color that someone had once thought was a good idea. She crossed her arms. "Peg told me you're a doctor for the outlying islands." *Why didn't you tell me? Why did I have to learn about it from Peg?*

He nodded. "The state of Maine made an offer I couldn't refuse. They'll pay off my enormous debt for medical school if I give them four years of service."

For as long as Blaine had known Artie, he had a dream to be a doctor, but it was a dream that came with a pretty steep price tag. Money was always a problem for him. He worried constantly about how to pay for med school, but it didn't stop him from pursuing it.

"So what does it mean to be a doctor for the outlying islands?"

"It means that I visit the unbridged islands with year-round residents to provide routine procedures, like flu shots."

"Thirteen unbridged islands," Dad said, putting a hand on Artie's shoulder like he was a favored son. "And he does a lot more than give flu shots."

"Yeah, maybe a few more things than flu shots. Like, checking up on injuries or concerns." Artie glanced at his watch and then up at the house. "Speaking of . . ."

"Oh," Blaine said. "Don't let me hold you up."

Artie tipped his head and walked past Blaine on the porch steps. *Man. Cold.*

She went down the steps to where her dad was pulling a box of groceries out of the back of the truck. "So why didn't anybody tell me Artie took a job here?"

"Not here, exactly. More like on the *Lightship*. It's a boat with specialized equipment."

"Dad, why didn't you tell me?"

He pointed to his throat and shrugged. His voice did sound pretty raspy, but Blaine couldn't be fobbed off that easily. She was no fool. He used his weak voice as an excuse.

"Fine. I'll just have to ask someone else."

Inside, Artie was seated in the large living room on the ottoman next to the sofa, his fingers gingerly probing Jean-Paul's knee. Artie, now a doctor, was in her living room. *Artie!* Her Artie. It felt so normal to have him here, so familiar, even after two long years. She watched him for a while, listening as he asked Jean-Paul some questions. He had a nice way about him, super smart without making you feel dumb, and the most *winsome* face. Endearing, solemn puppy-dog eyes. He'd always reminded Blaine of John Krasinski, the boy-next-door kind of guy.

He glanced over his shoulder at Blaine, then quickly looked away when their eyes met. Why was he acting like this? What was wrong with him?

They'd met as study partners in a biology class in a junior college. She was sampling every subject she could, like someone who was hungry and invited to an all-you-can-eat banquet. His schedule was overloaded with science-heavy prerequisites for medical school. Artie had his life entirely planned out. Blaine had trouble planning a day. Somehow, as different as they were, their friendship worked. He liked her laissez-faire spirit. She appreciated his earnestness. Here and there, they'd had a few misunderstandings, but they always worked it out. She assumed they'd be friends forever. Apparently, she was mistaken.

What had happened to them? What had gone so terribly wrong?

Clearly, Artie her college buddy was gone, replaced by this confident, no-nonsense professional. All business.

Artie pulled off his gloves. "Sometimes knees can take a long time to heal. Better stay off it another few days."

"Can't you get him crutches?" Blaine said. "Or a wheelchair? Maybe a walker?"

Artie glanced at her as if he'd forgotten she was there. "I think I have a pair of crutches on the *Lightship*. I'll leave them with Peg." He grabbed his bag, intent on ignoring her. "Now where is that older man who fainted?"

"My father?" Paul said.

"I just want to check in on him."

"He's in the kitchen," Blaine said.

She started moving toward the door, but he stopped her. "I know the way." He looked over at Paul. "What's your father's name?"

"Walter Grayson."

Artie left, the dining room door whooshing to a solid close behind him. Blaine looked at her dad. "What's that about?"

Dad shrugged. "Artie's a thorough doctor." He turned and left the house.

Blaine would have thought he'd go to the kitchen to see if Artie had any cause for concern about that fainting spell. After all, it had been a weird moment. Granddad Grayson just dropped like a stone. But then, the whole thing was weird. Why had her grandfather suddenly come to Three Sisters Island? What was the problem between them that caused Dad to keep making himself scarce?

Not that Blaine minded too much. She was happy to postpone a conversation about creating dining service at Moose Manor, because she still didn't know how to tell her dad that it wasn't going to work. Not a chance. Through the living room window, she watched him cross the yard to the boathouse, his refuge.

Jean-Paul held up an empty potato chip bag. "*Très bon*. Eez more?" He gave her a "poor me" smile. "*S'il vous plaît?*"

In Paris, he would have turned up his nose to a bag of potato chips. A few days at Moose Manor and he was turning into a junk food junkie. Disgusted, Blaine snatched the bag out of his hands. "Jean-Paul, maybe you should get up. Get some exercise. Fresh air."

"No no," he said, shaking his head woefully. "You heard. Zee bearded doctor, he says to stay off my knee." He peered around her and wiggled his hand. "Move, s'il vous plaît."

69

She swiveled and saw he was watching a basketball game on the television.

A few minutes later, Artie strode out of the kitchen, gave her a brief nod and kept going.

She trailed behind him like a puppy. "Hold on! Is Granddad okay?"

He jogged down the porch steps. "I don't discuss my patients."

"So then, that means he is your patient? There's something's wrong with him, isn't there? Just nod when I hit the right diagnosis. Diabetes? Heart trouble? Stroke?"

Artie opened the van door and tossed in his medical bag. "Nice try. Not working." He hopped in and drove off.

Artie was acting so strange! She gave it some thought. As frustrated as she felt with him right now, as indignant as she was by his coldness, his all-business attitude, his adultish-ness—despite all that, she found him to be . . . unexpectedly attractive.

Paul heard a funny sound and spun around. A big fat gray cat sat in the opening of the boathouse, watching him, swishing its tail. "Where'd you come from?" He walked up to it, recognizing the cat as the one that sat in front of the grocery store. Widely known and universally disliked. It stared at him and Paul stared back. "What'd you do, hop into the back of my truck for a ride to Moose Manor?"

The cat meowed and swirled around his legs.

"Oh no. Don't get any ideas about staying here. I am not a cat guy. If anything, I'm a dog guy. One hundred percent dog guy. I make fun of cats. I would never, ever choose a cat as a pet." He scooped the cat into his arms. "I'm taking you back to town."

Twenty minutes later, Paul took the cat into the diner and held it out to Peg. "Here."

She peered at its furry face. "Well, I'll be! Fluffy!"

"Fluffy?"

"That's Nancy's cat. He ran off when Nancy started packing up to move off island. Nancy was beside herself when that cat disappeared. I haven't seen hide nor hair of that cat since Nancy left town."

"I found it at Moose Manor. It must've jumped in the back of my truck." He held it out. "Here. You take it."

"Me? Oh no. Can't. Board of Health won't let me have a pet in the diner. In fact, you'd better get Fluffy out of here before someone tattles on me. I don't want that inspector nosing around here."

"Put the cat in the back room until Nancy can come get it."

"Nancy can't keep her. Her daughter is allergic to cats. That was the one deal breaker about moving off island. She wasn't going to be able to take sweet little Fluffy along with her." She scratched the cat's head. "Fluffy must've heard her talking and ran off."

Paul rolled his eyes. He opened the diner door and let the cat out. It sat on the sidewalk, right outside the door, staring at him. He stared back, watching it from the window.

Peg came up beside him. "I can't wait to tell Nancy that Fluffy has found a new home."

"Oh no. Not me. I would never, ever choose a cat as a pet."

"Well, that's the funny thing about cats, Paul. You don't choose them." Peg patted him on the back. "They choose you."

Six

IN THE BOATHOUSE, Paul was checking life preservers one by one. Maddie appeared at the open door, with the cat skirting behind her legs and twining around her ankles. She bent down to stroke its fur.

"Don't encourage that cat, Maddie. I keep taking it back to town and somehow it keeps turning up here."

"Why not? I like cats."

"They carry terrible diseases."

Maddie yanked her hand away. The cat left her in a huff and strode with purpose over to glare at Paul. If cats could talk, Paul knew just what it would be saying: *My pats. My people. My property. Why do you keep interfering?*

"Dad, I thought you agreed to have a talk with Granddad."

"I tried. It didn't work." Paul tossed the life preserver in the bin and picked up another. "Don't forget that he arrived without an invitation."

"But the fact remains that he did come here. There must be something he wants from you."

"He said he wants to get to know his granddaughters."

"Oh." She sighed. "Okay. I'll talk to him. But you should keep trying to spend time with him. You don't want to end up having regrets."

Paul paused for a moment to mull that over. It would be pretty hard to live any kind of life without some regrets.

"If it's okay with you, I'd like to invite Rick's mom up for a long weekend. She says she'll only come if she can pitch in to help get the camp ready for summer season. Maeve's a doer, not a sitter. She always wants to do her part."

"Sounds good to me. Maeve, you say her name is?"

"Dad! Seriously? You've forgotten the name of Rick's mother? Good grief! She was one of Mom's best friends. She was the one who got Mom to church. And then Mom got you to church."

"Ah yes, that's right. Maeve O'Shea. I won't forget."

Maddie gave him a look as if she wondered about the start of early dementia. "Maeve can sleep in the nursery on the daybed." She took a few steps into the boathouse, ran a hand along an upside-down canoe. "I'm hoping she can talk Rick into slowing down a little."

"I'm all for that." Maddie was a born worrier, plus she was pregnant, but this was one time when Paul heartily supported her concerns. Rick was a robust, energetic man, a former Marine. His schedule had ramped up the last few months to the point where even Paul felt alarmed by the pace his son-in-law kept. Rick was always in a hurry, always dashing off to another speaking engagement or meeting or to make a hospital visit. Juggling the needs of two churches, on two separate islands, was a Herculean feat. If anyone could make Rick listen to reason, it was his mother.

Maddie walked to the open door and pivoted. "So . . . then, you don't mind an extra body around Moose Manor? I know the house is pretty full."

"I don't mind." Paul smiled. *Actually, I don't mind at all.*

Blaine tried not to reveal how frustrated she felt each time she walked into the kitchen of Moose Manor. At first glance, she had thought it was at least designed for a home cook. But the more time she spent in it, the more she realized that its layout made no sense at all. As she opened the door . . . slowly . . . just in case someone was in the refrigerator . . . she saw Cam and Maddie's heads together, bent over the granite countertop near the sink.

"What's wrong?"

"A stain." Cam rubbed it with a paper towel. "I tried to clean it with bleach."

"You what?!" It came out like a shriek. "Bleach? On granite countertops?"

"Bleach works on everything."

Blaine took in a deep breath. "Never, ever use bleach on granite."

Maddie gave her a quizzical look. "Then how do we get rid of germs? Ammonia?"

"No! Nothing like that should ever be used on a natural stone. Just soap and water. If you absolutely need to annihilate germs on granite, you can try some rubbing alcohol on it. But never, ever bleach. It can harm it." Blaine peered at the stain. "And discolor it. Like it's done there."

"You mean," Cam said, "I did this by trying to fix it?"

"Exactly." Blaine took the bleach from her and set it below the kitchen sink, noticing what little space there was for cleaning supplies because a trash can was jammed underneath. When she turned around, her sisters were seated at the table, facing her like two matching pillars of sensibility.

Oh no. Blaine sensed an ambush. "What?"

Cam laid her folded hands on top of her rounded belly. "How long is Jean-Paul planning to stay?"

"Until the summer season. Why?"

"Does that mean," Cam said, "he has no job to go back to?"

Blaine's fingernails dug into the palm of her hand. Maddie, noticing, shot Cam a look as if to say, *Be careful, okay?*

"Of course he has a job. His father owns a bistro. He has a dream for Jean-Paul to take it over so he can retire, but Jean-Paul has his own dream for his life. That's why he's in America—to have time away from home to reflect on his . . . future." It was up to Jean-Paul if he wanted to tell her family more. "I'd think you'd be grateful. He's been keeping Granddad company." Watching sports on TV, but at least they provided company for each other. "No one else seems to be terribly concerned about Granddad. Especially not Dad."

"Granddad is a separate issue," Maddie said in that counselor-ish tone. "To stay on track here, we're all just mindful that there's a lot to do to get ready for the summer season."

"I know. I'm here, aren't I?"

"Are you?" Cam said. "Are you *really* here?"

Blaine was caught completely off guard by the question, and what did Cam mean by it, anyway? "If I'm not *really* here, where do you think I am?"

"You're away from the camp most every day." As Blaine opened her mouth to object, Cam lifted a hand to stop her. "For now, it's okay. I know you want to help Peg, and Jean-Paul is grounded. I get it. But as soon as I get the town's approval to move forward with the cell tower, then it's full steam ahead on the dining service at Moose Manor. We have to order tables, chairs, linens, flatware. You'll need to provide a menu and hire kitchen staff. The list goes on and on."

Blaine turned away to open the refrigerator, feeling the cool air cover her face. A literal cool-down moment, the equivalent of counting to ten. Was now the time for a "let's get real" conversation with Cam? To tell her that her big plans for Moose Manor's dining service would have to be scaled down, down, down . . . to the continental breakfast served on the porch that it had always been? That this kitchen could never, ever pass inspection by the state of Maine? Still facing the open fridge, she tried to put it into words, without having it backfire on her. But silence was a tricky thing . . . and she waited a little too long to respond.

"Blaine." Cam's voice took a conciliatory turn. "Try to understand. We've been waiting and waiting for you to return. Now, you're finally back."

Still, Blaine said nothing. She closed the refrigerator door and faced her sisters. She simply stood and stared. She had no idea how to start this conversation . . . and even less of an idea of how to end it. The wonderful idea everyone had of offering a dining service at Moose Manor was DOA.

Blaine hadn't noticed that Cam had a folder on her lap. She opened it to reveal a typed list. "I've taken the liberty to create a restaurant to-do list for you, complete with check-off boxes. This way, you can get started on things sooner, rather than later." When she looked at Blaine's expression, she added, "What? This is how I prefer to work. Ahead of the crisis."

She closed the folder and held it out to Blaine.

Cam, who had never been in the "back of the house" of any restaurant, who had no idea how to run or manage a kitchen, had created a to-do list for Blaine? She was fuming.

Maddie, growing uncomfortable with the unspoken tension, tried to intervene. "We just wanted to know how long your friend plans to stay, that's all. He's very nice."

"Yes. Very nice guy," Cam said. "But to be candid, we just want to make sure he doesn't distract you from everything we have planned for this season."

Maddie shot Cam another beseeching look. "Cam, I think we've said enough."

It was more than enough. Quiet descended, thick and cold. Blaine was at a loss for words, so angry that she made herself inhale and exhale so she didn't blow up at Cam. Into her head popped a Bible verse she had intentionally memorized before returning home, anticipating moments just like this one: *You must all be quick to listen, slow to speak, and slow to get angry.*

She went to the kitchen door and opened it. "If you'll excuse me, I need some fresh air." She went out past the pickleball court, circled around the house to head to the sea path, and took in a few deep breaths of the fir-scented air.

Blaine had intended to explain Jean-Paul's significance in her life to her family at the right time, the right moment. So far, that moment hadn't come. How *dare* Cam and Maddie, but especially Cam, dismiss Jean-Paul, her dear friend, the one who saved her from herself. Jean-Paul had given her the best gift in the world—he'd helped Blaine believe she was worthy of love, care, and respect.

BLAINE, AGE 20

Blaine was in trouble and she knew it. On a rainy day in Paris, she stood on a bridge overlooking the Seine River. She had thought that coming to Europe would bring the answers to life she was so hungry for. She gazed around her, at this beautiful city full of remarkable architecture. Here in Paris, of all places on earth, you'd think it would matter if a person lived or died. But here, of all places, she felt more of that gray fog of despair than she'd ever felt before. She desperately wanted to feel some kind of purpose, some kind of significance to her life. Instead, it all felt so random, so pointless. Nothing really mattered. She didn't matter.

Before she had left Three Sisters Island, Maddie had warned her about depression. "It has a way of following a person. And it can get much worse without a support system. You don't know a soul in Paris."

Blaine had assured her sister that she was not depressed. She had tricked everyone, herself included, into thinking she was doing just fine. It had become almost a game. Leaving the island, and her family, was necessary for her personal growth. She just needed time to find herself without everyone's expectations stifling her.

But Maddie had seen through her façade. Blaine wasn't doing well. She wasn't coping well. Depression, deep and dark, had not only found her in Paris but had curled itself around her. It settled on her like a backpack full of heavy stones, trying to drag her down. It was there when she went to bed, there when she woke in the morning. No wonder she hadn't been able to find a job. Who would want to hire such a gloomy cook? One who couldn't even speak French very well.

She dropped a stick into the river and watched it float, getting carried away. It seemed like a metaphor. A person's life just got swept along with the currents. Maybe there was no point in trying to make something of yourself. In between birth and death, you just hung on for dear life and hoped you didn't drown before you grew old and gray.

But her mom hadn't survived the currents. Libby hadn't.

And in the last month, Blaine had increasing thoughts that she didn't want to either. That Mom and Libby were the lucky ones. Life felt just too hard. Too pointless. The river was too cruel.

She gazed down at the water, leaning far over the bridge. Would drowning be painful? Would it be quick?

She leaned a little farther, sensing something surround her, envelop her, something coax her forward. Something promising her that peace she was looking for.

As her weight shifted over the bridge's railing, her heels lifted.

"Go on, go on," whispered that something. "You'll feel better."

She was on her toes now, leaning over, peering down into that swirling water. Would it hurt?

"Go on, go on," coaxed the something.

Would anyone care? Would they miss her? Would Dad? Would Cam or Maddie? Would Peg? Artie? Or would life just keep rushing everyone forward, leaving her behind?

"Go on, go on." The something's voice was changing, growing more urgent.

Blaine imagined all the air was escaping from her lungs, leaving them empty, lifeless. She felt herself start swaying forward, almost dizzy.

Suddenly a hand firmly grasped her upper arm and pulled her back to her heels. "No, no, *mon amie.*"

She turned her head and blinked a few times, trying to focus. A young man stood beside her, still holding firmly onto her arm.

On his face was a look of great concern. "*As-tu le cafard?*" He tried again. "You have the cockroach, no?"

Trembling, Blaine spun around to go, but he kept a firm hold of her arm. "Please. Eez raining. Come. I buy you coffee. We talk."

He didn't really allow her to refuse him. He kept his hand on her upper arm, gentle but firm, and led her to a little café near the river. They sat inside, next to the window, and he bought two espressos and two pastries. He sat across from Blaine without saying another word, though his face never lost that concerned look. His eyes, full of tenderness, understanding. No judgment.

And it was his gentle silence that cracked her. If he'd spoken, if he'd offered silly platitudes and empty reassurances, she would have shut down. But that silence . . . it was an invitation. Everything Blaine had been holding in these last few years—the grief she felt, the anger, the sadness, the loneliness, the feelings of abandonment, it all burst open.

"My mother died," she said, tears spilling down her cheeks onto her raincoat. "I'm here, in Paris, because of her. Because we'd always talked about coming here one day. But now that I'm here, I don't know why I've come." With that, she started bawling.

Blaine knew she was an ugly crier, eyes red and nose running, yet the young man seemed not to care. He untied the red bandanna around his neck and reached across the table to give it to her. She took it from him and held it in her hands.

"We were very close," she said, her voice cracking. "My mom meant so much to me. And then she was suddenly gone. Her absence left a huge crater."

"Cra-ter?"

"A hole. Normally a crater is in the ground. This hole is in my heart." She paused to wipe her face. "My dad and my two sisters, they seem to be able to move forward. I try, I really do try. But each time, I do something to mess it up and everything falls apart. My sister Maddie—she's a shrink—"

Confused, he said, "She shrinks?"

"No, no." Blaine almost smiled. "She's a counselor." She pointed to her head. "She says I self-sabotage. I can't seem to do what everyone expects me to do, so I ruin it, purposefully. Then I end up feeling like a giant disappointment to everyone."

He listened to her in a way that felt rare, privileged. Though the shop was full of customers, he wasn't distracted by anyone or anything, his attention didn't wander, he leveled his focus on her as she talked and cried and talked. She went on and on, until she emptied herself of words.

When she finished, he leaned back slightly, peering into his cup of coffee. "Zis big crater . . ." He made his fingers walk around the lip of his espresso cup. "You are tiptoeing around it?"

She lifted a shoulder in a shrug. "I suppose so."

"What makes you afraid of zat crater?"

Wasn't it obvious? "I'll fall in."

"Ah . . . ," he said, his eyes serious and pensive. "Like . . . on zee bridge?"

She looked away.

"I do not zink zat your mother would want you to fall in zee crater. She would not want you to waste zee life God has given to you, no?"

"No." Definitely not.

He took a sip of coffee and set it down in the saucer. "I wonder if you have not let yourself fully feel zee loss of your mama." Pronounced in the French way of ma-Ma. "You have just pushed her to zee back of your mind."

Blaine kept her eyes on her espresso, now cold. "It was five years ago. That's a long time." But long enough to know that she thought she would never be whole again.

"Time can pass without bringing healing, mon amie. I think you have only stuffed it down, down, down. But zat grief, it wants

80

to come up into zee light. Zat is how it can heal. Not in zee darkness. Zat darkness you felt . . . zat was not from God." Strangely enough, as he spoke, the sun broke through the clouds and a ray of sun streamed through the window onto their table. He clapped, delighted, as if it was cued. "You see, no? God, he eez light. And he has led you to Paris to find healing."

"God has led me *here*?" Blaine nearly scoffed out loud. She was the one who had insisted on leaving everything good behind, and look at the havoc she'd created. Her family was thoroughly disgusted with her for not finishing culinary school in Maine; Peg felt she had let her down at the Lunch Counter; Artie, her best and dearest friend, wasn't answering her calls.

They were all right. She'd let them all down. And now she was running out of money, still jobless, and thoroughly depressed. A minute away from throwing her life away. If there was a God, how did he have a part in sending her here? "I'm pretty sure God wouldn't want the blame for me being here. I'm really going nowhere . . . fast."

"You may feel as if you are going nowhere in zis world, but your spiritual journey eez another matter. God will never give up on you, even if you give up on him. His purpose for your life continues, wherever you are."

She tipped her head. "Do you *really* believe that?"

The young man seemed to sense all the layers of that one question. Her deep doubts, her hopelessness, her overwhelming feelings of insignificance, her misery. "Oui. God's power eez unlimited. He eez sovereign over all zings."

All things? Even dark depression? Thoughts of ending her life?

"All zings," he repeated, as if he could read her mind. "Mon amie, normally, I walk to work on a different path. But today, because of zee rain, God led me down another path. He led me to zat bridge where you stood, at just zat moment. A moment or two earlier, I might have walked right past and not even noticed you. A moment or two later . . ." He shrugged.

She might not have been there.

"So . . . do you see now? Oui? God wants your journey of healing to begin. Today."

It made no sense to Blaine. But two hours ago, she was miserable. Now, she was here, warm and dry in a charming little café, feeling cared for, and it was all because a complete stranger happened along the bridge at a certain moment in time. The river current of life did not seem so cruel and haphazard today.

"You are in God's country for a reason."

"God's country?"

His arm arced toward the window. "*En France.*"

Of course. A slight smile tugged at the corners of Blaine's lips. The first.

"In God's country, you will find healing. You will find hope. You will find faith." He took her hand in his and patted the back of it, a gesture to say that everything was going to be all right. "In time you will see wondrous zings." He rose from the table, left a few euros to pay for their coffees, and gave her a comforting smile. "Eez better now?"

"Much better." And she did feel much, much better. It was exactly what she had needed to hear. "Thank you . . . for everything. The coffee, the talk." The rescue. She held up his soggy red bandanna."

"You keep," he said, waving a hand. "Stay, have more coffee. I must go to work. A church lives down zee street. You can find me at zee church." He dipped his chin. "*Au revoir*, mon amie. Be well. And do not forget—'God comforts and encourages and refreshes and cheers zee depressed' . . . *and* . . . zee *sinking.*"

As the door closed behind him, she realized that she'd never even asked his name. "*Cet homme est un ange,*" said a server as she cleared their cups.

"Pardon?" Blaine said.

The server paused, searching for English words. "Zat man . . . he eez an angel."

Seven

PAUL HAD GONE TO TOWN in his truck to pick up Seth at school because his bicycle had a flat. While they were hefting the bike into the bed of the truck, Rick crossed the street from the church office to join them.

"Hello, stranger," Paul said.

"I know, I know." Rick wrinkled his face. "Hoping things will slow down soon."

"Fat chance of that," Seth said as he closed the trunk.

Paul looked from one son-in-law to the other. "Why do you say that?"

"First, there's summer coming," Seth said, "and second, there's a church on Isle au Haut that's interested in becoming a satellite to the Three Sisters Island church. Artie connected them to us."

Paul leaned against the truck. "How would that work?" Rick was already spread too thin.

"Like it works with the other island church," Rick said. "Visitations through the week, then preach on Sunday afternoons."

When Rick had taken on that second island church, his workload more than doubled. What would that mean for him if a third church were in the mix? Maddie's baby was due in September, just a few months away.

Paul stopped himself. These were meddlesome thoughts and he refused to be a meddler. His daughters did enough of that.

Rick hitched his pants up on his waist. Had he lost weight? *Stop it, Paul. Stop meddling.* "I haven't had a chance to talk much with Blaine's French boyfriend," Rick said. "He seems like a nice enough guy."

"She says he's not her boyfriend," Seth said, "and I believe her."

"No PDA?" Rick said.

"No PDA," Seth answered.

What did *that* mean? Paul would have to ask his friend on their next phone call.

Suddenly Rick gasped, eyes wide, and grasped the edge of the truck.

Paul and Seth exchanged a worried look. "You okay?"

Rick didn't answer for a while, too long a while, then he let out a long breath as color returned to his face. "I'm fine. Just fine." He took in another deep breath and released it slowly. "I'd better get back to work."

Paul watched him cross the street and head back up the church steps. An image of Maeve O'Shea, Rick's mom, filled his mind. He hoped she'd be coming soon.

The next day, Maddie sat cross-legged in a big comfy chair across from Jean-Paul in the living room, spilling out her frustrations. She had brought him an unopened bag of Hershey's Kisses, and out of the blue, he asked her what it was like to grow up in the middle of two strong-minded sisters. She stared at him, startled by his insight. And . . . suddenly, *Boom!* Out spewed her annoyances like a shaken bottle of soda pop.

"Each time I try to smooth over things between Cam and Blaine, it only gets worse. Cam says something in her blunt way and Blaine gets a wounded look." Jean-Paul nodded in all the right places, which only encouraged Maddie to keep going. "They're like oil and vinegar."

"*Se prendre la tête.*"

"Excuse me?"

"To take the head." Seeing Maddie's confusion, he patted his forehead and added, "It gives you a headache, no? You've had enough, oui?"

"No. I mean, yes."

"But . . . this is not new, oui?"

"Yes. I mean no. Not really. Well, maybe there's a little change. Blaine used to push back at Cam. But now, she doesn't react to her. Doesn't say a word."

He shifted on the couch, leaning forward to move a pillow under his swollen knee. "In France we have a saying—*changer de crèmerie*. It means . . . change your dairy shop."

What? "Um . . . what does that have to do with Cam and Blaine?"

He gazed at her, his look sweetly avuncular. "In France, if you change your dairy shop, it means you change your customs. Your patterns. It means . . . you let your sisters work zings out for zemselves."

"But . . . they need help." They needed *her* help.

"Oui. But it eez God's work." He lifted his palms in the air. "We trust God to do his work. His work. His time. Our work eez to pray . . . and release." He put his hands together as if in prayer, then split them apart. "Pray and release."

Cooper and Granddad came into the room from the porch.

"Boston Red Sox are playing," Granddad said, handing the remote to Cooper to find the channel. He stood in the middle of the room, his eyes darting back and forth from the TV to the chair Maddie was sitting in.

Okay, okay. She could take a hint. This overstuffed armchair had become Granddad's favorite TV viewing spot.

Maddie pushed herself out of her chair, mulling over Jean-Paul's unexpected advice. Pray and release, pray and release. So simple to say. So incredibly difficult to do.

⁓

This afternoon, Cam had asked Blaine if she'd had a chance to read through the to-do list she'd given her, and did she have any questions, and had she started on anything yet?

"No, no, and no," Blaine said, and darted out the back door.

By the time Blaine reached the beach, she felt less peeved. The repetitive sounds of the ocean waves were calming. The afternoon air smelled of salt and a changing tide, and she breathed it in deeply, congratulating herself for not overreacting to Cam.

While in Paris, Blaine had learned the power of silence. It was a lovely feeling to not rise to Cam's bait, to not lash back, to not argue, to not automatically sputter back, *You don't know what you're talking about!*

This was better, Blaine thought. This way she had a bit of control in their sibling dynamic, and that was a needed change.

Why did Cam always put her on the defensive?

Hold it. Blaine stopped her train of thought abruptly. Maybe the better question was, why did she let Cam put her on the defensive?

Had she learned nothing in the last few years from arrogant chef instructors who assumed all students were imbeciles and should be banned from the kitchen? She reminded herself of the thick skin for criticism she'd finally developed at Le Cordon Bleu after digesting that insight. The chef instructors would rant mercilessly at whatever had been done wrong, but then they would move on. Soon she realized that scorn was the chef instructors' chosen method of teaching. She began to pay closer attention—observing their methods, eavesdropping on the criticism given to other students. Blaine learned from her mistakes, each one, and grew determined to never make the same mistake twice.

As long as she could remember, Blaine had rested heavily on her talent in the kitchen, perhaps even with a hint of pride. It was the one thing that set her apart from her sisters, the one thing she could do better than them. But in Paris she had learned an important lesson about talent: it would take her only so far. While at Le Cordon Bleu, she needed to master the basics.

Gazing out at the water sparkling in the pale sun, Blaine thought of the countless times in her childhood that her parents had referred to this tiny strip of sand, the very place where Dad had once proposed to Mom. She tiptoed around the tidepools, absently looking for sea creatures.

She knew it wasn't going to be easy to come home again. She had survived the chef instructors by taking their criticism and learning from it. Maybe the same tactics, she pondered, could be useful with Cam.

BLAINE, AGE 8

Cam burst into the house, shouting Mom's name in her typical window-rattling way. "Where is Mom?"

Lying on the floor of the living room, Blaine looked up. "She's at church." She returned to reading her comic book. "Ricky O'Shea's mom picked her up. They're at a Bible study."

Cam clapped her cheeks, all upset. "Good grief. That's all Mom does lately." She dropped her hands.

Blaine rolled up her comic book and rose to her feet, quietly slipping out of the room. Cam was in one of her moods. She knew it was best to make herself scarce.

"Hold it!"

Blaine froze. Cam scared her a little.

"When is Mom coming home?"

"No idea."

"I'm supposed to bake three dozen brownies for our cross-country team's bake sale. Today. Starts in two hours."

Maddie came down the stairs and into the living room. "So, then, bake."

"I don't bake. I buy. I planned to, anyway, but the bakery seems to be closed." Hands on her hips, Cam frowned. "Somebody died there."

"Nobody died there, Cam," Maddie said in a long-suffering tone. "The baker's father died and they've gone to the funeral. You make it sound like he died just to make you upset."

"Well, they're running a business, aren't they?"

Maddie rolled her eyes. "Why can't you just go to the grocery store?"

"Because"—Cam paused, crossing her arms against her chest—"I promised to bring Mom's brownies."

Maddie coughed a laugh. "And you forgot to tell Mom?"

Cam took in a deep huffy breath, then let it out. "Maybe." She bit her lip. "Will you help?"

"Me? Bake? No way! Last time, Dad chipped a tooth."

Cam frowned. Blaine remembered. Maddie was trying to earn a Girl Scout badge for baking and had set the oven for a low temperature, then forgot about the brownies. They actually looked okay when they came out of the oven. Dad, passing through the kitchen, grabbed one and bit down, chipping a front tooth . . . which led to a very costly visit to the dentist.

Quietly, Blaine said, "I could try to bake Mom's brownies." They ignored her.

"What about Libby?" Maddie said, turning to Cam.

"She's already setting up the bake sale. All by herself." Cam plopped on the sofa. "I promised I'd help . . . and then I remembered that I also promised to bring Mom's brownies to sell."

"I'll bake them." Again, they ignored Blaine.

Cam leaned her head back to stare at the ceiling. "Think it'd be okay if I get Mom out of her Bible study?"

"No!" Maddie said, sitting beside her on the sofa. "Mrs. O'Shea is with her."

Cam's head jerked forward. "So what? Hold it. Do you still have a crush on Ricky O'Shea?"

"No!"

Oh yes, she *so* did. Blaine had read her diary. "I. CAN. BAKE. THEM."

Cam and Maddie swiveled to look at Blaine. "You?"

Blaine saw her sisters exchange a shared look of horror. "I've made them a bunch of times with Mom." *And neither of you ever complained.*

"Blainey!" Maddie said. "You're only eight years old!"

"Almost nine."

"Does Mom even let you turn on the oven?"

Blaine rolled her eyes. She'd baked with Mom for as long as she could remember. "Cam, go help Libby and come back in two hours. Maddie, you can be my assistant." Like she was with Mom.

Maddie gave Cam a gentle shove. "Better than nothing. Go."

Slowly, reluctantly, Cam went to the door. When she turned around with hesitation on her face, Blaine yelled, "Go!" And it felt pretty good to have something to hold over Cam.

But now, Blaine had to replicate Mom's famous brownies.

Mimicking her mother's calm, Blaine put the butter into the bowl and turned on the mixer, adding a thin waterfall of sugar. She watched the paddle beat its way to blend the two ingredients. One by one, she cracked eggs and let them slip into the mixture without a single piece of shell falling in, then poured teaspoons of vanilla extract. So far, so good.

In another bowl, she measured and sifted flour and cocoa powder, adding salt and baking powder. She folded the dry ingredients into the batter, watching shiny trails of yellow move through swirls of the cocoa mixture. Just enough folding, not too much. The last step, before baking, was to add Blaine's top-secret ingredients.

Two hours later, three dozen brownies were baked, cooled, wrapped individually in cellophane bags, tied with ribbons and sitting upright in two shoeboxes on the kitchen table. Maddie had been an excellent assistant—Blaine told her so. Helpful without being bossy, and she cleaned dishes and utensils along the way. Kitchen clean, Blaine washed her hands, wiped them on a dishrag, and turned to Maddie with a pleased look.

"Now what?"

"Now, we wait."

When Cam arrived to pick them up, she practically tiptoed in the kitchen. She examined the brownies in the shoeboxes. "Crackly tops. Dark chocolaty color. They look good, which means they'll sell. But the important thing is, how do they taste?"

Blaine was expecting doubt and disbelief from Cam and was prepared for it. She had made a few extra, of course (a wise cook always made more—Mom had taught her that trick). She handed one brownie on a plate to Cam, like a waiter serving a patron.

Cam picked the brownie up, looked it over, nibbled its edge. She took a full bite and chewed, darting looks at Blaine. Another bite, then another. She finished off the entire brownie in eight neat bites. After the final swallow, she said, "What'd you do? It's different than Mom's."

Uh oh. "Different?"

"Better."

Blaine let out the breath she'd been holding and shrugged, as if it was nothing. In truth, she added ground espresso powder and semi-sweet chocolate chips to bring out even more chocolate flavor. Mom never veered off a recipe, despite Blaine's many, many suggestions.

Cam lifted her hand to high-five Blaine. "I owe you, little sister!" She picked up both shoeboxes and headed to the door. "Someday, we're going to run a restaurant, you and me!"

Maddie snorted. "By that, she means you will do all the hard work, and she'll be the silent investor." She made a twisting motion in the air with her hand. "Knowing Cam . . . maybe not so silent."

Blaine twirled around, arms lifted high. "Works for me." It was the very first time that Cam's approval had landed, just for a flicker of time, on Blaine.

Eight

WOMEN, PAUL THOUGHT. Blaine was miffed with Cam who was miffed with Maddie who was miffed with Blaine. Or was it Cam who was miffed at Blaine? He wasn't sure.

Paul relayed all this to Peg during a visit to the Lunch Counter. "Nothing's out in the open." All three girls were shockingly polite to each other. But scratch the surface, and they were furious with each other. "I have to tell you, Peg, my daughters completely baffle me. They always have."

"Boy, that's completely understandable. Sometimes I've regretted having only one child, and a difficult boy at that, and I wonder what my life might have been like if I'd had a girl or two. But then I was down at the dock yesterday and watched a family with two very sullen teenage girls come off the ferry. I wondered, now what would it take to make those girls enjoy traveling with their family? And that's when I thanked my lucky stars for sparing me any children like them."

"Like them as in . . ."

"Ayup. Summer people." She turned to grab another muffin, setting it on the counter between them. "Your sweet dad came in the other day."

Paul released a shocked bark of laughter, then gaped at her in disbelief. *My sweet dad?* First time he'd ever heard *that* moniker for his father. "What did he want?"

"Just a good meal from my world-class chef. Say, how's that bad hip of his? Sure seemed to be giving him trouble. I told him to get Artie to check it out sometime."

A bad hip? Paul hadn't noticed his father had a bad hip. Now that Peg mentioned it, he had noticed him rubbing his side when he rose from that comfortable oversized chair in the living room he seemed to have claimed for television viewing. It used to be Paul's chair.

"Oh, and he said he's looking for a dog for Cooper. He said that boys need dogs for a whole lot of reasons. You know, Paul, I think he's right. It'll do Cooper wonders to have a dog."

Paul nearly rocketed off the stool. "No dog! That's the last thing I need at the camp. It's already filled to the brim with humans, not to mention one annoying uninvited cat." He could just imagine what it would be like to add a barking dog into the mix. How was he supposed to create a destination resort out of Moose Manor with every bedroom already filled? With cats and dogs everywhere?

His mind wandered back to thirty minutes earlier, when he'd been searching coat pockets for his truck keys to drive to town and the house was a hive of activity. Cooper had bolted through the living room, disappearing into the kitchen. Cam had taken over the dining room table as her office and was yakking away to someone called Mr. Thayer about a cell phone tower. Maddie was on the upstairs landing, her yoga mat on the floor, doing a prenatal exercise routine. His father was on the porch, reading the newspaper, ignoring everyone. Blaine's French boyfriend was on the couch, watching a baseball game on TV. Seth sat on the floor in the living room, papers spread around him, pretending he was grading them though his eyes were glued to the baseball game. Rick was upstairs in his bedroom, pacing the floor while loudly practicing Sunday's sermon—Paul could hear his footsteps creaking in the wooden ceiling over his head. As soon as Paul had located his truck keys hiding under Cooper's school backpack, he bolted. He needed a little breathing space.

Peg folded her arms across her ample chest. "Paul Grayson," she said in a tone that made him sit up straight and pay attention. "The reason you bought Camp Kicking Moose in the first place was to bring your family closer. Now you're complaining that they're too close? Do you realize how blessed you are? Most people would love to have family close by. I would! My son hasn't been home in five years. And you dare to bellyache."

"Whoa! Hold on. I'm not complaining." Not exactly. "But it's hard to figure out how to expand the use of Moose Manor when it's already a full house."

"Why do you have to expand?"

"Why?" It came out as a croak.

He'd been talking too much, too long without taking enough breaks. He'd pay for this today, but it was worth it. He wanted to make Peg understand. "There's a master plan. Improvements have been broken down in stages, all with an eye to making Moose Manor a year-round destination."

Peg held a hand up in the air, ticking off fingers as she talked. "You've fixed up the cabins. You've repaired and remodeled that old dinosaur of a house. You've spruced up the yards and cleaned out those old neglected carriage trails. Blaine told me that the camp even has a waiting list this year."

He nodded. Last year, the waiting list for this summer filled up before Labor Day.

"Cam said you've got some weddings booked for the fall."

"Two small ones." His voice sounded ground down. "Just in the yard."

"That big yard is a beautiful enough setting for a wedding, that's for sure." Peg leaned forward on her elbows. "So, Paul Grayson, tell me this. Besides those three daughters getting along, what else do you want that you don't already have?"

Oh. Put that way, Paul didn't have an answer. And he didn't have a voice left for the day either. Blast. *Women*.

Blaine looked up when she heard the bell jingle at the Lunch Counter the next afternoon, surprised to see her sister Cam come through the door. Since that day in the kitchen when Cam and Maddie had ambushed Blaine, they'd tiptoed around each other, polite but cool.

Cam eased onto a red leather stool. "I think these have gotten smaller."

"Probably so," Blaine said. Cam was not tall, with a very short waist. This baby was taking up most of her middle section. Her abdomen had become, in a word, beachballish.

"Blaine, I'm sorry."

Blaine stilled. She couldn't remember Cam ever apologizing to her. Not ever. This was a red-letter day. A signal-the-trumpets moment. She filled a glass with ice water and set it in front of her sister. "Sorry about what?" That was a Maddie tactic. Don't offer or accept vague apologies. To be sincere, get specific.

Cam cleared her throat. "I'm sorry for assuming that you needed help with a to-do list for the restaurant. You know what you're doing. After all, you're the one who went to culinary school. Not me. And I'm sorry for treating you as if you were still a child."

Blaine leaned on her elbows, eyes fixed on her sister. "Maddie's work, huh?"

Cam tugged her blouse down over her round tummy. "Well, yes. Maddie reminded me that my mouth is too often faster than my thoughts."

While Blaine picked up a fresh fork and napkin, she considered the apology. It seemed sincere, and it was specific. All trademarks of Maddie's influence. Well, good for her sister. Both sisters. "I accept your apology. And I am sorry I didn't give a heads-up about Jean-Paul. It was kind of a last-minute decision." Very last minute.

She had felt anxious about returning home, and he'd been told to go someplace to think and pray and ponder his future. It seemed like a perfect solution for them both.

"So . . . are we okay?"

Cam held her hand up in the air for a high five and Blaine returned it. "We're okay."

Cam smiled. "Then, what's on the menu today? I'm starving."

"Sweet or savory?"

"Yes, please," Cam said so sweetly the birds almost fell from the trees.

Blaine grinned. "I have just the thing to satisfy your pregnancy-induced craving. Grilled peaches glazed with maple syrup, and a scoop of vanilla ice cream on the side."

"You can grill peaches?"

"Yup. Split them in half, pop out the pit, leave the peel on, brush the cut surface with lemon juice and a dash of melted butter. Grill them for a minute or two, take them off, brush on the maple syrup." Blaine lifted her hand. "Voilà."

"I want it. I want two."

"Coming up. Let me just get the grill hot." She could sense Cam's eyes on her as she buttered the grill. She glanced over her shoulder. "What?"

"An indoor grill? I didn't know there was such a thing."

Blaine paused. Cam had hit a nerve without even trying. What Blaine wanted to say was, "Every commercial kitchen has an indoor grill. If you had only bothered to ask me, I could have told you. All that and more!" But she held her tongue. One by one, using tongs, Blaine set the peaches on the hot grill, leaving them in one spot to get grill marks. While the peaches were grilling, she got ice cream out of the big beautiful commercial refrigerator to let it soften for a few minutes. Taking a paintbrush (*Really, Peg? You can't spring for a kitchen brush?*), she coated the peaches with maple syrup. When she heard the syrup sizzle on the grill, she took the peaches off, placed them in a big bowl, added a generous scoop

95

of vanilla ice cream, and dusted them with cinnamon and brown sugar. She handed the bowl to Cam with a spoon.

"Why cinnamon?" Cam dug her spoon into the peach.

"Intensifies the flavor."

As Cam took a taste, her eyes closed. She chewed, swallowed, and opened her eyes. "This tastes . . . amazing! You'll have to add them to our menu."

"No indoor grill, remember?" Blaine couldn't resist.

"Then just grill outdoors."

Right. "No outdoor grill, remember?" Instead, there was a pickleball court.

"Just broil them then." Cam was halfway through her second peach when she looked up, as if she'd almost forgotten Blaine was there. "You didn't give much detail about how meeting Jean-Paul led you to a spot at Le Cordon Bleu."

"I tried. Cooper exploded Pepsi all over the living room."

"I remember. But there must be more to the story."

There was. Much more. But Blaine had, so far, avoided telling *that* story to her family through another lesson she'd learned: the Parisian skill of equivocation. Talking too much, saying not enough.

Right now, stalling, she went to the big stainless sink to turn the faucet on and start rinsing dishes.

"I'm waiting," Cam said.

Blaine wiped the counter near Cam with a cleaner and started rubbing. If done well, with just the right amount of detail, sprinkled with casualness, she thought the abbreviated version would suffice. "I'd been working for Jean-Paul's father at his bistro, and he . . . recommended me." More than that. As in, Henri worked part-time as a chef instructor at Le Cordon Bleu. As in, he pulled some strings to get Blaine in. As in . . . on full scholarship.

But she didn't really want to tell those details of the story to Cam. She was sure it would turn into an eyerolling "Blaine got another lucky break," which she had. She definitely had. But she had also worked hard, and for the first time in her life, she had finished what she started—something that had been a major complaint by her family. And she had prayed too. Most importantly, she had prayed.

"That's it?"

"That's it."

Cam polished off the last bite of peach and ice cream and put her spoon in the empty bowl. "If you served him *that*, I can see why." She leaned on her elbows. "Do you remember visits to Grandma?"

Washing a bowl in the sink, Blaine squeezed her eyes shut. Those summer visits were seared into her mind. It was during those happy moments in Grandma's kitchen when she had first felt the spark of cooking. Drying the bowl with a clean rag, she turned to Cam. "Why do you bring it up?"

"This dish reminded me of our last visit, the summer before she died. We'd spent the morning picking strawberries. It had rained the night before, and the ground was like a muddy sponge."

Blaine remembered. The sisters were barefoot, and the mud squished between their toes as they popped the sweet berries in their mouths. "We ate as many as we picked."

"Your fingers and face were berry stained for weeks," Cam said.

"Then Grandma baked a shortbread cake from her secret recipe."

"And smothered it with Cool Whip!"

"Um . . . that was freshly whipped cream."

"Was it? I just remember that she let us put as many dollops on it as we wanted to. And loads of berries."

"There's never been anything that tasted better, sweeter, than Grandma's strawberry shortcake."

Cam pointed to her empty plate. "Until this. It's just as good." Slowly, she eased off the stool. "Need a ride back to the camp?"

"No thanks. I have my car."

At the door, Cam turned and blew a kiss. "I'm glad you're home, Blainey." The door jingled as it closed.

Blaine picked up Cam's empty plate to find a crisp twenty-dollar bill folded underneath. A warm feeling covered her. One of her goals in returning home was to navigate a better relationship with Cam, to break deeply entrenched patterns of sibling roles that felt stifling. She hadn't wanted to come home until she was ready for that work; she knew it would have to start with her, and she knew it wouldn't be easy.

She smiled and added the twenty-dollar bill to Peg's old-fashioned register till. Maybe change was possible.

BLAINE, AGE 20, PARIS

A few days had passed since Blaine had that terrible Seine River bridge experience. She'd thought often about what the angel had told her about God leading her to Paris to fully heal. It helped. It buoyed her. Despite so many dead ends in her job hunt, she felt . . . better . . . than she had been feeling. More hopeful. Maybe there *was* something to what that angel had told her. Maybe God did know her. Maybe there was some kind of master plan going on.

Walking past a Catholic church with wide-open doors, she stopped. This was the place where the angel had said to go if she needed help. She didn't feel as fragile, but she knew she never *ever* wanted to feel that low again. She took a step inside, inhaling a mélange of scents. Candle wax and incense and mustiness and . . . something else. What was it? Sacredness, holiness, maybe?

She went to a pew and sat down, dropping her chin to her chest, murmuring, "Please God, please God, please God. I know it's been too long, but please, please, please, please, please help me find work." The strangest, most wonderful sensation covered her from head to toe, and she knew she was being listened to. Somehow she knew everything was going to be all right. Whatever this feeling was, whoever brought it to her . . . it was real. God, she knew in that moment, was real.

Someone touched her shoulder. "Mon amie? You are . . . okay?"

Blaine opened her eyes. "You!" It was him! The angel who had met her during her bleakest hour. He was here, just like he said he'd be. "I'm fine! I was, um, trying to pray. For a job. In a kitchen. Cooking."

The young man tipped his head. "Cooking? You have training?"

"Yes. Pretty much. Sort of. One year of culinary school in America. Mostly, to be honest, I was taught by my mother."

He pulled a key out of his pocket and held it up. "Come."

She followed him out of the church and two doors down to a little French bistro she must have passed dozens of times and never noticed. He unlocked the door, then held it open for Blaine. "Go in." Inside the bistro the young man called out, "Allô, allô."

A stern-looking middle-aged man poked his head around the corner and said something in rapid-fire French. The angel answered him, back and forth they went, too fast for Blaine to understand. Four years of high school foreign language class and her French was still iffy.

Finally the older man waved his hands in the air and disappeared behind the corner.

"Okay," the angel said, turning to her. "He says you can cook." He held up a finger. "He gives you one hour."

"Who is he?" Blaine whispered.

"Zis eez his bistro."

It turned out that a cook hadn't shown up for work, and the bistro had a large catering order to fulfill. Somehow the angel, who wasn't actually an angel but seemed like one to Blaine, had talked the bistro owner, who happened to be his pa-Pa, into giving Blaine one hour to cook or bake something, anything, and present it to him. If he liked it, she could have a job. For today, anyway.

"Follow me." The angel took her back to the kitchen where his father was deftly chopping onions with an enormous, terrifying

99

cleaver. He lifted his eyes to glance at her; she could understand *that* look without knowing French. It was full of doubt. *Man . . .* he was terrifying. His son could not have been more opposite. How was that possible?

The angel opened the refrigerator, and Blaine's eyes landed on a glass container of thick cream. Next to it was a box of luscious red strawberries.

Jackpot.

Nine

PEACE HAD APPARENTLY BEEN RESTORED between Paul's three daughters, though he was uncertain of how or why.

"What do you think happened?" Paul was walking along the beach near Boon Dock one morning after dropping Cooper off at school. He held the cell phone tightly against his ear as he walked because he didn't want to miss a single word from his friend. Not a single word.

"Sounds like they had a breakthrough. Those girls of yours always seem to find a way back to each other."

"Yes, but how and why and when. That's what I don't understand."

Silence.

He looked at his cell phone. *Blast*. No bars. The call had been dropped. *Double blast*.

Cam sniffed the air. Chocolate! Lying on her bed, she closed her computer and followed her nose downstairs to the kitchen. Empty, but the scent of chocolate lingered. She went back to the main room and spotted Jean-Paul and Granddad on the porch, eating something dark and brown and chewy. Her stomach rumbled.

She hurried outside, pleased to discover brownies left on a platter on the side table between the two rockers where Jean-Paul and Granddad sat. "I smell something wonderful."

"Come! Join us," Jean-Paul said, holding the platter of brownies out to Cam. She took two.

Cam tore off a piece of brownie and chewed slowly, then closed her eyes. "These are delicious," she said between mouthfuls. She took another brownie. "They practically melt in your mouth."

"Eez all zee butter," Jean-Paul said.

Her eyebrows lifted. "I'm so glad your knee is on the mend if this is what you do when you're mobile."

"I bake to celebrate zis big occasion. Food always eez needed to celebrate."

"What are we celebrating?"

"Look, Mom!"

She lifted her head to see Cooper on the grass lawn, playing with a small black puppy. "Oh no. Where did that puppy come from?"

"I got it for him," Granddad said. "Every boy needs a dog."

Cam cringed. "Dad will be furious."

Granddad frowned. "He had a dog when he was a boy." He pointed to Cooper. "Just about the same age as that one."

"But, Granddad, this camp is a business. It's different than a home."

Offended, Granddad rose from the rocking chair, one hand rubbing a hip as he stood. "Well, pardon me." His tone was hurt. "All I know is that every boy should have a dog. And that boy, most of all." He limped away and into the house.

"What did he mean by that?" Cam said, taking his chair before reaching for another brownie.

Jean-Paul's gaze was fixed on Cooper and the puppy. "He eez trying to help, I think."

"But help with what? What is he trying to imply about Cooper? Good grief, he's only been here . . . like, what, a week or so?" It came out a little mumbled as she talked around the brownie in her mouth.

Jean-Paul turned to her. "I zink your grandpa-pa, he wants to be a part of zee family."

She scoffed. "A little late for that."

"No, no, mon amie. It eez never too late."

Cooper, who had ears like a bat and an elephant all rolled into one, shouted from the lawn. "Jean-Paul's right, Mom. Granddad wants to be one of us. I promise I'll take good care of the puppy. Granddad's going to help me train it." The puppy bounded off toward the boathouse and Cooper chased after it.

Cam had to smile. The puppy's tail reminded her of a whirligig in the wind. "My dad," she said with a sigh, "will not be happy about this."

"Because . . . ," Jean-Paul said.

"Because Camp Kicking Moose isn't a place for pets."

"But," he said, his brow furrowed in confusion, "moose are welcome?"

She laughed and reached out for another brownie, her fourth. She was enjoying Jean-Paul more than she thought she would. She loved how words rolled out in his thick French accent. Softer, gentler, somehow.

The puppy tore out of the boathouse and Cooper ran after him. Such a normal scene. Just a boy and his dog. No hand sanitizer in sight. No can of Lysol.

Maybe Granddad did know something about what Cooper needed.

"You are happy about zis coming baby, no?"

She was startled by Jean-Paul's question. "No. I mean yes. Yes, I'm happy. Seth's happier, of course." Why did she have to add that?

"Why would Seth be happier?"

"He's a teacher, you see, and loves children," she said, a little too quickly. "And he doesn't want Cooper to be an only child. He's been eager for another child since we first got married. In fact, if it were up to him, we'd have a houseful. He's a natural father."

Now she was rambling, saying too much. She blamed Jean-Paul—he listened very carefully, as if what she was saying was the most important thing in the world. She grabbed another brownie and took a bite, just to stop herself from talking.

"And if it were up to you?"

She stopped chewing, swallowed. "Cooper's more than enough. In fact, it terrifies me to have a baby." She never intended to be so open with Jean-Paul—she hardly knew him!—yet there was something about the way he watched her, his eyes infinitely kind, gentle but observant. She felt safe, secure. Something about him spoke to her heart, like he was the brother she'd never had but always wanted.

"What makes you frightened?"

She felt a jab from the baby, first on one side, then another. Her hand rolled over her belly. "I'm a natural in the business world. But motherhood? Not so much." So far from it.

"So then, which role causes you to rely more on zee Lord?"

She opened her mouth, then closed it. She really didn't know how to answer him.

"Our limitations, zey provide an opportunity to rely on God all zee more. Zee Bible, it has a promise. 'I can do all zings through Christ who strengthens me.' All zings. Even being a good mama." He pronounced it ma-Ma.

Not only was Cam shocked to hear Jean-Paul quote Scripture to her like he had the book memorized, she was also shocked to realize she had not considered her weaknesses in light of God's strength. Never once had she thought to pray about her limitations as a mother. She let out a deep sigh. "Thanks, Jean-Paul. I needed to hear that." She reached out for another brownie, but the platter, somehow, held only crumbs.

"You sit. I get more." Jean-Paul picked up the platter and limped to the door. Just at that moment, the puppy tore up the porch steps, Cooper trailing behind him. Cam's mouth opened to warn Jean-Paul, but it all happened too fast. The puppy darted in front of Jean-Paul, he tripped, lost his balance, toppled down the porch steps, and the empty platter shattered. By the time Cam reached him, he was moaning in pain, gripping his bad knee.

Poor Jean-Paul. His knee had just started to feel better, the inflammation starting to simmer down. Thanks to the still-to-be-named puppy, that fall down the porch steps had caused a major setback. His knee had ballooned to the size of a softball.

"Oops, sorry," Blaine said as Jean-Paul winced when she replaced the bag of melting ice on his knee with a fresh one. "And I'm so sorry about the puppy collision today."

"Eez okay. My fault entirely."

That wasn't how Cam and Cooper had described the incident. The one silver lining was that Cam fussed over Jean-Paul all afternoon. She had called Artie to come by, but he was on another island. He repeated his advice: RICE. Rest, Ice, Compression, Elevation. Cam put it all into practice. She brought him fresh ice packs every twenty minutes, an unopened bottle of aspirin, any food he desired. Best of all, Cam seemed genuinely concerned about Jean-Paul. Such a change pleased Blaine. Maddie and Cam were finally getting to know her friend.

"Did you know," Jean-Paul said as if it was a startling discovery, on par with a medical breakthrough, "zat zee sports events are on zee TV all day long? All night long?"

Yes, of course she knew. Every American knew. Americans loved their sports the way the French loved their food and wine. And the French, being oh-so-French, looked down on Americans for their misplaced passions. Jean-Paul, in particular, had clear prejudices about the American way of life. He had hesitated when Blaine invited him, so she tried to convince him that Maine had strong historical connections with France. He remained skeptical until she threw out names like Cadillac Mountain and Calais and Isle au Haut. It was only then that he agreed to join her. She had wanted to open his mind to the real America, the way he'd opened her mind to real matters.

She gazed at him, lying there on the couch, surrounded by bags of chips and candy and empty soda cans, eyes glued to the television. What would Chef Henri have to say about this sight? His son was turning into an American couch potato.

Peg gazed at the sidewalk sign Blaine had dug up and dragged from the back room. She had lettered it carefully, using chalk, for today's diner special:

FRENCH SWEET MAUI ONION SOUP
$5/cup $8/bowl

"Honey, you've got a nice way of sprucing things up."

Here it was. The opening Blaine had been waiting for. Another lesson she had learned in Paris: timing was everything. She set down her chalk and followed Peg back into the diner. "I've been wanting to talk to you about something. I'd like to get the diner back to the way it was when I left for Paris. Bring back the refrigerated takeaways for the summer tourists."

"Nope. Not a chance. You can do what you want with the menu, but nothing else."

"I thought you liked the changes I made. I thought you were going to keep it up."

Hands on her hips, Peg sighed. "I tried, honey. That first summer after you left, I really did try. And then the sandbar went missing and in came those high-society summer people, and all my regular customers stopped coming. It wasn't long before I decided I just couldn't stand the summer people in here."

Blaine's eyes went wide. "So you intentionally drove them out? The very customers we were hoping to attract?"

"I sure did. I remember the day like it was yesterday. A husband

and a wife came in, all fancy and frippery, wearing matching Nantucket red shorts with those tiny little navy blue whales embroidered on them. I seated them over there"—she pointed to a corner booth—"and they asked to have their seats moved closer to the window because fishermen, they said, were smelly and coarse." She crossed her arms and frowned. "But don't you just know they love eating our lobsters. Anyway, the next day, back they come. The husband asked me where an airport could be built on the island so he and his hoity-toity friends could come and go in their private jets."

Blaine started to interrupt, but Peg wasn't finished. "Hold on," she said, "it gets worse. The wife sent back my scrambled eggs three times. Finally she told me that a dollop of beluga caviar on top might help." She stood with her hands on her hips, fuming. "Honey, I don't know what came over me. It was like a switch flipped! I was furious. Shaking so bad the fillings were jiggling out of my teeth. I told them to go, just go, that they were banned for life from the diner."

Astounded, Blaine said, "Did they go?" She had never once seen Peg get mad at a customer, never lose her cool, not even with the horrible Phinney brothers.

"They left in a huff and told all their snooty friends not to come here." She was trying to look remorseful, but the twinkle in her eyes gave her away. "Honey, it wasn't long until the locals came back. Kind of like how all the songbirds left my bird feeder when Seth's Lola was living in her cage out back. Lola left, and the songbirds came back."

Lola was Seth's rehabilitated goshawk. He'd found her as a baby with a broken wing and nursed her back to health. He used to take her for walks along the water before teaching school for the day. She had always returned to him of her own free will until the sandbar disappeared. When the yachts floated in, Lola left, horrified, and never returned. At least, that was Peg's version of the story. More likely, Seth said, Lola had found a mate, and was finally living life in the wild as she was meant to live.

Blaine knew what Peg was getting at. Some people were completely unreasonable just because they could afford to be. But Peg couldn't just paint an entire segment of the population with one broad brushstroke. That was stereotyping. And it wasn't true. Blaine had met plenty of very nice, very generous campers at Camp Kicking Moose who were well off and not a bit hoity-toity, not all fancy and frippery.

"Peg, the songbirds aren't going to feather your retirement nest." Wasn't that the whole point of giving the diner a major facelift? To build a success out of the diner and help Peg gain financial footing? She'd barely been able to eke out a living.

Peg scratched her forehead. "Well, honey, there's some truth to that. But at least I like my job again. Most days."

Blaine went outside to water the lavender plants in the window boxes (not plastic ivy—it was the only change Peg had let her make in the diner's shabby appearance) when she heard someone march up the hill from Boon Dock and recognized the person just by the sound of his gait.

She spun around, and there was Artie. She couldn't get over how much his appearance had changed, or maybe it was his confident countenance. Whatever it was, *man,* he looked good. She stepped out from under the awning eager to say hello, to make a connection, to begin the process of renewing their friendship, but he didn't slow his pace at all. In fact, he barely acknowledged her as he strode up the hill. Just a brief nod. "How's the bad knee?"

"About the same." She opened her mouth to say more, but he dashed on by.

"Remember to RICE. I'll drop by later to check on him. Can't talk. In a hurry."

Clearly.

She watched him disappear up Main Street and turn a corner. *Man!* He wasn't making this easy.

As Paul parked his pickup truck on Main Street, he tucked his keys in his pants pocket without locking the door. How absolutely weird it was, he thought, to leave a car unlocked. Completely counter-intuitive. In Needham, the town where he and Corinna had raised their girls, he would have never left a car unlocked. Or a house. But here, cars and houses were unlocked everywhere. Was there that much less crime on the island, or were the locals more honest? Paul didn't know, but it was an interesting thought to ponder.

He stopped in the diner to get coffee before making a phone call down along the beach.

At the stovetop, Peg smiled as he came in the door. "What's your pleasure?"

"Just a to-go cup of coffee." He hoped she wasn't in a very chatty mood because his mind was on that phone call, and he needed to save his voice for it.

"Paul, I've been meaning to talk to you."

Uh-oh. He glanced at his watch, hoping she'd take the hint.

"Sit down. We need to have a chat."

No hint was taken. Where were the other customers that usually filled the diner and captured Peg's attention? Where was Blaine? The diner was nearly empty.

"Rain expected. Blaine ran over to the grocery store to get a few things," Peg said, as if Paul had voiced aloud his question. She passed him his to-go coffee cup. "That girl's been working awful hard since she got back."

"I'll say." He couldn't get Blaine to sit still for two minutes to talk about plans for the dining service. She always had someplace else she needed to be.

"How's that little French fella? I heard he got reinjured."

Paul scoffed. "Don't worry about him. He's turned into a rabid Red Sox fan." He took a sip of the coffee. Drat. It wasn't Blaine's rich, dark coffee. It was hot water with a soggy herbal teabag. Women were conspiring against him. "Is that what you wanted to talk about? Because . . ." He really wanted to go.

"Look, Paul, there's something you should know." Peg leaned across the counter. "Baxtor Phinney's got something brewing."

He lifted his eyebrows in a way to say, "What?"

"This last winter, he created a committee called the Silent Opposition. At first I thought it wasn't much more than a winter pastime, but it started gaining momentum."

"What is Baxtor opposing? What more does he want?" A rasp edged Paul's voice.

"It's not what he wants. It's what he doesn't want. Now that the sandbar is gone, the island is turning into a playground for the summer people. He wants the island to keep its simpler way of life. Mostly, he talks about wanting to curb taxes, and that makes the locals take notice. And they are noticing. He's gotten a lot of support."

Oh no. He felt a hitch in his gut. "Cam's Phase 2?" He had a nagging feeling that Baxtor Phinney was going to mess it all up.

Peg drew a line across her throat. "Baxtor has folks believing Cam's Phase 1 is what started this . . . boom."

"Hold on. It was the disappearing sandbar that brought the boom. Not Cam's renewable energy program."

Peg lifted her palms in the air. "I don't disagree. I know that Cam's done a lot for this island. The Lunch Counter hasn't lost electricity since she got that whole thingamajig set up out there." She hooked her thumb in the general direction of the wind turbine.

"Hydropower plant."

"But I just don't want another summer season like the last one. I can't handle those summer people. If Cam could promise that those folks wouldn't be encouraged to come here, then I'd be all for her whatchamacallit."

"Cellular tower. And all the tower would do is provide Wi-Fi and cell phone connection for the island. That's all."

She leaned on her elbows. "But that's just what would make those summer people want to stay. I know that for a fact, because as soon as they try to check their email on their phones, they get a panicky look and head right back to their fancy-schmancy yachts. I'm sorry, Paul, those high-society folks are just different. If the sun is shining bright, they'll find the one cloud in the sky. I ask you, with all their money and all their stuff, where is their joy?"

He glanced at his watch again. He needed to go. "I recall a stern lecture you gave me about my bad attitude. You told me I'd been sounding old and crotchety. If I wanted to be in the service industry, you said that meant that I needed to *serve* my customers. Value each one. And if I didn't want to embrace that basic concept, then I should look for another line of work." He took a sip of the insipid tea only to keep his vocal cords lubricated for his important phone call. He'd been much more tolerant of the campers and their endless demands since that lecture. Many still bugged him, but not as much. Peg's upbraiding had jolted him into the perspective he'd been lacking.

Her eyes went big as saucers. "Oh boy."

He rose to his feet before another long conversation got underway. "What now?"

"If Paul Grayson is giving me advice that I once gave to him, that can mean only one thing."

"What's that?"

"I'm getting too old and crotchety for this line of work."

As Blaine drove up the gravel driveway, past the cabins, toward Moose Manor, she spotted a giant lump in the yard and did a double take. It seemed odd, out of place, peculiar. Had Dad been working in the garden and left a bundle of leaves? Wait. Did that lump just move? It did! And all at once she realized that the lump was not a thing but a someone, lying prostrate on the ground.

Blaine slammed on the brakes, jumped from the car, and bolted over to the lump.

Ten

"GRANDDAD!" Blaine dropped to her knees beside him. He lay in the grass, facedown, and she saw he was trembling. He muttered something incomprehensible, and for a chilling moment Blaine feared he'd had a massive stroke or a heart attack. What to do, what to do? She had absolutely no idea how to handle a medical emergency and vowed to take a first aid class this summer. She knelt close to his head and gently touched his cheek.

Awkwardly, Granddad turned his head. He needed a moment to answer, squinting at Blaine as if he did not recognize her. "Who are you?"

"It's me. Blaine. Did you break something? Hurt something? What feels most uncomfortable?"

Granddad spoke again, more slowly. "A bug flew up my nose."

Hold on . . . he wasn't trembling . . . he was . . . chuckling, a sound that surprised her for its rarity. He didn't have a massive stroke after all. Relief flooded her. She looked to the house and cupped her mouth. "Dad! Jean-Paul! Come help!"

"Don't waste your breath, kiddo. I already tried. No one's around."

"Even Jean-Paul? Where'd he go?"

"No idea. Can't you just help me get up?"

Blaine studied the situation. It wasn't quite so simple as rolling him over and helping him stand. "How are we going to do this?" Her grandfather was a rather good-sized man, with plenty of healthy padding, perfect for protection in a fall but difficult to shift.

She braced herself with her knees firmly on the ground, one hand on Granddad's shoulder, the other on his hip. "Ready? I'm going to try to roll you onto your back." She counted to three and pushed, but it was like moving dead weight. Blaine's heaving didn't budge him an inch. Plus it didn't help when he started chuckling again. This time, his whole body shook as he laughed.

She sat back on her heels to ponder what more she could do to help. "I have an idea. I'll be right back! Don't go anywhere." She jumped to her feet. "Oh . . . never mind. That was a stupid thing to say." She ran to the boathouse and had to stop short to allow her eyes to adjust to the dim light. Off the roof rafters hung neat and tidy rows of kayaks, canoes, and boogie boards. She grabbed a board and went back outside to discover that Peg's ancient green minivan had arrived. She hadn't even heard the loud engine rumble up the driveway. Blaine looked at her grandfather, expecting to see Peg. Beside him, there was Artie. *Artie!* Second time today. Both times, no warning. Heat dove through her, warming her cheeks.

Blaine took a few seconds to recover from the unexpected sight of him, then hurried over with the boogie board tucked under her arm.

"Oh good," Granddad said, still face-first on the lawn. "We can go surfing."

It was such a silly, unexpected thing for him to say that Blaine burst out with a laugh.

Artie frowned at Blaine. "This is hardly a laughing matter."

Her smile faded. "I found him like this."

"How long ago?"

"Maybe five, ten minutes ago."

Artie took Granddad's pulse, asked him a few questions, checked to see if he hurt anything in the fall, then rolled him gently into a sitting position. Blaine held her breath, watching to see if there was anything she could do to help. And noticing, in spite of herself, Artie. He looked sturdy, strong, brawny, so . . . male. Broad shoulders, not like a guy who worked out, but like a guy who worked.

She noticed the tension leave his face. "Granddad's okay, right?"

"I think so." Carefully, Artie lifted Granddad into his arms as if he weighed little more than a bag of potatoes. He carried him up the porch and to his favorite rocking chair. After he got Granddad settled, she noticed that he wasn't even winded.

Blaine crouched by the rocker. "What happened? What were you doing in the middle of the yard?"

Granddad brushed it off as nothing. "I thought I'd see what was in that boathouse where your dad spends most of his life."

"But what made you collapse?" She could see a lump beginning to appear where Granddad's forehead had hit the ground.

"I must have tripped on something. That's all."

That's all? She looked over at Artie and could see he had the same thought.

"Were you feeling dizzy?" Artie said. "Faint? Weak?"

Granddad clearly wanted this conversation to end. "I'm fine now. That's all that matters."

Artie wasn't finished. "Mr. Grayson, I'd like you to consider using a cane. I've got one back at the *Lightship*."

"No way. Not a chance." Granddad's light mood had soured. "I'm fine. And I don't need lectures from two kids. Stop fussing and just leave me in peace."

Ah. Her grandfather was back to his normal grouchy self. She glanced at Artie. "You came at just the right time."

"Just lucky," Artie said, hands on his hips, eyes on Granddad. "I was doing my rounds." His eyes flicked to her, then back again to her grandfather. "Blaine, will you get your grandfather something to eat? A sandwich, maybe. And a glass of water too. He looks a little pale to me."

She nodded and headed to the front door. She heard Artie talking to Granddad in a low voice, heard something about taking a few tests, and she paused halfway inside the door, leaning against the jamb, hoping to hear exactly what kind of tests he was talking about. Something didn't seem right with her grandfather. He'd collapsed twice now, with no explanation other than insisting he'd tripped.

To her surprise, Jean-Paul was not on the couch. Nor was he in the living room. And the television wasn't left on. She pushed the kitchen door and heard someone yelp in pain. "Oh no!" Jean-Paul had been searching for something in the refrigerator as Blaine came in. The kitchen door bumped against the open refrigerator side door, closing on his fingers. "I'll get ice!"

"Eez okay," Jean-Paul said, holding his hand, grimacing in pain. "Eez fine."

It wasn't fine. His fingers were already turning colors. "I'm so sorry, Jean-Paul. I didn't realize you were here." She helped him to a chair and got a bag of ice.

"Zee stove!"

The entire room smelled of semisweet chocolate. A double boiler on the stovetop had melting chocolate in it, so she turned off the burner and covered the pot. "What were you doing?"

He glanced up. "Suddenly"—he tapped his forehead with the palm of his uninjured hand—"inspiration hit. I felt zee urge to make truffles."

Blaine smiled. That sounded more like the Jean-Paul of Paris. "Can you bend your fingers? Artie's out on the porch with Granddad. I could ask him to see if anything is broken."

"No, no. All good," Jean-Paul said. Slowly, he unbent his swelling fingers. Nothing seemed broken, but his fingers looked bruised, seemed a little stiff.

Bummer. "Artie wanted Granddad to eat something. I don't think he meant truffles." She looked around for a space to work, but Jean-Paul had taken up the countertops for the truffle making.

There was no counter space to spare. Even the table was covered with cookie trays for the truffles to set. She finally decided to set a cutting board over the sink and threw together a roast beef sandwich for Granddad as quickly as she could. She made an extra sandwich for Artie, just the way she remembered he liked it—with a dash of horseradish—hoping he could be persuaded to stay for a while.

"And maybe one for me, perhaps? With a splash of Dijon?"

How could she refuse? She made one more for Jean-Paul.

She hurried as quickly as she could, but by the time she returned to the front porch with sandwiches, Peg's green minivan was gone and Granddad had fallen sound asleep.

Paul puttered around the boathouse, frustrated. His father's health worried him, the puppy bothered him, the cat annoyed him, but most disturbing was Peg's news about Baxtor Phinney's Silent Opposition committee. While Baxtor may not be well liked by most people on Three Sisters Island, he was a fifth-generation Mainer, and that legacy afforded him a ridiculous amount of grace. Baxtor had a tenure on Three Sisters Island as the self-appointed mayor to a town that didn't have a mayor, only a selectman. In Paul's opinion, Baxtor had never done much for the island. He resisted any and all change. Paul's purchase of Camp Kicking Moose had saved the island from complete bankruptcy, especially after Baxtor slapped him with an enormous bill for overdue property taxes.

Baxtor had a brief fall from grace among the locals when his sons had been tossed in jail for raiding lobster traps. Suddenly, he had reemerged, once again declaring himself as the leader of the town. And Peg, as the informal mayor, had essentially handed over the town "voice" to him. To Baxtor Phinney! This had all happened during this last winter—a rising tide that Paul had completely overlooked.

Missing the obvious was hardly new for Paul. It was a theme in his life, a bad habit that his late wife Corinna had tried to break. He was well aware of his lack of awareness. But how did his daughters miss the groundswell of resistance? Cam was tunnel-visioned, much like he was. But Maddie? She was extremely tuned in to the feelings of others. How had Maddie missed the rising surge? How had Seth and Rick, both very plugged in to the community, how had they missed it?

Paul let out a deep sigh. Now that he thought it all over, he knew the answer to the Grayson family obliviousness. They'd all been riding the wave of success that had hit Three Sisters Island. The church had exploded as people from Mount Desert ferried over on Sunday mornings to hear Rick preach. Maddie's counseling practice had grown so quickly that she had to turn clients away, referring them to a practice on Bar Harbor.

As for Seth, the school finally had a balanced budget with money from sales tax levied on tourists. Cam had successfully brought reliable energy to the island through a combination of an enormous wind turbine, solar panels, and a hydropower plant.

Best of all, Mother Nature added a bonus to the island. When that sandbar had been blasted away during a dramatic nor'easter, it created a tremendous opportunity to build tourist traffic. No longer did visitors have to rely on the Never Late Ferry. When the tide was out, that sandbar had allowed people, bikes, and cars to come back and forth from Mount Desert Island, but it also meant they were locked into tide tables.

But now? The harbor was just deep enough that large boats could enter and not have to worry about an ebbing tide. The way Paul saw things, once tourists came to Three Sisters Island and saw how it was no longer in a decline but making rapid improvements, they liked it. They came, they stayed, and when they went home, they told their friends about the island.

Things were looking up for Three Sisters Island, and the Grayson family could not be more pleased with the signs of progress. But the locals . . . they seemed to feel otherwise.

Blaine pushed the door leading to the kitchen just a few inches, then hit something and stopped. "Who's in the fridge?" She had learned to make a slow entrance after smashing Jean-Paul's fingers in the fridge.

"Me and Cooper." Dad closed the refrigerator and the dining room door swung open. He had a jar of peanut butter in one hand and a loaf of bread in the other. "We're making sandwiches to go."

"No jam on mine, Grandpa," Cooper said. "Only honey." He pushed his glasses up on the bridge of his nose. "Did you know that honey can kill bacteria?"

"No kidding, Coops?" Dad said.

Cooper nodded solemnly. "Egyptians used it as a natural antibiotic."

"Interesting trivia." Blaine couldn't help but smile. "Where are you two going?"

"We men are working around the property." Dad moved his shoes off the counter, opened the bread bag, and took out four slices.

Just as he put the slices on the counter, Blaine grabbed his hand. "Dad! First off, dirty shoes do not belong on a counter. Ever. And sandwich making requires a cutting board." She grabbed one from a narrow opening between the stovetop and the refrigerator—another cringeworthy place for kitchen utensils to be housed—and placed it on the counter.

Dad set the bread on the cutting board. "Since when did you get all germophobic?"

"Since I looked through a microscope at household germs in the average kitchen."

Cooper looked worried by her words. He went to the sink and washed his hands.

Dad held a peanut-butter-slathered knife in the air. "But *this* is not an average kitchen."

Oh boy. She braced herself, knowing what was coming next.

"Blaine," Dad said, carefully spreading the peanut butter to the edge of the bread, "we really need to get a plan for the dining service. I was thinking we could start small, offer a set menu, maybe just on weekend nights." He lifted the knife to scoop out more peanut butter. "Then, as we get the swing of things, maybe after the Fourth of July weekend, we could gear up to full service. Lunch. Dinner. Seven days a week." He squirted honey all over the peanut-butter-slathered bread and placed the other slice on top. "My vision is that we will be just like that restaurant at Jordan Pond."

"How so?"

"Reservations have to be made weeks in advance."

"Just like that?"

He snapped his fingers. "Just like that." He put his sandwich in a plastic baggie, searched through the refrigerator for an apple, and tucked everything inside a paper bag. "Sounds like a plan?"

"It definitely sounds like a plan." Not a realistic one, but it was a plan. Blaine still didn't know how to tell her dad that there was no way in the world this kitchen could provide the kind of service he had just described. She didn't know how to tell him that he had no idea what he was talking about. But then a thought occurred. "By the way, Dad, you've gotten a food and lodging license, right?"

He stopped, pivoted. "Uh, sure, the camp has a license. We've been serving food."

"Not for continental breakfast. That's different than full service."

He rubbed his chin. "I'm sure it's all covered with the camp's license."

"The *camp's* license?"

He cleared his throat. Not a good sign. "It came with one."

"Dad . . . please tell me that you've received a license under your ownership."

"Why?"

"Dad, you do have a license for the camp, right?"

119

Eleven

BLAINE MADE A PLAN, short and simple. Instead of always being surprised by Artie's unexpected appearances, she would surprise him. She would seek him out, find a moment when they could be alone, to talk. Operation Artie.

When she heard a customer mention that Dr. Lotosky's *Lightship* was arriving later this afternoon, she decided to wait for him at Boon Dock. Dr. Lotosky. *Man!* Artie must've doubled up on classes to get through med school in record time.

This was the first time Blaine had hung out by the harbor since she'd returned to Three Sisters Island. The day was warm, the air mild, the breeze gentle, the skies blue except for low, fluffy white clouds on the ocean horizon, looking for all the world like smatterings of heavenly sheep.

It was low tide, the water calm. Barely a whisper of wind to ruffle its surface. Seagulls cawed and dipped in and out of the water. Once she saw a heron. It was beautiful here, and she had missed it, more than she even realized.

She looked up and down at the ribbon of beach. A young mother and a little girl sat near the water's edge, peering into a plastic pail—filled with shells, maybe, or crabs. Or maybe it was just a bucket of sand. Give water and sand to a kid and magic happened.

Her gaze shifted past them to the harbor, at the location where the sandbar had gone missing. Memories rushed forward, happy ones. Jogging over to Mount Desert Island with Seth and his dog Dory and back again. Watching Rick, with Maddie strapped to him, float down under a rainbow parachute to a pinpoint landing on this very ribbon of beach. She grinned, thinking of Maddie's screams as they descended. Rick told her that Maddie had banned him from skydiving now that he was going to be a father, and he seemed a little sad.

Today, nearly every slip on the dock was full. There was the usual assortment of lobster boats and outboards, sailboats, including a catamaran, and quite a few pleasure crafts. She watched four sailboats head out to sea, swerving skillfully around lobster buoys.

One twenty-five-foot launch caught her eye and she sucked in a breath. A Hinckley craft—the epitome of style and quality, made of gleaming mahogany and polished brass. *Wow, wow, wow.* A Hinckley craft was worth as much as a half-million dollars or more. And it was *here*, tied to rickety ol' Boon Dock.

Gone from the harbor were rowboats and dinghies. No canoes or kayaks. The harbor traffic had grown too busy for that, Peg had told her, and she said it with a frown.

A cabin cruiser pulled into the harbor, slowing to a crawl as it approached the end of Boon Dock. She saw a red cross on its side and realized it must be Artie's boat. After a few minutes, she saw him hop out and tie the boat's ropes to the cleats. He reached back in the cabin and pulled out his medical bag, then walked up the dock with his purposeful stride.

She walked to where the dock met the beach and waved with her whole arm, probably looking like a stranded hiker flagging down a helicopter. Artie stopped short when he saw her, as if he had felt a shock, a jolt, then he recovered to approach her. Her stomach somersaulted and she felt breathless, even light-headed. What was that all about?

He glanced at his watch. "Did something happen to your grandfather?"

"No, he's fine." She tipped her head. "Why do you ask? Is something wrong with him?"

"Hello? HIPAA laws? I don't discuss my patients."

Good grief! So curt. So serious. "Those laws don't apply to family, Artie."

"Yes, they do."

She tried not to roll her eyes. "I'm not trying to be nosy, Artie. He is my grandfather, and you keep checking on him on a regular basis. We're concerned about him, but he won't tell us anything."

She could hear the water lapping against the dock pilings as Artie stood there, taking this in, saying not a word in response. Her gaze traced down his face, along his Roman nose, his cheeks framed by a trimmed beard, down to his lips. Nice full lips. She wondered what it might be like to be kissed by those . . .

"Anything else?" he said.

His abruptness burst the bubble of her ridiculous musings. *Pull it together, Blaine.* She held up the car keys. "I thought I could give you a lift to wherever it is you need to go."

"Peg lets me use her minivan as long as I leave her with a full tank of gas."

He was *not* making this easy. As they walked up Boon Dock to where Peg's minivan was parked, she searched her mind for some kind of an icebreaker. Anything to wring as much conversation out of him as she could. Questions about his work? About his dad and sisters?

Finally, nearly to the minivan, she opted for the direct method. "So I guess you're trying to make sure I get the message that our friendship is . . . uh . . . a thing of the past." When he didn't respond, she added, "But, Artie . . . we were friends for a long time." They stood near, so near she could have touched him by merely lifting a hand, could have brushed off a stray thread on his shirt, could have straightened the sunglasses that hung down from his top button.

Artie seemed to give her comment some serious thought. "That's true. It's also true that we used to tell each other everything. No secrets, that was our deal. That was how things were between us."

She remembered, she did.

"So how about not telling me that you'd gotten involved with a married instructor?"

Blaine's eyes went wide. "Hold on! Who told you that? That's NOT true."

"There wasn't a married instructor?"

"Well, yes, but—"

"Isn't that the real reason you ran off to Europe?"

Her hands shot up like she was stopping traffic, and she backed up to put a few feet of space between them. "Whoa . . ." But he wasn't stopping. She saw the look on his face, like a spark about to ignite.

"And as for inviting me to join you? I'd been breaking my back to accelerate through medical school so that we could—" He stopped abruptly and looked away.

We? We could what? "Why? What was the big hurry?"

"Why?" He glared at her, practically shouting the word. "Because I put myself through school, Blaine. I don't have a sugar daddy who funds my latest whim."

Her mouth opened wide. *Whim?* Le Cordon Bleu was no whim! And her dad was *no* sugar daddy. Artie *knew* that. He knew that her dad had sunk every penny he had into Camp Kicking Moose.

They faced off, color high, mouths set, while Blaine tried to hang on to a bare thread of self-control. She wanted to snap back at him, to defend herself. Her mind spun like a pinwheel, searching for a Bible verse she thought she'd need for Cam, not for Artie. *Don't sin by letting anger control you. Think about it overnight and remain silent.* She took a deep, calm-down breath, determined to not let her fury show. "It might be best to end this conversation now before one of us says something we regret." She turned and walked off. She had to get away from Artie before anything more was said.

Maddie had just finished for the day and was taking down a few notes. She couldn't wait to get home and put her feet up. Her mind was thoroughly preoccupied. Worried about the baby, but even more so, she worried about Rick.

If only he would slow down.

Maddie had even asked his secretary, Tillie, to make Rick decline additional speaking requests. She'd told Seth that Rick needed more balance for his health—and while they both agreed, they had no influence over him. Seth said it was like trying to stop a moving train.

That, she understood. But Rick had to understand this: he was about to become a father. They needed him. Home.

Rick was twenty-nine years old. His father had died in his thirties, a casualty of the same heart issue, and that fact was at the core of Maddie's deep-rooted fear. She had married Rick knowing about his heart condition and accepting his zest for life, despite the precaution he took with the ICD, the heart-regulating device. She and Rick had long talks about this very thing before they decided to get pregnant. She thought she was okay with the risks . . . but that was all in theory and practice. This was reality. Having a child, being responsible for another life, worrying that their baby may grow up without knowing his father . . . that fear kept returning to Maddie, and unsettled her.

She turned off the lights to her office as Blaine burst in and flopped on a chair. "I need one minute of counseling help."

Maddie turned the lights back on and sat across from her sister, noticing the messy bun of blonde hair at the base of her neck, the oversized T-shirt tucked casually in front of her jean's waistline. Maddie had no waistline. She noticed Blaine's slim ankles above her white sneakers. Maddie had no ankles. Blaine had a knack for looking so stylish without even trying. Maddie had to try so hard. She shook off her shortcomings to pay attention to her ridiculously beautiful little sister. "What's up?"

"I just bumped into Artie." Blaine explained the conversation they'd had. "It was like throwing a lit match at gasoline." She clenched the tips of her fingers, then splayed them. "Kaboom! I knew he was bothered with me for leaving for Paris, but I didn't know he was furious." She jumped to her feet, paced around the room. "I don't get it. He was in school on the opposite side of the country. It's not like we saw each other much."

"But you talked on the phone a lot."

"Yeah, we had regular calls. But why would he be so angry that he wouldn't even answer my texts? My calls. Two years of the cold shoulder. Black-hole silence. What kind of a friend does that?" She plopped back in the chair and squeezed her elbows. "So what do you think?"

"What do *you* think?"

"Oh no. Don't do that counselor thing. Tell me straight up."

Normally Maddie would try to help Blaine draw her own conclusions. That was a cardinal rule of therapy. Not today, though. She was tired, hungry, six months pregnant, and this individual wasn't a client. This was her sister. "I think, Blaine, that you hurt Artie."

Blaine gave her a startled look. "No way," she insisted. "Not possible."

The way her sister pushed back, so quickly and firmly, Maddie suspected that she must be onto something. "Badly. I think you hurt him badly."

Blaine stood up abruptly. "I'd better get home and check on Jean-Paul." She gave Maddie a wave at the door.

"Blaine! The things we protest against the most are often the very things we need to look at."

Blaine stopped and turned. "Did you tell Artie about that married instructor? You were the only one who knew the whole story."

"No," Maddie said, feeling a flush creep up her neck. She kept her eyes on her ankles. "No, I didn't tell Artie."

"Yeah, I didn't think so. I don't know how he would've found out. And he gave me no chance to explain." Blaine gazed at her sister's puffy ankles. "Your ankles are big, but not as big as Cam's."

Maddie smiled. Then the silence lasted a long time.

"Thanks for being there."

Maddie lifted her eyes. "Always."

On the drive home, Blaine couldn't stop thinking about Artie, about Maddie's remark that she had hurt him. Badly. About how different he seemed to be than the guy she used to know. The new Artie seemed preoccupied, always in a hurry. The old Artie had always made time for her. They told each other everything, he'd said today. No secrets. That was their deal. That was how it was between them.

She remembered, she did.

A movie reel of memories rolled through her mind. Meeting Artie during dorm move-in day at college when he offered to carry her boxes up the stairs. Discovering their mutual love of ice cream. Their mutual dislike of cafeteria food. Studying together in the library. Artie's willingness to be her guinea pig when she tried a new recipe. Artie painting over that hideous shade of Pepto-Bismol pink that covered Moose Manor. Phone calls every Thursday morning, like clockwork, after he left to continue his medical education in Oregon, even though it meant he had to wake up at three a.m. They talked and talked and talked. They told each other everything.

She remembered, she did.

BLAINE, AGE 18

Late one afternoon during midterms, Blaine and her roommate Dana took a break from studies to walk downtown to their favorite coffee shop and share a slice of boysenberry pie. Sitting in the booth, Dana held out a paper with a list of potential dates to her sorority's formal Christmas dance. Together, they whittled the list down to two possibilities for Dana.

"But . . . there is one more possibility," Dana said, digging her fork into the pie oozing with dark purple-red berries. "There is Artie."

Blaine stilled. "Artie Lotosky?" *My Artie?*

Dana took a bite of pie and closed her eyes. "Sheer perfection." She swallowed, opened her eyes. "Yeah, Artie. Unless, you know"—she flicked a glance at Blaine—"you've marked him."

"Marked him? No. No, of course not. Go right ahead, if you want. Ask Artie to the dance." Terrible idea. Dana was all wrong for Artie.

"But you don't mind? You spend a lot of time together. Really, a lot. I just assumed . . . maybe there was something going on between the two of you."

"Nope." Blaine took a bite of pie. It didn't taste as good as it usually did. Too much salt in the crust. Not enough lemon juice added to the berries. "We're just friends."

"Don't you think he's cute?"

"Cute? Sure, I guess. Like a brother is cute." Blaine jabbed her fork at the list of potential dates. "Not like Ben Austen. Now *there's* cute."

"Agreed." Dana took a bite of pie, a thoughtful look on her face. "I sort of think of Artie-types as a piecrust."

"How so?"

"You know, the piecrust is kind of like the guy in a movie who you don't realize is super hot until the final scene. Like"—she lifted a forkful of juicy berries—"if you think of this boysenberry pie, it's all about the filling. Berries are a wow. Eye candy. Sexy. You know, like Ben Austen. But the piecrust is what holds it all together." Dana pushed the plate toward Blaine to take a bite. "You're sure you don't mind if I ask Artie to the formal?"

"Go right ahead." Blaine pushed the plate back to Dana. This pie didn't taste like it should, or could. "Artie probably will say no, though. He's very focused on his studies." She wiped a crumb from her cheek with the paper napkin. "Probably best to just ask Ben."

Twelve

It was unfortunate that Blaine had accidentally squashed Jean-Paul's right hand with the refrigerator door. He had trouble grasping the crutches that Artie had dropped off, so he ended up mostly back on the couch, watching TV. Remarkably good-natured, he accepted his limitations with grace. "Eez okay," he told Blaine when she apologized again. "I sit. I watch American TV. I listen to your sister on zee phone." With his good hand, he made a yak-yak-yak motion. "And I learn about Americans. All zee time, I am learning."

She curled up in the chair across from him. "Jean-Paul . . . what if I made a mistake by coming back to Three Sisters Island?"

He pressed the mute button on the remote and gave her his full attention. "How so?"

"I'm just not sure I belong here."

"Because . . ."

"Because everything I came back for isn't going to happen. I worked so hard at Le Cordon Bleu so that I could come back and start a fine dining establishment. That's been my goal . . . ever since Dad bought Camp Kicking Moose." Her throat tightened. "And that dream is over."

"*La fin?*"

129

"La fin," she repeated. "Completely."

"So you are feeling dissatisfied."

All her emotions were riding close to the surface, and it took effort not to burst into tears. Eyes downcast, she knotted her hands together in her lap. "Massively."

"Saint Augustine says . . . . how do I say in English . . ." He put the fingertips from his unbandaged hand to his temples as if drawing out the words. "God eez always trying to give good zings to us, but our hands are too full to receive zem."

Blaine wrinkled her forehead. "Meaning . . . ?"

"Zee dissatisfaction . . . it eez a good thing. A gift."

"A gift," she repeated flatly.

"Oui. If you ignore it, or pretend zat all eez well when it eez not, zee dissatisfaction will grow and grow. It wants to get your attention."

"Why?"

"Because . . . zee dissatisfaction eez a *gift*."

"Right. So you said." She wrinkled her face in confusion. "But how?"

"It eez an invitation. To a new and better life. A new and better dream."

"But I thought coming home again *was* the better dream."

"No, no, mon amie. Dissatisfaction . . . it may not be calling you to go someplace or to do somezing different. It may be an invitation to somezing right here. Right now."

Staring down at her open palms, Blaine turned her ring around and around her finger.

"We are surrounded by possibilities zat only God can see. So what eez God calling you to now?"

Her hands fell still at the question. Chin still tucked down, she said quietly, "I have no idea." None. All that she knew was she felt limited at every turn. Moose Manor was never going to be what she had thought it would be. The diner belonged to Peg, and Blaine could sense Peg's resistance to any suggestions other than improving the quality of the food. Peg didn't want to attract the wrong people, she said, which meant summer people.

There were times Blaine felt like a bird in a cage. "How do I find out what I am here for?" That question—which she thought she had dealt with in Paris—had returned to plague her, nip at her heels.

A tender look came into Jean-Paul's eyes. "You must only ask, mon amie. God has not abandoned you. His hand eez on your shoulder, guiding and protecting you. He has dreams for you zat you could not even imagine." He lifted his hands in a big arc. "And when he eez ready, and when you are ready . . . God will show you zis new dream."

"But how? When? Where?"

"In my country, zere was a man, a humble monk. Zee humblest of all monks, in all zee world over. His name was Brother Lawrence. Someone asked him zee very same question, and he said, 'In God's will, zere eez always enough light to assure safe travel.'"

One step at a time, he meant. Blaine leaned back on the chair, pondering such wisdom. Jean-Paul was so good at seeing problems from a different view, so good at turning a bleak situation into one full of possibilities. "So . . . ," she said.

"So," Jean-Paul said, unmuting the remote. "I am wondering if more peanut butter eez in zee refrigerator? It goes so nicely with zee Hershey Kisses. And maybe you can bring more Hershey Kisses too."

She reached over to grab the empty bag. "You ate them all?"

"Plenty more bags in zee cupboard. I discover a big stash." Littered on the floor by the couch were bits of foil and paper. He lowered his voice to a whisper. "Your sisters. Zey eat zem all zee day long."

Blaine rose from the chair. *And so, mon amie,* she thought, *do you.*

Thirteen

THE FOLLOWING AFTERNOON, on a whim after work, Blaine walked right past her car down to the dock to her dad's slip. It was dead low tide, and not a breath of air was coming off the water. A perfect time to head to the lighthouse. She hadn't gone to it since she arrived on the island. She needed to clear her mind. Of the not-gonna-happen restaurant at Moose Manor, of Artie, of Maddie's opinion that she had hurt him. She hadn't!

Why did her thoughts keep veering back to Artie, like a school-girl with a crush? She annoyed herself.

She jumped into the outboard boat and pulled the motor's cord. The engine sputtered to life, spewing foul black smoke into the air. This old boat had seen better days, but it was still seaworthy. She glanced around the interior of the boat, at the puddles of rainwater and dead bugs. Looked like Dad hadn't used it in a very long time.

As she steered the boat out of the harbor, she felt a hitch of uncertainty. She hadn't been out on the water since she had left Maine. But soon it all came back to her like riding a bicycle, and the water was wonderfully cooperative—calm and windless. As she ventured out of the harbor, she turned the throttle to speed up. She passed the little beach below Camp Kicking Moose, the one where her dad had once proposed to her mom.

She slowed the engine down a notch or two, and turned the boat in a circle. In this area, she used to see color variations in the water, strange shadowy shapes like a sunken pirate ship or something weird like that. Once, in the fog, on a day of extreme tides, she could have sworn she saw the tip of a bow sticking up from the sea floor. Cam and Maddie laughed and laughed at her vivid imagination. They asked if she'd seen the Loch Ness Monster for weeks afterward.

She turned the throttle to speed up another notch or two and headed toward the north point of the island. Her thoughts wandered to Jean-Paul's advice, to be willing to ask God for a new dream. But she really wanted the old dream.

She wanted to be with her family, wanted to settle into a career that she loved. In her dream of returning home, she had imagined spending the summer working out plans for the remodel with a kitchen designer of her choosing—one well-schooled in commercial kitchens.

She'd expected coming home again to take some getting used to. She even expected that she'd need to be patient and persevering with her family, an uphill climb, until they started to see her as she now saw herself: as a full adult and not as the permanent baby of the family.

But she hadn't expected the illogical kitchen remodel at Moose Manor to squash her dream. She hadn't expected Peg to have crossed arms and a closed mind. She hadn't expected to find Artie Lotosky living here, treating her as if she meant nothing to him.

Had she made a mistake by coming home? What was the point of being here if she had no real purpose? At least not like she had hoped.

Why *had* she come home?

She'd come home because there was something Chef Henri had said to her that she couldn't shake off. It stuck to her like a burr on a long-tailed dog.

BLAINE, AGE 22, LE CORDON BLEU

Early one morning, Blaine had arrived at Chef Henri's bistro to prep for the day. She worked at the bistro before her culinary classes started each day, and then again after classes each evening. It had been important to her to not ask Dad to pay for anything, not even for living expenses. He'd offered, but she knew, via Maddie, that money was tight for him. He'd sunk his entire retirement into Camp Kicking Moose, and the camp was like a hungry bear in springtime. A bottomless pit of expenses. Besides, Dad had done enough for Blaine's fits and starts of higher education.

But even more than that, providing for herself was a fundamental part of being a grown-up. *If you do not make ends meet, then you will meet the end.* That maxim was a favorite of Chef Henri's, and it had completely redirected her concept about money. Up to this point, money was like water to her. Hard to hold, better to let spill.

Over a holiday weekend, she'd started working at Chef Henri's bistro, and one patron had left her a ridiculously generous tip, enough money for a pair of new shoes she'd been eyeing. But then she'd overheard Chef Henri declare that maxim to his son, Jean-Paul, who constantly exasperated him for oh-so-many reasons. While the maxim made no impact on Jean-Paul, who cared nothing about money, Blaine took the advice to heart. Instead of buying that pair of new shoes, she paid down the balance on her credit card, and then put her card away so she wouldn't be tempted to use it. She made a budget, revised it numerous times, and created monthly goals.

There was something about that personal exercise that gave Blaine a shocking sense of liberation. Independence. Maturity. She'd had no idea how wonderful it felt to live within one's means. To no longer have credit card debt nipping at her heels. To no longer lie awake at night, worry acting like a nagging toothache, wondering how she was going to pay next month's rent. It seemed so simple that she wondered how she'd missed that basic step of growth. Maybe because it wasn't so simple.

Normally, as she arrived early each day to prep for Chef Henri, she came with joy, with deep satisfaction. But on this cold, rainy winter morning, she arrived with her mind fully preoccupied. She was soon to graduate from Le Cordon Bleu and had her pick of enviable sous-chef jobs. She just couldn't seem to make a decision; nothing felt right. Her mind was spinning so that she hadn't even heard Chef Henri when he said good morning, not until he cleared his throat in that certain way he had of getting one's attention. She jerked her head up to find Chef Henri pointing his cleaver at her.

"You," he said. "What are you doing? It took less time for zee onion to grow."

She sighed, and set down her knife. "I'm trying to decide which job to accept."

Setting the cleaver down, Chef Henri leaned on the counter, his palms flat on the surface. "Zee young. Zey make decisions too difficult. You decide with your heart. So where does your heart tell you to go?"

Tears stung her eyes, or maybe it was the raw onion. "Home," she said weakly.

He clapped his hands. "You see? Not so hard."

"But . . ."

"No buts!" He picked up the cleaver and wagged it at her. "Every chef must gain footing at home. Zen, and only zen, will you become zee chef you are meant to be." He leaned close to pierce her with his gaze. "Zee other job offers will always come. But gaining confidence from home comes first. Like building zee basement of a house. Zee foundation."

She trusted Chef Henri implicitly. She turned down the enviable sous-chef opportunities at those renowned restaurants and called her dad to tell him she was coming home, ready to help him take Camp Kicking Moose to another level.

Fourteen

THE SUN BEAT DOWN on Blaine's shoulders, and the wind whipped at her hair. As the waves started hitting the boat head on, she braced her legs for the choppy jolts, steering the boat slowly toward the tiny ribbon of beach. Nearing sand, she cut the motor and let the boat beach itself. She jumped out, grabbing a line to pull the boat as far on shore as she could get it. The tide had ebbed; mud coated everything, oozing along the shore, which was draped in seaweed and kelp. Rickety wooden steps, gray and mildewed, led from the shore to the bluff above. Up Blaine climbed to the top step and there it was, just as she remembered. The lighthouse, with its cupola charred like a burnt marshmallow, a result of a lightning strike.

As lighthouses went, it wasn't particularly impressive. Short and stubby, but it had done its job to warn ships away from the small island's rocky point. Slowly, she walked all around the lighthouse and the small keeper's cottage, stopping a moment to read the proud little plaque:

SHIPWRECK SHELF LIGHTHOUSE TOWER
WAS CONSTRUCTED IN THE 1850s
AND DISCONTINUED IN 1933.

Cam had once spun ideas of turning the lighthouse into a unique bed-and-breakfast, an offshoot of the camp. Then she had decided it should be her energy control center—whatever that meant. But, like Peg always said, Mother Nature had the last word. When lightning hit the lighthouse, it became apparent to Cam that this north point was too exposed to be the control center. And so it had been abandoned.

Blaine pushed the door open and went inside. She stood for a moment, adjusting to the gloom, aware of a deep quiet. Although it was a sunny day, the interior was chilly and damp. That high ceiling, all that concrete. She went up the stairs cautiously, unsure of what she would find, though there wasn't anything to be afraid of but dust and a lot of cobwebs. Round and round she went, opening doors to small rooms near the top, struck by the way the afternoon light streamed through the windows.

Each room had a purpose for the keeper of the lighthouse. The watch room was the place where the keeper kept watch at night when the beacon was lit. In the gallery room, an octagon, she peered out the windows to the views below. In one direction was the wide-open Atlantic Ocean. On the opposite side was the island. If she squinted, she thought she could make out the rooftop and chimney of Moose Manor. She looked around the room and noticed a small door. She pushed with her foot, and it opened, so she crawled out onto the gallery's catwalk. There was a railing all around the platform, which looked secure, but she stayed close to the windows, just in case. She inched her way all around the platform, astounded by the gorgeous vistas in every direction. Imagine being here for a sunset or a sunrise, or a full moon. She felt as if she were on top of the world.

For a moment, she allowed herself to brainstorm, to create a vision. A destination restaurant at the top of the lighthouse. A cooking school in the keeper's cottage.

Fireworks exploded in her mind. She was trying to sort out her thoughts, which weren't thoughts so much as images. The vision that ran through her head was a crazy idea, full of obstacles.

Her sisters would shoot it down. Her dad would want her to focus on the camp.

Peg would worry it might attract summer people.

The cost to remodel it would be outrageous.

Getting to the lighthouse was difficult.

This wouldn't be easy.

She walked around the platform another time, more confident this time, less fearful. More determined.

Could this lighthouse be the new dream that God might have for her? Jean-Paul had said if she asked, it would come.

Lord, this really is a daring prayer.

Could this be it?

In the kitchen at Moose Manor, as Seth was rinsing off lettuce for a salad, Cam told him about today's phone call with Cooper's therapist. "She said that we should stop calling attention to his heightened awareness of germs."

"We?" Seth said, shaking the lettuce head in the sink. "But I don't call attention to it."

Cam grabbed a carrot stick from a pile he'd made for the salad. "Okay. Me." Her back felt tired, so she pulled out a chair to sit down. She looked at her tummy, astounded at its size. If this was how big she'd become in her second trimester, she shuddered to think what she'd be like in her third. She reined her thoughts back to Cooper. "She also said that the puppy could be a very good distraction for him."

"Oh yeah. That puppy's here to stay." He turned around and grinned at her. "Last night at dinner, I saw your dad sneak food to it under the table."

Her dad's reaction to the puppy was a shock. She would've thought he'd return the puppy to its breeder, the way he kept trying to return the gray cat to Peg. Just the opposite. Her dad picked that puppy up the first time he saw it and cuddled it like a newborn baby. "Does it seem strange that Cooper can't seem to settle on a name for it?"

Seth was chopping lettuce leaves. Midchop, he said, "Strange for most kids, but Cooper's not like most kids. He's working on finding the perfect name." He lifted the knife and pointed it to a can on the counter. "He forgot to bring his Lysol can to school today. I credit the nameless puppy for that welcome distraction."

Interesting. Cam was on the fence about keeping the puppy, especially after it chewed her favorite pink slipper. But that Lysol can left on the counter might've tipped her more toward keeping it. The puppy was still a nuisance, but a very cute one.

The kitchen door blew open and Blaine burst in, her long blonde hair tangled, her cheeks pink. She was glowing with happiness. "Cam! The lighthouse!"

"Is that where you've been?"

"Yes."

"What about it?"

Blaine clapped her hands. "Can I have it?"

"What? Why?"

"I'd rather not say. Not yet. But I definitely want it."

Cam shrugged. "Talk to Dad."

"I already did. He said to talk to you."

"Then . . . it's all yours."

Blaine shrieked. "Awesome!" And then she disappeared out the kitchen door, only to pop her head back in around the door. "Seth, lettuce should be torn, not cut."

He spun around, puzzled. "Why?"

"Brown marks." Then she disappeared.

Seth set down his knife and set to work to tear the rest of the lettuce. "What's that about the lighthouse?"

"No idea," Cam said, gazing down at her ankles. Were they swollen?

Seth finished tearing the last leaf of lettuce. "There's something about a lighthouse. Something about its beacon. A guiding light. It can be very . . . metaphorical."

Cam smiled, watching her husband toss the lettuce in the bowl. They were as different as the oil and vinegar dressing he'd made for tonight's salad. In that analogy, he was the soothing, calming olive oil. She, the vinegar. She knew that about herself.

Suddenly Blaine popped her head back in the kitchen. "Cam, I almost forgot. Peg said there's a village meeting tomorrow night to vote on your tower thingamajig. Peg's words." She vanished.

What?! Cam's mind started spinning.

Seth tossed the salad with dressing. "I didn't know you finished your presentation."

"I haven't."

"So you hadn't asked Peg to set up that meeting?"

Slowly, Cam shook her head. Dad had told her that Baxtor Phinney wanted to shoot down the cellular tower, but she had expected his opposition. In fact, she hadn't given Baxtor a second thought. But this unpublicized village meeting . . . it smacked of something more organized. Something more serious.

Blaine didn't tell a soul about her dream to turn the lighthouse and keeper's cottage into a restaurant and cooking school. It felt too fragile, too vulnerable, too spun-sugary. She needed time to herself to think it all through, to brainstorm, to create, to problem solve, to pray. And her best thinking happened while she was alone in a kitchen.

And that was why she remained at the diner after closing hours to make English muffins. It was the second time she'd made them for the Lunch Counter, and Peg said the customers hadn't stopped asking for them. "Honey," Peg had said, "I want to put a warning sign in front of their platter." She spread her hand in front of her like she was drawing in the air. "Once you try one of Blaine's made-from-scratch English muffins, you'll never be able to go back to store-bought."

Blaine skimmed the milk solids off the clarified butter and let the butter rest as she heated up the griddle. Carefully, she moved one puffy dough muffin onto a platter of cornmeal, turned it over, then onto the griddle. She set the timer for six minutes as Peg came in from the back room.

Peg's red hair was tucked in two pigtails and covered by a new bright yellow headband with a bow in front.

"Look at you! *Fancy.* Where are you off to?"

"To the village meeting. Honey, what's happened to that little French fella? All angles and knobs, that boy. Must not weigh more than one hundred pounds."

A little more than that, but not much. "Jean-Paul is planted on our living room couch. He's had a setback." Or two.

"Shouldn't you be home, with him?"

"I've asked, but he always encourages me to keep working. Turns out . . . he's discovered the addictive pull of American sports on the television. He and Granddad and Cooper watch ESPN like they're hypnotized by it." The timer went off, and Blaine flipped the muffin to its ungrilled side, then reset the timer.

"I'd better get going. You coming to cast your vote?"

"Maddie has my proxy." Blaine probably should've gone to the meeting, and would've if Cam pressed her, but she didn't have a strong feeling about the cellular tower. Cam seemed to sense that and didn't press her. In fact, her sister seemed happy to have her proxy over her presence. "I need to finish these muffins up. Besides, I thought this was the secret resistance meeting."

"Silent Opposition. And it's secret, but everybody knows about it who needs to be there."

"Does that include Camden Grayson?" Blaine hoped so. That's why she told her sister about the meeting. Cam had flown into action, staying up late in the night to finish whatever it was that needed finishing.

Peg stopped abruptly and turned back with an arched eyebrow. "Especially Camden Grayson." She lifted the handles of her enormous purse with a red lobster on the front over her head. She wore her purse like a sling. "Honey, why else do you think I told you about it yesterday?"

Cam gazed around the Baggett and Taggett store, the gathering place for the village meetings, and tried not to think about the buck's head mounted on the wall. From any angle, it seemed to be staring at her, accusingly. Creepy.

There was a pretty good turnout tonight, shockingly good, in fact. Most village meetings were never this well attended. Cam's concern heightened. She had purposefully chosen a seat in the front row so she could stare at Baxtor Phinney as he made his case against the cell phone tower.

Dad sat beside her in a show of support. Seth was in Augusta for a school conference that he couldn't get out of, but he'd given Dad his proxy vote. He said he was sorry to miss the meeting. Sorry for Cam's sake, sorry to miss the village drama. He told her he had no doubt she could persuade the locals to throw their support behind the cellular tower, and she counted on his optimism. Seth always had a better sense about the locals than she did.

At ten minutes after seven o'clock, Baxtor Phinney arrived. It was his custom to arrive slightly late, to make a grand entrance, and Cam never understood why people put up with it. Peg said it was because the Phinney family had been in Maine for generations and considered themselves as the founding family of the island, even though they weren't. "That's just the way it is here," Peg said once, when Cam had questioned the practice. "The longer you've lived here, the more respect you're given."

"Even if a person doesn't deserve the respect?" Cam had asked her. "Even then."

Cam didn't say another word after that. She knew that Peg came

142

from a long line of stubborn Mainers who felt the same way about outsiders. She wondered if the Graysons would ever be considered locals. Probably not.

Baxtor walked straight to the front, to the music stand that served as a podium, and clapped his hands to shush everyone. He wasted no time getting right to the point. "Our island," Baxtor said, "has been taken over by summer people." *Sum-mah pee-poh.* He pronounced it in his fake Boston Brahmin accent, his nose wrinkling up as if he were smelling something rotten. The room grew utterly silent. Not a peep. "Tourists, day-trippers, campers . . . that's one thing. Summer people are entirely different." From the hum of murmurs behind her, Cam knew locals were exchanging eyebrow-lifting glances of approval. "Summer people don't care about the quality of life here. They come and they go."

"They leave something behind," Captain Ed shouted from the back of the room. "Their dollars!"

"They leave more than that," Baxtor said. "They have altered the flavor of our island. A rise in petty crime. When have you ever had to lock the doors to your house? Last summer, a house was broken into."

"Turns out, Baxtor," someone standing at the back said, "that wasn't an actual break-in. A squirrel chewed through my window screen."

Baxtor frowned at him. "There've been reports of shoplifting—"

"Just one," the new grocery store owner said. "A six-year-old boy stole a candy bar."

Baxtor ignored him. "There's talk of adding cobbles to Main Street."

"Well, now that sounds nice!" Peg was also seated in the front seat, but on the opposite side of Cam.

"Sure, sure, Peg. It *sounds* nice. Until your *year-round* business has no revenue because Main Street is under construction."

"Now, Baxtor," Peg said, "how long could it take to cobble that little bitty street?"

"It took years and years in Nantucket."

"Oh dear." Peg's pigtails trembled.

"And then we'll be taxed for the cobbling. Every rock. Which brings me to the question of taxes."

Captain Ed cupped his mouth to create a megaphone. "No more taxes!"

"Unfortunately," Baxtor said, "the spike of summer people has caught the attention of the county. They want us to hire two full-time policemen. They want us to have a fire department. To have garbage service."

"Those are good things, Baxtor," Dad said, and a few murmurs concurred.

"They may sound good in theory," Baxtor said, shaking his head, "but the need for those services is due to *summer people*. They're flocking here from Boston and Portland . . . and *New York City*." A look came over his face as if he'd bitten into a sour apple. "They come to Three Sisters Island because it's nice and quiet and up close to nature. And then the developers catch wind of it. Developers are all about making money. They buy up land and build a bunch of houses. Worse, condos. Next thing you know, they'll turn Boon Dock into a big marina. And"—his voice dropped—"it won't be long before chain stores will be setting up shop. Walmart. Costco."

An arthritic, hunched-over old lady spoke up. "Here? A Costco?"

"Absolutely. And it doesn't stop there. The Lunch Counter will be replaced by . . ." He paused for so long that Peg ended up egging him on.

"Replaced by . . . what, Baxtor?"

"A Starbucks."

"No!" Peg gasped. A buzz started in the room, murmurs full of the locals' speculations, making a sound like a beehive in a tree.

"Captain Ed, your little canoe shop will become a Dunkin' Donuts shop."

Captain Ed jerked awake, like he'd been nodding off. "Huh? Something about donuts?"

"Exactly. Our little island will look like any strip mall in America. And then comes the day when the summer people will look up and down Main Street and wonder why it's not pretty anymore. Why it's not quiet. Why all the natural beauty has been paved over with asphalt." Baxtor gazed at Cam. "They'll move on to some other place, while the locals, those faithful Mainers who've lived here all our lives, are stuck with a town we don't even recognize anymore."

Dad stepped in. "Baxtor, something isn't adding up. You own the majority of real estate along Main Street. These chains can't come in and wipe out local businesses unless you sell out to them."

Baxtor's eyes narrowed. "I have no intention of selling my holdings. I'm trying my best to preserve our island." He pointed a long bony finger at Cam. "She's the one who's ruining our island. She's the one who is trying to ready our town for massive overdevelopment."

This wasn't going at all well.

Still, it wasn't time to despair. Not yet. Cam had been to the edge before. She'd had plenty of experience in controversial and hostile business meetings. She used to do it all the time. She would stare straight in the eyes of the audience, present her case, ready for a challenge, and they inevitably gave in to her. Her boss had nicknamed her "the Salvager." Truth to tell, she shined in this kind of challenge.

She rose to her feet. "A perfect segue, Baxtor. I'll take it from here." Adroitly, she moved the podium and spread out her presentation. "Would you mind passing out these papers for me?"

Baxtor, baffled by the takeover of his meeting by a small pregnant woman, started to hand out the papers.

Cam smoothed her white blouse over her very round tummy. Okay. *Showtime.*

Blaine had just finished grilling the last English muffin. She loved being in the diner when it was empty, when she could bake or cook without interruption. Or think. Here was a moment of calm, a pause, something so rare to find lately at Moose Manor. She indulged in an arched back, a full wing-span stretch, and nearly lost her balance and toppled over when Artie poked his head in the door.

"Oh, I saw the light and thought Peg was in here."

"No, she's not here."

"I, uh." He paused, looking flustered.

Seeing Artie flustered was a rare event. "What's wrong?"

"I missed dinner. I was hoping I could grab something quick."

"Come in," she said, waving him in. "I'll scrounge something up for you." She hadn't seen Artie since they'd parted in that spat after he called her dad a sugar daddy. "But do me a favor and lock the door. Peg must have forgotten to lock it when she left."

As he settled onto a stool at the counter, she rummaged the fridge. "There it is. I knew I had some soup left." She poured it into a bowl and popped it into the microwave.

"Where is Peg?"

"She's at the village meeting over at the Baggett and Taggett. It's quite the buzz."

"So I've heard. Cam left a message in the middle of the night last night. Something about coming to the meeting to provide medical expertise."

"Cam was burning the midnight oil over it. I shudder to think what will happen if it doesn't get voted in."

An awkward silence followed, waiting for the microwave to beep.

"Blaine . . . I'm, uh, sorry. About our last conversation. I shouldn't have . . ."

Been so accusing? Blaine thought. *Jumped to conclusions? Or how about you shouldn't have refused to answer my calls in Paris when I needed a friend so desperately?*

". . . brought up things I don't know about."

Thank you! I heartily agree, she thought. Let the past stay in the past. Artie had offered an olive branch, and she should accept it. "And I shouldn't have stomped off like that. It was childish." She set a bowl of hot soup and handed him a spoon. Their hands touched just so slightly and she jumped back.

He didn't say anything, just looked at the steaming bowl of soup set before him. He stirred the soup before tasting it. One spoonful, then another. He looked up, pleased. "This soup is good. Really good. What is it?"

"Clam chowder," Blaine said.

"It doesn't taste like the clam chowder I'm accustomed to." He grinned. "That would be . . . out of a can."

She lifted her eyebrows in mock horror. "This was made from scratch. I added fresh dill, which makes all the difference."

"How's the knee?" Artie kept his eyes lowered on the soup bowl.

"Jean-Paul? It still looks swollen and sore."

At that, Artie glanced up. "I'll check on him. Knees can take a long time to heal because they're constantly in use. Remind him to keep his weight off his leg."

That wasn't a problem. Jean-Paul was happy as a clam on the couch. Yesterday, she came home and found him watching *General Hospital* . . . and crying!

Blaine remembered the English muffins she'd made and turned to slice a cooled one, then pop it in the toaster. She brought a dish of butter and the toasted muffin to Artie, and watched as he spread some butter on it.

"That cell phone tower," he said, taking care to spread butter from edge to edge, "there's a lot of opposition to it."

"I know."

"It would make my job much easier if the tower goes in. Sometimes I don't know how we ever lived before cell phones."

"We probably moved more slowly and had better concentration."

Artie laughed. She'd forgotten how much she loved his laugh, a nice easy, low rumble.

147

His chewing slowed. "I've never had an English muffin taste like this. They could be . . . addictive."

She leaned her elbows on the counter and rested her chin in her palms, trying to mask how pleased she felt by his praise. Not that Artie was hard to please; he'd always been a fan of her cooking. But to be together like this, comfortable and easy again, felt like a major milestone. She had missed him, more than she let herself realize. Until now. She didn't want this quiet time together in the diner to end, wanted him to stay and talk to her, but she could tell he was completely focused on his meal, in a hurry to be someplace else.

He finished the bowl without stopping. "I guess I was hungrier than I thought," he said as he put down the spoon.

Artie left his hand on the counter. She wanted to touch it, just brush her hand over his for a second. Where in the world did that thought come from?

"I'd better head over to the meeting and see what's going on." He looked up at her. "You're not going to it?"

"No, I need to finish cleaning up here. But I did give Maddie my proxy. Honestly, I'm kind of on the fence about that cell phone tower. When Dad first bought Camp Kicking Moose, I was desperate for cell phone service. It felt like we had moved to Timbuktu."

"And now?"

"I suppose I see the benefits of getting away from it all."

"If there is such a thing. Somehow the *all* has a way of finding you." He tipped his head. Their eyes met, held. Even in the dim lighting of the diner, she felt a sudden charge as if he'd reached out and brushed her flushed cheek with his fingers. With effort, she looked away.

From the first day she'd met Artie, she had felt a special connection to him. She knew she wanted him as her friend. But she'd never considered him as a boyfriend. Friendship, to Blaine, wasn't a consolation prize. It wasn't less than. It wasn't second best. Unlike romances, friendship lasted. So she had thought, anyway.

He glanced behind her at the stack of pans and bowls on the counter, dusted by cornmeal. It was a mess. Their gaze met momentarily. A soft smile curved his lips. He had nice lips, she thought.

"Those English muffins were definitely worth the trouble," he said, pushing off from the counter.

As she locked up after he left the diner, it occurred to her that he used to say that very thing about her.

Fifteen

CAM ALLOWED EVERYONE a moment or two to read through the one-page proposal, giving her an opportunity to scan the room and take a read on her audience. The door opened and she saw Artie enter, finding an empty seat in the back. Oh good! He'd gotten her message. As soon as she saw a face or two look up from reading the report, she took charge. "As you can see from the report, because of our swelling summer population, we do have the numbers to support a cellular tower."

Captain Ed waved an arm in the air. "I've heard the government uses those towers to spy on us."

Peg turned to give him a look. Then she held the paper. "Hon, where's that tower gonna be? I can't figure it out."

"Communication is needed most where people live and work," Cam said. "Happily, we have ample room for the tower in the downtown area. Up the hill."

"Hold your horses a minute." Euclid, a thin, elderly man with round glasses, rose to his feet. "Near the school? Now, that's a problem, right there. Cell phone towers spew out dangerous radiation."

Baxtor, still standing, inched his way back to the podium. "For once, Euclid said something worth listening to. Cell phone towers leak radiation, causing all kinds of health problems."

Cam looked at him, nonplussed. "Baxtor, there have been decades of studies about the concerns for radiation and cell phones, and results are always inconclusive." She glanced over the sea of heads to Artie. "Perhaps you can chime in on this, Dr. Lotosky?"

Artie rose to his feet. "I was just reading about this topic in a medical journal. The power levels are relatively low, the antennas are mounted high above ground level, and signals are intermittent, rather than constant. Exposure of radio frequency from towers is very minimal."

"Speak English," Captain Ed said.

"In other words," Artie said, "I understand the need for caution, but we need to make sure it's a real risk, and the science is showing that it isn't."

Euclid jumped back up. "She's probably paying him as a key witness!"

"What?" Artie said.

"Are you crazy?" Cam said. Yes, of course he was.

Turning around to address Artie, Euclid said, "Oh, by the way, Dr. Lotosky, since you're here, I need a prescription filled."

Peg told Euclid firmly to sit down and not say another word or she'd have him tossed out. "Go ahead, Artie, honey," she said. "We're listening."

"I just wanted to leave you with one more piece of scientific data," Artie said. "On its website, the American Cancer Society agrees that towers pose little risk."

"Maybe so," Baxtor said with a scoff, "but I don't want our schoolchildren to be the ones who find out differently."

Oh, ouch. How could Cam argue that? Everyone cared about children's welfare. Baxtor had the crowd in his pocket, and he knew it. He had inched his way closer to the podium, and suddenly Cam realized she wasn't even standing behind it any longer. When had that happened?

Baxtor banged his fist on the podium. "Beside the radioactive danger to our dear little ones . . ."

Seriously? Cam could barely contain an eyeroll. Baxtor had never, ever called any child a "dear little one." He complained bitterly to Seth about the schoolchildren of Three Sisters Island. They were too noisy, too unruly, too omnipresent.

"We haven't even begun to discuss the appearance of the cell phone tower. They look hideous. Thoroughly unattractive. Not the least bit convincing."

"But, Cam, honey," Peg said, "it'll look like a tree, right?"

Cam exchanged a look with her dad. "The thing is, these cell towers cost about $150,000 to build. If we were to camouflage it, that could add another $100,000."

"Honey, do you mean to tell me that we're not even getting a tower dressed up as a tree?"

Silence.

Cam barely stifled a sigh. "What you are all getting is reliable cell phone coverage. Wi-Fi connectivity."

"What we're getting with this ugly tower," Baxtor said, "is more summer people, overdevelopment, fast-food joints, chain stores, and"—he swept the room with his piercing gaze—"children who glow in the dark."

"Hold on, now," Cam said.

"Time for a vote," Baxtor said, ignoring Cam's objections. "All in favor raise your hand." Artie, Cam, and her dad raised their hands. "All opposed, say nay." The entire room erupted in a no. Baxtor left the podium to join a cluster of people.

The meeting, apparently, was over. Cam packed up her papers, discouraged. She hadn't expected it to be easy, considering it was a meeting spearheaded by the Silent Opposition. But she hadn't expected such firm resistance. She would regroup and try again.

Then she realized someone was waiting a few feet away to talk to her. She lifted her head and smiled, hoping for a friendly face. Her smile faded. It was Mr. Thayer, the representative of the telecom company. "Mr. Thayer. I, um, didn't know you were here tonight. How did you find out the meeting was happening?"

Mr. Thayer took a few steps closer. "I received a phone call from Baxtor Phinney, inviting me to attend."

Cam swallowed.

"We didn't expect such a contentious public forum. I've never seen anything like it."

"Forum?" Cam cleared her throat. "Not really a forum. Not at all. It was just an airing of opinions. A time of reflection. It's very healthy, actually." She swallowed again. Her palms started to sweat.

"Our company doesn't like to be where we aren't wanted."

Oh no. No, no, no! "The locals on this island just need a little time to adjust to change. In the end, they're always grateful for progress." Pretty much. Most of them, anyway.

"I'm sorry, Cam, but we're going to have to reconsider."

"Reconsider?" Her heart started pounding.

"It's likely the company will decide to back out."

"You mean . . ."

"No tower."

She was afraid that's what he meant.

Paul and Cam followed Peg over to the diner. They sat on the red stools at the counter while Blaine finished cleaning up.

Paul eyed the English muffins cooling on a tray. "Can I buy one to take home for breakfast?"

Blaine pointed to one that was slightly burned. "You can have that, Dad. First one, worst one."

He grinned. "Works for me." He loved to be around when Blaine was baking.

"How'd the meeting go?" Blaine asked. "It was . . . shorter than expected."

"Terrible," Cam said with a sigh. "Awful. Worse than I could have ever imagined. The telecom carrier representative said that he'd never been to a public forum that was so contentious." Cam covered her face with her hands. "What made it so contentious?"

"You really don't know?" Peg said.

Cam dropped her hands. "No."

"You."

Paul looked at Peg, shocked. Cam slapped her hand against her chest. "Me?"

"Cam, honey, you can't go around saying the kinds of things you say in a small town. Locals are very territorial."

"What things?"

"Just the other day you were sitting right in that booth"—Peg jabbed a thumb behind her—"and you called our island 'Back of Beyond.'"

"I was working on a presentation to the telecom company."

Blaine whirled around. "I remember. I was refilling coffee and you yelled at me from across the room to ask what I thought of the title—'Back of Beyond into the Twenty-First Century.'"

Paul tipped an eyebrow Cam's way. "You said that?"

"I didn't yell," Cam huffed. "I was asking Blaine if she thought it would be considered offensive."

"And it was," Peg said. Even Paul could detect a slight frostiness to her tone.

"I told her I didn't know what she meant by it," Blaine said. "I'd never heard it."

"Back of Beyond," Peg said, "is a mean way of calling Three Sisters Island a dull, unimportant place. There was a big heated discussion about it in here after you left."

"Oh," Cam said in a flat tone.

Peg wasn't done. "A couple of days ago you told Captain Ed that he should change the name of his ferry from *Never Late* to *Never Around When You Need It*."

"Oh Cam," Paul said. "You didn't." Captain Ed was very sensitive about his ferry.

Cam folded her hands on top of her belly. "Please. You all have to admit that the ferry is very unreliable. Peg, even you can't deny that."

"It's part of the island's charm."

"Charm?" Cam scoffed. "Not when you have a meeting to get to on the mainland."

Peg kept her blue eyes fixed on Cam. "Running down our dear old Captain Ed, who works so hard and so faithfully, got the locals grumbling. Me along with them."

"But I'm a local too!"

Peg lifted a shoulder in a slight shrug. "You're a resident, not a local."

Cam lifted her hands up in frustration. "Three years I've lived here now! I'm married to the local schoolteacher. My dad owns the local camp. I'm here to stay. I'm doing all I can to improve the daily life of this island. What will it take to be accepted as a local?"

"Locals have been here for generations. Many of them have never been anywhere else. The last thing they want to hear is someone from elsewhere telling them how things should be done."

Paul could see that *this* forum was also turning contentious. Time to redirect. "Something just isn't adding up with Baxtor Phinney. If things played out the way he described, with Starbucks and Costco and McDonald's coming in—"

Peg held up her hands in mock surrender. "If that happens, then I'm outta here."

Paul waved that off. "It would never happen, Peg. But let's just say for the sake of discussion that a few chains did decide to come to the island . . . Baxtor would make a fortune. He'd be sitting pretty."

Peg folded her arms against her chest. "Not everybody is interested in making money."

"Come on," Paul said. "Everyone has a price."

"Not Baxtor."

"But he's such a penny-pincher," Blaine said. "He never even leaves a tip when he's here."

"That's all due to a Yankee upbringing," Peg said. "Now, I don't deny that Baxtor Phinney is tighter than most. He holds on to a dollar bill so tight, it makes the eagle squeak. Even still, he's not motivated by money."

"Then what else could it be?" Cam said. "Control? Does he just want to remain as the king of the island?"

Peg glanced at Cam. "That's probably part of it. But there's more to Baxtor than that."

"What?" Cam said.

"I think it would be best if you figured that out for yourself." Peg covered a yawn with her hand. "I need my beauty rest." She rose from the stool and walked toward the back room that led to her living space. "Blaine, honey, lock up when you're done."

Blaine squirted down the counters with a cleaner and wiped them dry, then tossed the rag in a basket to wash in the morning. Paul stared at her until she finally looked up. "What?"

"Interpret Peg's meaning for us."

"About Baxtor?" Blaine put the burned English muffin in a to-go container and handed it to Paul. "Peg wants you to figure him out for yourself."

"That, I got," Cam said. "But what's there to figure out?"

Blaine grabbed her purse from beneath the counter and flicked off the lights. "There's something you're missing."

Paul walked to the door and held it open for Blaine and Cam to pass through. "But you think you know what it is?"

"I think so."

Cam frowned. "And you won't tell?"

"Peg's right," Blaine said, locking up the door to the diner. "It's the kind of thing you need to figure out for yourself."

Paul felt mildly confused, which he often did around these kinds of conversations. Gossamer girl talk, he called them. Vague and hazy, like a thin cloud.

Very early the next morning, Paul sat on the bench at the beach along Boon Dock, holding his cell phone up against his ear, hoping the call wouldn't drop like it did so often. He replayed the entire conversation he'd had with Peg about what motivated Baxtor Phinney to keep the brakes on the island's growth. "Why? I just don't get it."

"I think what Peg meant to say," his friend said, "is that people tend to glorify the illusion that more is always better."

"But isn't more always better?"

No answer. *Blast.* The call dropped.

Sixteen

WHEN HER ALARM CLOCK CHIRPED in the morning, Cam shut it off and forced herself from her bed. She felt exhausted, listless, a result of the disastrous village meeting. But she refused to allow herself to wallow in a puddle of self-pity.

Then she caught sight of her reflection in the mirror. Overnight, it seemed her middle section had ballooned, stretching the T-shirt she'd borrowed from Seth after her pajamas started to feel snug.

"Oh no," she said to herself in the mirror. "Aren't you a treat for the eyes."

"Actually," Seth said, coming into the room from the bathroom after a shower with a towel draped around his neck, "you are indeed a treat for my eyes." He slipped his arms around her, and his hands didn't even meet in the middle.

"Seth, ever since Blaine came home, I can't stop eating."

"That started long before she came home."

Cam elbowed him. "I'm serious. Those English muffins she makes are irresistible. I'll have to take one to my next doctor's appointment so I don't get scolded for gaining too much weight in a month."

"I can think of something else that's irresistible." He kissed her neck once, then twice. "Alas, there's a field trip today to Artie's

Lightship, and I need to get to school early. I'm not sure all the kids turned in their permission slips."

He disappeared into the bathroom and Cam gave herself one more appraisal in the mirror. Maybe she wasn't so big after all. On second thought, she was big. She was huge.

A little later, Cam went downstairs for breakfast, thinking about last night's meeting. Frustrated, she gave the kitchen door a hard push, not realizing Jean-Paul was on the other side. He let out a yelp.

Oh no, oh no. "I'm so sorry!" she said.

Blood started to trickle down his nostrils onto his chin.

"Sit. No wait, don't move." He was on crutches. "Let me bring a chair."

He covered his nose. "Eez okay," Jean-Paul said. "Eez my fault."

Cam brought him a rag to press against his nose and propped a chair under him to sit on. "Jean-Paul, I'm really sorry. I didn't realize you were there." It dawned on Cam that the placement and style of the kitchen might not have been the best idea for a waitstaff to serve food or carry dirty dishes back in.

"No sorry. Eez all good." He pointed to the table setting. "I go searching for someone to taste my creation and no one eez here. Zee family eez always in a hurry. All go-go-go."

Cam stared at the dish on the table and her mouth started to water. "Eggs Benedict."

"Oui." With a flourish, he sprinkled freshly minced chives on top of the rich, oozing Hollandaise sauce.

So much for willpower. She picked up the fork and dug in, then closed her eyes as she tasted it. One bite, then another. "Jean-Paul, this is *sick*!" As soon as she saw the confused look in his eyes, she clarified. "I mean, it's delicious! You've spoiled me for Eggs Benedict forevermore."

Behind the rag pressed against his nose, his eyes smiled. "Good, good."

She tried to slow down her eating, but she couldn't hold back.

159

When she polished off the last bite, she barely stopped herself from licking the plate. With a satisfied smile, she set down the fork. "You'll have to give Blaine the recipe." *This* should be on the menu.

"*C'est facile.*"

Cam wasn't sure, but from the casual shrug of his shoulders, she guessed he meant *easy*. "No wonder Blaine's cooking has gone up a notch after being around you."

He shook his head. "No, no. Blaine, she has zee magic."

"Different from you?"

"Oui," he said definitively. "*Elle ne casse pas trois pattes à un canard.*"

"Which means . . ."

"She has broken three legs on a duck."

"But . . . ducks only have two legs."

"Oui. Blaine . . . she is an extraordinary chef. As noteworthy as a duck with three legs."

An odd analogy, Cam thought. She pointed to her empty plate. "If this is any indication, you're every bit as extraordinary a chef as Blaine."

"Blaine, she eez a chef. My pa-Pa, he eez a chef. I am but a cook."

Same thing, Cam thought. Cook, chef. Tom-ay-to, tom-ah-to. "Isn't this kitchen great?"

His eyes, above the rag held against his nose, swept the room. "Good for a cook. Easy for a one-legged man to hop around."

"But just right for a chef. You know, for the restaurant." Maybe that's what Cam would do today to cheer herself up. Get started on ordering tables and chairs for the restaurant.

"A restaurant?" Jean-Paul said, sweeping the kitchen with his gaze. "A restaurant," he repeated, a puzzled look on his face. Then he shrugged and lifted the bloody rag in the air and said, "But you have sadness about it."

"Not about the kitchen. *That* is perfect. I'm bothered about something else. A big project I'd been working for over the last year has been . . . derailed."

He nodded knowingly. "Blaine told me zee village meeting did not go so well."

"It was horrible. A complete and total disaster."

"You did not get what you wanted."

"Not at all. Not even close." She felt the baby move and ran a hand over her round belly. "It's frustrating, you know? It's such a good thing for the island's future."

"And for you?"

"Not monetarily. I have no stake in the cell phone tower. But I would benefit in the same way that everyone would benefit. We'd all have reliable cell phone coverage. We'd have Wi-Fi connectivity."

"But zee island, it said no."

That was a rather poetic way of putting it. She let out a puff of breath. "The island said no."

"Why did it say no?"

She shrugged. "Same as always. The locals resist change. They're afraid of it."

"Most people do, oui?"

"Not me. Not my dad. It feels like we keep trying to pull this island forward, but the current keeps pulling it back again." She picked up her fork, scraped her plate, and licked off the last little bit of delicious Eggs Benedict.

He pointed to her empty plate. "*L'appétit vient en mangeant.*"

"What does that mean?"

"Zee appetite comes with eating."

She mulled that over for half a minute. Another French idiom! Suddenly its meaning seemed clear. "YES! You're right! You're *so* right! Amazing! How did I miss it? It'll be just like the renewable energy program—the locals will embrace it in the end. Somehow, someway, I will get a cell phone tower on this island. Thank you, Jean-Paul. I'm so glad we had this little talk. You are a wonder!" She rose to leave.

"But, but . . ." he said, his eyebrows furrowed in confusion, "when I said zee appetite comes with eating, I meant zee Eggs Benedict."

Oh. "That was a wonder too." She gave him a rolling finger wave goodbye. "Toodles. Sorry about the nosebleed." She smiled. Her wind was back.

———

Maddie hung up the phone and turned around to see her dad standing there, near the staircase, an enigmatic look on his face. "That was Rick's mom," she said.

"So I gathered," Dad said. "Is she planning to come up soon?"

"She's trying to find someone to cover her at the church. You probably don't remember, but she works as the secretary."

"Of course I remember. Mollie, right?"

"Maeve. Dad, her name is Maeve. I don't know why you can't remember her name."

"Maeve. Got it." Dad cleared his throat. "So when is she planning to come?"

"Within a week or so."

"Good, good. The sooner the better." He looked pleased. Very pleased.

"Why do you say that?"

"Well, if anyone can get through to Rick, it would be his mother." Dad's voice grew scratchy and he suddenly seemed nervous. "That was a little scary the other day. You know, when Rick almost passed out."

"He *what*?"

"Didn't he tell you?"

"Tell me what?"

Dad's voice was down to a whisper. "Seth and I were in front of the school, loading a bicycle in the truck bed and Rick crossed the street to say hello. Suddenly he stopped and turned as white as a ghost. I'm sorry, Maddie. I figured he had told you."

No, Rick hadn't said a word about it. Maddie clutched her elbows tightly. What else wasn't he telling her?

It was low tide as Cam walked along the strip of beach near Boon Dock, searching for the most bars on her cell phone. She wanted to call Mr. Thayer and tell him she would be willing to finance the cell phone tower if his company would provide its construction and ongoing service. How could he refuse such an offer?

A contentious forum, he'd said. What did he expect? Change was always contentious.

She stopped in front of the bench to watch a flock of seagulls rest in the warm sand. Other tiny birds, sandpipers mostly, darted around the water's edge. For a moment, she grew mesmerized with the birds and forgot why she was there. *Cooper would love this,* she thought. *I should bring him here after school today.*

"Well, well. How goes the cell tower?"

Cam's good mood fizzled. Slowly, she turned around to face Baxtor Phinney.

He was an enigma to Cam. A small, bespectacled man with a jiggly Adam's apple, Baxtor resembled a New England college professor and spoke like one too. Nasal twang, clipped words, Boston Brahmin accent. Walking along the beach—a beach!—he wore a bow tie and penny loafers. "Hello, Baxtor. The cell tower is . . . currently under discussion." That wasn't far from the truth. She was trying to discuss the tower with the cellular company. No one was returning her calls.

He smiled, smugly, and it looked weird on him. No wonder he didn't smile much. "Pity."

"Baxtor, why are you against progress?"

The Never Late Ferry tooted its horn and he turned to watch it approach the dock. "Do you know how Camp Kicking Moose got its name?"

"No, I don't." She should know, though. It never occurred to her to find out why.

He peered at her over his spectacles. "When I was a boy, a bull or two would drive a herd of cows over to the island every spring. Usually, they're solitary creatures, except for mating season. They like cold weather, and the island's cool temperature was to their liking. Cows would deliver their calves on the island, because it was such a quiet, safe place to be. Then in the fall, they'd head back over to the mainland to winter. My father would bring me to this very place, spring and fall, and we'd watch for the herd to arrive. It was the signal of the seasons changing."

"So why did someone name the camp Kicking Moose?"

"Get anywhere near a bull moose and you'll know why." His gaze lifted to follow a circling seagull. "There hasn't been a moose on this island in years and years." There was a wistful tone in his voice, as if he was longing for those days of boyhood. Suddenly he twitched, snapping his attention back to Cam. "Mustn't tarry. The ferry awaits. Good day, Camden."

"Goodbye, Baxtor." Now Cam understood. Baxtor Phinney was trying to protect the island *from* progress. That's what motivated him. Not personal wealth, not creature comforts, not conveniences. Just . . . conserving nature's beautiful legacy on Three Sisters Island.

Couldn't conservation and progress work together without canceling each other out? Did it have to be one or the other?

"Hey there, Cam!"

She turned to see Artie Lotosky walking up from Boon Dock, his ever-present black bag in his hand. "Sorry about that meeting the other night," he said as he approached her.

"Yeah, me too," she said with a sigh. "I was just thinking about it."

"Change comes slow here."

"I know. But change is coming, whether they want it or not. Look at the sandbar." She pointed out to where it used to be. "Mother Nature swept it away, and that's created all kinds of change here."

"Well, Mother Nature doesn't ask for permission. She just does what she wants to do."

"No kidding." She felt a swift kick from the baby and let out an "Oof." As she rubbed the spot where she felt the kick, she said, "This baby is going to be a soccer player."

"Cam, how far along are you?"

"Around four months. I'm not exactly sure." She didn't keep track of her menstrual cycle. There were too many other things on her mind to keep track of.

A pair of creases appeared between his eyebrows. "Haven't you had an ultrasound yet to pinpoint the date?"

"No. There was supposed to be one early on, but the machine wasn't working. They heard the baby's heartbeat, though. Loud and strong." The baby did a somersault, and she automatically put a hand to her belly. Busy and active.

"That's good."

But his expression didn't line up with his words. "What?"

"When is the anatomical ultrasound scheduled?"

"In a week or so, I think. Maybe two." She sat down on the bench. "Why? You're looking at me in a funny way."

"Am I?" He shook his head, as if trying to convince himself of something. "No reason."

"Artie Lotosky, I know you well enough to know there is a reason for that look. Tell me what you're thinking."

He took in a deep breath, then exhaled. "Do multiple births run in your family? Or Seth's?"

She bolted upright. "WHAT? NO! Absolutely not. Don't even say such a thing. Don't even think such a thing. That's ridiculous." She slipped her cell phone in her purse. "I'm just showing early, that's all. Short waisted. That's the only thing that runs in our family. Not twins."

"Right." He stroked his beard. "Interesting that Maddie is due sooner than you and—"

"I know, I know. I'm showing more than she is, and she's farther along than I am. That's because I am eating a bowl of ice cream every single night and she eats a bowl of celery. Okay?" She pointed a finger at him. "You should know better than to compare sisters, Dr. Lotosky. Especially pregnant ones."

"You're right. I should know better." He started backing up, holding up his hands in mock surrender. "I'd better run. See you around."

Cam pulled her cell phone out of her purse and stared at it. What did Artie know? He was a recent graduate from medical school, a doctor who rode around in a ship all day and checked people for poison ivy or high blood pressure. What could he possibly know about women and how quickly they showed? She felt another kick, this time from the opposite side of her abdomen.

Twins? No. Way. Not happening. Impossible.

By now, she had all kinds of troubling thoughts.

Seventeen

OVER THE NEXT FEW DAYS, Blaine made calls to contractors about fixing up the lighthouse. She was learning so much, so fast. The best lesson she was learning was that as long as the county gave its approval, anything could be done . . . for a price.

On Mondays the Lunch Counter was closed, so Blaine spent the day at the County Planning Department to find out what would be required for the county to approve plans to turn the lighthouse into a restaurant and cooking school. A small one, she admitted to the county official, who asked Blaine to repeat herself, and still looked as if he thought she was pranking him.

"I've spoken to a contractor," she reassured him. "I've consulted an architect. It *can* be done."

That was followed by a long silence. "Okay," he said, finally taking her seriously. "Okay, first things first. Its use is changing, so the lighthouse has to first be rezoned so it can later be approved as commercial space."

She smiled. "Then let's do it. Let's get it rezoned."

The official asked the background of the lighthouse, when it had been decommissioned, who owned it now, and how long he had owned it. Three times he asked about the property's owner, Paul Grayson, repeating the name back to her to verify spelling.

Then he took out a huge property map and had her show him exactly where the lighthouse was located. He drew a red line around Camp Kicking Moose's boundary lines and asked Blaine to confirm it. "I'll send someone out there," he said, rolling up the map.

It was late afternoon by the time Blaine got home, feeling pretty pleased with the day's results. She found Jean-Paul not on the couch watching TV but out on the porch with Granddad Grayson. That was a victory in itself.

"What are you two up to?" she said. She thought that Jean-Paul's bruising under his eyes from Cam's nose bash looked a little better. Less purplish, more yellowish.

"I'm teaching him how to play Twenty-One," Granddad Grayson said, shuffling the deck with a practiced dexterity.

Blaine's eyes went wide. "You're not playing for stakes, are you?"

Jean-Paul looked up, half grimacing. "Eez unfortunate. I owe your grandfather ten million dollars."

"Granddad!"

"Not to worry." Her grandfather's eyes twinkled. "I told him I'd take it in yearly installments."

"Oh, well, that changes things," she said, smiling. "I'll go get you both some iced tea."

Alone in the kitchen, Blaine took three glasses down from the open shelf (trying not to cringe at its location near the stovetop—what if a glass broke?) and smiled at the thought of her grandfather fleecing poor Jean-Paul in poker. Granddad could actually be pretty funny. He had a different humor than Dad's, whose jokes required a waving flag so everyone had fair warning. And *man*, it was so good to see Jean-Paul up and about. His TV addiction was worrying her.

The door to the kitchen opened and Dad appeared with a preoccupied look on his face.

"What's up?"

"I just received a phone call from the state of Maine. They're sending an inspector to the camp. A health inspector. Why?"

Cutting a lemon into slices, Blaine stopped and looked up. "That's their job."

Cam walked into the kitchen and was just about to place her purse on the counter near the sink when Blaine snatched it away. "Not on the surface where food is prepared." When Cam rolled her eyes, Blaine added, "Don't blame me. It's the kind of thing a health inspector will zing you for."

"Health inspector?"

Dad told Cam about the phone call he'd just received. She looked at him, stunned. "What is this about?"

Blaine filled the glasses with ice, poured cold tea into them, and added lemons. "Counties do regular inspections to make sure businesses are in compliance."

"Yes," Dad said, "but why now?"

"Probably," Blaine said, searching through cupboards for a tray to put the glasses on, "because the season is about to start." She found a tray tucked under dinner plates and squeezed one hand into a fist, frustrated. She would have to completely rearrange the kitchen before Memorial Day when the camp opened. Nothing made sense!

Cam shook her head. "Inspectors have never come nosing around here."

Blaine spun around. "What about the permits for the kitchen? That must have triggered a bunch of inspections. Plumbing, electrical . . ." Her voice drizzled off as Dad and Cam exchanged a look that spoke volumes. *Oh no.* "Don't tell me you didn't get any permits? The contractor had to get permits!"

Dad looked away, out the window, up at the ceiling, anywhere but at Blaine. "Seth knew a guy, who knew a guy . . . someone who needed the work. He came after-hours."

"Do you mean to tell me that the kitchen guy wasn't a licensed contractor?" Blaine squeezed her eyes shut, then opened them. "Dad, not only did you neglect to have the camp's business license transferred to your name, but you've also remodeled the cabins and

169

Moose Manor without any permits." She covered her face with her hands. "You are going to be in so much trouble."

"Blaine," Cam said, "I really think you're making a big deal out of nothing."

Nothing? This was nothing?! Blaine dropped her hands. "Cam, how could you—*you* of all people—have let this happen? You're a businesswoman! You know there are rules to follow."

"In the business world, we do whatever it takes to get things done. If you get the government involved, everything grinds to a halt." She gasped. "Government!" Turning to Dad, she said, "Baxtor Phinney! I'll bet he's the one who turned you in to the county."

"You're missing the point," Blaine said. "Inspectors can make your life miserable. Trust me. I've taken food safety classes. I know that the job of health inspectors—in any country—is to make sure that a business is compliant with safety codes. Especially businesses in the food service industry." She slapped her fingers into the palm of her other hand. "I repeat. The first rule of running a commercial kitchen is to *not* get on the wrong side of inspectors. At best, they'll cause you sleepless nights. At worst . . ."

"What? At worst . . . what?" Dad's voice had gone raspy.

"They can shut you down."

Cam and Dad exchanged a look, followed by silence. Then Cam waved her hands in the air, like shooing a fly. "But that was in Paris. You know the French. They love government regulations. This is Three Sisters Island. This is Maine. We'll be fine."

Blaine gave up trying to make her understand. Cam lived by her own rule: what she believed to be true was true, even if it wasn't. And one thing she knew about her sister—it was useless to try and convince her of anything. And even if she didn't say it aloud, Blaine knew she would always lack knowledge and experience in Cam's eyes, no matter how old or educated she became.

Even if Blaine knew otherwise.

BLAINE, AGE 7

Being ignored by Blaine's older sisters had its rewards, particularly when it came to snooping on them. Since Cam and Maddie considered Blaine to be invisible, she used it to her advantage and even became skilled at it. She was rarely caught at spying and had developed a knack for being at the right place at the right time.

Take this summer. Blaine had made an important discovery. Most nights, Cam's best friend Libby stayed over at their house because her grandmother didn't care where she slept. The two friends would wait until Mom turned off her bedroom light (Dad, a sports radio announcer, was on the road all summer long with his baseball team), then they would climb out of Cam's bedroom window and onto the roof of the garage. There the two teenagers would sit, smoking. The house was on a corner lot and built with a turned garage, like an *L*, giving Blaine an ideal vantage point of the front of the house from her bedroom. She saw it all.

Smoking terrified Blaine. She had seen pictures on television about what would happen to someone who smoked. One commercial showed a woman with half her face missing, a strange surgical distortion from cancer, all because she had smoked. Cam was Blaine's least favorite sister, but they were still sisters. She felt a loyalty to her. And she felt troubled for her. She wanted to cure her of smoking before it was too late. But how? That was the problem. Tattling to Mom and Dad was Maddie's way of handling such news, but Blaine had observed how often tattling would backfire on Maddie. Cam was shrewd. Last time she wanted to get even, she waited until an afternoon when Maddie's friends were over. When Maddie left the room for a few minutes, Cam told embarrassing stories about her. True stories, like Maddie wetting her bed until she was seven years old. The kind of insider information only your family knew, and it should stay that way.

Blaine knew it was best to be sly with Cam, to do things in such a way that her older sister was never really sure what had happened. Things like soaping up her toothbrush or coating her hairbrush in Vaseline.

Breaking the smoking habit would require extreme cleverness. So Blaine hopped on her bike and went to the best source in town for mischief: Ricky O'Shea.

First, she waited until she saw Mrs. O'Shea drive away for work. That woman had eyes in the back of her head. Second, she made Ricky promise to keep her secret, which he did. Secrecy was never a problem for Ricky, something she admired about him. So few people could keep a secret. Third, she explained the situation. "It's not enough just to get Cam and Libby into trouble."

"Why not?"

"They'll only keep smoking in other places."

"So what do you want?"

"I want them to quit so they don't die of lung cancer like on TV."

Ricky stroked his chin. "I've got an idea, but it'll cost you."

"How much?"

"Five bucks."

She nodded. It was time to raid her piggy bank.

"Do you know where they keep their stash?"

"Stash?"

Ricky rolled his eyes. "The cigarettes?"

"Oh yes." Under Cam's bed in a box.

"Bring them to me on a day when Cam is gone. I'll need a few hours. Then you'll need to get it back where you found it and make it look untouched. Absolutely untouched."

Blaine nodded solemnly. Cam and Libby were running in a cross-country match on Saturday, boring events which took hours and hours. She already knew that Maddie was staying home so she could work on a Girl Scout merit badge. Dad was out of town, so Blaine would ask Mom if she could stay home with Maddie.

On Saturday morning, everything went according to plan. Mom didn't blink when Blaine pleaded to skip the boring meet. Cam was thoroughly preoccupied with being Cam, her usual focus. This morning, that meant she was psyching herself up for the meet—whatever that meant—and couldn't be bothered with anyone. As soon as they left the house, Maddie went to the basement to work on the merit badge. Blaine slipped into Cam's room, pulled the box from under the bed, memorizing how everything looked in the box before she took the cigarettes out—just like Ricky had taught her. Despite everyone's complaints about Ricky O'Shea, Blaine liked him. He was smart and funny and clever, and he could keep a secret. She biked over to his house and held out the baggie of cigarettes.

Ricky stared at her. "Those aren't cigarettes."

"Sure they are. I've seen Cam and Libby smoke them."

Ricky rolled his eyes, frowning. "This is going to cost more."

"How much?"

"Ten dollars," he said, holding out his palm for the money.

Blaine sighed. That would take her entire life savings. But still, this was Cam's life.

As soon as the money was exchanged, he smiled and took the baggie. "Come back in two hours."

Blaine biked back to Ricky's house two hours later, was handed the baggie—which looked exactly the way she had given it to him. She wondered, for a moment, if Ricky was pulling the wool over her eyes. She didn't really know why her dad used that phrase, but she knew what it meant. She looked him straight in the eyes. "You sure you did something to these cigarettes?"

"Trust me. It will give them the surprise of their life."

They shook hands, swearing to keep this act between them to their dying days, and Blaine biked home. Carefully, she put the baggie back in the box under Cam's bed, and even had time to eat a bag of Cheetos before Mom, Cam, and Libby returned. Maddie, still in the basement working on the merit badge, was none the wiser.

"Everything go okay?" Mom asked.

"Yup," Blaine said truthfully. "Everything went great."

Not so much for Cam. Libby had beat her again, which always

put her in a foul mood. But on a happier note, this summer Blaine had noticed that Cam was more likely to smoke those cigarettes after losing to Libby in a race. Later that night, Blaine sat kneeling under her window to peek over the sill, watching and waiting. Finally, long after Mom's bedroom light had gone out, Blaine saw Cam crawl out the window, followed by Libby. The girls settled onto the roof and one of them lit a match. Blaine watched Cam light her cigarette, then put her lips to the cigarette, breathing in deeply. She passed it to Libby to smoke. Hot and sticky, Blaine brushed her bangs off her forehead, watching, listening, though she wasn't sure what she was waiting for. It was so quiet tonight, not even the sound of a car driving on a nearby road. Now and then, Cam would whisper something and Libby would giggle, and Blaine wondered what they were saying. Those two were thicker than thieves, Dad often said. Like so many of Dad's sayings, Blaine had no idea how it had come to be, but she knew what it meant. Cam's sisters weren't good enough for her.

She yawned, growing bored, wondering how to get her ten dollars back from Ricky O'Shea. Suddenly . . . *BOOM!* Cam yelped, just as Libby's cigarette exploded too. Blaine heard the girls utter a few choice words that she knew Mom would object to, then burst into giggles, then she saw another flicker of light as a match lit up. Were they going to try another cigarette? They were! This time, Cam had barely taken a puff when her second cigarette exploded.

"Cam? What's that noise?"

Blaine smiled. The sound of the exploding cigarettes in the quiet of the night had woken Mom.

"Why are you on the garage roof? Is there a fire? I smell smoke. Hold on. That's *not* smoke I smell . . ."

Blaine saw Mom stick her head out of Cam's bedroom window. And then her voice went up an octave, and her volume grew with it. "CAMDEN GRAYSON! LIBBY COOPER!!! *WHAT* ARE YOU SMOKING?!"

Lights flicked on around the neighborhood. Dogs howled. Cats meowed. Children cried. Blaine thought she even saw a bat burst from a tree.

Whatever Ricky had done, it cured Cam of smoking. It might have helped that Mom and Dad threatened to tell the cross-country coach (Libby begged them not to because she was counting on a scholarship to college and needed her cross-country team success to make that happen), plus they threatened to not let Cam go to college if she continued smoking, plus they took her car privileges away for the rest of the summer, plus Libby was not allowed to spend the night for the rest of the summer. That might have been the worst punishment of all for Cam and Libby. Thick as thieves, those two.

Happily, no one ever suspected Blaine had a role in this situation. After all, she was only a kid.

Eighteen

PEG LEGG. She, more than anyone else, would know what to do about Paul's phone call from the county. First thing on Tuesday morning, Paul hopped in his truck to drive to the Lunch Counter. Halfway there, he felt something warm and fuzzy slither across his ankle and, startled, practically drove off the road.

The cat! It must have spent the night under the driver's seat. Far away from Cooper's still-to-be-named puppy that kept wanting it to play.

By the time he got to town, he forgot about the cat and hurried into the diner to talk to Peg.

Happily, she didn't seem at all concerned. "They're just doing their job. The health inspector comes to the Lunch Counter a couple of times a year."

"A year?" It came out like a croak. It was only morning and his voice already sounded like gravel.

"How often have they come to the camp?"

"Never."

Peg's eyes went wide. "Never? Even though you've been feeding breakfast to your campers?"

"Nope. Never. So why now? They've never bothered Camp Kicking Moose before."

She shrugged. "Something must have caught their attention."

"Cam thinks Baxtor Phinney turned us in."

"Turned you in for what?"

"The kitchen remodel wasn't permitted."

Peg frowned at him. "I warned you about that kitchen."

"Think it was Baxtor?"

She rubbed her chin. "I don't know. He's never been a fan of the Graysons."

"So you do think he turned us in?"

"I wouldn't put it past him. He doesn't like change, and you folks are all about change."

"Should I talk to him?"

"Not today, not with the way your voice is grinding down to nothing. Besides, what would it matter? What's done is done. If I were you, I'd hightail it back to the camp and start looking around for anything that might be considered a violation. Follow every regulation."

"What do you mean? What kind of regulations?"

"What kind!" She looked at him as if he had just landed from Mars. "There are dozens and dozens of regulations, and they change each year. They change per inspector! Some inspectors are real friendly and nice and understanding, some are in a hurry and just blow in, sign off, and blow out." She lowered her voice. "But then there's one, in particular, who takes his job way too seriously. He should've been an FBI agent. Pray that they don't send that one out to you. He'll be looking for any little thing that might cause problems for your campers."

"Like what?"

"Well, let's see. Last time he came around here, he fined me for storing dishes too close to food. Oh, and my glasses weren't stored upside down. Then I got fined for cross contamination of food. Captain Ed had just caught a sea bass and tossed it in a bucket full of ice on the day the inspector happened to stop in. That cost me two hundred bucks. And what really irked me was that Captain Ed brought this particular fellow over on the ferry."

Unfortunate timing, which was often the case when Captain Ed was involved. "So . . . you're saying I should expect a fine or two."

"A fine or two? Paul, if you happen to get that particular inspector . . ." She snapped her fingers in the air. "The camp could get closed down."

That's just what Blaine said. "What's this particular fellow's name?" He would pray *that* one wouldn't be sent to Camp Kicking Moose.

"Donald Dominski. But everyone calls him Dr. Doom."

Paul's voice was simply exhausted now, exhausted and sounding defeated. He left the diner, climbed in his truck, pushed the cat over to the passenger side, put the key in the ignition, and drove back home. His home, where he lived, with a cat.

Paul stared at the business card that the inspector, who had been waiting for him back at the camp, handed to him. Donald Dominski, county inspector, health and public safety. An unsmiling man, grim and gray-haired, with jowls like a bulldog. "Have you been to the camp before?"

"Five years ago," Dr. Doom said as he pulled out his clipboard.

"Ah, that was before I bought it. It was going bankrupt. In derelict condition. Instead of Camp Kicking Moose, it should have been called Camp Needing-Life-Support Moose." No reaction from the inspector. Whenever Paul tried making a joke, it fell flat.

"Yes." Dr. Doom peered at Paul over his glasses. "I well remember."

Suddenly it dawned on Paul that *this man* was the reason the camp had been shut down. *He* was the reason Paul had been able to buy it for a song from the previous owners, who were desperate to make a deal. *As is.* He cleared his throat. "Lots of improvements since then."

"So I see," Dr. Doom said in a tinny, accusing voice. "And yet there is no record of improvements at the county permitting department."

Flustered, Paul started to explain, tried to defend himself. In doing so, he made enormous blunders. One after the other. "It was all in terrible condition. Virtually uninhabitable." He waved an arm toward Moose Manor. "The house, in particular. We remodeled everything. Top to bottom. The kitchen, in particular. Brand new. All ready to become a fine dining establishment for the summer season."

Dr. Doom looked at Moose Manor. "Dining?" He glanced at Paul. "This summer?"

"Yes, indeed." *Stop talking, Paul. Stop talking!* But in his desperate situation, he couldn't seem to stop, even though his voice was wearing out, down to a scratch. "You can be our first guest. You and your wife. My daughter, you see, is a Le Cordon Bleu–trained chef."

"Hmm." Dr. Doom wrote something down on one of his many, many forms on the clipboard.

Paul glanced at the clipboard. *Attempted bribe.* What?! "Oh no! No, no. I wasn't trying to bribe you. I would never!"

"Hmm."

Then that awful cat jumped out of the truck and strolled right toward Paul. It twined gracefully around his ankles like a warm feather boa, then lifted its head and meowed.

"House pets." Dr. Doom wrote something down.

"No, no! It's a stray cat. It just keeps hanging around. I take it to town and back it comes. I'm not a cat guy. If anything, I'm a dog guy." *Stop talking, Paul. Stop talking!*

Dr. Doom started walking toward Moose Manor. "I see there's no ramp." He stopped and wrote something on his clipboard.

Paul saw he made the note under a section for ADA compliancy. "But . . . ," he called to the inspector in his raspy voice, "aren't you here to see the cabins?"

"Oh, I'll get to those," Dr. Doom said. "Whenever there's more than four steps, double railings are required." He put his hand on the wooden porch railing and paused.

Paul stared at it, as though he might will those loose screws at the base of the railing—the very ones he had meant to tighten but kept forgetting—to remain firm.

The inspector gave the newel post a little shake and the entire railing wobbled. Dr. Doom let go, the railing sagged to one side, and he wrote something else down on his clipboard.

Just at that moment, Cooper came out of the house with the black Labrador retriever puppy in his arms. The puppy saw the cat and wiggled free out of Cooper's arms, then bounded down the steps to bark at the cat. The cat responded by snarling and hissing.

"No house pets, eh?" Dr. Doom said with a hardened smile.

A sinking feeling started in Paul's stomach and spiraled through his entire body. Apparently, this was destined to be a day of exasperations.

On Monday afternoon, just six days after Dr. Doom's inspection, Paul stared at the letter from the county that had just arrived via registered mail. His senses reeled, his mind staggered with the ramifications of what he was reading. He thumbed through page after page of the report by Dr. Doom.

This man's dour personality made him perfectly suited to the task. There was no detail too small, no flaw to overlook. That persnickety inspector could find one dandelion in a field of grass.

Paul walked into the kitchen and sat at the table, defeated. "Forty-five violations."

Blaine was peeling carrots at the sink. "What? No way!"

"A lot of them are for ADA compliance. A ramp is needed for Moose Manor. At least one cabin must have wheelchair accessibility. We need fire exit plans to be posted everywhere. And exit signs. And smoke, fire, and methane gas detectors have to get installed in the cabins."

"Dad, you don't have smoke detectors in the cabins?"

He shook his head. "Then there's other things. Some windows

don't open easily in the cabins. The path to the bathroom needs better lighting. On and on. He says we can't open up for the season unless these violations are fixed." He held the last page of the letter up close. "And he's slapped a huge fine for lack of permitting. Huge." He hung his head.

Blaine slunk into a chair next to him to peek at the report. "What did he say about the kitchen?"

"Apparently Dr. Doom believes this kitchen isn't up to snuff for a restaurant. He said it could jeopardize the public health." Paul looked around the kitchen. "What is wrong with a man like that? It's like he takes pleasure in finding obstacles."

"Well, finding problems *is* his job description." Blaine read a lengthy page focused entirely on the kitchen. "Undefined space for food for guests and food for family. Poor drainage. Lack of ventilation. Not a commercial dishwasher. Animals in the house."

"I could take care of that one right now. That puppy and the cat can go to the animal shelter."

"There is no animal shelter on Three Sisters Island." Blaine settled back in her chair and skimmed the letter again. "Dad, the kitchen . . . it has the most violations."

"Yes, I know." Paul's chin was tucked as he read the letter a second time. His gaze swept the room, thoroughly disappointed. "We've got to keep the camp running. Somehow I'll keep it going." He raked a hand through his hair and turned to face his youngest daughter. "But this kitchen . . . Blaine, I just don't know if we'll ever be able to get the green light from Dr. Doom to allow for fine dining. He seems to think it's not a commercial kitchen and never will be. I'm so sorry, honey. You came all the way home from Paris for *this* kitchen." He felt terrible. Sick to his stomach.

Lifting her palms in an *oh well* gesture, Blaine said, "*Qui vivra verra.*" She kissed him on the top of his head and left the room with a spring in her step.

Poor Blaine. Poor sweet Blaine. She was putting up a good front, but Paul knew she must be devastated.

181

~⌢

Early the next morning, Maddie sat at the kitchen table, steeping her chamomile tea bag in a mug of hot water, thinking about church on Sunday, about how it was bursting at the seams. About how people who couldn't find a spare seat inside sat outside on the front steps, and how Seth set up a speaker so they could listen to Rick's sermon. They were like hungry people waiting for a meal. Hungry for the love of God. How could she ask Rick to do less, stay home more, when it was so clear that what he was doing was making such a difference?

"Do I interrupt?"

She lifted her eyes to see Jean-Paul standing at the door. "Please. Come in. I didn't even hear your crutches."

"Your head, it eez very deep in zhought."

She stared at the tea bag in her cup. "I'm trying to solve a problem that feels unsolvable." She took a sip of tea and watched him hobble over to the coffeemaker, pour a cup, then add a teaspoon of sugar and stir. Then another teaspoon, and another, and another.

"At your wit's end. Zat's zee expression, oui? At wit's end?"

"Yes, I suppose that's exactly right. I'm at my wit's end." She leaned back in her chair. "My husband, Rick . . . he's got a heart condition and yet he just won't slow down. He feels he's needed everywhere."

"*Il a les chevilles qui enflent.*"

"Excuse me?"

"How do I say . . . zee swollen ankles."

She pushed back her chair to peer at her ankles. "Are they? Maybe a little. Not as bad as Cam's."

"No, no! I mean . . . your husband. Zee French we say when someone eez proud, he has swollen ankles."

"Oh. Odd. But I guess I understand what you're trying to say. He wants to do all that he can, as long as he can. He knows he might not have a long life, and it makes him live full steam ahead."

182

"Full steam ahead," Jean-Paul repeated.

"Pedal to the metal."

"Pedal to zee metal," Jean-Paul said, utterly confused.

"What I mean is . . . he just won't stop. He says yes to everything and hardly sleeps and is always in a hurry."

"Oui, I have noticed." He took a sip of coffee, then added another spoonful of sugar.

She lifted her head. "Blaine says the French are famous for not worrying. So how do they handle anxiety about the future?"

"Ah, eez easy. We French, we live for today. Just one day at a time. We live and we count our blessings. Each day. You see, a grateful heart protects you from worry." He snapped his fingers. "Just like zat."

"Just like that?"

"Oui. Eez impossible to worry when counting blessings. *C'est impossible.* Zee zhankfulness . . . it sets us free." He lifted a finger in the air. "No. It eez God who sets us free."

For the rest of the day, Maddie considered Jean-Paul's words. That night, as she climbed into bed, she turned to Rick. "Say yes as often as you feel God wants you to."

Rick had been reading a book and let it drop on his chest. "Maddie, do you really mean that? Really and truly?"

"I do." She did. This inner battle had to end. She had to make peace with it. She had married Rick for better or worse, and she had to trust God with their future . . . all that it held.

Rick seemed vastly relieved. He set the book on the nightstand and turned the light off, then reached for her.

Cam had to go to the bathroom so badly that she felt like she was going to explode, right here and now, in the waiting room for the ultrasound. The nurse had called yesterday to remind her to arrive early and come with a full bladder, because doing so would lift the uterus up, and that would help the sonographer view the baby. So she drank three glasses of water and regretted every sip. "Seth, if we don't get in soon, I'm going to lose it."

He looked up from his magazine. "Don't think about going to the bathroom."

"What should I think about?"

He set the magazine down. "Peaceful things . . . like a waterfall. A fountain. A hot shower."

She swatted him. "Don't make me laugh!" She squeezed her eyes shut. "I'm not kidding, Seth. My bladder feels like a balloon that's about to burst."

"I'll go find out how much longer you have to wait."

As he rose from the chair, the door opened. "Camden Walker?"

"Thank heavens." Cam pushed herself up out of the chair and followed the nurse into a room with the ultrasound equipment.

"You can have a seat. The sonographer will be in soon."

"When can I go to the bathroom?"

The nurse gave her a look like she was running through a drill, having heard this a thousand times before. "As soon as the sonographer completes the ultrasound."

Ten minutes later, Cam's belly was lathered with a lubricant, and the technician began to move the wand all over her abdomen.

Cam watched the screen carefully, but all she could make out were squiggly lines on a black-and-white screen. "We don't want to know the gender."

"We don't?" Seth looked puzzled. "I thought we decided we did."

"No. We definitely don't. At least, not today. We're going to have a gender reveal with our family. You know, take your results to a baby store and choose two outfits and let them decide. Then you open up the box at the reveal. It's how everyone is doing it now." Cam felt her neck straining, so she laid her head back on the table. "At least, that's what my sister did. She's having a boy."

The technician's brows furrowed as he moved the wand all over her big belly. Horizontal lines appeared on his forehead.

Cam's head lifted. "What? What is it? Is something wrong? Is the baby all right?"

The tech kept his eyes on the screen. "Would you please stop talking? It's very distracting."

"Oh." She dropped her head back on the table. She'd always heard that sonographers went into this medical specialty because they weren't people persons.

The tech removed the wand. "Is this your first ultrasound with the pregnancy?"

Cam nodded.

"Hmm." He placed the wand back on Cam's belly and moved it around. "You've had blood work done, haven't you?"

"I'm . . . a little behind schedule on a few things. It's been terribly busy, you see. But I'm going to get it done today."

"Hmm." He moved the wand to the side of her belly. He glanced at the computer that held her records. "Quite a weight gain."

Seth snorted. "A quart of ice cream a day will do that."

Cam kicked him.

"Your records don't indicate IVF."

Cam popped her head up. "In vitro? We didn't have any fertility treatments. Dr. Potter wanted us to try for a year before we considered any treatments. That year was just about up and . . . well . . ." She pointed to her middle. "This happened."

"So this is your first pregnancy?"

"Yes."

"And you're how far along?"

"Well, I'm not one hundred percent sure about that, either. My work, you see. It's quite consuming."

"I'll say," Seth added.

"Have you had many symptoms?" the tech asked.

"Meaning . . ."

"Nausea? Fatigue? Heartburn?"

"A little here and there. Nothing like my sister. She's the one with all the pregnancy ailments. She can hardly talk about anything else."

"Moody?"

"Maddie? Oh, a little, I suppose. But nothing out of the ordinary."

"You, I meant."

"Oh yeah," Seth said, drawing out the words. "Very moody."

Cam lifted her head to frown at him until he looked away. "Is this going to take much longer? Because I really, really have to go to the bathroom."

The tech moved the wand side to side. "Hmm."

"Hold it." Seth's eyes were glued to the screen. "Is *that* . . . what I think it is?"

The technician gave a slight nod. "Mm-hmm."

Did that mean their baby was a boy? She didn't want to know the gender! Cam lifted her head to watch Seth. He seemed calm enough, Cam thought, although he kept a tight grip on her hand and inhaled less frequently than she thought was normal. Then his eyebrows shot to the top of his forehead.

"And that?" Seth's voice rose an octave.

"Mm-hmm." The tech gave a brisk nod.

"What?" Cam said. "What does that mean?" She couldn't make out anything from the ultrasound picture. The shocked look on Seth's face alarmed Cam. Seth was never shocked. He was cucumber calm in all situations, completely unflappable. "What do you see? Is something wrong with the baby?" Tears started to sting her eyes. Their baby had to be all right. Of course he was all right. "Please tell me the truth. I can take it. I'll be okay. We'll be okay, right, Seth?"

Seth didn't say a word. She looked at the technician. He, too, appeared stunned. His mouth opened and shut, then he said, "The doctor will discuss the results with you."

Now Cam was sure that something was definitely wrong.

Nineteen

SETH HAD NEVER LOOKED so serious. He reached out for Cam's hand, and she was surprised at how icy cold his was. After a trip to the bathroom, they were sent on a short walk over to her obstetrician's office. On the way, she tried to get him to tell her what he thought he'd seen on the grainy ultrasound, but all he would say was that everything was fine. "Let's just let the doctor explain the ultrasound."

Fear and worry warred inside her. What had Seth seen that caused such a reaction? Cam looked at the same screen and couldn't see anything recognizable. Was their baby missing a limb? Or two?

She tried to remember what had been effective during Maddie's panic attacks. Breathe in, breathe out, slow and steady. She tried it a few times. It didn't work. Her heart was pounding, her palms were sweaty. *Let's just get this over with.*

"Okay," she told the doctor as she settled herself in the chair. Seth sat stone still, his hand gripping hers. "Give it to us straight. Tell us what the problem is with our baby."

Dr. Potter was staring at the computer screen that showed Cam's ultrasound. "Actually, Cam, everything looks good. This anatomical ultrasound ruled out all kinds of potential problems. I'm happy to say that every landmark is checked off."

Oh, relief! "Then . . . why do you seem so concerned? If the baby is fine . . ." She felt a jab and instinctively placed her free hand over her belly.

"Not 'baby,' Cam." The doctor pointed to the screen. "Bab*ies*." He pointed to the blurry ovals on the screen.

"Twins?" Her eyes opened wide. *Oh. My. Gosh.* So Artie was right.

"No, not twins."

She glanced at Seth, confused. With his other hand, he held up three fingers. "Triplets," he said hoarsely, and exhaled with a whoosh.

Cam heard sounds, but everyone seemed to be talking underwater, slowly. *Triplets?* It wasn't possible. Was it? She shook her head, looking down again with wonder at her belly.

"Cam—now listen, this is important." She heard Dr. Potter's voice rise above the watery sounds. "You need to get your blood work done, double up on fruits and vegetables, take prenatal vitamins, and get more rest. A lot more. Each and every day."

"What? Bed rest? I can't! I can't possibly lie in bed all day. I'll go crazy."

"Cam, the chance of conceiving triplets naturally is tiny. It's a 1-in-8100 shot. You're now deemed a high-risk pregnancy."

"High risk?" Cam's voice shot up an octave.

Seth leaned forward in his chair. "But everything's been going so well."

Cam nodded. "I've been a little tired, but I haven't even had terrible morning sickness. Not like my sister, and she's only having one."

"Any heartburn?"

"A little."

"That will get much worse. Much, much worse."

"Oh."

"These babies are putting substantial demands on your body. The chance of developing high blood pressure or diabetes is significant. Your blood pressure is already higher than I'd like it to be."

Cam blew out a puff of air. "Well, that seems reasonable considering I just found out I'm having triplets."

"I know this is a lot to take in, but there's an even bigger concern to keep in mind. The main risk is delivering the babies prematurely. The average length of a pregnancy with triplets is only thirty-two weeks."

"But that," Seth said, with concern in his voice, "means they'll be premature."

"Exactly. And that can create all kinds of problems. We want those babies to stay put as long as possible. If all goes smoothly, I'd like you to make it to about thirty-five weeks. And then we'll schedule a cesarean."

"What?"

"It's very rare to deliver multiples vaginally. But let's worry about that when we get to the last trimester. For now, I'm going to bring in a specialist. And we'll do a lot more scans, a lot more prenatal visits. In fact, I'd like to get your blood pressure checked in between weekly appointments."

"Hold on. I live on Three Sisters Island. It's half a day to get here and back. That alone will spike my blood pressure."

Seth squeezed her hand. "Artie."

Cam turned to Seth. "Artie!"

"Artie Lotosky is the doctor with the *Lightship*. He's on the island a couple of times a week. I'm sure he'd help us out."

"I know Artie," the doctor said, scribbling something down. "He's dating my nurse."

Cam and Seth shared a look.

"I'll connect with him to see if he can take your blood pressure twice a week and send me the results. That'll save you a couple of extra trips into Bar Harbor." He pointed at Cam. "But no more skipping appointments or postponing blood work. Keep up the quart of ice cream. Your only job is to keep those babies safe and sound. Lots of rest, lots of naps, plenty of fluids. Feet up. Avoid all stress."

"But . . . what about—" Cam started.

"No buts," the doctor said. "No stress. No pressure."

Seth sat back in his chair. "Wow. Talk about a sea change."

Blaine set a big bowl of steaming orecchiette pasta in the center of the table. She paused, noticing the look that passed between Cam and Seth. Like something big was about to be unveiled. Most likely, the cell phone tower got passed. She grabbed the Parmesan cheese and grater, set them on the table, then turned to ladle the Bolognese sauce into another bowl.

"So," Cam said, holding Seth's hand, "we have news."

"We're all ears," Dad said, though all eyes were on the thick red Bolognese sauce. "Wow, that looks really good, Blaine."

"It sure does," Rick said. "Smells good too."

"Please," Cam said. "All of you. Please set aside your appetite for a moment to listen. We were given some news today at the doctor's office."

Maddie gasped. "Oh no. There's something wrong with the baby."

Blaine finished the last ladle of sauce into the bowl and turned to see another weird look pass between Seth and Cam.

"Babies," Seth said.

"Twins?" Dad croaked.

Seth held up three fingers.

Cooper smiled widely. "Triplets!"

Silence fell. Then, a happy chaos, with everyone chiming in. "No way!" "Impossible!" "That's awesome!" "Identical? Fraternal?" "Boys? Girls?" "Both?" "Cam, you are SUCH an overachiever!"

Laughing, Cam held up her hands. "Slow down, slow down. We'll tell you everything over supper." She turned to Blaine. "I'm so hungry I could eat a bear. Is dinner ready?"

"Coming!" Blaine picked up the heavy bowl of Bolognese sauce with two thick mitts and started toward the table, pleased that one of her specialties would honor this big event. As she stepped toward the table, she heard Cam say, "And guess what the doctor mentioned? Artie is dating his nurse. Small world, right?"

Suddenly the bowl of Bolognese slipped out of Blaine's mitted hands and landed upside down, spewing her wonderful homemade red sauce all over the new wood floors, splattered on cupboards and walls, up on the stainless steel refrigerator. Everyone stared.

"Wow," Cooper said. "It looks like a crime scene."

Jean-Paul took a step forward to grab a cleanup rag and slipped on the sauce, hurling to the floor, his full weight landing on his elbow as he tried to instinctively protect his bad knee.

Seth carried Jean-Paul to the couch in the living room while Dad called Artie on the landline. "He said to put a bag of ice on the swelling," Dad reported. "Fifteen minutes on, fifteen minutes off. Artie's still on the island and will be here as soon as he can."

Blaine and Cooper mopped up the Bolognese sauce all over the kitchen; the puppy helped by licking the floor. It did look like a bloody crime scene, but that wasn't going to stop Cam, nor Maddie, nor Granddad, from eating cold and gummy and sauceless orecchiette pasta.

As Blaine wrung out the rag in the sink, she turned to those left at the table. "I'm so sorry about dropping the sauce."

"Not as sorry as the little French guy," Granddad said. "He's starting to look like he's been through a war. And lost."

Blaine winced. She felt terrible about Jean-Paul's additional injury. She also felt terrible about Artie's girlfriend. But why shouldn't he have a girlfriend? "Butter and Parmesan cheese might help the pasta."

"Good idea," Cam said. She started to get up, but Seth had returned to the kitchen and stopped her. "Stay put. I've got it." He bent down to give her a quick kiss on the lips.

Unlike Cam, Seth seemed to be coming out of his reverie. He couldn't stop smiling, or fussing over Cam, or glancing at the ultrasound pictures that were left on the table. He could not be happier about these babies. Cam still seemed shell-shocked, stunned . . . and speechless. A shockingly rare affliction for her sister. Blaine hoped for some kind of follow-up about the nurse Artie was dating. What was she like? How long had they been dating? How serious were they? But Cam volunteered nothing else, other than a request for more cold, gummy pasta, and Blaine dared not ask for information.

She heard Artie's voice in the other room and hurried out. He was sitting on the coffee table directly across from Jean-Paul, examining his elbow. While Artie asked questions, Blaine studied him carefully, noticing how confident were his actions, his manner. She noticed that he needed a haircut. His hair was curling around the back of his neck, and she wondered if the nurse-girlfriend gave him haircuts. She was surprised to find herself fascinated by him, his profile, the crisp, straight line of his nose, the trimmed beard that wrapped his jaw, the hollow of his cheek, the darkness of his eyebrows. He made a rather fetching sight, no question about it, and she wondered if the nurse appreciated his good looks. As he checked out Jean-Paul's elbow, Blaine saw that a blue vein ran along the inside of Artie's wrist. She felt a sudden desire to trail a fingertip along that vein and . . .

Suddenly he glanced up to find her studying him, and she turned away, blushing.

Oh my gosh. What was her problem?

Paul watched Artie carefully examine Jean-Paul's elbow like a seasoned professional. Minutes earlier, Cam had come into the living room waving her ultrasound pictures.

"I didn't believe you," Cam told him. "How in the world did you know?"

Artie examined the pictures with a modest grin. "Well, I didn't know there'd be *three* babies."

"But you knew there was more than one," she said. "My own doctor missed all the signs until the ultrasound today."

"Did you find out the babies' gender?" Artie said.

Cam and Seth exchanged a sheepish look. "We told him we didn't want to know."

Paul's father walked past them, newspaper in hand, out to the porch. He was limping again, favoring his left hip. Ever since Peg had mentioned it, Paul had noticed how often his father rubbed that hip, how he winced as he settled into a chair. When Paul noticed Artie move the bag of melted ice off Jean-Paul's elbow, he handed him a fresh bag.

"Thanks, Paul. You would've made a good medic."

Not really, but all Paul heard was *would have*. Like his best years were behind him. Sixty-two seemed awfully young to him.

And then Artie made a sudden jerk with Jean-Paul's hand and popped the dislocated elbow back into joint. "It's going to be sore. You'll need to wear a sling for a few days."

Paul marveled at this young man, freshly out of medical school, already exhibiting remarkable expertise. Or maybe some people had a natural gift for their vocation, a head start, like Blaine and cooking, like his own voice and a radio career. Maybe the tricky part in life was aligning the gift with the vocation. He rubbed his throat. And trickier still was what to do when the gift left. He gazed around the large living area—Maddie and Rick sat on the bottom step of the stairs talking, Cam and Seth were over by the fireplace, showing ultrasound pictures to Cooper. The puppy was curled up against Cooper's feet, sound asleep. Blaine kept fussing over the placement of Jean-Paul's ice packs. Artie packed up his bag, his eyes on Blaine with an inscrutable look on his face.

And suddenly Paul's late wife Corinna's face swam into his view. One thing he knew for sure, life kept moving on.

And so, perhaps, should he.

Cam couldn't sleep. Her mind was spinning like a top. Triplets! No wonder she felt as if there was constant movement going on in her belly. There was! One baby was always awake, kicking and jabbing the others. She covered her face with her hands. Was this what it would be like after they were born?

She finally gave up trying to sleep and went downstairs to get a glass of water. Blaine was at the kitchen table, papers spread out everywhere. The end of her blonde ponytail feathered against her shoulder, she had no makeup on, and yet she looked like a fashion model. Drop-dead gorgeous. Thoroughly dazzling.

Cam, hot and sweaty, wearing one of Seth's baggy T-shirts, felt like a fat, plain duck next to a swan. "Hey there. What're you doing up so late?"

Blaine closed her computer, as if she didn't want Cam to see what she was doing. "Just a little alternative planning."

Cam coughed a laugh. "That seems to be a recurring theme around here lately."

"Mm-hmm," Blaine murmured.

Poor Blaine. Dad's letter of violations had killed any plans for a restaurant, at least for this summer. Cam got a glass of water, added crushed ice from the oh-so-wonderful new refrigerator, and settled into a chair. "Blaine, I think we can fight this."

"Fight what?"

"Fight the violations, of course. Apply for a variance. Prove to the county that the restaurant will be an economic benefit to the island."

"Cam, um . . ."

"I know, I know. It's a longshot for this summer. But maybe for next summer."

Blaine's eyes flicked to Cam's belly. "Sure, sure. Definitely. Maybe for next summer." She opened her computer and said, "In the meantime, as long as we're both wide awake, I'd like to pitch a business opportunity to you."

Cam eyed her, taking a sip of water, then another. "Go ahead."

"I want to turn the lighthouse into an exclusive restaurant."

At that, Cam practically spewed her water out. Coughing, she said, "You *what*?"

"I want to turn the lighthouse into a restaurant, with a cooking school in the keeper's cottage." Blaine held her hand out as if pointing to the words written in the air. "At Lighthouse Point. On top of the world." She smiled. "I've got it all planned out. The kitchen will be in the keeper's cottage. Restaurant patrons will have to book reservations in advance. A set menu will be served." Blaine turned her computer around. "I've spoken to a contractor. I've met with an architect. I've already had the planning department at the county rezone the lighthouse so it can be approved as commercial space. I've run all the numbers. My plan is to host a dining experience in the gallery of the lighthouse. I've worked it all out, right down to the china and flatware." She clicked a page. "It will look like this."

Cam looked at the picture Blaine had mocked up of a lighthouse, set against a setting sun, with a soft candlelight glow coming from the lantern room. It looked lovely, but it made no sense. "Blaine, you can't be serious."

"I'm very serious."

"How many people do you think you can fit in that . . . lantern room?"

"Probably just four in that room. A few more tables could fit in the gallery room. Like I said, it's very exclusive fine dining. A once-in-a-lifetime experience."

A wave of fatigue swept over Cam. The day was finally catching up with her. "I can't even imagine how much it would cost for one dinner to just . . . break even!"

Blaine looked her directly in the eye. "People like unusual dining experiences. And when they're on vacation, they're willing to spend more."

She tilted her head. "How much do you think you can charge for a meal?"

Blaine cleared her throat. "It depends on what's being served. But for high season, let's say a lobster dinner, I think it'll start around, um, three hundred and fifty dollars."

Cam leaned back in the chair, shocked.

"People in Paris spend that much on a bottle of wine. Everyone in France appreciates food, and slows down for it, and savors time at the table."

"Blaine, this isn't Paris. This is Three Sisters Island in Maine."

"How many people can go home from their summer vacation and say they've had dinner in a lighthouse? Think of the special moments in their lives. Proposals, anniversaries. Think of going on vacation to a cooking school, and eating what you make at the top of a lighthouse. I'd charge locals less, of course." She turned her computer back around. "You were the one who had the idea of turning the lighthouse into a bed-and-breakfast."

"That was before the top got blown off."

"Cupola. And it's replaceable."

"What about supplies? How do you schlep them up to the lighthouse?"

"Those aspects are, well, um, still to be determined."

"Have you given any thought to the total cost?"

"Yes. Of course. I've gotten bids."

"Well? How much? I'm thinking it's at least fifty thousand dollars."

Blaine's eyes went to her keyboard. In a very quiet voice, she said, "One hundred thousand."

Cam's jaw dropped open. Double!

Blaine cleared her throat, straightened her back, and looked right at Cam. "Would you be willing to make a loan? I promise to pay you back, with interest."

Feeling extremely uncomfortable from sitting too long on a hard chair, Cam eased herself up. "I'm sorry, Blaine. Even if I wanted to, I don't have the money to help this . . . project." As she walked to the door, she stopped and turned. Something niggled at the back of her mind. Then a momentary flash of shock. "Did you say you've been to the county to ask to rezone the lighthouse?"

"Yes."

"So they must have checked to see who owned the land?"

"Yes."

Cam leaned against the door. "Oh. My. Gosh. So it wasn't Baxtor Phinney after all."

"What wasn't?"

"You."

"Me?"

"Blaine, you must have triggered the county to send an inspector to Three Sisters Island. To Camp Kicking Moose." Cam shook her head and blew out a puff of air. "Tomorrow. We'll fix this tomorrow." A wave of weariness traveled over her, head to toes. She was exhausted. "I have to get to bed."

Twenty

What have I done?

Blaine watched the kitchen door shut, her mouth wide open. Could it be true? Had she unwittingly tipped off the county about the lack of permits at Camp Kicking Moose?

What have I done?

Of course. Of course she had. She dropped her forehead to the tabletop. It hadn't dawned on Blaine, until now, that the county official had seemed unusually curious about the camp. She was so focused on getting the lighthouse rezoned that she answered every single question. Argh, what an idiot! What had she done to her dad? To her family? She banged her head against the counter three times, furious with herself.

Finally, she turned off her computer and went upstairs to her bedroom to sleep. To try, anyway.

Just before dawn, Blaine left the house to head to the Lunch Counter. She couldn't face her family this morning. She assumed Cam would tell Dad that she'd triggered the inspections for the camp, and she dreaded the look of disappointment in his eyes.

By the time Peg came into the diner, coffee was made, biscuits

198

were out of the oven, and berries for cereal had been washed, hulled, and sliced.

"Peg," Blaine said. "Would you mind if I took a few hours off?"

Peg, being Peg, sensed an undercurrent. "Honey, take the whole day."

Blaine grabbed her purse, gave Peg a hug, and shot out the door. She had to get out to the lighthouse. She had to be there, to see it, to feel that same feeling of excitement she had when she first came up with the idea of converting it into a restaurant. Cam's reaction had doused her enthusiasm, cast doubt on the whole thing. Was it a crazy idea?

Blaine rushed down Boon Dock to the slip that held her father's outboard and jumped into the boat. She pulled the engine cord once, twice, three times, and paused. "Come on, engine." She checked and saw the gas tank was full, so she pulled one more time and it coughed to life. She let it idle while she untied the ropes from the cleats and then turned the throttle to reverse, backing it out of the slip.

The tide was out, the water was calm. She steered the boat out of the harbor and headed north, staying fairly close to the island. She loved seeing it from the water. It gave her a completely different perspective. She felt protective of it; it seemed small and snug and vulnerable. When out hiking, it could seem almost hostile. Dark and shady, with trees that blocked the light.

But from any angle, this island was breathtakingly beautiful. Blaine's parents had fallen in love with it when they were college students, and that love affair had never died. No wonder Dad had bought the camp when he had the chance. No wonder at all.

And Blaine had spoiled his dream.

As she passed the little ribbon of beach below Camp Kicking Moose, she wondered if she could risk a quick dash up to the house to get Jean-Paul. She wanted his opinion on the lighthouse, and she wanted his company too. He had a way of making her feel as if everything was going to be okay. She needed a dose of that today.

It was still early; with a little bit of luck, everyone might still be asleep. She turned off the engine and made sure the boat's bow was securely anchored in the sand, then ran up the trail to the house to get Jean-Paul. He was awake, watching a tennis match on TV.

"Come with me," she whispered, handing him a cane borrowed from Artie's *Lightship*. "I have an adventure planned."

Startled, he pointed to the television. "But . . . but . . . eez Coco Gauff!"

"Trust me. She'll be around for a while. She's only a kid. Let's go."

She helped him off the couch. He hobbled slowly behind Blaine, using only one crutch because the other arm was in a sling. Slowly, oh so slowly, he made it down the hillside, down the rocky cliff, through the sand, and next to the boat, where he stopped like a dog at the vet's office.

"I cannot." He rubbed his tummy. "I get zee mal de mer."

"It's a super short ride," she said, and reluctantly he climbed into the boat. She didn't even want to tell him about what lay ahead—a steep climb up narrow old stairs on a rocky cliff to reach the lighthouse.

As soon as Jean-Paul got settled in the boat, she pushed the bow into the water and jumped in the back. She pulled the cord and the engine roared to life.

He slapped at a mosquito on his chin, noting the bloody smear on his palm with a look of grim satisfaction. He pulled out a tube of insect repellent. "I learn fast. I am never without zis now. I sleep with it." He slathered the insect repellent on his arms, legs, neck, and face.

A grin tugged at her lips. She couldn't believe this was the first time he was out on the water. He'd been here weeks now. She should've taken him out first thing. But of course, his injured knee prevented doing much of anything at first. And then his hurt hand, slammed in the refrigerator. And then his bloody nose. And then his dislocated elbow.

Well, she was glad she was finally showing him this beautiful island. As she headed north along the coast, she told him how she saw strange shapes appear in this area. "One time, I could have sworn I saw the skeleton of a shipwreck. There's a reason the waters around lighthouses are nicknamed graveyards."

Jean-Paul turned his head, eyes wide. "Graveyards?"

"Currents and shoals and shifting sand. Powerful stuff. There's a reason the lighthouse was called Shipwreck Shelf."

"So sad." He peered over the edge of the boat into the dark water. "A shipwreck . . . it eez zee end of someone's dream."

"Sit tight! We're heading into choppy waters." And boy, were they ever. As the little boat rounded the tip of the island, they were moving away from the protection of the island and straight into the open ocean. The water went from calm seas to choppy, roiling waves that splashed the sides of the boat, accompanied with hair-raising headwinds that churned the water's surface into frothy whitecaps. The vast, great Atlantic Ocean.

She loved this moment! It made her feel terribly insignificant to face the power of the open sea, and yet also full of awe. So filled with the intense awareness that she was in the presence of something greater than herself.

She cut right through the waves until she turned the boat slowly toward the little beach below the lighthouse, then slowed the engine so he could see it from the water. "Behold paradise!" The lighthouse, minus its cupola, stood tall in the wind.

"Paradise?" Jean-Paul sounded skeptical. "But where did its head go?"

"A lightning strike."

"It looks like a birthday candle without zee flame."

She docked the boat up on the exposed beach and helped Jean-Paul climb out. She led the way over the slippery gray polished pebbles, through the seaweed, helping him make his way to the stairs. The old wooden steps were so small, so fragile, each one covered in chicken wire.

"Eez safe?"

"Yes. I'll go first." At the top, she turned and looked down at him. He gazed up the stairs as if facing a mountain. She'd thought about the tides, but she hadn't thought about his ailing knee. "Maybe this wasn't such a good idea."

"No, no. We are here. I come." Good sport that he was, he took one step at a time, leaning all his weight on his crutch, dragging the other leg, huffing and puffing.

It took an enormously long amount of time until he reached the top, hoisted himself up onto the bluff, and collapsed on the ground.

After he stopped panting, she pointed to the lighthouse. "Look. Look at that beautiful building up close."

He lifted his head to look, and rocked his hand in the air. "Maybe not so beautiful."

"Let's go explore it."

He pulled himself up to sit and turned to peer down at the boat on the beach. "But . . . zee tide. It will take our boat. We will be stranded."

"Not to worry. I'm watching the tides." It was part of island living, knowing those tides. She might not know the exact hour that the tide ebbed, but she could feel a general sense of change in the air. The air, the water, had a different smell at low tide. Sounds were different. Birdsong was different. She couldn't really explain it; it was just part of being an islander. She took a deep breath of fresh sea air. She was glad she'd come. That deep-down thrill had returned to her.

"Jean-Paul, I brought you here for a reason." She walked a few feet, then spun around. "I have a plan for this lighthouse."

One hand was tenting his eyes from the sun as he gazed up at the lighthouse. He dropped his hand and turned to her. "Bomb it?" He made the hand motion for blowing something up. "Kaboom!"

"Bomb it? No," she said, a little miffed. "I want to turn it into a restaurant."

His eyebrows shot up, but he listened carefully to her as she explained her idea. Jean-Paul was a good listener, something she'd always appreciated about him, and nodded in all the right places.

"I know the problems, Jean-Paul. Schlepping food in, cooking it, getting it up to the top . . . which doesn't currently exist." She looked up. "But I can see it. Not as it is, but how I imagine it to be. And I even have a name for it. I want to call the restaurant 'Lighthouse Point. Dinner on Top of the World.' I've got it all figured out in my mind." Almost all. "Dinners will be a set menu. Gourmet cuisine. Imagine special events, anniversaries, marriage proposals. Oh, imagine proposals. Especially marriage proposals. How romantic! Overlooking a glittering ocean, watching the sun set over the waves." She could see it all, right in front of her, even the sunset. "Well? Thoughts?"

He was staring at the lighthouse with a skeptical look on his face. "It will be . . . lots and lots of climbing for zat special dinner."

"Yes. True. You have to climb fifty-five stairs to the top." She held her hands in the air when she saw the fear in his eyes. "Not you! I won't make you climb up to the top today."

He turned to check on the little boat on the beach. "How do zee dinner guests get here? You expect zem to climb up zee stairs?"

She scratched her forehead. "I don't have that part figured out yet."

"It will take much money."

What does that matter? Money had never been an obstacle to Jean-Paul, even though he didn't have any. "Yes. Much money."

"How much money eez needed?"

"Probably around . . . one hundred thousand dollars." Her enthusiasm was starting to evaporate again as she realized that he wasn't buying into her vision. She hadn't expected a buzzkill from Jean-Paul.

He squeezed his eyes shut, as if trying to visualize that much money in one pile. "Zat eez . . . five hundred thousand . . . no, nearly six hundred thousand . . ."

He was converting the amount into French euros. *Good grief!*

203

"Jean-Paul, don't think about the cost of it. I'll figure that out." How, she had no idea. For the time being, she wanted to marinate in possibilities.

"But how? What will you do for zis money?"

"Not sure. I asked Cam, but she shut me down." She pivoted to face him. "So," she said with a big smile, "putting aside all of those still-to-be-figured-out pieces of this plan . . . what do you think?" She was excited to get his reaction.

"Zee rest of your life, on zis little min-i-sque speck of land?"

Miniscule? "It's so much more than a speck of land. It's my family, and my friends."

He turned to face the Atlantic. "Blaine, eez a big wide world out zere. So much to see. To learn about."

Then she said something that she hadn't even realized, not until that moment. "I think, Jean-Paul, that this is my world." She wasn't just here because of a promise she'd made to her dad. She was here because she wanted to be here. She loved this island.

Something came over his face she could only describe as pensive. "Zen, mon amie," he said as a soft smile lit his eyes, "you must find a way to make zis world work."

Twenty-One

ON THE RETURN TRIP TO BOON DOCK, Jean-Paul asked to be dropped off at the beach below the camp. Blaine pointed to the sea path that wound up the hill. "Straight up to Moose Manor."

"Straight up," he repeated, sounding uncertain.

"Are you sure you wouldn't rather go to town? I can drive you home. I just have a few things to take care of at the diner first." She had to talk to Peg. She was the likeliest to know how to fix this.

"No, no. Eez okay." He placed a hand on his tummy. "Zee mal de mer. It visits me."

It dawned on Blaine that he really hadn't minded staying on the couch because he didn't really want to be here. Not in America, not on Three Sisters Island. She had persuaded him to come. "Jean-Paul, is this lighthouse restaurant idea . . . is it a ridiculous dream?"

He tipped his head. "Maybe a dream should be a bit *ridicule*." Even the word sounded better in French. Ri-dee-que.

"Sure, but turning it into reality? It'll be one obstacle after another." No money, for one.

"If God has given you zis dream, zen he will take care of zee obstacles. Pray and release. Pray and release." He gripped his crutch and limped away, through the rocks and sand.

205

Encouraged, Blaine let the boat drift a moment before pulling the engine cord. Pray and release. Pray and release.

When she arrived at the Lunch Counter, she was pleased it was empty of customers. Peg saw her and pointed to a red stool. "Sit. Sit and tell me everything."

Blaine sank onto the stool and explained it all, leaving out nothing. When she finished her sorry tale, she looked at Peg. "Dad has worked so hard to make Camp Kicking Moose a success. I've essentially destroyed his plans for the future." She snapped her fingers. "Just like that."

"Honey, there's something you need to grasp. Something that took me a long time to learn, but it makes a big difference in life."

"I'm listening."

"That is *not* the whole story. Has it occurred to you that your dad and sister ignored all the regulations? They just barreled ahead, doing what they wanted to do. Look, I'm all for keeping the government out of my personal business as much as I can, but I know the good that comes out of government too. They're trying to keep things safe and sound. Seems to me that your dad and sister could've saved themselves a heap of trouble if they'd just done things right the first time. I don't think you should be beating yourself up." Peg wrapped an apron around her ample middle and pulled the container of coffee off the shelf. "This whole mess could've been avoided. They brought this on themselves. Rules apply to everyone, including those two."

A tiny ray of light broke through Blaine's self-recrimination. Still, she dreaded going home. "How do I get Dad and Cam to see it that way?"

"Well, that's the tricky part."

"Peg, the inspector has threatened to shut down Camp Kicking Moose this summer. THIS summer. It's almost May. Memorial Day is on the horizon."

Peg took a while to respond, pulling the coffee beans out of the container and pouring them into the grinder. It whirled once, then twice, and Peg was about to tip the contents into the filter when Blaine jumped up and grabbed it from her. "Peg, remember to wait until the sound is smooth. No grinding of beans. That's how you know the beans are properly ground. Doing it right makes all the difference."

Peg gasped, then her face lit up. "Blaine Grayson, you did it again!"

"What did I do?"

"What you just said. Doing it right makes all the difference. *That's* what your dad and sister need to be reminded of. Fix every one of those violations so the camp can get right back on track for the summer."

Blaine slapped her chest with the palm of her hand. "Me?"

"You."

"How?" How in the world could she fix forty-five violations by Memorial Day weekend? A little over a month away!

"That . . . I don't know. But I do know you'll figure it out." Peg smiled. "Just like you're the only one on this island who can make a perfect cup of coffee."

Peg started humming to herself as she readied the kitchen for the next day. Stacking to-go coffee cups and lids, piling up fresh paper napkins. She went to the pantry for more napkins, and Blaine watched her go. An excellent solution, she thought, but with it comes a new problem. A big fat one. *Because, my sweet wonderful Peg, the only way to get those violations fixed in time is to bring in the man who broke your heart.*

Twenty-Two

IN THE BOATHOUSE, Paul sat on a wooden trunk that held the life preservers, rereading Dr. Doom's letter of violations, fretting, trying to figure out how he could get things fixed by Memorial Day weekend. It was a Sisyphean task, even deleting the apparently-not-commercial kitchen from the list.

What a mess. And it was his fault. His name was on the property deed. He didn't pay attention to licensing or permits because he didn't want to bother with them.

He heard an odd noise and peered out the opening to see Jean-Paul hobbling up the sea path with his cane, huffing and puffing. "Where have you been?"

Breathing hard, Jean-Paul pointed a crutch in the ocean's direction.

"Well, good for you to see more of the island, now that you're feeling better."

Jean-Paul hopped over to the boathouse. "So zis eez where you go to hide. My pa-Pa, he goes to zee kitchen. And farmers, zey go to zee barn."

Was Paul hiding? He sighed. Yes. He loved the boathouse all throughout the year, loved its cool shade in the summer, loved its quiet protection from the elements in the winter. He loved having a place where his daughters didn't go. He watched Jean-Paul make his way down the aisle, looking at the canoes and kayaks hanging upside down.

Jean-Paul came back up and stopped near Paul. "Blaine has told me about your voice."

"My voice?"

"She said it was your ticket. To life."

Paul nodded. "To a career in radio. It worked out well . . . until it stopped working."

"And now you are working at listening."

Paul cocked an eyebrow.

"Most people are very bad at listening. I zink it eez a skill. It needs practice. Listening eez learning to pay attention." Jean-Paul gave him a smile. "Have you ever zhought zee loss of your voice eez . . ." He pointed to his head.

"Psychosomatic?"

"Zere's never been a cause for its loss, no?"

"No. I mean, yes." Sticking a yes or no at the end of a sentence confused Paul. "Laryngitis."

"But most laryngitis comes and goes, yes?"

"Yes."

"I have noticed zat your voice . . . how you say . . . weakens . . . when you are under stress."

"What? I don't think so." Did it? Could that be true? Paul would have to give that some thought.

After Jean-Paul hobbled off to the house, Paul couldn't stop thinking about what he'd said. He decided to just go ahead and call his speech therapist in Bar Harbor, but he didn't want to use the landline, not with his father in the house. So he drove all the way down to Boon Dock, deeply annoyed that there was no cell service on this island.

He walked to the spot that provided the most bars on his phone and called his speech therapist. He explained Jean-Paul's theory. "So what do you have to say about that?"

"Interesting you should bring it up, Paul. I was just reading a journal article that said under periods of stress, the muscles that control the voice box become tense, and that leads to an incoordination of the vocal control system."

"Translate, please."

"Your voice can get worse under stress."

Hmm. "Does that mean it can improve without stress?"

"As in, a full recovery? It's hard to say. But it's definitely heading in the right direction."

Paul felt cheered up. This was the first good news he'd had since Dr. Doom arrived at the camp. He started walking up the hill and stopped when he saw Blaine leave the diner and bolt down the dock, running so fast she didn't even see him. His eyes followed her as she hurried onto Boon Dock, to where Artie's *Lightship* was pulling in.

He smiled and slipped his cell phone in his pocket. Now that was the second-best news he had in a long while. He'd always had a soft spot for Artie.

Blaine had overheard a lobsterman at the Lunch Counter say he was expecting Dr. Lotosky to arrive by four o'clock, to take a look at his gouty foot. She had absolutely no interest in that gouty foot, but she was very interested in talking to Artie. She went down to Boon Dock to watch for his boat to come in. One of the good things about Artie is that if he told you he'd meet you at four o'clock, he meant four o'clock. On. The. Dot. It was uncanny how accurate he was, even as a college kid. But then, Artie never really seemed like a kid.

When Blaine saw a boat approaching in the harbor with a big red cross on the side, she went down the dock to the slip and waited for Artie to disembark. He saw her, threw the rope to her to tie to the cleat, and took care to lock up the interior door of the boat that led to the downstairs where the pharmaceuticals were kept.

Other medical equipment too. She could tell he was proud of this boat, this floating medical office.

When he jumped onto the dock, black bag in one hand, he looked at her. "Is your grandfather having trouble?"

"Granddad? He's fine." She tilted her head. "Isn't he?"

Artie didn't answer her question. "Jean-Paul? Is his elbow giving him trouble?"

"Not too bad." Though he did slip a few times going down the stairs today.

Artie frowned. "Then what do you want?"

His voice still had a bit of an edge to it, Blaine thought. "I want to ask your father to come to Camp Kicking Moose."

"Dad? Why?"

"We need his help. I want to ask him to come, but I thought I should check with you first."

"Why do you need my father's help?"

"The county is threatening to shut down the camp unless the violations are corrected by Memorial Day. Dad has some basic handyman skills, but nothing like Bob Lotosky. He's always depended on your dad's help."

Artie ran a hand over his beard. "Well . . . there is Peg to consider."

"I know. But I think she would understand that this is a desperate situation."

Artie didn't seem so sure. "Ask Peg. If she's okay with him coming, then so am I."

"Great. Thanks." He started down the dock, and she hurried after him. "Artie, I have an idea."

He slowed, but didn't stop, didn't turn. "What?"

"I want to turn the lighthouse into a fine dining restaurant."

At that, he pivoted. "A restaurant in a lighthouse." He seemed to roll the idea around like he were tasting a fine wine. He brought his eyes back to her face. "Interesting. Complicated, but interesting."

Shocked that he didn't dismiss her idea, she smiled. "I've already been to the county planning department to get it rezoned."

"Will they do it?"

"Yes, but apparently I triggered the county into conducting a long overdue inspection of Camp Kicking Moose with their most ardent inspector." She waved her palm in the air. "Hence . . . the need for your father's immediate help."

The tiniest of grins started on Artie's face, first with his eyes, then it spread to his mouth. "Bet Cam's not happy."

"Oh, yeah. On top of that, I asked her for a loan to remodel the lighthouse."

"I take it she said no."

"A resounding no." She lifted her shoulders in a cringe. "It didn't go well."

His eyes softened. "Well, you've never let anything stop you before."

She melted at his words. "Cam said you're dating a nurse. I wonder if that's smart, you know. I remember once you said that when doctors and nurses dated, all they did was talk shop." She quickly regretted her words as he raised an eyebrow at her.

"Seriously, you did not just say that."

"What do you mean?"

"You don't see the irony? You're a chef and you brought your French-chef boyfriend home to meet your family."

"Jean-Paul is *not* my boyfriend!"

"And the nurse is not my girlfriend." Artie glanced at his watch. "I'm running late." He turned and sprinted down the dock.

Bob Lotosky didn't even let Blaine finish explaining when she called him to ask if he'd help fix the many violations of the camp.

"I'll be there. We'll get it all done."

"Even the paint is peeling."

"Probably the salt air." He pronounced it *salt eh-ah*. "I'll bring my tools."

The very next afternoon, Bob arrived on the Never Late Ferry and walked into the Lunch Counter like a local.

Peg nearly dropped her coffeepot. "So you came after all," she said.

"So I came after all," he answered. And then suddenly they were in each other's arms, and Blaine had to look away.

There was a part of her that had always held out hope Peg and her dad might find their way to each other. But apparently, Bob Lotosky beat him to it.

Bob Lotosky and Peg Legg acted like they were teenagers—holding hands, whispering to each other, exchanging smiles when there was no reason to. It was both embarrassing—after all, they were past middle age, edging near old age—and endearing. And, Blaine had to admit, it was charming to witness how love knew no age boundaries.

But then there was Dad. Alone. She looked for any signs of regret or remorse from him, any hint that he was disappointed he'd missed his chance with Peg. There were none. Just the opposite—he had a skip in his step whenever he was around Bob Lotosky. The two of them would go off to repair things, which meant that Bob fixed things and Dad carried his tools, handing him each one when needed, like a nurse to a surgeon.

Poor Dad.

There were two reasons Paul enjoyed spending time around Bob Lotosky. First, the man had an uncanny knack for knowing exactly how to repair things. Anything. Artie said it came from the farming life. You learned to make do or do without, because you couldn't stop work to go find a part. Paul had never realized that duct tape was a man's best friend, but after shadowing Bob, he would never be without it again. It could even fix a leak in a canoe.

The second reason Paul was happy to trot behind Bob all day long was that it gave him an excuse to stay away from his father, the world's laziest man. He was either on the front porch reading a newspaper or sitting in Paul's favorite chair, watching TV in the living room. His presence irked Paul to no end. Whenever Paul asked how long he planned to stay, his father would respond with an enigmatic, "As long as it takes."

What on earth did that mean? Paul didn't even want to know.

Blaine sat in the chair across from Jean-Paul in the living room, waiting for a commercial in the golf tournament on TV so she could ask him a question. Waiting until he could be "unglued" from the TV was a change.

As soon as the commercial began, she broke in. "Do you want to go outside for a while and get some fresh air?"

"No. Eez safer here."

Twice now, Jean-Paul had tripped over Cooper's puppy as it dashed around the house, leash-free. Blaine knew she had to talk fast before the commercial ended and boring golf resumed. "Jean-Paul, when you spend time with my grandfather . . . do you think that he . . . well . . . is he . . . ?" Her voice drizzled off.

He set the remote down and looked at her. "*Ça sent le sapin?*"

It was a common French expression. Literally, it meant that one sensed the fir tree, the wood commonly used for coffins. In Americanese, it meant having one foot in the grave. Slowly, she nodded.

He looked out the window at her grandfather on the porch, reading the newspaper. Then he turned to Blaine. "Oui."

Bob Lotosky had studied Camp Kicking Moose's forty-five violations and made a plan. He organized the family into teams and gave them daily work assignments—if they weren't at work, they were expected to do their part at the camp. Bob's edict included Granddad and Jean-Paul, Cam and Maddie. The four of them were given the task of finding tradesmen who could get to Moose Manor fast: carpenters, plumbers, electricians, roofers. Cam's job was to set up delivery schedules of gravel, lumber, and other materials. None of it was physically demanding, but at least they were contributing. Dad, Cooper, Blaine, Seth, and Rick (when he was home) were given hard labor tasks but they dared not complain; Bob worked more than all of them combined. He was up at dawn working, took brief meal breaks for sustenance, and kept working until the day's light was gone. He slept on a sleeping bag on the floor in the living room. And he did it all because the Grayson family were friends of Peg.

Today's focus had been rerouting the rainwater that pooled underneath the cabin called Never Enough Thyme by installing a French drain—which pleased Jean-Paul to hear, though he had no idea what it was.

By six thirty, Blaine and Cooper needed a break and went to the house. They kept working. It was a perfect spring evening in Maine, so ideal that even the ever-present mosquitos were elsewhere. Cooper had a craving for lemonade, so Blaine helped him make it, and they took the pitcher to share with Jean-Paul and Granddad on the porch.

"This is a pretty special property," Granddad said, with a trace of awe in his voice.

Blaine smiled. She would have to tell Dad about that all-too-rare compliment from his father. "Beautiful, don't you think?" It almost looked like a painting. The large expanse of grass in front of the house had a velvety lime-green sheen, recently fertilized by Bob Lotosky. The pine trees that rimmed the property had been properly trimmed, recently pruned by Bob Lotosky. But the sunset that filled the sky with streaks of pink and purple and orange, that was God's handiwork. Sunsets were a special time for Blaine, almost a sacred one.

Granddad nodded. "Beautiful."

"But not," Jean-Paul said with a smile in his voice, "so lovely as Paris."

"To the French, if you dropped a pin in the center of the universe," Blaine said, "it would . . ." She waved her palm to cue Jean-Paul.

"Land on Paris," he said and everyone laughed.

They were quiet for a while, watching the sun inch its way slowly toward the horizon until it disappeared, and the vibrant colors in the sky deepened.

Blaine let out a contented sigh. "The only kinds of sunsets that I don't like are the ones I miss."

"Oui," Jean-Paul said. "Sunsets should never go unnoticed."

Cooper pointed to the first star now visible in the sky. "Reminds me of popcorn," he said. "I'm gonna go make some." He jumped up and ran inside.

They sat quietly for a moment or two, until Jean-Paul said, "Light eez different here."

"Different than Paris?" Blaine said. "The city of lights?"

"Oui. Everyzing here takes on a gray-blue hue in zee morning—"

"We call that fog," she said.

"Late in zee day comes zee yellow cast. But in zee middle of zee day, zere's a glare in zee sky coming from zat direction." He pointed past the carriage house.

"Maybe because the ocean is over there."

Jean-Paul seesawed his hand. "Maybe so. But zee light, it eez changing all zee time."

Pretty perceptive, Blaine thought. She'd never really noticed how the light took on different hues throughout the day.

Jean-Paul picked up his crutch and pulled himself up. "I go after my little friend. Last time he burnt zee popcorn bag and zee aroma offended my sensibilities for zee entire day."

After he'd hobbled inside, Blaine turned to Granddad. "Pretty

sure he meant to say the burnt popcorn aroma offended his senses."
She fished a lemon seed out of her glass. "I wish lemons didn't
have these bothersome seeds."

"I wish a lot of things," Granddad said.

"Me too."

"So tell me," Granddad said after finishing off his lemonade.
"What's the deal with that little French guy? And what about the
doctor with the beard? Who's in love with whom? I can't really
tell."

Blaine nearly choked on her lemonade. What? Where was the
small talk?

Fortunately, at just that moment, out came Cooper with a big
bowl of popcorn, Jean-Paul hobbling not far behind him. The
smell of popcorn brought Cam downstairs—and happily she was
no longer in a tizzy about the camp violations once Bob Lotosky
arrived on the scene. Dad and Seth and even Bob came up from
the cabin where they'd been working, and Maddie drove in from
town and joined them. The gray cat showed up, though he kept
one eye on the puppy sleeping by Cooper's feet. Rick was the only
one missing. They all sat on the porch and chatted about their day.
And in that moment, Blaine noticed, the world felt still.

Twenty-Three

CAM PERCHED ON THE STOOL at the Lunch Counter, polishing off an English muffin sandwich, Blaine's specialty. In it was a fried egg, crisp, thick apple-smoked bacon, white sharp cheddar cheese—melted just the right amount—and avocado. It was her second sandwich this morning.

"Want another?" Blaine said. "A triplet special?"

"Very funny." Still hungry, Cam was actually considering a third sandwich. "I like Jean-Paul."

Putting dishes in the dishwasher, Blaine grinned but didn't glance at her sister. "You love his cooking."

"Yes. And his advice. He gives great advice."

"That he does."

"He should consider being a life coach."

"Tell him that." Blaine seemed pleased. "I'm glad you're getting to know him."

Cam drained the last of her iced tea and pulled out her wallet. "Actually, what I really think is that he should be the father of your children."

"What?" Blaine slammed the door shut on the dishwasher.

"He's perfect for you."

"Except for the fact that we aren't in love. Jean-Paul and I are

218

only friends. Entirely platonic. He will return to Paris, and I have my life here."

Cam leaned forward. "Blaine, don't let this one get away. Trust me. I know these things."

"But you don't. In fact, you have a terrible track record with relationships. It's a miracle you're married to Seth."

"That's my point exactly. You're just like me. You're lucky to have Jean-Paul. Guys like him and Seth don't come along every day. Especially on a tiny island off the coast of Maine." Cam grabbed a peach out of a bowl and sank her teeth into it. "Don't blow this one, Blaine, like you did with Artie."

"Artie?"

"Just remember . . . a good man is hard to find."

Cam eased off the stool as delicately as possible, blew a kiss at Blaine, and left the diner. Standing by her car, hunting through her purse for keys, she heard Blaine call her name. When she turned around, she saw her sister striding toward her.

"Cam, did you tell Artie why I left the culinary school in Maine?"

Hand still rooting around inside her purse, Cam glanced at her. There were two bright pink spots on Blaine's cheeks. "You mean, because of the mess with the married instructor? Yes. I told him."

"How did you find out, anyway?"

"Maddie told me."

"Maddie!" Blaine's voice jumped a decibel. "And so you told Artie?"

"He asked why you left. I told him." Cam pulled out her keys. "I would have thought you'd told him yourself." She opened the car door. "If you're just friends, then it really shouldn't matter, right?"

As she saw Blaine whirl around and head back into the diner, she realized she shouldn't have added that last part.

Blaine knew Maddie saved ten minutes for herself in between clients, so she waited on the church office's porch steps for the door to the basement to open. She waited, and she mentally rehearsed a number of Bible verses she had memorized about anger, thinking she would need them to keep her cool upon returning home. But she assumed she'd need them for Cam, not Maddie.

A fool gives full vent to his anger, but a wise man keeps himself under control. . . . In your anger do not sin. . . . A hot-tempered man stirs up dissension but a patient man calms a quarrel.

The door opened and a teenage girl walked out, holding a box of tissues. Blaine's heart softened. There were bigger problems in this world than hers.

As soon as the girl reached the street, Blaine knocked on the door and went in. "Maddie, why did you tell Cam about the married instructor?"

Maddie looked up from her desk in surprise. "Blaine, you're my sister. Cam's your sister too. It's not right to keep secrets from each other. Not those kinds of secrets."

"I don't know what you told her, but she interpreted it all wrong. And *she* told Artie. *That's* why Artie is so angry with me. That's why he didn't speak to me for two years." Upset, disappointed, betrayed, she turned to leave.

"Blaine! Wait. Please wait."

She stopped at the door, but she didn't turn around.

"I apologize for breaking your trust. I really do. I should have told you sooner. But why *didn't* you tell Artie? Maybe that's the core of what's really wrong between the two of you. So why didn't you tell him yourself?"

Blaine dropped her chin. "I don't know."

Paul drove into town with a long list of items from the hardware store over in Mount Desert Island. He parked his truck just as the ferry pulled away from the dock. *Blast.* These were the moments when he missed that large sandbar that had appeared twice a day when the tide receded, as it was now. Large enough to drive his truck over and back again. He decided to pop into the Lunch Counter to say hello to Peg and Blaine while he waited for the ferry to return. As he walked into the diner, he inhaled the smell of coffee, and it lifted his spirits. Coffee had that kind of restorative power. Standing over in the kitchen, Peg gave him a wave and held up a mug.

"Is Blaine here?"

Peg frowned. "She went up the road to talk to Maddie about something. But she made the coffee, if that's what you're really asking."

"In that case, I'd love a cup. To go, please." He sat on a stool and held up a long list. "Bob sent me on errands."

Peg grinned. "If he sends you off on errands in the morning, then what he really wants is a little peace and quiet. He likes to work alone." She poured hot water into a paper to-go cup, dropped a tea bag in it, and held it out to him. "He says you follow him around like a puppy."

What? Could that be? Had Paul been managed? Frowning, he took a sip of the too-hot tea from Peg and winced, just as the bells on the door jingled.

"Well, if it isn't Dr. Lotosky," Peg said, smiling at Artie as he settled onto a stool next to Paul. "Full breakfast?"

"Morning. Just one cup of coffee in a to-go cup, please." He paused, looking around. "Hold on. Who made the coffee?"

Peg frowned at him. "Blaine did. And I'm going to charge you double just for asking that." She poured a to-go cup of coffee as Paul watched longingly, and handed it to Artie.

Artie swiveled on the chair to face Paul. "Tell your father I'll be out at the camp later today to see him."

Paul took another sip of tea. Still too hot. "Why do you keep coming out to check on my father?"

"I can't tell you. Doctor-patient confidentiality." He sipped the coffee. Looking pleased with its taste, he took another sip. "Your voice is sounding pretty solid these days."

Paul thought so too. Still a ways to go, but he could carry on longer conversations without his voice wearing out or sounding grainy. "So . . . you consider my father to be one of your patients?"

"Well, didn't he faint right outside the diner?"

"That was over a month ago."

"Was it?"

Answer a question with a question. Paul recognized the strategy. "So you're not going to tell me, are you?"

Artie gazed at him unflinchingly. "Tell you what?"

Paul scowled, drank back the rest of his horrible tea, and walked to the door.

"That man needs help finding a good woman," he overheard Peg tell Artie. "He's getting real tetchy."

Tetchy? Me?! Paul had stopped in for a friendly visit and ended up with nothing close to friendliness. *And no, Peg Legg, I do not need anyone's help to find a good woman.*

What bothered him most was Artie's deflection about his father. It certainly wouldn't surprise Paul if his father had some health issues. Good grief, the man had been a functioning alcoholic for most of his adult life. Liver cirrhosis? Diabetes?

Paul glanced over Bob Lotosky's list and realized that, indeed, he was getting sent off on a fool's errand. There was nothing on the list that couldn't be found somewhere at the camp, probably in the carriage house. These items could wait for another day.

Maybe a certain conversation with his father, he finally admitted, was overdue.

When Paul pulled his truck to a stop at the camp, he saw Bob Lotosky disappear quickly into the cabin with stuck windows. So Bob *was* trying to ditch him! Just the way Paul was avoiding his father.

Enough of this contagious avoidance strategy. He used it, his father used it, Bob Lotosky used it. Maybe most men in America used it.

How many times had Maddie warned Paul that avoidance was ineffective, a poor coping method, that it only backfired. As usual, she was right. When would he ever learn to listen to his wise, meddlesome middle daughter?

There was his father on the porch, hiding behind a large newspaper, so Paul shut the door of the truck and climbed the porch steps. He sat in the chair beside him. "Are you sick?"

Behind the paper, his father grunted and Paul remembered that particular grunt. It was the closest his father could get to a yes.

"Is that why you're here? Do you need money to help with medicine? Treatments?"

"Don't need your money." He went back to reading the newspaper. "Besides, from where I sit, I wouldn't think you have a penny to spare."

A small truck drove into the driveway and parked. Bob came out of the cabin to greet the electrician he had hired for a few problems too complicated that even he couldn't untangle them.

"This must be the costliest summer camp to maintain on the eastern seaboard."

Felt like it lately. "So then, why did you come to Three Sisters Island? Why now? And how long do you plan to stay?" Paul's voice was holding up quite well. "Don't say 'as long as it takes,' because I don't know what *it* means."

"What it means is . . . I'm staying as long as it takes to patch things up before I kick the bucket."

Paul shot a look at him. Was he being serious? His father had never been a man to share personal feelings. Was he actively dying . . . or was this just a vague and general remark? A plea for attention? He had absolutely no idea how to respond to a comment like that. Finally, he decided to take the "blunt for blunt" tactic. "Elaborate." *Blast*. The rasp returned in his voice.

His father was hidden behind the newspaper. "The ol' body is wearing out."

"That's not what I meant." *Double blast*. His voice was grinding down to gravel. "If you really think you're dying, why are you here?"

"Just to tidy up a few loose ends." He dropped the newspaper so he could glare at Paul. "Not to worry. I won't interfere with your precious camp. Just like I never interfered with your precious family. Or your precious radio career."

My precious camp. My precious family. My precious radio career. It was hard to feel empathy for the man. *Don't say it, Paul. Don't say it.* "But you did interfere once, Dad. The time you put my youngest daughter in grave danger." Argh. He said it.

Utter, cold silence. His father returned to his newspaper. Paul rose and turned to the house. And there was Blaine, standing at the open window, staring at his father with an odd look on her face.

A forgotten memory emerged, diamond sharp. Blaine had completely blocked out that horrible visit from her grandfather. The last visit. For a long time afterward, she would overhear Mom bring it up, always in a worried tone. Then Dad would shut down the conversation. "No more what-if's, Corinna," he would say. "It's over, it's done, it won't happen again."

Also for a long time afterward, Cam took pleasure in telling the story through her lens. Blaine was *this close* to being kidnapped and held for ransom—*this close*, she emphasized by holding her thumb and index finger together—and she had strongly recommended that her parents not pay the ransom. "Nev-ah negotiate with terrorists," she would say in her Winston Churchill voice, wiggling her chin like it was full of wattles. Maddie would frown at Cam and reassure Blaine that they would definitely have paid a ransom, if there'd been one. But then Maddie admitted that she wasn't really sure if there was or wasn't.

Only Blaine had known the whole story. Only Blaine and Grand-dad Grayson, Mom and Dad. Memories streamed down like rain.

BLAINE, AGE 5

On her fifth birthday, Blaine had been given a golden retriever puppy named Winslow. The pup was sweet natured, but overly enthusiastic about most everything. He'd grown so big that he was hard to manage for everyone but Dad, who was seldom home. Mom complained, Cam complained, even Maddie complained . . . but Blaine adored Winslow.

Granddad Grayson visited the family once a year, in February, before Dad's baseball season started. Mom wouldn't let Granddad Grayson come to visit unless Dad was home. Something about Granddad made Mom and Dad cranky, even though he just sat in a chair and read the newspaper.

But that was before Winslow came into their life. It turned out that Granddad Grayson, who showed little interest in his granddaughters, did love dogs. He volunteered to take Winslow on walks, tossed a ball outside with him to tire him out, and even showed Blaine a few training tricks, like how to teach the pup to shake his paw. The visit had been going well, really well, and Blaine had noticed that Mom and Dad were acting less jumpy, less prickly, and more like themselves.

Until the afternoon when Granddad Grayson offered to take Winslow for a walk and Blaine asked to go along. Her mom hemmed and hawed, but her dad said to let them go. "It would be good for Blaine to work with Winslow on a lead." Blaine wasn't allowed to walk the dog on her own because she couldn't control him. The last time she tried, she came home with bloody knees after he'd wrapped around and around her with the leash and she fell.

On this afternoon, Winslow was behaving so well on the leash that they walked and walked, all the way into town. Granddad Grayson noticed a bar, and licked his lips, and asked Blaine if she might like to wet her whistle before they headed home. Blaine liked whistles.

225

So Granddad tied Winslow to a bike rack outside and in they went. It was dim inside, and overly warm, and smelled musty—a stale cigarette smoke stink that reminded her of Libby's grandmother's house. Blaine asked if she could take Winslow home, but Granddad promised they'd just be a minute and then head straight home. He ordered a lemonade for Blaine and something for himself. Then another something for himself. Blaine finished her lemonade and asked again if they could go home. "In a minute," Granddad said, ordering another something for himself. She went to a plastic-covered booth—so sticky!—and sat down while Granddad watched a football game on a large television. She rocked her feet, waiting. And waiting. And waiting.

The next thing she knew, Mom was shaking Blaine, hugging her tight, sobbing. Dad was yelling at Granddad, telling him to leave and never come back.

Apparently, Granddad had eventually left the bar and gone back to the house. He'd remembered Winslow, but he'd forgotten all about Blaine, who'd fallen sound asleep on the plastic-covered booth.

Twenty-Four

PAUL WALKED UP AND DOWN the beach, phone pressed to his ear. "All three daughters are mad at each other again. I don't know what happened. When they were children, at least they would shout at each other and get it over with. As young adults, the anger goes quiet and smolders."

"The good thing," his friend said, "is that they seem to find their way back again. Maybe the nice part of having adult children is relinquishing the parent-fix-all role."

Good advice. They talked for a few more minutes before Paul glanced at his watch, shocked to realize they'd been on the phone this morning for over an hour. The time always went too fast.

Bob Lotosky was waiting for a certain drill bit to come in on the Never Late Ferry, and this wasn't just a fool's errand kind of tool. Paul picked up his pace, climbing the hill to where he'd parked his truck. "Gotta run," he said, hurrying past Peg as she watered the plants in the window boxes outside her diner. He hopped into his truck and slipped the key in the ignition. Something jumped through the passenger window and into the truck, landing on the seat with a sudden thud.

"It's you!" Paul cried, startled. "Why do you follow me everywhere I go?"

The cat. He was staring at Paul persistently. He was making some kind of point.

"I know, I know," Paul said, stroking his head. "She's very special."

The cat turned around three times and curled up in his lap.

On Sunday morning, Blaine came down the stairs, curling her hair into a knot at the base of her neck. She saw Jean-Paul and Granddad sitting on the porch together. Cooper and the puppy were down on the lawn near the boathouse. Cooper took daily training sessions with the puppy very seriously, far more seriously than the puppy took Cooper. She saw Jean-Paul drop his cards on the table between the chairs, shaking his head, laughing. The window was open, and Blaine wondered what Jean-Paul and Granddad were talking about. She tiptoed over in an effort to listen.

It was not at all what she expected.

"It eez very brave of you," Jean-Paul said, "to reach out to your son."

Granddad grunted. "It's not working."

"Eez working. Eez just not easy."

"I don't blame Paul. I wasn't much of a father."

Blaine watched through the screen to see Jean-Paul reach out and place his hand on Granddad's shoulder. "Oui. You are broken and flawed . . . and yet you love your son Paul so much zat you pursued him here. It eez zee same with God, who has no brokenness, no flaws, only love. He pursues you. He chases you down. Imagine, Grandpa-Pa. Just imagine how much God loves you."

Granddad was quiet for so long that Blaine stepped away, intending to leave, then pivoted when she suddenly heard a strange sound. Her grandfather was sobbing.

"Not me. Not after the life I've lived." His shoulders shuddered as he wept.

Jean-Paul let him cry, until his sobs finally subsided. "God's

love eez a mystery, Grandpa-Pa. It eez unchanging. It eez uncon-
ditional."

"Too late." Granddad shook his head. "It's too late for me."

"No, no. Eez never too late, Grandpa-Pa. Some are drawn into
relationship with God early in life, others at zee end of life, and
some along zee way. Eez another mystery. All zat matters eez zat
you cling to him now. When you hear from God, your heart must
respond. Eez easy as zat. *C'est facile.*" He patted his shoulder
again, like a father with a child. "So then. Come to church with
us today."

Another long silence. At long last, Granddad gave a short nod
of his head. Then the puppy ran away from Cooper and down
the driveway, and he chased after it, yelling, and the moment was
over. Blaine tiptoed away.

Granddad Grayson did not reveal much about himself, but
Blaine had discovered that he rose at six o'clock in the morning,
no exceptions. And she also learned, from Peg, that he loved om-
elets. Since she found that out, she had started to make him an
omelet before she left for work at the Lunch Counter. She would
take it to him out on the porch and explain what was in it, as if he
had asked. "Today's selection," she said, "includes Havarti cheese,
which has a mild, nutty flavor. Spinach, lightly sautéed in garlic
oil. Mushrooms, roasted just to the point of caramelization." She
handed him the plate, along with a fork and napkin. "I'll get you
a refill of coffee before I head out."

He looked up at her. "Sit for a moment."

Why not? She had a few minutes to spare. As she sat, he took a
bite of the omelet, then paused. Swallowing, he nodded his pleasure.

That was enough thanks for Blaine. "I agree. Just the right
combination for a foggy morning."

Her gaze swept the front yard and she soaked up the evidence of springtime at Moose Manor. Purple lilacs bloomed in the yard. Blue hydrangeas, with their large green leaves against the house's foundation, were just starting to blossom.

Spring. A lovely reminder of how beautiful change can be.

Granddad polished off the omelet and set the empty plate on the small table. "I've been hearing something about a lighthouse."

She snapped her head to look at him. "How did you hear that?"

He pointed to the window behind him, where Jean-Paul lay sleeping on the couch. "He told me, and I quote, that 'you're a brilliant chef and you have a brilliant idea for this lighthouse.'"

Blaine sighed and leaned back in the rocker. "Not so sure about the brilliant part. And there are lots of obstacles to this idea." A serious lack of cash, for one. A complicated location to get to, for another. Then she slapped her knees. "But I'm not giving up. Just because something isn't easy doesn't mean it isn't doable." She rose and picked up his empty plate.

"So show me this lighthouse."

"You want to see it?"

"I do. I want to see what the big fuss is."

"Really?" She smiled, pleased. "I get off work at three o'clock." And high tide would ebb around ten this morning, so that would be perfect for their timing. But could Granddad get up and down the stairs? "I have to warn you that it's not an easy climb. The stairs from the beach are steep, and then there's the steps in the lighthouse. Jean-Paul barely made it on crutches."

He dismissed her warning with a flick of his hand. "I'll be at the diner at three."

Granddad Grayson arrived early at the diner to flirt with Peg, he said, which delighted her to no end, so much so that she refused to accept his money for the iced tea.

"You just keep coming back and fill my head with compliments," she said with a wink.

Blaine led him down the hill to Boon Dock, holding on to his elbow as if he were the gentleman and she were the lady. In truth, she was worried he would slip and fall. She helped him get settled into Dad's motorboat, found a life preserver for him, hopped back on the dock to untie the ropes from the cleats, and jumped back in. Happily, the water was calm this afternoon, with hardly a breeze. Still, she knew that rounding the tip of the island was a different story, even in low tide, even in mild weather. She bit her lip, wondering how to manage getting dinner guests to and from the lighthouse. That was the piece of her dream that she couldn't seem to work out. Would it end up like this? She imagined a well-dressed couple, eager to celebrate a special occasion, having to be delivered to the lighthouse in a humble outboard motor by Cooper, entirely dependent on the tides. That didn't sound terribly . . . sustainable.

The slap of the water against the bow of the boat tugged her out of her musing. "Hold on, Granddad. We're rounding the island. In a minute, look left and you'll see the lighthouse." She slowed the boat until she saw his hands grasp the side rails. Then she turned the handle to a higher speed and plowed ahead, into the Atlantic, carefully turning the boat until she was heading it straight to the beach, a gorgeous view of the lighthouse. Once the bow dug into the sand, she hopped out with a line and pulled it as far up the beach as she could.

Granddad looked up at the stairs. "That thing will hold?"

"It will. I promise." She wondered if he would change his mind, but he never flinched. Up the stairs he climbed—not quickly, but not bad for an old guy. Quicker than Jean-Paul did.

When he reached the top, he said, "Reminds me of my army days."

Blaine stopped. She'd never known her grandfather had been a soldier. "World War II?"

He scoffed. "I'm not quite that old. Nope. Vietnam."

Interesting. She climbed up behind him, then spread her palm in a grand gesture. "Behold . . . the future restaurant at Lighthouse Point."

He gazed up at it, and she wasn't sure what was running through his mind. Whatever it was, it was okay. It wouldn't stop her if he thought this was a ridiculous idea. This wasn't some hobby. It wasn't some whim. She'd been working toward this moment her whole life. She wanted this lighthouse. From the moment she first saw it, she'd felt some kind of strange connection to it. Period. It was her God-given dream. She wasn't going to let anyone discourage her from pursuing it.

"A little tricky to get here."

"Yes. I haven't quite got that part of it figured out yet."

He pointed to the meadow. "That reminds me of the army too."

"How so?"

"Could be a helicopter pad."

She whirled around. "You think a helicopter could land there?"

"I don't see why not, assuming the weather behaves. You know what they say. 'A cockpit is no place for an optimist.'"

A helicopter! Interesting. How would that work? She thought of the Nantucket couple that Peg had banished for life from the diner. If he had a private jet, he probably had a helicopter . . . or access to one. But wouldn't that mean Blaine was pandering to the summer people? She would be dependent on the very people Peg and other locals didn't want on the island. She wanted locals to come to the restaurant. She wanted the campers at her dad's camp to come.

She glanced at the motorboat. Maybe it could be both. The locals were comfortable with boats, narrow stairs, tide tables. The summer people . . . they could helicopter in. The menu—and the cost per meal—could adjust for the customers.

She looked at her grandfather. "Thank you, Granddad."

"For what?"

"For taking me seriously." She pointed to the lighthouse. "Want the nickel tour?"

"Let's go."

She showed him everything, starting with the keeper's cottage.

232

"This is where the cooking school will be held. I've got it all planned." A commercial kitchen she would design herself. One that would sail through Dr. Doom's persnickety inspections with flying colors. It was so much easier to start with the county planning department and work with their rules rather than go to them afterward, expecting to pass all the inspections. There was no such thing as the county making accommodations. They didn't bend. You had to do the bending.

"You planning to live here?"

"In the keeper's cottage? I . . . hadn't thought about it."

"You don't want to live at Moose Manor your whole life, do you?"

She walked to the small bedroom and peeked inside. Her mind started spinning with ideas. Why hadn't she thought of living here? It was brilliant!

They walked over to the lighthouse and went inside. "Dumbwaiter goes in here." Blaine pointed to an opening in the ceiling.

"Pulley system?"

"Yes. I've found a company that will put it in." She went to the stairs, then hesitated and pivoted around. "We don't have to go to the top. You can get the idea from here."

"You go, I'll follow." The look on his face told her he wasn't going to be dissuaded.

It took a while for her grandfather to climb the spiraling staircase to reach the top. He would pause now and then to peer out the window, an excuse to catch his breath. "Are we there yet?"

"Close." Not really. She tried to distract him. "Did you know that all lighthouses have a similar anatomy? All over the world, the design is nearly identical. Right down to landings every fifteen steps."

Plodding slowly up another level, he was breathing heavily.

Concerned he was getting winded, she stopped. "Should we take a break?"

"No. Keep going. Keep talking."

Oh boy. This climb was hard for him. "Um, did you know that the world's first recorded lighthouse was in Alexandria, Egypt?"

"Nope." He stopped at the landing and leaned on the stair railing.

Oh dear. She was going to have to find a way to accommodate older guests to the restaurant. "It was one of the Seven Wonders of the Ancient World."

Granddad started up the stairs again.

Okay, Blaine thought. The power of distraction was working. "Every night, they lit a huge bonfire at the top. It's said you could be thirty miles away and still see it."

"What"—*gasp*—"what happened to it?" *Gasp, gasp.*

She stopped to let him rest. "Earthquake. Wiped it out. But it was in use for, um, I think over fifteen hundred years." She went up a few more steps and stopped at the landing. "This is the watch room."

"What's it for?"

"The watch room is where the keepers kept their log." She started up another spiral of stairs and he groaned. "Not much farther. We're close." She stopped at the next landing. "This is the service room. It's where keepers would store cleaning equipment and tools or spare parts for the beacon."

"Why can't people eat in here?"

"I was thinking of using the gallery room. There's even a gallery deck that you can access that circles the tower. In fact, that platform might be better than the widow's walk." They went up another level. Waiting for her grandfather to join her, she glanced inside the gallery room, imagining tables filled with patrons, hearing the clinking of silverware and glasses.

He was puffing hard. "What's . . . a widow's walk?"

"It's another platform that lets you walk around outside. This one is outside of the lantern room, but the name isn't unique to lighthouses. A lot of coastal houses have a widow's walk. It comes from the wives of sailors who kept watch for their husbands' ships to return from the sea."

"Are we at the top yet?"

"Nearly. The lantern room is up here. This is where I thought people would dine too."

"What about the beacon?"

"It's been removed. The light had been permanently out since the lighthouse was decommissioned."

"Maybe you could add some kind of light coming from the cupola. Not so bright that you'd blind your patrons, but enough to give the lighthouse some authenticity." He nudged her elbow. "Besides, your sister can provide the electricity to light the lamp, right?"

Actually, yes. "Granddad, I'm glad you came today. You're giving me all kinds of ideas." He looked embarrassed, and she wondered if he hadn't had many compliments in his life. They walked out on the widow's walk and around the lighthouse, and it couldn't have been a more perfect day. Breezy, but not windy. The ocean looked blue-green, with just the right amount of light whitecaps. As she walked around, she pointed to the rooftop and chimney of Moose Manor, barely visible through the trees.

"Guessing it'll take some money to make this happen."

"Oh yeah. Plenty of it." Of which she had none. She remembered what Jean-Paul said. *Pray and release, pray and release.*

"What else would you do here if money wasn't a problem?"

Now, *that* was a wonderful question. She turned around and leaned her elbows against the windows, overlooking the large bluff. "Over there, I envisioned as a large vegetable and herb garden. Choosing seasonal foods, freshly picked and vine ripened, well, it's the best way to cook. It brings such integrity to the dishes. Plus, when I get the cooking school going, there's just no better classroom for a cook than the garden."

"How so?"

"A garden is the way to engage someone in the kitchen, just the best way. It wakes up the senses to taste and texture. Color too. I think students gain a direct appreciation for quality of fruits and vegetables and herbs when they pick them in the garden. Imagine the first bite of just-picked corn or vine-ripened tomatoes that are still hot from the sun. They're such basic pleasures, and they have a way of not only making you truly hungry but also truly satisfied. Then, when students go home, they'll be better prepared to evaluate food in the market. Is it fresh? Is it in season? What does it smell like? Where did it come from? And most important of all, does it make me hungry?"

He peered out the window. "You love this, don't you?"

"Passionately."

"You're fortunate to have something you feel that way about. Not many people do. Your dad did, with that radio career."

"Granddad, did you ever find something you were passionate about?"

He didn't answer for a long time. "I suppose so, but it came with a cost." He tipped his hand above his mouth like he was chugging from a bottle.

Ah, yes. Dad had spoken of his father's love of drinking.

"Blaine, if there's one piece of advice I could pass on to you . . ."

"Please do. I'm all about life lessons."

"Don't get to be my age and wonder how your life might have been different if you'd done one thing and not another."

Now it was Blaine's turn to remain quiet and introspective.

"So you need money for this project?"

She laughed. "Just a little." She had spoken to one bank in Bar Harbor and was shocked to learn the interest rates on small business loans. Tomorrow, after work, she thought she'd go down to the beach and call around to a few more banks.

Granddad put his hand in his jacket pocket and pulled out a check, folded in half. "Here you go. Make this place what you want it to be. Build your dream."

Blaine took the check. It was made out to her, in the amount of one hundred thousand dollars. Her eyes went wide with shock. "Granddad . . . oh no. I can't accept this."

"What else am I going to do with it? Let the government nip away at it? No ma'am. They've stolen enough from me in taxes. I want to see something from my hard-earned bucks. Something real. Something that lasts. And your lighthouse is just the thing."

She stared at the check, stunned.

"But . . ."

"No buts. No strings attached." He lifted a finger. "Actually, there is one string. I don't want you to tell anyone about this. Keep it between you and me, at least until I'm dead and buried."

"They'll ask, though. Everyone in the family will wonder where the money came from." She wondered if her dad would even want her to accept money from her grandfather. And such a vast amount! This was no small thing.

"Tell them that a silent investor came through. That's all they need to know." He looked down at his hands, and she saw that he had tremors. His hands shook ever so slightly.

"Granddad, is this because of that time you forgot me at the bar?"

He looked away. A long moment passed. "I was hoping you were too little to remember."

"Granddad, I forgive you. I really do. I've made plenty of mistakes in my own life. Plenty. You don't need to give me this money. You and I . . . we're good. We're okay."

He looked back at her. "I want to do this for you. It would make me happy if you'd accept." He reached over and squeezed her hand. "Just do your best with it."

She looked down at his hand, covered with blue veins and liver spots. It dawned on her that this was the first time he had ever touched her. First time. He wasn't one for hugging or kissing or even handshaking. Blaine wanted to hug him but was afraid he'd go into shock. "I'll do my best," she whispered. "My very best."

Twenty-Five

BLAINE STILL FELT A LITTLE DAZED about the money her grandfather had gifted her. Still dazed, still overwhelmed, but not so much that it prevented her from moving forward on the lighthouse at warp speed. She had learned a lesson from watching Bob Lotosky: make a plan, and then make it happen.

She spoke to all the tradesmen who came in and out of the camp, knowing their work had passed Bob's approval, and offered them work on the lighthouse. She decided to act as the general contractor, like Bob had done, and went out to the lighthouse a couple of times each day to check on activity and progress. Peg, bless her, was fully supportive even though it meant Blaine was in and out of the diner.

In another gift, Peg had also encouraged Bob to help Blaine as a consultant. Each evening, before Bob left Moose Manor, he would sit with Blaine outside on the porch, away from listening ears. She had decided to not tell her family that she had started to renovate the lighthouse. Not yet. Together, she and Bob would go over the day's work at the lighthouse. Mostly, Bob would help problem solve.

Blaine learned some other valuable lessons from Bob's tutelage. Most problems had solutions. Most mistakes could be fixed.

She had just tied her dad's boat to the slip when she saw Artie's *Lightship* come toward the dock. She didn't even wait for him to jump on the dock to tie the ropes to the cleats. "Artie, I think we need to have a talk."

Artie glanced at his watch. That habit of his reminded her of the way her dad would point to his throat when he didn't want to talk anymore.

She wasn't buying it. "I'd like you to set aside some time to have a conversation with me when you're not about to bolt off. Is that really asking so much?"

"I can give you five minutes now while I lock up."

He helped her onto the *Lightship* and walked into the cabin. She followed behind.

Five lousy little minutes? She knew she'd have to talk fast, but she was distracted by the telemedicine equipment inside the cabin. It looked like the interior of an ambulance, with monitors, a bed, several computers. It was . . . impressive.

Artie turned off a machine that was making a humming sound, then locked a cabinet that she assumed was full of pharmaceuticals. "So what is it you want to talk about?" His expression revealed annoyance, which worried Blaine more than a frown.

She drew herself up as tall as she could, as he was quite a bit taller than her. "I should have told you why I left for Paris."

"I agree." His lips compressed and a muscle twitched in his jaw. "So . . . why didn't you?"

Why didn't she? She'd given that question a great deal of thought ever since Maddie posed it but couldn't puzzle it out. Standing there in front of him, a shaft of understanding hit her. On an unconscious level, she had been aware that she had kept that information from Artie because she was afraid it would harm their friendship if he knew. She was terrified of losing it.

So she didn't tell him. And she lost the friendship anyway.

She stepped close to him, scowling, her hands balled on her hips. "I didn't want to make more of a mess of everything by telling anyone about it." That was as close as she could get to telling him the whole story.

Even that wasn't enough for him. "Blaine, I can't do this. I'm here to do a job. I just can't add you into the mix. It's too much." His look was long and steady. "I think we just need to accept that that was then and this is now. Some people are just meant for a specific time in a person's life."

Some, maybe. But not us. "Artie, I know I hurt you and I know you didn't do a thing to deserve it. I just don't know why you feel hurt."

Artie looked hard into Blaine's eyes, in a way that made her heart do a somersault. "You really don't," he said flatly, regarding her with dismay.

A moment of silence filled the room, like the quiet right before a shock of lightning hit the sky. From low in his throat came a rumble of frustration. Artie stepped forward, grasped her face in his hands, and kissed her.

Emotions flooded her in swift succession, one thought after the other. Soft, firm lips. Artie's lips. Against hers. Glowing, sparkling, warmth. She'd had no idea, no idea, that kissing Artie would be like this, fire and ice and—

Artie pulled back abruptly.

His chest hitched with his breath. "I'm sorry," he said, his voice hoarse. "I shouldn't have done that." He stepped back, his hand raking through his hair and then draping around his neck as he looked around the floor. His eyes landed on his black bag and he grabbed it, then steered her out of the cabin, locking it behind him. He climbed on the dock and turned to give her a hand up, avoiding her eyes.

As soon as both of her feet were on the dock, he tried to release her hand, but she held on tight, forcing him to look at her. "Why did you kiss me?"

"I don't know."

"Why?" she asked again.

His eyes traveled to her lips and stayed there. "I guess . . . I always wondered what it would be like to kiss you," he said. He pulled his hand away and strode down the dock, leaving her there.

So . . . did it knock you out like it did me? Or did it disappoint?

If his answer was supposed to make her feel better, it didn't. Things had gotten even weirder between them.

All that day, as Blaine worked in the diner, her mind wandered back to that moment in the cabin of the *Lightship*. To Artie's face. His eyes. His deep voice. That kiss.

That kiss. She had never, ever, *ever* felt affected by a kiss like that.

For Pete's sake! It was just a kiss. One little kiss. One magical kiss. One lightning-boltish, shocking, yet tender and—stop! She had to *stop* reliving that moment. She had to stop thinking about Artie! Why was it so difficult to get him out of her head? She wished she could reach into her mind with a broom and sweep away all knowledge of him. Something. Anything!

Rick jolted the bed so abruptly that it woke Maddie out of a sound sleep. He was sitting up, panting, hand splayed on his chest.

"What's wrong?"

"Just . . . a shock."

She sat upright. "Should I call 911?"

He took his time answering, as if he wasn't sure he wanted to say too much. "No, no. It'll settle down."

"Promise me you'll see the doctor about it."

"I will. I'll call her."

Facing Rick, Maddie rested her head in the palm of her hand. "Now."

He blew out a breath and slowly lay back down. "Everything's fine now."

Maddie knew that the doctor had warned Rick to expect shocks, as the ICD implanted in his chest was constantly monitoring his heart rate, and shocks were sent out to slow the heart, to restore it to its normal rhythm. Shocks were to be expected.

But not one like that.

"Rick, if you don't call the doctor now, I'll do it myself."

He rolled his eyes and went downstairs to use the landline phone. A few minutes later, he came back up to their bedroom. "She said it's probably nothing to worry about."

"And?"

"And she wants to see me."

"When?"

He cleared his throat. "Now."

She stilled. "I'm coming with you."

"Nope, nope. You have a full day of clients. I've got things I can do over in Bar Harbor. I'll jump on the ferry and be back by noon." He kissed her on top of her head and left, eager to get on with his day and avoid more worrisome questions.

Blaine had just come out of the Lunch Counter to water the window boxes when she heard someone call for help. She spun around to see Artie, close to the dock, leaning over an unconscious body. She ran down the hill and stopped abruptly when she recognized Rick, lying on the ground.

"Blaine—go get Maddie!" Artie was digging into his black bag.

"Is Rick . . . ?"

Artie kept his head down. "Get Maddie." He glanced up at Blaine. "Now."

"What do I tell her?"

He barely paused to fix his eyes on hers. "That she needs to hurry."

Normally, Maddie didn't go to her little office in the basement of the church until closer to nine, but on this morning, she had felt anxious and restless and decided to go to town, to prepare for a busy day of clients. She knew she'd be distracted until she heard from Rick about his doctor's appointment—*Please, Lord, let it be as simple as replacing a battery. Let it be nothing, Lord.* Deep down, she sensed a foreboding.

So when she heard footsteps pounding and somehow knew the reason for the pounding footsteps was Rick, she wasn't at all surprised to hear, through Blaine's panic, that Rick was unconscious on Boon Dock. A calm covered Maddie, as if whatever she was dreading was finally here. She grabbed her purse and dashed out the door, saw Tillie on the porch steps with a worried look on her face, told her to please cancel all her appointments for the day, then raced down Main Street toward Boon Dock as fast as a six-months-pregnant woman could race. By the time she reached the parking lot that lined the beach, someone had brought Artie a stretcher from the *Lightship* and they'd moved Rick onto it. Artie glanced up when he saw her approach. "He's alive, but still unconscious. His heart is in arrhythmia. I'm taking him over to Mount Desert Hospital. You can come along in the ship." He noticed Blaine had joined them. "Blaine, can you pilot the boat?"

"I think so." Then, more confidently, "Yes. Yes, of course."

Maddie and Blaine followed behind the men who carried the stretcher. On the *Lightship*, she stayed out of Artie's way as he hooked Rick up to all kinds of equipment and radioed over to the hospital. As Maddie listened to Artie's description of her husband and the request to have an ambulance to meet the ship, the feeling of peace continued. So much so that Blaine, at the helm, kept taking second looks at her.

"Are you all right?" she whispered. "You seem strangely all right."

Eyes glued to Rick's face, holding his hand—it was so very cold—Maddie said, "I'm all right for now." She hadn't stopped praying since Blaine had arrived in her office. *God, keep him alive. Make him well, Lord.* Prayer was her lifeline right now. Each time she stopped, icy fear started to overwhelm her.

"What can I do to help?"

Maddie grabbed Blaine's arm and said, almost fiercely, "Please, pray, pray, pray."

"I am," Blaine said.

Moments later, the *Lightship* docked and the paramedics were moving Rick onto the ambulance. Artie seemed to know them, and when they asked if he'd like to come, he said to go on ahead and he'd follow with Maddie and Blaine.

"Wait," Maddie said. She didn't wait for permission but clambered into the ambulance and kissed Rick on the forehead. "I love you. I love you so much, Rick O' Shea. Please don't leave us. We need you." She thought she saw his eyelids flicker a little, but maybe not. Then the paramedics made a motion and she hopped out.

Watching the ambulance go, she turned to Artie. "He'll be all right, won't he?" She searched his eyes. Blaine did too.

"He'll get good care at the hospital. The best."

"But he'll be all right? Artie, I need the truth."

Artie kept his eyes on the ambulance. "These are the facts that I know: Rick's heart is racing, his breathing is shallow, his pulse is faint."

"But, Artie, you know Rick," Blaine said, in a voice of authority that surprised Maddie. "He's more than a body with facts."

Artie gazed at Blaine, and Maddie could see his eyes soften. "Then I would say he has a better chance than most."

How would Blaine ever forget the hours that followed? She stayed quietly by her sister's side in the waiting room of the hospital's ER, watching the door each time it swung open, hoping for news about Rick. Artie stayed as long as he could, until he knew that Rick had been stabilized and admitted as a patient, and promised to return.

Blaine walked him out to his car. "Did Rick have a heart attack?"

"Dr. Turner will fill you in when she has all the tests back."

Blaine gave him a look.

"What?"

"You know more and you aren't saying."

"Honestly, Blaine, I don't. Myocardial dysfunction is concerning."

"Speak English, please."

"There's something funny going on with Rick's heart."

"But it was caught in time, right?"

"I sure hope so."

"You were there, right when we needed you."

"That's what the state of Maine pays me for."

"Artie, do you always have to act so cold and professional?"

"I am a professional. But I didn't realize I am acting cold."

"You are. Chilly. Like the wind from a heavy fog."

He paused, then a slight smile lit his eyes. "I'll try to warm up." He unlocked his car and opened the door. "How's it going with the lighthouse restaurant?"

"Slow. But good. I . . . have an investor."

"Who?"

"Can't tell you that." When he rolled his eyes at that, she said, "See how it feels? A chilly wind." They locked eyes. "Artie, thank you. For everything. For Rick, for Jean-Paul's injuries, for Granddad—"

Artie tossed his medical bag on the passenger side. "Quite an eventful summer for the Grayson family."

"It is."

"Glad you came back?"

She wouldn't change a thing. Leaving for Paris was the right decision. But oh my goodness, she missed Artie. She'd been missing him for a very long time. "There's no place I'd rather be."

Without another word, he slipped into the driver's seat. But she caught the smile on his face.

It was nearing midnight, and Maddie could see Blaine's eyes start to droop. No wonder. She'd been working so hard lately at the diner, and she'd been up since five a.m. Maddie had encouraged her to go home, but she refused to leave the hospital, not until someone else came. Dad wanted to come, but Maddie said no, to stay at Moose Manor and keep working on the violations. She didn't really want everyone crowded in this little room, waiting for news. Cam said she was coming in the morning whether Maddie wanted her or not. As Blaine nodded off, Maddie covered her with a blanket, feeling a sweep of love for her two sisters. They didn't always get along, but when push came to shove, they were there when they needed each other.

Maddie couldn't sit still. Every nerve taut, she paced around the room, arms held tight across her middle, absolutely unable to settle her soul.

Rick's eyes, the shocked hollow of his mouth, stayed with her. The peace she had felt earlier had left her, replaced by an endless spin of what-if's? She almost suffocated with the physical symptoms of fear, a racing pulse, a churning stomach, and pounding heart.

Suppose Rick did die . . . How could Maddie live without him? How could their baby grow up not knowing him?

At one o'clock in the morning, Rick's mother arrived at the hospital. Blaine had called Maeve O'Shea while they were following the ambulance. She was planning to come up next weekend but dropped everything and drove all evening. Maddie couldn't remember ever feeling so glad to see anyone. She hadn't seen Maeve since Christmas and was happy to see she looked just the same. Maeve never changed, and Maddie was so grateful for that. Grateful for everything about her mother-in-law. Her strength, her solidness, her faith. Calm and comforting. Rick had so many of his mother's qualities—her strength and her rock-solid faith—yet he also had such a desperate restlessness, a sense that time was running out.

Maeve held her arms out wide and Maddie sank into them, even before she asked any questions about Rick. That was Maeve O'Shea.

Twenty-Six

CAM MADE A NEW DISCOVERY today. She realized that they should always take the ferry at the crack of dawn because Cooper wasn't alert enough at that hour to get nervous. He wiped down the germy spots around his seat on the ferry, but then he settled down to read, which was a big deal, considering they were on the way to the hospital to see Rick.

He glanced up from the book he'd borrowed off Cam's night table, *What to Expect When You're Expecting.* "We're going to need more Clorox wipes for when the babies come. We don't want the babies exposed to germs."

"Add it to the list," Cam said. A list Cooper had started when she first told him she was pregnant, and had grown exponentially when he learned of the triplets. "Coops, how come you aren't bothered by the puppy's germs?" She'd seen his puppy lick him right on the face.

"Granddad says puppy germs are good germs. So it's okay for the babies to be around the puppy."

Cam and Seth exchanged a look. They'd been trying to help Cooper understand the difference between germs for a long time. She leaned over and rubbed his knee. "Cooper, you're going to be a wonderful big brother." As he tucked his chin to read again, she imagined how attentive he would be to the babies, how lucky they were to have him. Cam had always wanted a big brother. It wasn't easy being the eldest. First at everything meant just that . . . you had to go first. Through everything.

A forgotten memory surfaced, a time when she had led Maddie and Blaine on a hike through a grassy meadow. At day's end, she was the one who had fourteen ticks on her legs. Maddie and Blaine didn't have a single tick on them, and didn't fully appreciate that they'd been spared. A metaphor, she thought, for being the eldest. You had to clear the paths for siblings.

After Rick had been wheeled away for tests, Maddie and Maeve went to the cafeteria to get some breakfast. Blaine had left to catch the ferry. They sat near a sunny window, and Maeve sipped her coffee while Maddie tried to eat a bowl of yogurt and fruit, but food would not go down.

"You need to try and eat something. The baby needs nourishment."

Maddie picked up her spoon and took a few bites. It tasted disgusting, and she wasn't sure if that was because it was hospital food or because Blaine had spoiled her palate for anything but her own homemade yogurt.

"Hopefully," Maeve said, trying to make small talk, "Rick just needs the battery replaced."

"Hopefully." Then fatigue and worry overtook Maddie, and her eyes filled with tears. "But what about next time? What if . . ."

"What if Rick ends up like his father, with a much too short life?" Maeve set down her coffee cup and reached out to take her hand. It felt so warm, that hand, after holding the coffee cup. Or maybe it was warm because it belonged to Maeve. "Maddie, when my husband died, and I had two little ones to raise all by myself, it was the worst thing that ever happened to me." She squeezed her hand. "And it was the best thing that ever happened to me."

Maddie glanced at her, thinking she heard her wrong. "The best?"

"Sounds strange, but yes. Best in that it brought profound blessings, ones that changed my life. After he died, I found I lost my fear of death. And when you don't fear death, you truly live the life you're meant to live."

Maddie reached out for a paper napkin to wipe her eyes.

"There's something else that happened to me when I became a widow. I realized that the resource I had depended on most was gone. The Lord told me, 'I'm your resource now.'"

"But has that been enough?"

"More than enough." She released Maddie's hand. "You're not really trusting God until you are trusting him for the ultimate things in life." She picked up her phone. "If you'll excuse me for a minute, I'm going to call my daughter and let her know what's going on with Rick."

Maddie sat alone in the cafeteria, the morning sun streaming through the window on her, while her husband was somewhere in this hospital, having his heart examined by all kinds of machines. They were trusting those machines to find out what was wrong.

Trust—trust—trust—the word kept coming back to Maddie, a boomerang.

She thought of Christ's promise to give peace, "not as the world gives." Her eyelids fluttered shut and she asked God to simply give her that peace right in the middle of her fears about Rick, right in the middle of this crisis with his heart.

By the time Maeve returned to the cafeteria, Maddie had her answer. Tension and fear slipped away; in its place was peace. A calm courage to face whatever the day's news held. It didn't make any sense, but it was real.

Dr. Turner came into Rick's room with a big smile on her face. "It's the device," she said. "It's malfunctioning."

Thank God, Maddie breathed. *Oh, thank God, thank God, thank God.* "So it's not his heart?"

"No. We'll replace the battery this afternoon. I've already booked the procedure. And then, if all goes well, as I think it will, you'll be released tomorrow morning."

"And back to business as usual," Rick said, grinning ear to ear.

"No, no," Dr. Turner said, wagging her finger at him. "Not business as usual, not if you want to live to be an old man." After she emphasized the importance of reducing the outside demands on Rick's time, Maddie could have hugged her, though the doctor wasn't really the hugging type.

"Rick, I am very serious about this," Dr. Turner said. "You must make changes. Plan for rest and relaxation. Get proper exercise. It's essential to get eight hours of sleep. As it is now, you're burning the candle at both ends. Your heart has been trying to tell you how much it can take, and you aren't listening to it. It's been telling you, 'Stop, stop! You ask too much of me.' Our bodies have limitations. We must respect those limits." She glanced at Maddie's middle. "You want to see this little one grow to be a man, yes?"

"Yes," Rick said. "Indeed I do." After the doctor left, he reached over and took Maddie's hand in his, then he leaned back, smiled, and closed his eyes as his body sagged into the embrace of the pillows. Maeve quietly opened the door and saw herself out, into the sunny late afternoon.

Maddie looked over at Rick as he slept. She saw those familiar crow's-feet wrinkles around his eyes, and she loved every single one of them. Every single one.

The next day, Cooper's black Lab puppy came bounding toward Maddie's car from the boathouse as she returned home from the hospital with Rick and his tuned-up heart and his mother. Maeve bent down to greet the dog, giving the pup a more enthusiastic greeting than Dad ever did. By the time Maddie had helped Rick carefully emerge from the back seat, Dad had walked up from one of the cabins to welcome them home.

From the opposite side of the car, Maddie watched the interaction between Dad and Maeve. First they were all smiles and big hellos and handshakes. Then, they remained side by side, and that's when Maddie saw what she saw. Dad and Maeve's eyes met. They met . . . and they stayed.

At first Maddie thought she had imagined it, but then she noticed Dad sucking in his stomach and standing a little straighter. Then Dad said something that made Maeve laugh, and she batted him on the shoulder.

A slow revelation dawned on Maddie. *Maeve.*

Twenty-Seven

AFTER A LONG HOT SHOWER, Cam pulled her nightie over her round body and wrapped a towel around her wet hair. She walked into the bedroom to find Seth sitting in the armchair in the corner, an open book on his lap. "Quite a day, huh?" She sat on the edge of the bed to comb out her thick hair. It felt even thicker during this pregnancy. Triple-thick.

"Cam, I've been thinking a lot about Rick's heart condition."

She tossed her hairbrush down and picked up her laptop that she'd left on the bed. During her shower, she'd had a brilliant idea. Maybe the tower could be placed behind the Unitarian Church instead of next to it. That way, it would be less obvious. "I thought," she said distractedly, "that Rick had been given a clean bill of health."

"The battery of his ICD was replaced, but the doctor also told him he has to scale back, to respect his body's limitations." He rose from the chair to sit on the bed beside her. "I think there's a message in that for you too."

"I catch your drift." She nudged him with her elbow. "But pregnancy doesn't last forever."

"I wasn't talking about pregnancy."

"Oh. Then maybe I didn't catch your drift. Explain."

"Cam, you . . ." He started slowly. "You have trouble respecting limitations."

She sighed. "Seth, I'm resting twice a day. I'm walking. I'm taking those horrible prenatal vitamins that are as big as horse pills."

"Yes, you're doing a great job. But I meant the cellular tower."

"What about it?"

"The locals don't want it."

As she opened her mouth to object, he cut her off. "No, Cam. They really, really don't want it. They want to preserve what this island is known for—peace and quiet. For all the benefits of cell phones and Wi-Fi, there's a price. These people don't want cell phones ringing all over the place. Not everybody wants to be accessible twenty-four hours a day."

"Seth, this is the future. They can't pretend it's not coming. Progress is unavoidable."

"True, but maybe it's okay to slow it down."

She kept her eyes downcast. "Go on."

"The pace of change brings burdens too. The locals want to be the ones to decide what is acceptable change and what they're not ready for. So they've voted down your tower. Respect that decision. Don't force it. Don't pay for it, hoping that one day they'll be grateful. Sometimes . . . no just means no."

Feeling a kick, she rolled a hand over her stomach. "Why haven't you said something about this?"

"You've been . . . busy. And listening isn't exactly your greatest strength. So when you're really busy, you're really not listening. In a way, I think God has brought these babies to us at just the right time. It's a major lesson in understanding limitations."

A word she'd always ignored as much as possible.

Cam felt a trickle of shame run through her. Seth was right. She didn't run the world; she didn't have the right to interfere with what others wanted for their island home. Most had lived here all their lives; the Grayson family had been here only four years. She felt all three babies kick her at once.

"I guess . . ." She closed her file and pressed the off switch on her computer. "I guess no means no."

He took her in his arms and hugged her warmly, placing a kiss on her forehead.

Two weeks until Memorial Day and Camp Kicking Moose was more than ready for campers. At least, that's what Paul thought. Bob Lotosky disagreed and drove the Grayson family at a relentless pace. Each day, they were assigned tasks to do, and each night, he would check on their progress. Rick was on the injured list, so he cut him some slack. Jean-Paul, Bob gave up on as accident prone, a potential liability. And Bob didn't seem to expect much from Blaine, which baffled Paul, but he supposed it had to do with her lighthouse restaurant—which Paul knew about but had been too busy to pay much attention to. Besides, Cam had reminded him that most of Blaine's big ideas usually fizzled out. More likely, Bob was giving Blaine a pass because she worked for Peg during the day.

If ever a man was besotted, it was Bob Lotosky. Whenever Peg stopped by the camp, he morphed from a stern Army sergeant into a cuddly teddy bear. It was embarrassing to watch.

Then again, with each passing day of Maeve's visit, Paul was feeling more besotted himself. She had rolled up her sleeves and joined right in, helping alongside him with tasks that his own daughters happily avoided. Today she had climbed a ladder to clean out debris from cabin gutters. Impressive.

When they had finished cleaning the last cabin's gutters, Paul carried the ladder back to the boathouse as Artie drove up the driveway in Peg's green minivan.

Paul stopped. "Looking for Cam?" Artie came by the house every few days to take Cam's blood pressure and sent the information to her obstetrician when he returned to the *Lightship*.

"No," Artie said, and didn't elaborate. He went straight to the house and over to Granddad, sitting on the porch.

Paul hung the ladder on the boathouse wall and crossed the lawn to join them. "I think it's time to let me know what's going on."

Artie was unrolling a blood pressure cuff out of his bag. He kept his head down. Paul looked directly at his father, noticing the fatigue on his face, the wince in his eyes as he lifted his arm for Artie.

His father gave a nod to Artie. "Go ahead," he said. "A man has no privacy around here."

Artie wrapped the cuff and paused. "I've diagnosed Lyme disease in your father."

"From the tick?"

"Yes. A tiny insect, but it wreaks havoc on a body. In your dad's case, it causes constant fatigue and joint pain."

Paul fixed his eyes on Artie. "But curable. That's what I've always heard about Lyme disease."

Done with his task, Artie released the valve and unwrapped the blood pressure band. "If it had been caught early, antibiotics could have cured it. But the disease has been advancing for a while."

"Dad," Paul said. "Why didn't you see a doctor sooner?"

His father shrugged, giving Paul his answer. His own stubbornness had brought him an enormous loss in quality of life.

Paul felt a surprising flood of emotions for his father: pity, regret, sorrow for time lost between them. And forgiveness, or the start of it. Like light shining through a crack in the roof rafters.

Artie took a bottle of pills out of his bag and handed it to his father. "These painkillers will help on days when your joints feel unbearable." He glanced at his watch. "Gotta go."

Paul waited for a long moment. He should get back to the work crew. But he needed to finish this up. He sat down on the rocker across from his dad. "Do you need a place to stay until you . . ."

"Die? You can say it. No, I don't. There's a veterans' home I'll be going to."

"You could stay here if you want to."

SUZANNE WOODS FISHER

"Thanks, but no. It's getting a little crowded."

No kidding. Paul didn't even want to think what Moose Manor would be like with four babies living in it. "Dad, what did you hope to gain by coming here? I really want to know. And no more deflection."

His father's attention was fixed on the line of cabins. Bob had Maeve and Seth and Cooper in a huddle, giving them instructions. Paul needed to get back to work. He cleared his throat, trying to egg on his father.

It worked. "Seemed like the time had come to make peace." His father looked at him. "I'm the only father you'll ever have, you know."

"I got the impression that you never considered yourself a family man."

"I supported you, didn't I? You were fed and dry and had a place to sleep."

There was a lot more to parenting than that. But then it occurred to Paul that he'd never even known his grandparents, nor hardly knew anything about them. Maybe . . . giving his son food and shelter was his idea, albeit limited, of being a good father. "You did, Dad." He relaxed a little. "What do you remember of your dad?"

His father looked away, visibly stiffening. "The back of a hand across my cheek. A belt across my backside."

For all the complaints Paul had about his father, he had never laid a hand on him.

"I know what you're thinking."

"What's that?"

His father turned his piercing gaze on him. "You're a better parent than I was."

Paul wasn't exactly thinking that, not right now, but he had thought it before. Many, many times.

His father leaned back in his rocking chair. "And if you're lucky, your girls will be better parents than you."

257

Paul gave that some thought. Then he smiled. "Let's hope you're right about that." He reached out his hand and set it on top of his father's.

Work was underway on the lighthouse. It was fascinating for Blaine to see how the tradesmen carried on work in a nautical setting. These construction workers had to adjust to the tides, plus the complexity of reaching a steep lighthouse. Each time they faced an obstacle, they figured out a solution. They reminded Blaine of Bob Lotosky's masterful, practical logic. Like Bob, these workers had no college degrees, nothing that the world might deem as necessary for success, and yet, in Blaine's view, they were brilliant. Beyond brilliant.

Today she watched them create a human chain to bring supplies from their boat on the beach, up the stairs, and over to the lighthouse. At that point, they created a pulley system from the lighthouse's gallery platform to haul up equipment. *Genius.*

Blaine still hadn't figured out how restaurant guests could arrive at the lighthouse without depending on a low tide, or without having to climb up those steep stairs, but she felt inspired after watching the dogged creativity of these workers. Somehow, she would find a solution.

Paul sat on the porch steps of Moose Manor, next to the newly installed ADA approved railings, watching Maeve toss a Frisbee to Cooper on the lawn. The still-unnamed puppy charged back and forth between them. Maeve was teaching Cooper a powerful tool: a good puppy is a tired puppy.

A man like Paul Grayson just didn't meet a woman like Maeve O'Shea every day.

Maeve was in her midsixties with salt-and-pepper shoulder-length hair, dark brown eyes, and a laugh that sounded like music.

She was fun. She had presence. And most important, she was strong. Widowed early in her marriage, she had raised two little children all alone.

Paul might've expected a woman in her situation to have grown bitter. After all, life had dealt her an unfair hand. But instead, Maeve radiated a calming confidence, a sense that somehow, someway, everything would turn out all right.

"I think," Paul said out loud, "that I might just be growing smitten." The gray cat came charging out of the bushes and up the steps, its tail as straight as a poker. "I wasn't talking about you." But the cat only preened, pretending not to hear.

After dinner, the family lingered at the kitchen table. Paul and Maeve slipped out quietly to sit in the living room, a rare moment alone. It was a chilly night, so Paul made a fire in the fireplace and they sat on Jean-Paul's couch, watching the flames.

"Something I noticed the last time I was here," Maeve said. "There is no picture of Corinna."

"No. Strangely enough, I don't have many pictures of her. She was always the one taking pictures." Paul paused. "To be entirely candid, I just didn't know how to bring her into this new chapter. It was easier to keep her in the old one." After a moment of reflection, Paul added, "Sometimes my memories of her seem to be fading."

"I used to feel the same way. Every year that passed, it seemed a little more of my husband had slipped away. I began to fear that one day I would come to forget him altogether. But the truth is that no matter how much time passes, those we've loved never slip away entirely." She got up and went to her purse, hanging on a hook by the front door, took something out of it, and returned to the couch. She handed a small package to Paul.

"For me?"

"For you. For your daughters."

He tore off the wrapping to discover a framed picture of Corinna, smiling, with a familiar look in her eyes, a look he had loved.

"I found this picture of her when I was cleaning out a drawer. I remember taking it. We had just finished the church women's summer Bible study and Corinna had gathered everyone together to take a group picture. But then she wasn't in it, so I grabbed my camera and snapped a picture of her when she wasn't looking."

"She didn't like getting her picture taken."

Maeve set the picture of Corinna on the mantel of the fireplace. "She's a part of this family, Paul. She'll always be an important part of this family. She belongs in a place of prominence. Not forgotten. Not fading. Still with you. Still loved. Her influence continues."

Paul rose from the couch, scooped Maeve into his arms, and kissed her swiftly on the mouth. And suddenly there was a chorus of loud gasps. There, standing just a few yards away, were Cam, Maddie, and Blaine, all three, wide-eyed, jaws open.

This wasn't exactly the way Paul planned to tell his daughters that he had a girlfriend, but then again, he had no plan. Chagrined, he reached out for Maeve's hand. "Should we tell them?"

Maeve blushed. "After Maddie and Rick's wedding, we started calling each other. That led to a few visits now and then."

"When?" Cam said. "Where?"

"We saw *Hamilton* in New York City," Paul said, adding proudly, "on Broadway."

Maeve smiled. "That was the first thing on our bucket list."

"Dad!" Maddie said. "You told us you were meeting your accountant."

"I did. And then I met up with Maeve."

"Hold on," Blaine said. "What exactly are you saying? Are you two . . ."

Paul looked at Maeve and she looked at him. He grinned like a silly schoolboy. "We are. We're dating."

Blaine looked at Maddie, then Cam. "Did you know?"

"No idea!" Cam shook her head. She turned to Maddie. "Did you?"

"Not officially. I had an inkling, just the other day, when I saw how Dad sucked in his stomach when he greeted Maeve."

Paul frowned.

"Dad," Cam said, "why didn't you tell us?"

"Didn't want you girls to meddle."

The sisters exchanged shocked looks. "Us? Meddle? When do we ever meddle?"

Twenty-Eight

ON SATURDAY EVENING, Blaine brought a bowl of ice cream to Jean-Paul—his third—and sat across from him in the living room.

"I have been learning from you, mon amie."

She smiled. "What could I possibly have to teach you?"

"Everyone eez against your lighthouse restaurant. But you keep at it. You do not let your family—how to say—deflate your dream."

"I think you mean, pop my balloon."

"I came here for a purpose. Watching you, I think I have found it."

She lifted her head. "Ohhhh. You're ready to go back?" The thought made her sad.

"Oui. I am ready."

"You're going to tell your father no to the bistro?"

"Oui. I am a cook. I am not a chef. I must do what I was born to do." He lifted the empty bowl of ice cream and patted his stomach. "I will miss zis."

Not nearly as much as I will miss you, she thought.

Before he went to bed, Paul checked the weather report. A spring storm was moving up the East Coast, bringing rain and strong winds. Weather was something you worked around in Maine, but Maeve thought she'd better get home before it hit in full force. She decided to catch the first ferry out on Sunday morning.

Early the next morning, Paul drove Maeve to Boon Dock. It was chilly, so they waited in the car for the ferry to arrive. They held hands and talked about their next visit, about the babies coming, about Rick's heart. Then Paul saw the ferry approach in the harbor, and he knew their time together was coming to an end. It was hard to say goodbye to Maeve.

"Paul, just a thought, but it occurred to me that the carriage house looked big enough to convert into a residence."

His head snapped up. "You mean . . . big enough for a home for triplets, a big brother and their parents?" He hadn't thought of it, but it could be a brilliant solution.

She laughed. "I guess I was thinking more for you. If you needed a little space from a houseful of darling but noisy grandchildren."

Oh. But it seemed a little lonely to live in the carriage house all alone. Unless . . .

"You know," she said, interrupting his train of thought, "I think your voice sounds better than last time."

Paul shrugged, like it was no big deal. "Good days, bad days." The truth was that he'd been working diligently to care for his vocal cords. He found he had a lot he wanted to say to Maeve.

"I remember how it used to sound. Rick and I would listen to you on the radio. I hadn't been much of a baseball fan until I realized Rick was crazy about it. Those games on the radio, they became a way to connect with my son. Thank you for that."

"I miss that voice."

She looked at him and smiled. "Actually, Paul, I think I like this one even better."

Eyes stinging, he felt a surge of love for Maeve. He leaned over and kissed her, a really good kiss, he thought. But then the ferry blasted its horn and the moment was over.

Church that morning was led by Seth, since Rick was still under doctor's orders to rest. Sunday was the one day that Bob Lotosky took off, and they were all grateful for the reprieve. After church, Cam and Seth stayed in town, along with Maddie and Blaine. By the time Paul and Cooper arrived back at Moose Manor, where Granddad and Jean-Paul were watching a baseball game on the television, clouds had closed in, and the sun vanished.

After lunch, Artie arrived at Moose Manor to take Cam's blood pressure. From the boathouse, Paul saw Artie stop to talk to his father on the porch, and he crossed the yard to join them. The cat strutted alongside him.

Artie and his father were looking in the direction of the Atlantic. Off in the distance, Paul could see billowing black storm clouds rolling in, heading straight to the island. "I thought this was supposed to be a typical spring storm."

"I just heard an update on the radio as I drove out here," Artie said. "Two upper-level troughs in the Mid-Atlantic have joined together to create a massive low-pressure system, moving north. At the same time, cold air from Canada is heading south. Added to all of it is the super moon."

"So what does all that mean?"

Artie turned to his father. "It means the typical spring storm could turn nasty."

Paul felt a hitch of worry about Maeve, and that brought a tender awareness. He had a sweetheart to worry about. He thought he'd call Maeve soon and see how the drive was going. "Dad," Paul said. "It's cold out here. Come inside. I'll start a fire in the fireplace. You can finish up that baseball game with Jean-Paul."

Cooper appeared on the porch. "Jean-Paul sent me out to ask you if you think he's ready to travel."

"Travel?"

A gust of wind lifted the newspaper and scattered it around the porch.

"Back to Paris," Cooper said, helping Paul pick up newspaper pages.

Artie closed up his bag. "When?"

Cooper stopped. "Soon, he says. As soon as Blaine is ready."

Paul had been bent over and bolted upright. "As soon as Blaine is ready? What does that mean?"

Artie rose, turning, to look through the large picture window at Jean-Paul on the couch, watching television, mindlessly eating a bag of Fritos corn chips. "Where *is* Blaine?"

"She stayed in town with Seth and Cam and Maddie."

"No," Artie said, his expression growing troubled. "I saw the three of them at the diner with Peg and Bob. They didn't know where she'd gone. She just told them she'd see them at home."

Blaine didn't like what she saw. Winds ripped at the little boat as she steered it toward the tip of the island, but it was the gusts that pushed the boat off course. The water was really rolling, frothed with whitecaps, as she approached the lighthouse, and she wondered aloud about wave size. A storm was coming, that she knew, and that was why she wanted to get to the lighthouse as quickly as she could to board up the broken windows and protect the new wooden floor in the lantern room. She had hoped to get the new windowpanes in on Friday, but the glass guy hadn't arrived and the floor guys had shown up early to lay the floor. Blaine hadn't wanted to slow anything down, so she gave them the go ahead to sand and stain the wooden floors.

Stupid, stupid, stupid. This was what happened when you didn't exercise patience. Bob Lotosky had warned her about that very thing. Hurry, but don't rush.

For a fleeting moment, she felt uneasy and wondered if she should turn back, the seas were that rough. But she pushed aside those worries and pressed on, bracing her feet in the boat to withstand the spray of the waves as the bow cut its path. She knew just what to do, so if all went well, she could get in the lighthouse and out again, and she'd be heading back to the harbor within fifteen minutes. Before the rain started.

Her whole heart was in this project. Thanks to Bob Lotosky, so far she was under budget, right on schedule to open around the Fourth of July. Perfect.

As she positioned the boat to make its mooring, she was alarmed to discover the beach was nearly submerged. She had thought the tide was ebbing, that the sea would be reducing, but could she have misread the tide tables in her haste? Normally, landing here was easy; this was treacherous. She guided the bow of the boat as close to the beach cliff as she dared, then cut the engine and let it drift in. The tide should be heading out, but she had to move fast. She climbed up the stairs and ran to the lighthouse. She closed the door behind her and rested against it to catch her breath and wipe the sea from her face.

For that brief interval the lighthouse was an oasis, a private moment of calm.

A rumble of distant thunder broke, and Blaine popped out of her reverie. She dashed up the spiral staircase, taking the steps two at a time. When she reached the lantern room, she opened the door carefully and breathed a sigh of relief. The floor guys had boarded up the windows with plywood. She would have to find out who had gone that extra mile for her and make sure they were given a voucher for a free dinner. She reached down to press a finger on the wood floor. It was dry to the touch. She was told to leave it untouched for at least forty-eight hours. She closed the door and went down to the gallery room. She walked inside, thinking of how this room could be laid out with tables. She didn't like to have tables right up against each other, where it felt as if you were constantly being eavesdropped by other patrons. She went down to the watch room and peered inside. This was larger than the gallery, but the windows were high, meant to provide light and cool the tower, but not for creating views. The watch room would be claustrophobic for restaurant patrons. Thunder rumbled again, sounding closer, so she peeked out the window and saw that the rain had started.

Out of the corner of her eye, she noticed a nice-looking leather toolbelt left by a workman on the gallery platform, probably forgotten as he was lifting plywood up to cover the windows. She knew she should get down to the boat before it really started to pour, but she wanted to get the toolbelt in out of the rain. It was the least she could do for those floor guys. As she pulled open the gallery door, a tremor ran through her. This wind was much stronger than it had been fifteen minutes ago. It was pushing her against the lighthouse as she inched her way to the toolbelt.

BANG! The door whooshed to a close behind her. Another tremor shot through her. She grabbed the toolbelt and crawled back to the door.

It was locked. No, no, no, no!

Blaine started to shiver from the biting, icy wind. Rain pelted her. She tried to make herself as small as she could, leaning against the lighthouse, zipping up her windbreaker, pulling the hood over her face. Calling this a windbreaker, she decided, was stupid. It didn't break the wind at all. One moment, the wind blasted from the east. The next moment, from the west. She couldn't even tell which direction the wind was blowing. It swirled.

She tried to keep her mind steady and calm. This gale had come up so fast, surely it would blow through quickly. Surely she could outlast it. She searched through the tool bag, hoping to find a hammer or screwdriver, something to break the lock with, but all that was in it was nails. A wave of disgust filled her. She had put herself in a terrible spot for a bag of nails. A bag of nails!

Crashing thunder made the gallery platform quiver. She lifted the collar of her coat to pull around her jaw as another gust of wind blew past, sea spray flinging in every direction. She felt the power of this storm, and it frightened her. *Dear God,* she prayed. *Help me.* Her mind repeated it like a chant: *Dear God, dear God, dear God. Help me, help me, help me.* She could think of nothing else to say, or think, or hope for.

BLAINE, AGE 16

It was the one-year anniversary of Mom's death. Blaine assumed the whole family would gather so they could have a little ceremony. Put flowers on Mom's and Libby's graves. Clean the graves up. Have some kind of recognition that they had all made it through the year. They had survived the worst year of their lives.

Blaine's assumptions were all wrong. Dad had to travel at the last minute to sub in for some announcer at a baseball event, Maddie had a big paper due on Monday and felt she should stay at college. When Blaine called Cam to find out when she'd arrive at their home, her sister had forgotten all about it. "It's best for Cooper to stick with a routine, sleep in his own bed. He's barely been sleeping through the night without nightmares. Bringing him back to Needham would only start them all over again."

"So I'm alone for this weekend?"

"Blaine, stop being dramatic," Cam said in her no-nonsense way. "It's just a day like any other day."

No, it wasn't. Not to Blaine anyway. But at least Winslow was with her, though he spent most of his time curled up and asleep on his bed in the kitchen. She bent down to stroke his head and ears. His gray muzzle. "Okay, old man. Will you come with me to the cemetery?" He thumped his tail twice, which she took as a yes.

She helped him into her car to go out to the cemetery, and helped him out again. His back legs weren't what they used to be. He curled up in the sun, leaning right against Mom's gravestone. Blaine didn't think Mom would mind at all. She had brought some tools to clean up the grave, and Libby's. She swept Libby's grandmother's grave with a broom. Even as she swept, despite the warmth of the day, she felt cold near this particular grave. It was a strange feeling, to the point where goose bumps cascaded down her arms.

The last thing she did before she left the cemetery was to leave flowers on her mom's grave, and on Libby's. None on Libby's grandmother's. She probably should have, but she had never liked that grandmother and she'd only thought to buy two bouquets.

She helped Winslow back into the car and went home again. Blaine made dinner for herself and watched a movie, Winslow curled up by her side. She had made popcorn and Winslow licked the salt off her hand. The movie was boring and Blaine nodded off, jerking awake suddenly when Winslow licked her hand. She yawned and stretched, and got up to go to bed. "Come on, Winslow. Off to your bed." Before she flipped off the light, she called to him again. His head was down, his eyes closed. He didn't budge. "Come on, buddy."

She walked over to him. "Winslow?" She bent down. *Oh no. Please, please no. No, no, no. Not today. Not when I'm all alone. Please God, please God, please God. Don't take him today. Not yet.*

And suddenly she saw Winslow's chest fill, then he lifted his head, shook his ears, and slowly got to his feet, stretched, and ambled to his bed.

Blaine knew she had been . . . heard.

Twenty-Nine

CURLED UP IN A BALL, Blaine tried to block her face from the rain with her windbreaker, tried to fill her mind with calming thoughts. She imagined she was in Hawaii, lying on a beach in a bikini, working on a tan. It didn't work. She had never felt so cold in her life, despite a childhood in New England. Her teeth couldn't stop chattering, her body couldn't stop shivering, her fingers had turned husky blue. Her lips probably were too. But she wasn't frightened, wasn't fearful. She sensed she'd be okay, sooner or later. But *man*! She was cold.

"Blaine!"

She squeezed her eyes shut, tried to imagine someone was calling her name.

"Blaine! Blaine! Down here!"

Her eyes opened.

"Blaine! Over here!"

Down below was Artie, shouting up to her. She reached for the railing. "Artie! The door is locked! I'm stuck!"

"Crouch down low! Hang on to the door handle. I'll be right up."

Within minutes, he was at the door of the gallery platform, holding it open, pulling her inside. A gust of wind blew the door shut again. He yanked her wet coat off, undid his jacket, and wrapped it around her shoulders, zipping it up front. The lining felt thick and cozy and warm like a fleece blanket, and it smelled like Artie—Irish Spring soap, like always.

"Oh, Artie," she said, trembling, teeth chattering, "h-h-how d-d-did you know?" *How did you know I needed help? How did you know I needed you?*

"I stopped by Moose Manor to check on your grandfather and you weren't there. Cam and Maddie had said you'd see them at home, but I remembered noticing your dad's boat wasn't at its slip at Boon Dock. I put two and two together . . . and then I started to—I mean, everyone is worried about you."

"H-how d-did you g-get here?"

Lightning lit the room, quickly followed by a crack of thunder so loud it shook the sky. Artie waited until the thunder passed. "I took one of your dad's ATVs as far as it could go in the mud on the carriage road. Then I ran up and over the hill."

Warming up, little by little, she rubbed her arms and stomped her feet, took in deep breaths, exhaled; she was okay. Thanks to Artie, she was okay. Without thinking, she took a step toward him and grabbed his hands, and she thought every muscle in his body froze. His eyes met hers, but then he yanked his hands away. "So I hear you're leaving with the Frenchman."

"Jean-Paul . . . he wants to leave. He says that America is too dangerous."

"He hasn't left Moose Manor."

"Well, yes, pretty true." She smiled, and even the smile warmed her up. "He says America is turning him into someone whom his *pa-Pa*"—she gave the word a French accent—"would not recognize." She let out a deep breath, so thankful to be sheltered from that bitter wind. "Funny thing is, he's absolutely right. America and Jean-Paul are not a good fit. He belongs in France." A shock of lightning lit the sky; thunder followed, but not on its heels. A sign that the storm was passing. She hoped, anyway.

Artie's eyes were on the sky. "You're in love with him."

"I'm not. Artie, please look at me." A bit reluctantly, he turned to face her. "It's not like that between us. Jean-Paul wants to be a priest. A Catholic priest. His father wants him to be a chef, to take over his bistro. That's the real reason Jean-Paul came to America—to have time to search his heart before he took his vows."

"A priest? Who wants to be a priest in this day and age?"

"Jean-Paul does. It's been the longing of his heart. It's his true calling. I've known it from the first time I met him. He just had to see it for himself."

Artie still had that cautious look in his eyes. It was time to tell him the whole story. And for once, thanks to a storm, they had time for it.

"I owe you an apology." She stuffed her hands in her pockets and stepped closer to him. "I'm sorry I didn't tell you about that married instructor hitting on me. I should have told you, but I felt too ashamed. So scrambled. Depression can do that."

"Depression? You never seemed depressed. Not to me, anyway. Easily distracted, yes. Depressed, no."

"I hid it well." Blaine had convinced everyone into thinking she was fine, just fine. It had become almost a game to her. And while playing the game, she did all she could to quench those parts of her that weren't doing fine. Oddly, it worked . . . until it didn't. "I thought that by going to Paris I could escape my depression, but it came with me. Those early days and weeks were . . . incredibly difficult." They seemed a lifetime ago now, as though lived by someone else. "I tried so hard to stuff it all down, but it kept coming back. Again and again."

"Blaine . . . I'm not following you. What was the 'it'?"

"Grief. My mother's death. I'm not trying to make excuses, but I was only fifteen when she died. Still at home, and it had become a very lonely home. Cam and Maddie had moved on, and Dad's radio career was still going strong . . . and I don't think I ever really dealt with how sad and lost I felt. I lost my mom, but I also lost my best friend, my best cheerleader."

His eyes softened.

"If it weren't for Jean-Paul, I wouldn't be here. I don't mean *here* here. I mean . . . I probably wouldn't be alive."

He stared at her intently for a moment before repeating, "Alive?"

"One day I realized that there was nowhere in the world I could go to escape how bad I felt." Blaine couldn't bring herself to look at Artie as she explained her bleakest moment on the bridge over the river Seine. She leaned against the wall, grasping her elbows with crossed arms. This was hard to say aloud, so hard. "Jean-Paul happened to come along, and he stopped me from doing any harm to myself, and later he helped me get a job at his father's bistro. And that led to a spot at Le Cordon Bleu. He's been so good to me. I brought him to the island because I wanted everyone to meet him and understand how wonderful he is."

Artie regarded her with astonished concern. "Blaine, I . . ."

"I know." She kept her eyes on the tips of her boots. "It's not something I'm very proud of, yet that moment was so profound. I was at the lowest of lows, and it was like God met me on that bridge, like he scooped me up and held me close. That was the turning point. It was the moment I started to heal, to truly heal, from the inside out." She forced herself to look at him, and it took more courage than she could have imagined. She had never been able to tell anyone that story. Not anyone.

"Blaine." Artie's voice caught and he stopped for a second. "I can't even imagine a life without you in it," he whispered as he closed the gap between them.

In one determined move, the palm of his hand was on her jaw, and his fingers were grasping the back of her neck to pull her lips to his. All thoughts of the rain pounding the lighthouse were forgotten as his arms wrapped around her.

"Artie, I love you," she whispered when their lips finally parted. Then she realized what she said, what she had admitted *out loud*. She said it first! She was never going to say it first. But she also knew the words came straight from her heart.

He pulled away, which was the last thing she wanted. But there was something in Artie's eyes that she hadn't seen in a very long time. Maybe she'd never seen it, or maybe she'd never noticed it before.

He bent to pick up a small metal washer left on the ground, a thoughtful look on his face. "I have tried and tried to get over you, and I've never been able to. So I give up."

He lowered onto one knee.

Her breath caught in her throat.

He looked up, a gentle smile in his eyes, and asked, "Blaine Grayson, will you marry me?"

Tears flooded her cheeks, but still she said nothing.

"Um, Blaine, I'm not sure how long my knee can stay on this cold floor."

She leaned down to kiss him. Once, then twice. "My answer is yes."

Later, on the long, muddy, slippery, rainy, and windy walk down the hill to Moose Manor, she learned a new lesson about weather: it's a lot easier to handle when you're euphoric.

The only thought that dampened her high spirits was wondering how to tell Dad that his boat had been swallowed up by the sea.

Thirty

NATURE COULD BE FECKLESS. The storm took a toll on Camp Kicking Moose, knocking down tree limbs, ripping shingles off cabin roofs, turning the golf course–like grass lawn in front of Moose Manor that Paul had carefully babied all spring into a soggy pond.

But it could've been worse. Nothing was catastrophic, and with the storm came two gifts.

Gift number one: Blaine returned home unharmed. It took Paul two full days to stop hugging her each time she passed by him. Thank God for Artie Lotosky's dogged determination, something Paul had realized was a trait passed to him by his father, Bob Lotosky. The Lotosky grit.

And that brought Paul to gift number two: Artie Lotosky. Something had happened up in that lighthouse between Blaine and Artie, and they wouldn't say what. All they said was that they were a couple now, with plans to marry. But there was no date set. Paul wanted to nail it down before Blaine changed her mind.

Maeve advised him to stop planning and start enjoying life. "You've an embarrassment of riches, Paul. Think about it. Each of your daughters has found a wonderfully suited life partner. All three are happy, reaching their potential in their chosen fields, all three with a bright future ahead of them. What more could you want?"

"You're right," he told her. Like most of the women in his life, she was often right. He was often wrong. "But there is one thing I want. When are you coming up for your next visit?"

Soon, she told him, and it couldn't be soon enough. He missed her. He wanted her here, part of his everyday life.

"Ready?"

Paul turned to see his father standing at the door. "You're sure about this, Dad?"

"I'm sure. I said my goodbyes last night, so let's go before the blubbery tears start all over again."

Those would be Blaine's blubbery tears. She didn't want her grandfather to leave. The two of them had developed some kind of close connection that baffled Paul.

His father had chosen to live in a home for veterans over on the mainland, and he insisted on leaving Camp Kicking Moose before Memorial Day, before campers arrived and peace and quiet—which was in a shortage to start with—left for good.

So Paul drove his father all the way to the veterans' home. Sea View Village, which actually had a view of the sea. To his surprise and relief, his father felt at home from the moment he saw it, or pretended he did. He settled into his room and flirted with a nurse's aide, and shooed Paul away.

"Dad, if you change your mind . . ."

"I won't. Look, I know I'm going to need extra help and my pride won't let me ask it of my family. So come visit now and then, bring a box of Bob's potato candy, take me over to Three Sisters Island later this summer so I can eat on the top of Blaine's fancy lighthouse . . . but don't make this difficult."

"Got it."

His father stuck out his hand for a handshake, and Paul looked at it for a long while, then reached out and engulfed him in a hug.

On the drive back to the camp, Paul felt a swirl of emotions about his father. The familiar feelings of guilt and sorrow and frustration, but new feelings were coming to the forefront. Maybe not enjoyment, exactly, but respect. Gratitude. They had found a path back to each other before it was too late.

And then all thoughts of his dad disappeared as he pulled into the driveway of Moose Manor and saw Dr. Doom walking around the cabins with a clipboard. Paul had asked the county to send an inspector prior to Memorial Day weekend, hoping the camp could pass inspection. Hoping they wouldn't send Dr. Doom. He hadn't had a chance to clean up the camp from the storm.

Paul's heart sank like a stone.

Blaine stood with her family on Boon Dock to say goodbye to Jean-Paul. She wished he would stay longer, but she knew he didn't belong here. He joked last night at dinner that he had to leave soon because, he said, "Eez dangerous here, in America," and everyone laughed, even Dad.

It was hard to see her friend leave, knowing she wouldn't see him again for a very long time, if ever. But she felt a deep-down peace that he was making the right decision. Her family had helped him settle his doubts about becoming a priest. If he could help *them*, which he did, each one, then he could help anyone. That, it turned out, had been the stumbling block for his becoming a priest. It had amazed Blaine when he told her that last evening as she helped him pack. "You really didn't know you had a gift to help people?"

"Now I do," he said.

Jean-Paul said goodbye to each member of the family, kissing each one on their cheeks, taking a moment to stroke the puppy in Cooper's arms.

"I've decided on a name for my puppy," Cooper said. "I'm going to call him JP. So we remember you each time we call him."

Jean-Paul's eyes grew shiny. "Eez an honor, my little bespectacled friend."

Then the ferry tooted its horn. Time to go. Blaine walked

him down the dock to board it, tucking her arm companionably through his.

She searched for a way to express the fullness in her heart. From finding her on the bridge filled with despair, to sticking his neck out to get her a job at his father's bistro, to coming back to the island with her to help her settle into a new chapter. There was just no way to express all he had given to her. "You saved me, Jean-Paul. And then you gave me what I needed to come home again."

He put his palm on her cheek. "Zis is where you belong, mon amie. Do not forget zat God will never give up on you, even if you give up on him." He smiled. "And I am happy for you and zee bearded doctor. Stay well."

She tried not to cry as Jean-Paul boarded the ferry. He was her angel. As it pulled away from the slip, Dad walked down the dock and put his arm around Blaine's shoulder. "So he's really going to become a priest?" That, too, had been shared with the family at dinner last evening.

She nodded, wiping tears off her cheeks. "He wasn't completely sure of his calling, so he came to America with me, hoping that God would make things clear to him."

"And?" Cam said, as she walked up alongside Blaine to join them.

"He's leaving with no doubt. He feels called to a life of service." She grinned. "After a few months of living with the Grayson family . . . he no longer has any questions about his calling."

Cam reached down and slipped her hand into Blaine's. "I owe you an apology."

Blaine's eyebrows lifted in surprise. A second apology from her sister Cam? Wonders never ceased.

"Jean-Paul has been a wonderful friend to you, to all of us. So I stand corrected. A man and a woman can be friends without it being romantic."

They can, Blaine thought. But when a friendship blossoms into romance, it's the best of all.

The van was quiet as it returned to Camp Kicking Moose. Jean-Paul had insisted on a simple goodbye, leaving everyone where they belonged, he said, and wouldn't even let Blaine take him to the airport. He walked onto the ferry, crutch-free, sling-free, bruise-free. Finally ready, Jean-Paul said, to go home to Paris and take his vows. His *pa-Pa*, he said, will not be so *hap-Py*, but he was ready to face him.

As he neared the camp, Paul's mind started turning to Memorial Day. It was just a few days away and there was plenty of clean-up to do from the storm before the first guests arrived on Friday evening. And that was only with a wing and a prayer that Dr. Doom's inopportune assessment of the camp hadn't ruined all Paul's hopes and dreams. And livelihood. And future.

On the Thursday before Memorial Day, Peg's green minivan arrived at Moose Manor. Paul started down the porch steps to greet her and stopped abruptly. Baxtor Phinney climbed out of the passenger side of the minivan and opened the sliding door. Paul couldn't remember Baxtor ever stepping onto the camp's property, so he knew something important must be brewing. Important in Baxtor's eyes anyway. And then out of the minivan climbed Dr. Doom, a thick envelope in his hand. A very thick envelope. Paul's heart started to pound. Approaching the house, Peg gave a hearty wave to Paul, smiling. Beaming, actually. Paul relaxed, but just slightly. Peg might be part of the Silent Opposition, but she was also his friend, a bit like a sister, and she wouldn't be smiling if he was about to receive some horrible news about the camp's violations.

"Paul Grayson," Peg shouted, "we have some news to tell. You won't believe it. You just won't believe it." She clambered toward the porch steps and waited.

By this time, everyone in the house had heard Peg's rally cry. Blaine had come to the door, and Maddie and Cam. Cooper and his puppy appeared around the corner of the house, coming from the pickleball court.

"What's going on?" Paul said. "This looks rather official."

"It is," Peg said happily. "It's an official meeting with the selectmen of Three Sisters Island along with a representative from the state of Maine." She jammed a thumb in Dr. Doom's direction.

Blaine was first down the steps and slipped around Paul. "What's happened?"

Peg looked like she was about to burst, but she waited until Maddie and Cam joined them. "Honey, didn't I tell you? Mother Nature always has the last word."

"The sandbar," Blaine said. "It's back?"

"It's back," Baxtor said, looking pleased.

When had Baxtor Phinney ever looked pleased? Paul was intrigued.

Peg glanced at Baxtor. "Go ahead. Tell them."

Baxtor took his sweet old time, even adjusting his glasses and clearing his throat. "The storm caused a shift in currents and the movement of sand."

"Tons of sand," Peg said. "Tons and tons of it. Go on, Baxtor. Go on and tell them."

"And then the moon, a super moon, it's called, created a gravitational pull on the tides. All of this together, well, it moved the sandbar that used to be in the harbor and is now further out. Creating a shallow seabed for the harbor and—"

Peg waved him off. "Oh good grief, Baxtor. We don't need a lesson in tides. Guess what that storm churned up? Go on. Guess!" She clapped her hands. "An old shipwreck."

Blaine gasped. "I knew it! Once or twice, during low tide, I thought I saw something strange in that area. Dark and shadowy. One end pointing up."

Paul's eyebrows lifted. Imagine that! A shipwreck, so close to the camp. "Why didn't you tell someone?"

Exasperated, Blaine lifted her palms and gave them a little shake. "I did! I told all of you! No one believed me."

Baxtor cleared his throat, annoyed that Peg interrupted him. "It's not just any shipwreck. It's a . . ."

He shouldn't have paused for dramatic effect. Dr. Doom jumped in, full of authority. "A German U-boat."

"Here?" Paul was flabbergasted. He knew there'd been U-boats around the coast of Maine during World War II, but here? Around Three Sisters Island?

"Here!" Peg was overjoyed. "And that's not all. Go ahead, Dr. Doom, tell them your news." Her eyes went wide. "I mean, um, Mr. Dominski."

"The state of Maine has, naturally, an interest in this discovery. The Parks Department is expediting plans to have it declared a National Historic Site so scavengers can be kept away."

"Scavengers?" Maddie said.

Dr. Doom peered at her over his glasses. "Treasure hunters."

"Blaine, honey," Peg said, practically quivering with excitement, "this is the best news for your lighthouse diner."

"Restaurant," Blaine corrected. "How so?"

"Go ahead, Dr. D—um, Mr. Dominski," Peg said. "Go on and tell her."

Dr. Doom cleared his throat. "The state of Maine would like permission to build a floating dock off Lighthouse Point. We realize the lighthouse property is now private, thus it can only be done if the owner's permission is granted."

Paul scratched his forehead. "Why does the state of Maine want a dock there?"

"So they can nose around the German sub!" Peg said.

"*Hardly* the correct vernacular for a maritime project of great importance." Dr. Doom frowned at Peg. "But she is correct in stating that the state of Maine will be undergoing a period of archaeological discovery at the site."

"And," Baxtor added, almost gleefully, "no additional building permits will be allowed on Three Sisters Island during this archaeological discovery."

"How long does the discovery last?" Paul said, thinking of all the plans he had to expand the camp. The swimming pool, the indoor gymnasium for rainy days.

"Discovery is quite extensive," Dr. Doom said. "And of course we are dealing with an international wartime finding, hence, the world will be watching. You can rest assured that not a single stone will be left unturned."

"So," Paul said, "maybe . . . more than a few months?"

"Years and years and years," Baxtor said, grinning. "A U-boat was found off the coast of New Jersey. It's taken decades."

And *now* it made sense to Paul why Baxtor Phinney was happy. He got what he wanted. No growth for the island. No change. No progress.

"Cam, honey," Peg said, "there is one building permit that the state of Maine will grant the island." She put her thumb against her ear and her pinkie against her chin, like she was holding a phone.

"You're kidding me," Cam said in a flat voice. "The cellular tower? *Now* you want it?"

"Now we want it," Peg said. "The state of Maine wants it too. For their . . . what's it called again? Archaeological discovery."

"So all this time," Cam said, disgust in her voice, "the locals have resisted everything I do to try to help move this island into the *next* century. But with a shipwreck in the harbor from the *last* century, you're suddenly ready and willing." Both hands rolled over her expanding belly, and she winced as if she'd just been kicked, inside out. "Do you not see the irony?"

"This way," Peg said, oblivious to Cam's tone, "the changes aren't taking something important away from us. This way, we can control the change." She walked up to Cam and placed her hands on her shoulders. "Cam, honey, I know you—more than any other Grayson—have a hard time understanding us, but Three Sisters Island is a special place because of the *very* things you call backward. On this island, time slows down. It gives folks a little space in their life to think and reflect, and treasure how precious their life is. How fleeting it is." She clapped her hands. "So, honey, what do you say? Will you call your tower people and ask them to come back? Tell them we're not a controversial forum any longer. Tell them we're all in. Maybe . . . we could even talk about Wi-Fi."

"Wi-Fi?" Cam was shocked. "Wi-Fi!"

"The state of Maine would like that available too." Peg glanced down at Cam's abdomen. "And maybe get it all done before those little ones arrive?"

Cam shrugged. "Maybe." Then a smile tugged at her lips. "Fine," she huffed. "Fine. I'll do it."

Dr. Doom handed Paul a thick envelope.

"What's this?" A shiver of foreboding tingled down the back of Paul's neck. What else could Dr. Doom have found that needed to be fixed? What else could possibly go wrong?

"I could have mailed it," Dr. Doom said, one eyebrow lifted in Paul's direction, "but I thought you might like to get it before the season begins on Friday."

Paul opened it to find page after page of the violations all checked off. He flipped through the pages, as joy started bubbling up. "We're okay? Good to go?"

"For now," Dr. Doom said. "But I've got my eye on this camp now. I'll be back for periodic inspections." He turned to Peg. "My work here is done. Shall we go?"

"Ayup. I'd better get back to the diner. Bob's been making potato candy this afternoon, and I can't stop thinking about it. Yum."

"Potato candy," Paul said. "Very Bob-like."

Peg winked at Paul. "Turns out Bob isn't so fond of his potatoes that he can't leave 'em."

Paul's eyebrows lifted. "So he's staying on?"

"Sure is." She scurried to the minivan, in a hurry to return to Bob and his potato candy.

Wonders never ceased, Paul mused, hands on his hips, watching the green minivan rumble down the driveway, taking Dr. Doom along with it.

Cam stood at the bottom of the porch stairs. "I have so much to do. I don't even know where to begin." She lifted a finger in the air. "Yes, yes I do. A call to Mr. Thayer." She clambered up the step at a rather slow, plodding pace. Very un-Cam-like.

Blaine watched her go, then turned to Paul with an ecstatic look on her face. "Funny, isn't it?"

"Funny?" Did she mean Cam's waddle? It was quite amusing, but Paul didn't want to say so. Not aloud.

"Jean-Paul was right. Most things work out in the end if you leave them in God's hands and don't try to meddle. 'Pray and release,' he would say. 'Pray and release.'" Blaine mimicked a thick French accent perfectly. "Dad, who could have imagined such an outcome? The dock is the answer I've been waiting for to make this lighthouse restaurant work."

"I'd like to know more about this lighthouse restaurant. Like, how are you getting the money for it?"

"We can talk about the lighthouse later," she said. "But back to the outcome. Isn't it amazing? The thumbs-up from the locals is the answer Cam's been waiting for. A win-win."

"And I've been waiting a long time for you to realize Artie Lotosky is the one for you. The storm brought that too."

She lifted her palms in the air. "A win-win-win."

"But what about me? My big plans to expand Camp Kicking Moose have been severely hobbled."

"Ah, but Dad, this allows time for you to properly court Maeve O'Shea." She thumped him on the arm. "You know, before you're ready to join Granddad at Sea View Haven."

"Very funny."

At the bottom of the porch steps, Blaine paused. "Peg called it. As usual."

"Called what?"

"Mother Nature. She always has the last word." She grinned, and her whole face lit up. "And thank God for that."

Then Paul watched his beautiful youngest daughter take the stairs two at a time, her steps full of purpose and intention, and she disappeared into the house.

Epilogue

It was a perfect October day. Azure-blue sky, vast and empty. Morning frost that brought a crispness to the air, followed by an unseasonably warm afternoon. So warm the wedding guests wouldn't need sweaters and coats. Even the waters surrounding the lighthouse seemed to be cooperating today. The Atlantic provided just the right amount of waves crashing against the rocks to lend authenticity to the Maine coastline.

In the gallery room of the lighthouse, Blaine finished dressing, smoothing out her wedding dress and slipping into shoes. She put on her mother's pearl earrings, turning slowly around to face her sisters. Maddie's eyes were on the bundle in her arm, four-week-old baby Johnny, named after Rick's father, sound asleep. Cam sat by an open window, fanning herself, peering at the guests as they arrived. Nearly nine months pregnant with triplets, she looked like she might topple right over.

Blaine's heart was suddenly too full for words as she let her gaze roam lovingly over her sisters, out the window to the grass below where so many friends had gathered to celebrate her wedding to Artie. Where Rick would stand under the wooden arch covered with lime-green chrysanthemums—created by Peg and Maeve—to perform the ceremony. Where her grandfather sat in the front row, next to Seth and Peg and Maeve. Where Jean-Paul and

Chef Henri sat, having just flown in yesterday from Paris. Where her dad, her wonderfully dear dad, waited to walk her down the path to her groom.

Artie was the one who insisted they squeeze the wedding in this fall, after Blaine wrapped up her first summer season of opening a restaurant at the top of this very lighthouse. They had to postpone the Labor Day wedding because Maddie surprised everyone by giving birth two weeks early. Artie set another date, undeterred, determined to get married to Blaine before Cam delivered her babies. He told Blaine he'd waited long enough for her.

It still amazed Blaine that Artie loved her so, that he never gave up on her. He said he fell in love with her the minute they'd met, that he knew she was the one for him. "It just took you a little while to figure out I was the one for you," he said.

In a way, that was true. She'd certainly had a lot of growing up to do. Yet in another way, her heart had been woven with his for a very long time. Probably starting, she realized now, from that first day they'd met in college and their friendship had begun.

Blaine lifted her eyes and met Maddie's gaze across the room.

"Oh, wow," Maddie said. "You are a breathtaking bride. Seriously. My breath is gone."

Cam turned from the window. She didn't speak, she only nodded, her eyes filling with tears. She put her hands over her heart and let out a deep sigh. "I wish Mom were here," she whispered.

"She is," Blaine said with confidence. With a healed heart. "Remember that saying Maeve told us at her funeral?"

"'If loved ones are with God,'" Maddie quoted, "'and he is with us, they cannot be far away.'"

"Oh! I see Artie," Cam said, pointing out the window. "His boat's coming in. His dad is with him. Look! Cooper's running to meet them. Oh my gosh, the puppy is tagging behind him." She turned with a smile. "It's gonna take me a while to get down those stairs. We'd better start now." Slowly, she eased herself out of the chair.

Man. Blaine hoped the steep lighthouse stairs wouldn't trigger Cam's labor. Chef Henri had spent all morning preparing a wedding feast, with Jean-Paul and Cooper acting as sous-chef and dishwasher. As Cam waddled past, Blaine ran a hand over her enormous belly. "Please stay put, little baby girls."

"No kidding, you three," Cam said. "Listen to your aunt." She squeezed Blaine's hand. "You look absolutely stunning."

"Ready?" Maddie said, waiting by the door with a baby tucked in one arm and a huge diaper bag draped over the other. "Ready to get married?"

Was she ready to marry Artie? Her mom had often said that love was friendship set on fire. Blaine wasn't just marrying the man she loved today, she was marrying her best friend.

Was she ready?

Oh yes. "So ready," Blaine said. She smiled at her sisters. "Let's go."

Questions for Discussion

1. Early in the novel we learn that Blaine had been in serious emotional trouble when she first arrived in Paris. How did that flashback at the end of chapter 6 affect your perception of her?

2. The theme of this novel is that God will never give up on you, even if you give up on him. Name a few ways in which that theme played out over the course of the story.

3. Paul's speech therapist had warned him to not waste his words, to save them for what's truly important. How did that advice affect Paul? First with his daughters, and then with his own father. It's good advice for all of us to keep in mind, to think before we speak. What might change if you took that advice to heart?

4. Though he was never particularly good at it, "listening" became a theme in Paul's life after he lost his voice. Listening well, giving someone undivided attention, isn't easy; there's much that competes for our focus. The ding of an incoming text on a cell phone, for example. How are your listening skills? How could you improve them?

5. Peg reminded Blaine that life didn't always turn out the way they planned. She might have been thinking about her stalled romance with Bob Lotosky, or maybe about

changes in Three Sisters Island. But why was it something that Blaine needed to hear, rather than sympathy?

6. Blaine wanted to change a negative sibling dynamic—not an easy thing to do. She had anticipated challenges, so she memorized Bible verses to help her refrain from saying something to her sisters that she might regret. What kind of wisdom did she display? Did it create instant change? Or lasting change?

7. What role did Jean-Paul play in Blaine's life? How did he affect others in the Grayson family? Have you ever known someone like him? Better still, have you ever been Jean-Paul-esque to others? Please describe.

8. Pray and release, Jean-Paul suggested, whenever someone faced a problem. Pray and release. What are your thoughts about his advice?

9. Artie had given up on Blaine, or tried to. And Blaine couldn't quite let him go. Why do you think they were meant for each other?

10. What do you think friendship adds to a romance?

11. Maddie didn't seem to have a large role in this story, though in a behind-the-scenes way, she had a significant influence. Where did you see her impact?

12. On the phone, Paul's friend reminded him that people glorify the illusion that more is always better. Why is that true? What makes it difficult for you to feel contentment? When did you catch on that Paul's early morning cell phone calls on the beach were to Maeve O'Shea? Some had hoped that Paul and Peg would end up together. Why, or why not, is Maeve a better fit?

13. How did the flashback elements at the end of some chapters enhance the novel? Do any of them stick out as especially poignant or impactful?

---

14. What did the lighthouse represent in this story?

15. What made it particularly satisfying to know that Mother Nature had the last word for Three Sisters Island?

16. Fast-forward a few years. What do you think has happened to each member of the Grayson family? To Camp Kicking Moose? To Blaine's lighthouse restaurant and cooking school?

17. Last question . . . how do you think Cam is managing triplets? ;)

⌒ Blaine's Outrageous Fudgy Brownies ⌒

These were the brownies that eight-year-old Blaine made for Cam's high school cross-country team's bake sale. Shrewdly, Cam doubled the price per brownie and still sold out.

¾ cup	unsalted butter
2 cups	semisweet chocolate chips
1½ cups	sugar
½ cup	light brown sugar
3	large eggs (room temperature)
2 teaspoons	vanilla extract
1 tablespoon	instant coffee granules
1 cup	unsweetened cocoa powder
1 cup	all-purpose flour
1 teaspoon	salt

Preheat the oven to 350 degrees and grease a 9x13-inch pan or line with parchment paper, leaving an overhang on the sides to lift the finished brownies out. Set aside.

In a microwave-safe bowl, combine the butter and 2 ounces of chocolate chips. Melt 30 seconds at a time, whisking after each increment until completely smooth. Whisk in the sugar until completely combined. (Whisking the sugar into warm butter will help the sugar, during baking, to rise to the top of the batter. That's the secret to the shiny crackly tops.) One by one, whisk in the eggs, vanilla extract, and instant coffee granules.

Add the cocoa powder, flour, salt, and remaining chocolate chips. Fold it all together with a rubber spatula or wooden spoon. Batter will be very thick. Spread evenly into prepared pan.

Bake for 25–30 minutes. (Do not overbake! A little underdone is better than a little overdone.)

Remove from the oven and place on a wire rack to cool completely in the pan before cutting into squares.

Optional add-in: 1 cup chopped walnuts or hazelnuts.

Loved This Book?
Turn the Page for a Special
SNEAK PEEK of Suzanne's Newest Novel,

A SEASON ON THE WIND!

COMING SOON

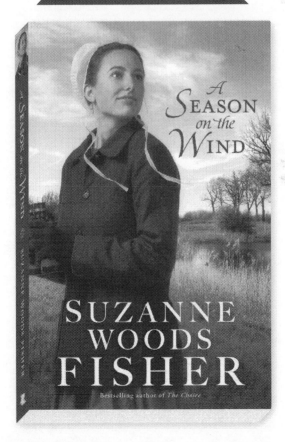

One

PENNY WEAVER STAYED SO STILL that the brown robin in her yard didn't seem to know she was there. It was better in the early morning, when she could see the blush of rose against his proud chest. In this late afternoon light, a robin seemed like an ordinary Little Brown Job. After he flew off, she crossed the yard to the old milking stable that her brother Micah had converted into a guesthouse with the help of a few men from their church.

Inside the guesthouse, Penny took one last look around. On a whim, she had cut a handful of late blooming chrysanthemums from the garden and put them in a mason jar to set on the small table. The guesthouse was made up of two small bedrooms, a tiny but functional bathroom, and a sitting area with a woodstove. Against the wall, near the table, was a kitchenette of sorts: a sink, a mini refrigerator, and a microwave, with power provided by a generator. It wasn't fancy, certainly nothing like these Englisch strangers were probably accustomed to. But it was clean, tidy, warm . . . and the strangers had asked the bishop, David Stoltzfus, for a place to stay while birding with Micah. She had to remember that, especially if they were the complaining type. *They* had asked.

If this worked out, it might provide needed income. The bishop had come up with the notion of adding a guesthouse at the Weavers' farm for birders, to encourage longer guiding trips for Micah than the usual one-day outings. "This could be a good thing for Micah," David had said. "It could be just the thing to bring him out of his shell. And it's good for Stoney Ridge too. Micah's eye and ear for rare birds seems to be God's means to bring blessings to our town."

It did seem as if the Almighty was working overtime lately to bring Micah out of the shadows. Last January, he'd spotted a Black-backed Oriole pecking away at Penny's kitchen feeder. The Black-backed was a stunning cousin to the Baltimore Oriole, but this one lived in central Mexico. It was only the second time the Black-backed Oriole had been spotted in the United States. Ever. That little bird created a major attraction during its two-month stay, drawing bird lovers from all over the country.

As if that wasn't enough, in early March, Micah spotted a Roseate Spoonbill. While it wasn't hard to notice—goodness, it stood nearly a yard tall with pink feathers like flamingos—where Micah had found it *was* remarkable. An overlooked, hard-to-get-to creek that ran along the northern edge of town. It had been nearly fifty years since the last Roseate Spoonbill was spotted in Pennsylvania. Why it had traveled from Florida—remaining for nearly a month in the insignificant no-name creek—was a mystery. Then again, that's what made birding so intriguing. Birds didn't always act or play according to the rules.

And now, in November, Penny's brother had sighted the White-winged Tern, a vagrant bird, rarely seen in all of North America. Suddenly it seemed that birders everywhere knew the name Micah Weaver.

She heard a noise outside and peeked out the window. The sound of a car coming up the long, steep drive always startled Penny, so different a sound than the gentle clip-clop of a horse pulling a buggy.

Opening the door of the guesthouse, she spotted the dark brim of Micah's hat as he peered around the edge of the barn. She let out a sigh. That boy. Nearly nineteen and still so shy. He was as gentle in nature as he was tall in height.

She hoped David was right to add this whole venture of hosting birders at Lost Creek Farm to Micah's field guiding. She hadn't slept well last night, tossed and turned, anxious. It wasn't typical for Penny to feel unsettled, which only made her even more uneasy.

She smoothed down her apron, tucked a stray strand of hair inside her prayer cap, took a deep breath, and crossed the yard to greet the guests. A small man climbed out of the driver's side of the car and waved his arm, smiling.

"Welcome. You must be the man coming to find the bird," Penny said.

An awkward silence followed. Something seemed off. What had she done wrong?

"Um, my name is Natalie Crowell. My cousin is the birder."

Oh no! Penny realized this man was actually a woman with a startling haircut. Crewcut-short like a man's, spiky on top, white-blonde. "Welcome to our farm. Lost Creek Farm. It's where my brother Micah and I live. Micah is the field guide you've come for." She was babbling now, nervous, embarrassed.

Out of the passenger side of the car, another person emerged and popped his head over the top of the car. "I'm the one you were told about. Don't feel embarrassed. People confuse us all the time."

"Very funny," Natalie said. She pulled her big purse out of the car and turned to Penny. "Ben's my cousin, but we look nothing alike."

That did not need pointing out. Ben had longer hair than Natalie's—thick, dark brown, wavy. He raised his arms onto the top of the car, folding them, leaning forward slightly as he cupped his elbows, and as he did, Penny's stomach dropped.

"The name's Ben Zook. I've come to see that White-winged Tern that everyone in the bird world is buzzing about. I sure hope it's not a one-day wonder."

Penny's heart gave one huge thump and then started beating wildly.

It was *him*.

Her Ben Zook.

Even after two decades, she would know him anywhere.

She'd always believed that one day, somehow, somewhere, they'd meet again. And here he was. He was here for a bird.

Of course the Lord would entice him back home with a bird. A rare bird. Just as birds found their way in the sky, so God had found a way to bring Ben Zook here.

Ben walked around the car to greet her, holding out his hand to her. His movement was quick, graceful, and Penny suddenly remembered that was the way of him. He was tall, so tall she had to raise her chin to see his eyes. He was so fine to look at that she couldn't help but stare at the sheer wonder of him. His deep voice made Penny think of a waterfall, fast-moving and fluid, unable to hold on to, yet so mesmerizing.

Ben Zook was standing just a few feet away from her!

Still dumbstruck, she gazed at him, then at his offered hand. *Do something, Penny! Pull yourself together.* But she couldn't budge, couldn't move a muscle. His eyes registered no recognition of her. Not a flicker. Penny could see she was a complete stranger to him. Eyes couldn't lie.

When too much time had passed, Ben dropped his hand with an awkward smile, then turned away to take things out of the car. He opened the trunk and pulled out suitcases, handing one to his cousin. He paused, leaned one hand against the car, swayed a little, and suddenly folded to the ground like a rag doll.

Ben felt a gentle touch on his forehead before his eyelids could open. He felt as if he were waking up from a sweet dream, so sweet that he didn't even want to be roused. He couldn't remember what he was dreaming about, only the feelings it evoked. It covered him in calm, his soul felt settled, utterly safe. He could scarcely remember ever feeling that way.

Wait. He did remember. He was a little boy, maybe five or six years old, sick with some dreaded childhood illness like chicken pox, and his mother had put her cool hand on his hot forehead. Just like now.

Eyes opening, he blinked up at a woman. She wasn't his mother. And he wasn't six years old. And he had absolutely no idea what had just happened.

From somewhere far away, he heard warbling sounds, and the world started slowly coming back into focus.

"Ben. Ben! Are you okay?" The warbling sound had become words and belonged to Natalie.

He lifted his head, then pushed himself up on his elbows. "Was ist los?" *What happened?*

A Plain woman, the one who had touched his forehead, leaned back on her heels, a stricken look on her face. "Sie is bletzlich umechdich warre." *You fainted suddenly.*

"Zwaar?" *Truly?* Argh. *Not again.* He felt himself color and shrugged, feigning nonchalance. "I had a bout of the flu recently. Still recovering, I guess."

He tried to get himself up and felt two large hands under his arms, hoisting him to his feet. Still a little unsteady, Ben brushed himself off, embarrassed. *What a way to meet people.* He turned to face the man who helped him up and realized this must be Micah. Tall and thin, more so than others had described him, but still a boy. Ben could see that in his eyes, mostly. They remained downcast, shy and reserved, even as the two shook hands.

"So you're Micah Weaver. I'm Ben Zook."

The boy gave a brief nod. Just a brief, awkward nod of greeting, despite the fact that Ben had traveled long distances to meet him. Over the last few years, Ben had heard Micah Weaver's name circulated around the Pennsylvania birding community, always with a sense of awe. Apparently, the boy had an uncanny ability

301

to spot birds, especially migrating ones blown off-course during storms. Ben hoped Micah Weaver would live up to his reputation. He had a book manuscript due in, one that was anxiously waiting for this White-winged Tern.

Ben Zook had only two loves in his life. Books and birds. In a stroke of good fortune, he'd stumbled onto a way to cobble together those two loves into a career. He wrote books about rare birds. The market wasn't exactly mainstream, but there was a steady and faithful readership for it, and for that he was grateful. As Natalie often pointed out, he'd bought himself a job. Happily, it was work that he loved.

Penny Weaver, the woman who had first seemed frozen in shock at the sight of Ben, snapped out of her odd stupor and jumped into action. "Micah, would you take their luggage to the guesthouse? You must be thirsty from your travels. If you'll follow Micah to the guesthouse, I'll bring you something to refresh you."

Ben glanced at the Plain woman as she hurried off to the main house, half walking, half running. Scurrying. Just the way he remembered how Amish women moved. Quick, purposeful, nononsense. He felt strangely touched by her care for them, two strangers, until he remembered that this was a business arrangement and he owed her a sizable check for her hospitality—regardless of whether or not he was able to photograph that rare bird. The bishop had made that clear. He had retained Micah's help to find that bird, effectively stopping other birders from hiring him for the duration.

Micah lifted all their luggage like it was made of cotton balls and was halfway to the guesthouse by the time Ben reached into the trunk of the car to retrieve his optical equipment bag. That, he didn't let anyone touch.

"Ben, are you all right?" His cousin looked at him with concerned eyes.

"I'm fine, Natalie. I just need some water. I didn't drink enough today."

"You spoke in tongues to Penny Weaver."

He scrunched his face in disbelief "What?"

"You did! And she understood you too. It was freaky."

Oh no. Could he have spoken in Penn Dutch? No way. There was no way. He hadn't used the dialect since he left the Amish as a teenager. Hadn't spoken a single word of it.

"Well, believe it or not, you did." She looked around, sniffing, scrunching her face at the smell. "What reeks?"

He chuckled. "That is the sweet aroma of farm life." When her eyebrows knit together in confusion, he added, "Fertilizer." When she still looked puzzled, he added, "Manure on the fields."

"Oh."

It was common knowledge for a man who spent his childhood less than a mile away. A man who might've easily become an Amish farmer himself, were it not for his father.

But Penny Weaver and her brother Micah knew none of that, and he had no intention of telling them. He wouldn't lie, but he believed the past belonged in the past.

Besides, Ben had always loved change. After growing up in a town that never changed, he loved it even more. Stoney Ridge, in his opinion, was the kind of town that was better to come from than to stay in, but then again, he wasn't really the staying type. He was a man on the move, all the time. Like a bird in that way, migrating eight months of the year.

He doubted there was anyone left in Stoney Ridge who might even remember him. So many had passed away, like his mother, or moved away. Maybe that's the real reason he felt he could return at last. He could be here, could bag this rare bird, yet remain anonymous. He could stay on the fringes, irrelevant to a community that cared only about their own.

Then again, maybe he would've followed that bird anytime, anywhere. It was an extraordinary find—the first sighting of the Eurasian species in the United States this year and the first ever reported in Pennsylvania. It was his nemesis bird, his Dip. A bird that continually eluded him. "Fische un Yaage macht hungrigen Magen," he said softly. *Fishing and hunting make an empty stomach.*

He clapped his forehead. Why in the world did *that* saying pop into his head? It was one his father had often said. The mind was such a strange thing. And how it affected the body—that was strange too.

The last year or so, Ben had felt a world weariness that dampened his enthusiasm for most everything, even birding. He hoped this super-rare White-winged Tern would snap him out of his funk. Assuming . . . the Micah Weaver kid could find it again. The way he slipped out of sight after dropping off their luggage in the guesthouse, Ben got a funny feeling he was as elusive as the bird.

Trudy Yoder. *She* was the one who had told Micah about the White-winged Tern. He'd taken the word of a fifteen-year-old girl. Stupid, stupid, stupid!

Trudy was absolutely positive she'd seen it, described it in great detail—startlingly specific. She'd never been wrong before. As annoying as Trudy could be in practically every way, she knew her birds. So Micah took her word for it without verifying the find with his own eyes and posted it as a confirmed sighting on the Rare Bird Alert. Then he added his own name to the confirmation.

News of the vagrant, spotted by Micah Weaver, traveled like wildfire.

That was when Micah got the first jab of guilt to his gut. A few days later, the moment lost even more of its shine when his sister Penny told him that a twitcher was coming to the farm, an author on bird books, expecting Micah to locate this rare bird like he could snap his fingers and it would appear. Paying him handsomely so he wouldn't take other birders out in the field. Micah had been out at dawn every morning, out again each twilight, regardless of the weather, trying to locate that bird. So far, nothing.

As a birder, he was honorbound to tell the truth. It was a cardinal value among those who loved birds. If you cheated about finding a rarity, who did you cheat? Even more important, he was honorbound to tell the truth because he was Plain. It was woven into the very fabric of his soul.

The whole thing made Micah feel sick to his stomach.

Why had he taken Trudy Yoder's word for it? He knew how easy it was to misread birds. He'd done it himself, many times. He certainly knew better than to post it on the Rare Bird Alert as a confirmed sighting, adding his name. In truth, only Trudy had seen the bird, so it should have remained an unconfirmed report. He should never have attached his name to it.

So what made him do such a shameful thing?

Because his reputation as a crackerjack field guide impressed others, especially Trudy's older sister, Shelley Yoder, who sang like an angel and looked like one too. Because spotting rare birds was easy for him, unlike getting words out from around his twisted-up tongue.

It was a sinful thing, a worldly thing, to act like he was a big somebody. But, as he well knew, it was even worse to be a nobody.

Acknowledgments

WARM THANKS to Lindsey Ross, who has an amazing ability to do a "flyover" of an unfinished, choppy manuscript and provide encouragement *plus* valuable edits. You're a wonder!

A high five to Dylan, my hydropower go-to guy. Your expertise was invaluable, especially for a nonengineering type like . . . moi. Any blunders were mine, all mine.

I am privileged to have the benefit of the Revell team—Michele, Brianne, and Karen for fresh and innovative marketing and publicity, Andrea and Barb for skillful, wise editing.

Artie's role as a roving doctor was inspired by the Maine Seacoast Mission, founded in 1905 by two Congregational ministers to serve the communities in Maine's unbridged islands. The *Sunbeam*, a seventy-five-foot vessel, is equipped with state-of-the-art telemedicine equipment, and even serves as an icebreaker to help clear harbors. Such a remarkable way to keep isolated locals cared for and in community.

Suzanne Woods Fisher is an award-winning, bestselling author of more than thirty books, including *On a Summer Tide* and *On a Coastal Breeze*, as well as the Nantucket Legacy, Amish Beginnings, The Bishop's Family, The Deacon's Family, and The Inn at Eagle Hill series, among other novels. She is also the author of several nonfiction books about the Amish, including *Amish Peace* and *Amish Proverbs*. She lives in California. Learn more at www.suzannewoodsfisher.com and follow Suzanne on Facebook @SuzanneWoodsFisherAuthor and Twitter @suzannewfisher.

"Memorable characters, gorgeous Maine scenery, and plenty of family drama. I can't wait to visit Three Sisters Island again!"

—IRENE HANNON,
bestselling author of the beloved Hope Harbor series

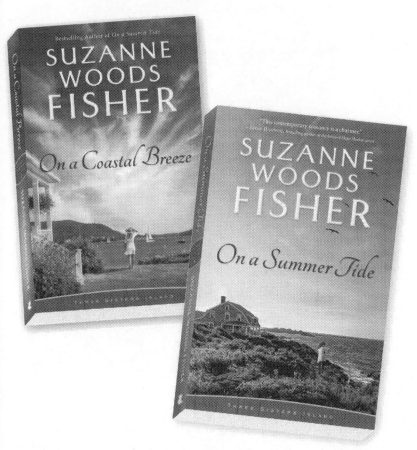

Following the lives of three sisters, this brand-new contemporary romance series from Suzanne Woods Fisher is sure to delight her fans and draw new ones.

"An unforgettable story about love and the transforming power
of words and community. Deeply moving and uplifting!"

—LAURA FRANTZ,
Christy Award–winning author of *Tidewater Bride*

Based on true events, a young woman used to the finer things in life
arrives in a small Appalachian town in 1911 to help her formidable
cousin combat adult illiteracy by opening moonlight schools.

Ɍ Revell
a division of Baker Publishing Group
www.RevellBooks.com

Available wherever books and ebooks are sold

"There's just something unique and fresh about every Suzanne Woods Fisher book. Whatever the reason, I'm a fan."

——SHELLEY SHEPHARD GRAY,
New York Times and *USA Today* bestselling author

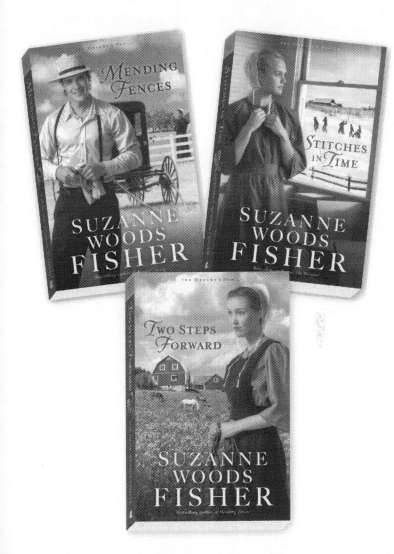

DON'T MISS ANY OF
THE BISHOP'S FAMILY

"Suzanne is an authority on the Plain folks. . . .
She always delivers a fantastic story with
interesting characters, all in a tightly woven plot."

—BETH WISEMAN, bestselling author
of the Daughters of the Promise and the Land of Canaan series

IMMERSE YOURSELF IN THESE HEARTWARMING—AND SURPRISING—TALES OF *young love*, *forgiveness*, AND *healing*.

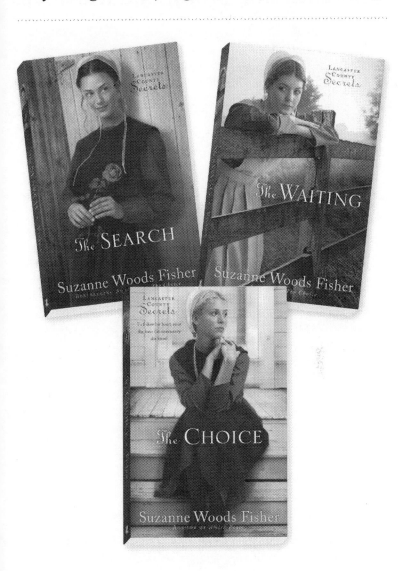

Fisher intrigues and delights with stories that explore the bonds of friendship, family, and true love.

Stoney Ridge Seasons

Connect with SUZANNE

www.SuzanneWoodsFisher.com

LET'S TALK ABOUT BOOKS

- Share or mention the book on your social media platforms. Use the hashtag **#AtLighthousePoint**.

- Write a book review on your blog or on a retailer site.

- Pick up a copy for friends, family, or anyone who you think would enjoy and be challenged by its message!

- Share this message on Twitter, Facebook, or Instagram:
I loved #AtLighthousePoint by @SuzanneWFisher
@SuzanneWoodsFisherAuthor // @RevellBooks

- Recommend this book for your church, workplace, book club, or small group.

- Follow Revell on social media and tell us what you like.

> 📘 RevellBooks
>
> 🐦 RevellBooks
>
> 📷 RevellBooks
>
> 📌 pinterest.com/RevellBooks

Printed in the United States
by Baker & Taylor Publisher Services